Tournament
of Witches

Jack Massa

 Triskelion Books

Published by
Triskelion Books
www.triskelionbooks.com

ISBN ISBN: 978-0-9976461-7-7

Print Edition published June 2020

Cover Design by Shaun Stevens, https://www.flintlockcovers.com/

Preface

Tournament of Witches is Book 3 of *The Glimnodd Cycle*. It continues the story begun in *Cloak of the Two Winds* and continued in *A Mirror Against All Mishap*. The author has attempted to provide enough of the backstory in the opening chapters that you can begin reading here with pleasure. For information on the world of Glimnodd, including a Glossary and access to a map, see the Afterword.

Cast of Characters

Amlina - Wandering witch from Larthang, a nation of great witches. Victorious in acquiring the Cloak of the Two Winds, now seeking to recover from what the adventure cost her.

Eben - One of Amlina's Iruk warriors, sharp-witted and mercurial, with a certain poetical bent. Squandering his loot on a life of ease; enjoying it less and less.

Eben's mates, members of his klarn:

Glyssa (f), brave and loving. Trained by Amlina in the magical arts.

Lonn (m), the klarn leader, strong, passionate, stoical. In love with Glyssa.

Draven (m), Lonn's cousin, brave and optimistic. In love with Amlina.

Karrol (f), brawny, decisive, outspoken. No longer sure where she belongs.

Brinda (f), Karrol's sister, quiet and reserved.

Kizier - Scholar and friend to Amlina. Ruminating over his past life as a sentient sea-fern.

Buroof - A talking book, once a human. Three thousand years old and full of knowledge.

Beryl Quan de Lang - Amlina's great enemy. Now a ghost that haunts her.

Belach - Iruk shaman and sometime mentor to Glyssa.

Witches of Larthang

Drusdegarde - Archimage of the West. Supreme witch of the Golden Land.

Trippany - Bee-winged lady of the drell people. Envoy from the Archimage.

Clorodice, Keeper of the Keys - Powerful and strict. Adherent of the austere Thread of Virtue faction.

Arkasha - Clorodice's subaltern and member of her circle.

Elani Vo T'ang - Clorodice's favored apprentice.

Melevarry, Mage of Randoon -Chief witch of the port city.

The Seven Witches in the Tournament and their Sponsors

Amlina, sponsored by Melevarry.

Elani Vo T'ang, sponsored by Clorodice.

Shen Tra Lo, sponsored by Kanshi, Keeper of the Forge.

Von Lui-Tong, sponsored by the Mage of Long Mountain.

Tolanga of Gon Fu, sponsored by Wicksa, Keeper of Swords.

Liska Quenn sponsored by the Mage of Hanjapore.

Ulleena Tuvari, sponsored by Crandora, Keeper of the Books.

Larthangan Military and Court

Duke Trem-Dou Pheng - Supreme Commander of the Larthangan Forces. Leader of the militarist faction, the Iron Bloc.

Shay-Ni Pheng - Admiral of the Larthangan Navy and the Duke's nephew. Unhappy with his current assignment.

The Tuan (Me Lo Lee) - Supreme Ruler of Larthang. A nine-year-old boy with access to the memories and knowledge of his 154 dynastic predecessors.

Prince Spegis Besu Keli - drell ambassador to the Court. Cousin to Trippany.

Ting Fo - gentleman tutor and interpreter for the Iruks at the Court.

Part One

On the
South Polar Sea

One

C old wind tickled his eyelids. Eben blinked, painfully waking. Squinting into the gray dawn, he recognized the worn brick wall of an alley, smeared with frost. Rime and icy winds were normal enough in Fleevanport at the end of Third Winter. Waking from a drunken sleep in an alley was also, regrettably, typical for him these days.

Not typical was the sparkling woman floating over him in the air, her vibrating insect-wings blowing a cold breeze on his face. Eben shut his eyes and rubbed the back of his head. At least the drunken dreams were growing more interesting. Groaning, he reached inside his fur over shirt, fingers groping for his purse.

Gone. Robbed again, no doubt by some doxy he had stupidly followed from a tavern. How often had he fallen for that ploy these past two seasons—roaming the waterfront, drinking too much, squandering his hard-won loot? At least this time the thief had left his fur cape and hunting knife.

Persistent humming made him open his eyes. Startled, he sat up and squinted hard.

The gleaming lady still hung in the air, her wings a blur. Her slim body was dressed in gauzy garments that could have offered little protection from the cold. Black hair, bound by a gemmed silver band, a slim and angular face, coppery complexion, eyes that turned up at the corners—eyes like black onyx beads watching him.

Vision or real, Eben thought her the most beautiful creature he'd ever seen.

She floated down, dainty belled slippers settling on the cobblestone. Bending to peer at his face, she spoke in halting Low-Tathian.

"You are ... all right?"

Stiff and aching, Eben struggled to his feet. He was small for an Iruk warrior. Even so, the top of the lady's head just reached the level of his chin. He examined her wings, still now, blue-veined, translucent, rounded like bee wings sprouting from her back.

"Oh, I am all right," he said. "And how are you?"

She smiled, revealing white pointy teeth.

"And *what* are you?" he added.

The wings fluttered and she rose into the air, stopping when her eyes were level with his.

"I am named Trippany. Are you an *Iruk*?"

"That is so, my pretty flying girl. But from what nation do you hail? For, assuming you are real and not some phantasm, I have never seen the like of you."

Her tone grew solemn and proud, the words coming like a speech she had rehearsed. "I am an envoy from the House of the Deepmind in Larthang."

That might make sense. Larthang was far away and strange, known as a land of great witches. Who could say they had not bred such creatures as this by their arts?

"That is odd," he said. "You do not look Larthangan."

Her mouth quirked in a half-smile. "My people are the *drell*. You know ... how Larthangans look then?"

Suddenly Eben realized this was leading into dangerous territory. He rubbed the back of his head. "Well, of course. Their trading ships sometimes sail these waters."

The lady seemed to sense his secretiveness—and was having none of it. "I seek the Cloak of the Two Winds," she stated. "Do you know where it can be found?"

Eben tilted back. He forced himself to show a puzzled frown. "Why no ... How should I know such a thing?"

Of course, he did know. The Cloak was in the possession of the witch Amlina. She, along with three of Eben's former mates, lived in hiding at a farmstead in the hills half a day's journey from here.

The lady floated a bit higher, glaring down at him now. He hoped she could not read his thoughts

"I've heard tales of it," Eben muttered casually. "A great thing of magic, is it not? Stories have reached this port that it was stolen some time back, taken from some mighty witch who was slain in the battle."

"Tales also reached Larthang," the bee-lady said. "Some of them say the Cloak was stolen by a witch of Larthang, in league with warriors of the Iruk folk. Some tell how that same witch used the Cloak to scatter a Tathian fleet ... at an island called Alone."

Eben shrugged, wondering if he should reach for his knife. He would hate to harm this lovely creature—but he was sworn not to reveal Amlina's hideout. "You seem to know more about it than I do."

"I am not so sure." The lady peered hard into his eyes. "*You* are Iruk. And you were heard boasting in a tavern last night that you had once seen a whole Tathian fleet blown away by magic."

Casually as he could, Eben slipped his hand toward the knife handle. "I don't remember saying that. To be honest, I've been told I can be a terrible liar when I've had too much to drink."

She eyed his hand on the knife hilt. "I see. Perhaps also you lie at other times?" She flew higher, floating out of reach. "So then, you cannot help me find the Cloak?"

"I fear not."

"You ... disappoint me. But I *shall* keep looking."

The angle of her wings changed, and she looped higher into the air. Light flashed, and Eben thrust up an arm to shield his eyes. When he looked again, the lady was gone.

Eben wiped his forehead and heaved a deep breath. He glanced suspiciously up and down the alley.

Had the winged lady been real? Certainly, the conversation was too prolonged for a simple drunken dream. But perhaps she was a vision, sent by some sorcerer or witch to interrogate him? Amlina had predicted that many deepshapers would seek the Cloak of the Two Winds once it became known that it was loose in the world. Eben vowed to be careful.

He really should avoid so much drinking.

Streams of light and shadow—some drifting slowly, others pouring in torrents, crashing in waves, spinning into whirlpools—so, in her meditation, Amlina the witch perceived the currents of the *Deepmind*, the realm below the surface of appearances.

In her immediate vicinity she perceived dense curtains of power, sparkling on one side, utterly dark on the other. But the curtains were separating, rips appearing in their fabric.

Once again, her concealments were coming undone.

Daily now, they grew flimsier, harder to maintain. Of course, she had known this must happen sooner or later. One could not hide a source of power so great as the Cloak forever—no matter how carefully the designs of concealment were woven, no matter how much energy fed those designs.

Amlina's hands rose from her lap, fingers pointing and circling as her mind summoned power to repair the barriers. But even as she envisioned the fabric mending, the tattered weave thickening again, pain burned in her heart and throbbed behind her eyes.

Too much power.

That, of course, was her real problem—the dark power that seethed in her body, growing stronger, more insistent, no matter what measures she took to disperse it, to bleed it away.

Bleed it away.

Amlina opened her eyes, staring at the red lamps arranged around the room, the feathered *desmets* and glittering balls that hung suspended on threads. She sat cross-legged in her closet-bed, alone.

Below the floor, she could faintly hear her friends in the great room downstairs—talking, the clatter of pots and dishes as they prepared breakfast. Draven, Glyssa, Lonn, Kizier—friends who had become her family. This farmhouse in the hills south of Fleevanport was such a peaceful place, belying the turmoil of the outer world, the fear and chaos that had filled Amlina's life for so long—chaos that was closing in on her again.

Half a year had passed since their arrival. At the start of First Winter they had sailed into the harbor of Fleevanport, their Gwales raiding ship a unique sight in these parts. That and the unusual crew had been more than enough to attract attention—scrutiny Amlina did her best to fend off with witchery. As soon as possible, they used some of their treasure to purchase this house in the hill country south of the town. Originally built as a hunting lodge by a Tathian merchant, it had become a farmstead and passed through the hands of several owners who tried breeding sheep and woolgoats—a difficult proposition in the frigid climate. Set on a wooded hill overlooking an inlet of the sea, the place made a perfect hideout for a renegade witch and her pirate companions.

The first months had been peaceful, Amlina grateful for victory, able to rest at last. Together with her warrior crew, her *klarn*, she had defeated Beryl, the Archimage of the East, reclaimed the Cloak of the Two Winds, which Beryl had stolen long ago. Amlina planned to return the Cloak to Larthang. She only meant to linger in Fleevan a short time, long enough to recover her health. The great ensorcellment she had forged, the Mirror Against All Mishap, had taken its toll, left her weak and sick.

At first, she seemed to be recovering, nourished by the peace of this place, by the presence of her friends, and by her love for one of them, Draven. That love had proven all she could have hoped for and more. So many nights she had fallen asleep beside him, satiated from lovemaking, warmed by his body, contentment filling her heart.

But even as her strength returned, her energies lurched farther out of balance. The Mirror was forbidden magic, *blood magic*. By invoking it, Amlina had raised fearsome, dark power. She had thought that when the Mirror expired, the evil force would drain away.

That hope had proven false. Instead, as her vitality was restored, hunger for more power grew. Food no longer satisfied her. Her coupling with Draven became by turns frantic and repellent. When she started imagining biting him, tasting his blood, she knew how deep the sickness ran.

With the arrival of Second Winter and the ice-sailing season, Amlina had planned to depart for Larthang. But in all her treasured imaginings, she had returned in triumph, presenting the Cloak at the House of the Deepmind, victorious and honored. Instead she was now a broken, tainted thing. Were she to return in that condition, she would likely be an outcast still, reviled because of the evil magic that possessed her.

So she had delayed longer, trying every method she could to overcome the sickness—meditations, purification rites, imbuing herself with light. She had consulted with the scholar Kizier and with Buroof, the talking book, who knew the magic of ages past.

All the time she had studied and fretted, others were searching for the Cloak. The Iruks had reported stories from Fleevanport of war in the Tathian Isles. On their voyage here, Amlina's party had used the Cloak to unleash a storm that blew away the fleet of Hagan, Prince-Ruler of Kadavel. With the disappearance of Hagan's fleet, rival city-states had moved to fill the void, seizing Kadavel's lands and ships. In the midst of these skirmishes, the navy of Larthang had suddenly invaded the Island of Gon Fu—forcing the Tathians to abandon their differences in the face of a common foe.

To all of the rulers of the Three Nations, the Cloak would be an enviable prize. As a weapon of war, it could freeze whole cities, scatter fleets. Increasingly, Amlina had sensed the minds of deepshapers searching—Tathian State Sorcerers, magician-priests from Near and Far Nyssan, witches of Larthang.

As the pressure mounted and her concealments frayed, she still hesitated, indecisive, unsure. A few days ago she had invoked the *Bowing to the Sky*, the ultimate surrender to the Deepmind. But that ritual gave her no answer at all—except that she must wait and accept.

It was the *Bowing* that originally told her to go forward with the blood magic. At least, that had been her interpretation of the message at the time. And that course *had* led her to defeat the Archimage and win the Cloak.

But at what cost?

Despondent, Amlina wondered if she had vanquished the bloodthirsty Queen of Tallyba only to become like her.

"That is right, little Larthang, little fool." Beryl's voice crept into her mind.

Amlina lurched out of bed, clutching her skull with both hands. The voice came often to torment her. Was it the product of her imagination, or the Archimage's actual ghost? She did not know.

"You are not real," she said. "You are dead and have no power over me."

"I have no power, it is true," the voice answered. "But the blood magic, *that* has power, power you cannot deny. The cravings grow and grow. Sooner or later they will overwhelm your paltry qualms and then ... your lover, your friends, victims you lure from the town, it will not matter."

"No," Amlina whispered through closed teeth. "I will not become like you."

"You were *always* like me. You just refuse to see yourself."

That much might be true. Amlina had often thought herself lacking in self-awareness, blinded by ambition, an exaggerated sense of her own importance and power. Ambition had brought her to this ...

"There is no other way to still the cravings," Beryl taunted her.

"Oh, but there is." Amlina crossed to a dressing table, pulled open the top drawer. Reaching to the back, she extracted a small bone-handled knife with a razor-sharp edge.

"Cutting yourself is no solution," Beryl whispered.

"Begone," Amlina said, and used the knife to trace a sign of banishment in the air.

Pulling up the sleeve of her dressing gown, Amlina stared at her forearm. The tiny scars were growing numerous, a pattern like a spider's web. She used a cosmetic and a *cantrip*, a mind-trick, to hide the marks from Draven and her friends. How long would *that* concealment last?

No matter, she must relieve the pressure. She must balance her energies, restore her equilibrium, so she could make plans to return the Cloak to Larthang.

Time was running out.

Deliberately, she sliced the steel edge along the skin above her wrist. Holding her arm over a porcelain basin, she squeezed the spot above the cut and watched the red droplets fall.

Two

Three ships ran before the north wind, tilting as they skidded over gleaming ice. Imposing warships, they had fortified hulls and raised forward- and rear-decks suitable for battle. Still, they were elegant vessels, with gilded carvings along the rails and ribbed ice-sails arrayed in fore-and-aft rigging on three tall masts. Indeed, they were among the finest ships the Larthangan navy could put to sea.

Yet Admiral Shay-Ni Pheng's mood was sour. Scowling, he stood with hands clasped behind his back, dressed in dark quilted wools and golden cuirass, his booted feet spread wide on the rear deck of his flagship, the *Satin Cobra*.

Behind him, the ship's captain manned the ice-tiller, occasionally calling orders through a megaphone to sailors who manned sheets and stays on the forward decks, keeping the wind to port, the ship balanced on keel and starboard ice-runners. At the rails and gunwales, sea-troopers stood guard in armor and helmets, while on the wide main deck a detachment of the men drilled in unison, stamping and lunging with long pikes, staying battle-ready.

Pointless exercise. Pheng's eyes scanned the horizon—desolate ice in all directions.

Far to the north, he knew, the bulk of the navy was engaged in blockading the island of Gon Fu or skirmishing against the ships of Tathian cities. Perhaps some were already winning glory by invading the Tathian Islands.

While he, Shay-Ni Pheng, son of one of the noblest military houses in all the Golden Land, had been sent on this fool's errand.

Accompanied by a witch and her aides, his flotilla sailed the bitterly cold South Polar Sea searching for the lost Cloak of the Two Winds.

Rumors had begun months ago. Seers at the House of the Deepmind perceived that the Cloak might no longer be held by Beryl, the Archimage of the East. In Second Winter, the ice-sailing season, the news was confirmed by mariners returning from abroad. The tyrant queen had fallen and some of her treasures, including the legendary Cloak, had been carried off. Larthangan spies, residing in the Tathian Islands, reported that several of the rival city-states were sending ships to search for the prize. Skillfully used, the Cloak of the Two Winds amounted to a supreme weapon of war. Naturally, the authorities in Minhang arranged their own expeditions. Flotillas were dispatched to Near and Far Nyssan, to Gwales and other remote places.

Including even the South Polar Sea, Admiral Pheng fretted. Why had the *simning* cursed him so? No, he could not blame the deities who administered human fates. It was his own uncle, Duke Trem-Dou Pheng, who had chosen him specifically to lead this voyage. The Duke, supreme commander of the Tuan's Forces, had claimed it was an opportunity for his nephew to win glory by returning one of the great magical treasures to Larthang. Was the Duke sincere in this? Shay-Ni doubted it. No, his uncle either wished to spare him the dangers of combat in hope of preserving his life for some later role in service to the family, or else the Duke despised him and wished to prevent him winning any honors at all. Perhaps Shay-Ni was viewed as a possible rival to the Duke's own sons. It was hard to tell; Trem-Dou Pheng was an inscrutable man. Indeed, life in the upper echelons of the Larthangan aristocracy was forever a shadow-play of intrigue, deception, and betrayal.

The admiral's grim musings were interrupted by the noise of hurried footsteps coming up the deck ladder. A young man appeared, dressed in a loose-sleeved gown and square hat—one of the witch's servants. He spotted the admiral, hurried toward him, made a deep bow.

"Lord. A message from the Duke."

Pheng wasted no time in following the messenger below decks. At the end of a dim passage, they entered a space completely unlike the bright, sparse, military world above. The air in the chamber was warm and close, smelling of incense. Red lamps glowed and magical trinkets hung from beams, leaning with the tilt of the ship. The servant bowed and backed away, joining others who stood in the shadows, their arms folded in sleeves.

At a table in the center sat the witch Arkasha and her two apprentices, dressed in elaborate robes of different colors. With them was a fourth person, a skinny girl in servant garb, barely out of her teens. Her jaw hung slack, and she stared through glassy eyes. This one was a *thrall*, a mind-slave.

Even Pheng, who generally shunned knowledge of witchery, knew that the art of enthrallment was forbidden in Larthang. But he also knew that—among witches and mages, as among the nobility— forbidden practices often flourished when they might give the practitioners some advantage.

The witches stood at his approach and gave curt bows, eyeing him warily as they always did. Arkasha gestured for him to sit in a broad chair at the head of the table.

Taking the seat, Shay-Ni allowed his eyes to wander to the young girl across from him. A pretty little thing, despite her vacant mien. What was her body like under that drab apparel? The admiral shook himself and dismissed the thought. He knew himself to be overly prone to lust, especially for girls who were helpless and easily dominated.

Arkasha spoke in the direction of the thrall.

"Lady Clorodice, my Lord Duke: Admiral Pheng has arrived."

Clorodice was a high witch, a member of the Inner Council at the House of the Deepmind. For her own reasons, she had allied herself with Duke Pheng and his militarist faction, the *Iron Bloc*. She had also enthralled this young woman and now used her as a conduit to communicate across the boundaries of normal space. Thus, seated in some richly-appointed chamber in Minhang, the Celestial Capital, she and the Duke could speak directly to the Admiral and his party.

The girl's mouth fell open, and a hollow voice issued from her throat. "Duke Pheng speaks. Nephew, I have two important pieces of news to convey. But first, your report."

The Admiral cleared his throat. "Our ships are fit and seaworthy, my lord uncle, we are on course ..."

Through the thrall, the Duke interrupted. "Did you search the Iruk Isles yet?"

Shay-Ni frowned. "As ordered, lord. We visited each of the main islands, made anchorage and contacted the village elders. As instructed, we made peaceful gestures, offered gifts of iron and oil. Most of their warriors are at sea in this season. We did encounter several groups of Iruk hunting boats. In one case they refused to parlay and attacked us with spears. We answered with crossbows and easily drove them off. In all, we found no one who admitted any knowledge of the Cloak of the Two Winds. Nor did the witches find any trace of it."

"That is so, my Lord Duke," Arkasha confirmed. "Our deepseeing found no trace of the Cloak's emanations in those places."

"I am not surprised," the Duke replied. "This matches new impressions that have reached us through Lady Clorodice's deepseers. It seems the Cloak is indeed in that region, but to the east of the Iruk Isles. Most likely on the peninsula called Fleevan, where a Tathian colony has existed for some time."

"Clorodice speaks now." The tone of the thrall changed to a higher pitch. "That is so, and the emanations grow clearer. This likely means that our concentrated efforts to weaken the concealments around the Cloak are at last succeeding."

Immediately, the thrall's voice dropped again. "Pheng speaks. That is the first important news, nephew. Here is the second: You are no longer alone in seeking the Cloak in that region. The House of the Deepmind has sent its own agent."

This was ill news to the Admiral. The controlling interests in the House of the Deepmind were opposed to the Duke's faction and their policy of military expansion. But the military controlled the navy, and in the icy seasons, Larthangan merchant vessels almost never ventured to these waters.

"How could they without a ship?" the Admiral demanded.

"Fool," the Duke snapped. "By witchery of course. This envoy witch is a *drell*, one of the winged people. More, she has the gift they call *second flight*. She can travel outside of normal space."

Shay-Ni was appalled. The earlier news had led him to hope he might actually succeed in bringing the prize back to Larthang. But now— "Then how can we hope to thwart this drell witch?"

"You must not fail!" The girl's head shook as she shouted the Duke's command. "You have deepshapers of your own on board, as well as Lady Clorodice's retinue here. Failure is unacceptable. The Cloak must come to us and not the obstructionalists in the House of the Deepmind. Do you understand?"

Shay-Ni bowed his head, cowed. "Yes, lord uncle."

"Be prepared," the Duke continued. "Whoever holds the Cloak will likely defend it with force—unless you are lucky enough to take them by surprise. They might even use its magic against your troops. In that contingency, assault the enemy with crossbows, striking from a distance. Lives may be lost, but that is of no consequence."

"I understand," the Admiral muttered, trying to keep anger from his tone. His uncle did not need to advise him on these tactics. They had been over these points before.

"As for the drell witch," the Duke went on. "If you encounter her, treat her with all deference. But you must *insist* on the military's rights to the Cloak, as it is a weapon of war. Kill her if you have to, but *do not let her take the Cloak!*"

Lady with wings
Lady with wings
Where did she fly
The bright lady?

The haphazard lyric drifted through Eben's mind as he wandered the streets of Fleevanport. It was his habit, when some question troubled him, to compose a verse or two. Once he had loved the chants and story-songs of his people, had been deemed to have some talent as a drummer and song-maker.

But that was before he and his klarn voyaged north and saw so much more of the world. That voyage had changed everything.

Twilight was settling over the waterfront, the air chilling, the faint polar sunlight gone, leaving only the witchlight of the harbor with its blue, frosty glow. Eben had just left the hostelry where he rented a small room in the attic. All day he had lain in bed, sleeping some, otherwise staring at the ceiling, brooding.

With this latest robbery, his money was running low. He would have to pay a visit to the farmstead where some of his former klarnmates still lived with the witch, Amlina. Eben had left his remaining share of treasure in their keeping. He didn't even know how much was left.

Of course, it would be pleasant to see his mates again. And Eben found it interesting sometimes to converse with the scholar Kizier, and even Buroof, the foul-tempered talking book. But it would also be embarrassing to see Lonn and Draven and Glyssa. The Iruks would not discuss it openly, but Eben knew they worried about him, disapproved of how he was wasting his loot and his life in Fleevanport.

No doubt, they had a point.

After resting and feasting for a time in Fleevan, the klarnmates had gone their separate ways. The sisters, Karrol and Brinda, had returned to their home island and joined a new klarn, determined to resume the Iruk way of life. Wilhaven the bard had sailed north, to fulfill his promise to sing Queen Meghild's saga in all the halls of Gwales. Glyssa had stayed with Amlina, to continue studying the magic of Larthang. Lonn and Draven had also chosen to stay, Lonn because he loved Glyssa, Draven because he was in love with Amlina.

That left only Eben at loose ends. He had no wish of joining a new klarn, of resuming the hard Iruk life of hunting and raiding. With his share of the treasure of Tallyba, he had thought to live at ease, drinking and feasting and sleeping with tavern girls. That was how he had always spent his gold in the past, when he'd been lucky enough to gain any.

But after many drunken nights and bleary, head-sore days, that life palled. Over Second and Third Winter, he had wandered back to the farmstead twice, stayed and hunted a bit with Lonn and Draven, told tales over the fire to Kizier, who was writing a scholarly work on the Iruk people. But soon boredom stirred again in Eben and sent him marching back down through the woods to the taverns and brothels.

Lady with wings
Lady with wings
Will you fly me away
Bright lady?

Eben grunted at the silliness of the thought. He had to find something worthwhile to do with his life, to occupy his mind and satisfy his restless heart. Sooner or later, his money would be gone. Then, like Karrol and Brinda, he supposed he would have to join a new klarn and hunt again. The notion held little appeal.

Coming to the waterfront, he noticed a dozen or so *dojuks*, Iruk hunting boats, tied up at the docks along with the fishing craft of the Fleevaners. At this time of year, the klarns sailed into port with cargoes of hides, frozen meat, and rendered yulugg oil to trade. These dojuks were among the first arrivals.

Eben's steps quickened, his boots crunching on the hard-packed snow, his mood brightening. He headed for the *Sea Lion*, an inn and hostelry frequented by Iruks. Perhaps he would meet Karrol and Brinda, or other of his neighbors from Ilga. If so, they would talk and laugh, and he would buy drinks for everyone. He still possessed enough coin for one good night of carousing.

The *Sea Lion* stood on a narrow street one block from the harbor. Approaching the lamp-lit doors, Eben heard loud talking and raucous laughter. Three Iruks in hunting garb and fur capes leaned on the outside walls, drinking from tankards. Not recognizing the man and two women, Eben nodded and stepped past them.

The main room was wide, low-ceilinged, and noisy. Lamps hung from black iron chandeliers and a wood-fire blazed in a hearth along one wall. The long bar and tables spread over the floor were crowded with Fleevaners, Tathians, and Iruks, their nationalities immediately apparent by their different clothing styles. The air smelled of smoke and spilled liquor.

Eben wound his way to the bar, where a party of broad-shouldered Iruks stood drinking. But when he spotted their faces he paused, then sidestepped toward the far end of the bar. Two of the men glanced up. But they were already well into their cups, and Eben could not tell if they had noticed him.

Casually, Eben moved to the end of the bar and ordered a tankard of mead. The man he had spotted was Harful, a klarn leader from Ilga. Bad blood simmered between them. When Eben and his mates first joined Amlina's crew, they had been forced to defend the Larthangan ship from the Iruk hunting party that they had left a few days earlier. Harful and the other boat skippers assumed Lonn's klarn had captured the ship and refused to share their loot, as required by Iruk law. Lonn and the mates bluffed them away, but not before Harful and the other captains vowed reprisal. When Lonn's klarn was away in the north, these vengeful neighbors ransacked their lodge house on Ilga. Later, after returning from their adventure in Tallyba, Lonn and his klarn had visited Ilga, met with the island's elders, and paid restitution for the infraction. But several of the klarn leaders had declared the payment inadequate. Harful in particular seemed humiliated that Lonn and his five klarnmates had faced down twenty boats and turned them away. He made no secret that he still nursed a grudge.

Now, Eben quietly sipped his mead and avoided looking at Harful or his companions. Instead he strained his ears to listen, picking up snatches of conversations. It seemed three Larthangan ships were in the region and had recently sailed around the Iruk Isles. This was rare news, as Larthangan ships seldom plied these waters—and especially not in the icy seasons. Eben wondered if those ships might have some connection with his lady of the wings. It seemed a logical conjecture.

A heavy hand clapped down on his shoulder.

"Here's one who is a friend to Larthangans!" A surly voice roared.

Eben spun around and stared up into the besotted face of Harful.

"He's sailed on their vessels, made friends with one of their witches. Maybe he knows why they've come."

Angrily, Eben flung up an arm to disengage Harful's grip. The taller Iruk grimaced. He was backed by two of his mates, all staring belligerently.

"Actually, I know nothing about it," Eben said calmly. "I've not been sailing this season."

"*Ooo. I've not been sailing this season.*" Harful repeated his words in a mocking, childlike voice. "I should have known that. You and your outlaw klarn have no need for plying the seas and hunting. Not with all your Larthangan treasure—loot that you cheated your own neighbors out of."

Eben clenched his lips. After a judicious pause, he answered quietly. "We cheated no one. The witch's ship at that time held no treasure, as we said. The loot we won came long after we parted from the hunting fleet. And we are not outlaws, since we paid fair shares to the village, as judged by the elders of the island." With a mild nod to Harful's companions, he turned back to the bar.

But Harful gripped his shoulder again and angrily spun him around.

"Don't turn your back on me, you little sea worm! I say you are a liar and a cheat."

The area nearby had grown quiet, everyone watching the dispute between two Iruks. Eben glanced at Harful and his two bulky mates. His wits told him this was not a battle he could win.

"I don't want to fight," he murmured, and reached to pick up his tankard.

"Ha!" Harful roared. "So he is not only a liar and cheat, but a *coward*."

Eben sighed. His wits told him one thing, but his warrior's pride said something else. Not listening to his wits was almost always a mistake.

Despite this wise thought, Eben thrust up his hand, splashing the mead into Harful's face. Next moment, he twisted and ducked. His foot lashed out, connecting hard with Harful's knee. Eben hoped the kick might tear a tendon or crush bone, but he had grown soft these past months, neglected his fighting practice.

Still, the knee snapped straight and Harful roared in pain, stumbling backward, his mead-splashed face contorted. Immediately, the two klarnmates grabbed Eben, each getting hold of an arm.

"Leave him! He's mine!" Harful snarled, a knife whipping from his belt.

"Stop it! Stop at once!" The barkeeper lifted a heavy cudgel over his head. "Take it outside, if you please. We'll have no damages here." Two of his waiters, stocky Fleevaners, were pushing through the crowd to add force to his request.

"Yes! Bring him out to the alley." Harful told his mates. "We'll soon make an end of one lying Iruk."

Mixed with his panic as they hustled him toward the back of the tavern, a stray thought ran through Eben's mind: *At least this isn't boring.*

Three

The alley was five paces across, cobblestones dusted with snow. The windows of the tavern kitchen and the rooms overhead cast a dull illumination. The air was frigid, a steady breeze coming up from the ice-laden harbor. The tavern noise, restored to a jovial babble, sounded faintly from inside.

Set free by the two warriors, Eben drew his hunting knife and watched Harful walk toward him. Mind racing, he calculated his chances. Harful was somewhat drunk, though a long way from stumbling. He was taller than Eben and much heavier—a bulky, hardened warrior. In duels with sword or knife, Eben's skill lay in speed and agility. But he had seldom handled weapons these past six months and knew himself to be woefully out of shape.

He crouched, pointed his knife, grinning.

Harful wasted no time, stalking forward, stabbing at Eben's face. Eben tilted just enough, nearly losing an ear, and thrust at his opponent's arm. But he was off balance. The blade scraped a sleeve but failed to even pierce the fur. Eben spun out of reach, crouched again.

Harful came on, swinging this time. Eben ducked low and took a gamble. He lunged, wrapped his arms around Harful's leg and lifted sideways. Harful, his reflexes not at their best, slipped, toppled, and fell sprawling on his back. Eben also stumbled, but managed to land on top of the bigger man. He pinned Harful's knife arm down with the weight of both legs and brought his point up to Harful's neck.

"Yield," Eben hissed.

Suddenly Harful's mates joined the fray. One of them kicked Eben over onto his back. The other warrior held Eben down while Harful righted himself and crawled over beside him.

Now it was Harful's knife point poking under Eben's chin.

"So!" he crowed. "Now I will free the world of one Iruk cheat!"

The point pressed closer.

Why didn't I listen to my wits? Eben wondered.

The tapered point of an Iruk hunting sword slid before Harful's eyes. The knife drew back from Eben's throat.

"That was *not* a fair fight," a woman's voice said.

Eben's eyes rolled up. Brinda, one of the women from Lonn's klarn, stood with her sword held firmly at Harful's nose. A glance to the side showed Karrol, Brinda's sister, pointing sword and spear to hold the other two men at bay.

Dressed in a quilted robe, her white-blond hair in disarray, Amlina descended the steps to the great room. Glyssa, Lonn, and Kizier watched her from the dining table. Draven stared moodily from a chair at the fireplace.

Amlina lowered her eyes, avoiding their gazes.

None of her friends spoke as Amlina walked to the hearth and lifted the lid from a cauldron. She took a bowl from the mantel and used a ladle to serve out some stew. She hadn't eaten all day, keeping to her room, claiming she was meditating. She felt no hunger now, but knew she must eat in the hope of regaining her strength.

Crossing to the table, she could feel their emotions—worry, fear, perhaps a sullen anger. Amlina hated herself for causing them to suffer. When she was seated, it was Kizier, the normally quiet scholar, who broke the silence.

"Amlina, we must talk."

"I am listening, my friend." She raised the spoon to her lips. The venison broth was hot and savory. Her stomach cringed.

"We cannot go on like this." Draven had stalked over to stand at her shoulder. "*You* cannot go on like this. You are destroying yourself."

Amlina set down the spoon. Lonn and Kizier stared at her solemnly, Glyssa with love and deep worry. She dared not even look at Draven, opening herself to his grief would be unbearable.

"I am not destroying myself." Her voice faltered. "I am coping as best I can."

Draven gripped her wrist, yanked up her arm so the loose sleeve dropped, showing her skin. "This is how you are coping? By bleeding away your life's blood?"

Amlina's cheeks burned with shame. "So you know."

"How could I not know?" Draven raved, jerking her wrist harder. "I share your room, your bed. Do you think me so stupid? A witless barbarian?"

"Steady." Lonn told him.

With a growl of frustration, Draven released her and stamped back to the hearth. Leaning an arm on the mantel, he stared into the fire.

"All of us know how you are suffering," Glyssa said softly. "We want to help you. There must be a way."

Amlina stared blankly. "I have tried everything I know to do."

Kizier had stood and walked over to a writing table near the fireplace. He returned carrying a large book bound in leather and iron. Draven followed him and sat down beside Amlina.

"I *have* conferred with Buroof," she said.

"So have we," Kizier answered. "I think you need to hear his perspective on this matter."

Setting the book on the table, he opened the cover. A cloud of light rose from the parchment. "Buroof, I, Kizier, summon you."

Once Buroof had been human, a scholar of vast learning. Long ago, his mind had been captured and bound into the book by a sorcerer. For nearly three thousand years, Buroof's mind had continued to live, absorbing knowledge from every mage, sorcerer, and witch who possessed the book.

"I am here," a hollow voice answered.

"With me is Amlina," Kizier said, "and also our Iruk friends."

"Yes. So?"

"I want you to repeat what you told us earlier, concerning techniques of healing those who suffer imbalance and unnatural hungers caused by residues of blood magic."

Buroof heaved a sign. "Really, it is most annoying to constantly be required to repeat myself."

"Nevertheless," Kizier answered patiently.

"Oh, very well. The most extensive records are of course from ancient Nyssan, among both the Nagaree and the cities of the Far East. In both places, the practices of blood magic were common, and often the hungers you term "unnatural" resulted. Of course they were not then deemed unnatural, merely appetites to be satisfied. However, there were treatments devised for when these appetites became unmanageable. Typically this involved a circle of practitioners drawing both blood and a measure of life essence, thus restoring physical and psychic balance."

"Drawing blood and energy to restore the balance," Amlina said. "I've consulted Buroof too, and this is exactly what I've been attempting."

"Obviously without success," Lonn stated bluntly.

"What about the records from Larthang," Kizier prompted the book.

"Yes," Buroof answered. "Before the Time of the World's Madness, blood magic was also practiced in Larthang, though to a much lesser degree. It was already condemned by many as nefarious. History tells of certain formulations that were devised to cure blood mages by transmuting their unbalanced energies, turning them into power aligned to principles of right practice as defined by philosophies of the time."

Amlina eyed Kizier skeptically. "Are you suggesting I should sail to Larthang?"

"Isn't that what you always intended?" Glyssa asked her gently.

Amlina fretted, raking a hand through her hair. "Yes, but that would mean ..." Her voice trailed off. It would mean going back, not in triumph as she had always hoped, but as a tainted witch, a pitiful failure, throwing herself on the mercy of the House of the Deepmind, the establishment of high witches—they who had scorned her long ago.

"How do I even know they could help me?" she said. "Just because certain practices existed in the remote past ..."

"It seems your most likely place to find a cure," Kizier insisted. "And isn't it said that all magic that was ever practiced in the House of the Deepmind abides there, in the very foundation stones and the ground below?"

"Yes, so it is said," Amlina answered. "But even if that is not merely a poetic conceit, finding a witch able and willing to raise such ancient designs for my benefit ..."

"... Seems your best hope of finding a cure," Kizier insisted. "Besides, you can't hide here forever. I know you've woven concealments, but sooner or later one powerful mage or another will penetrate them and discover the Cloak."

"I believe this is all stupendously obvious," Buroof interjected. "In my opinion, Amlina, you should sail to Larthang immediately and deliver the Cloak and the Scrolls of Eglemarde to the House of the Deepmind. I'd prefer that you also present myself, as a gift to them. Frankly, I am enormously bored with the lot of you, and would welcome a chance to converse with wiser, more engaging minds. In fact—" Kizier closed the book cutting off Buroof's developing tirade.

"There you have it." Glyssa smiled. "Even our kind and courteous friend Buroof sees this as your wisest course."

Amlina regarded her sullenly, then glanced around at the others, her gaze coming to rest on Draven. The pain and love she read in his face melted her resistance.

"Perhaps you are right," she murmured. "Would you—would all of you sail with me?"

Before they could answer, a buzzing sounded above, at a corner of the ceiling. Between the timber beams a ball of light appeared, growing as it drifted down. A figure coalesced in the light, a small black-haired lady lifted by the blur of bee wings.

"How did you find me in that alley, mates?" Eben asked. "Not that I am not excessively happy that you did."

Karrol snorted. "You mean, behind a tavern, in over your head in some stupid brawl? It seemed an obvious place to look."

Eben and Brinda both laughed.

The three Iruks soaked together in a wide tub of steaming water. They had walked to this bath house several streets from the harbor immediately after leaving the *Sea Lion*—deeming it wise to put some distance between themselves and Harful's crew. Of course, Eben had insisted on stopping along the way at one of his favorite wine shops to purchase several bottles of mead.

Now he passed one to Karrol, who took a long swallow.

She was tall for an Iruk woman, and strongly built. Brinda, her sister, was leaner, though both had muscular physiques that made Eben glance regretfully at his own thin limbs and soft belly.

"We just landed at sunset," Brinda explained. "We were going to bathe first, then buy some dinner. But something made us stop at the *Sea Lion*."

"It might have been the klarn-soul," Karrol added. "It had that feeling."

A klarn was more than the crew of a hunting boat. It had a group soul, formed by all of the members. That group soul bound them together and gave them strength.

Eben scratched his head. "You mean from Lonn's klarn?" They had disbanded the klarn months ago, after settling in at the farmhouse.

"Of course," Karrol said. "What else could I mean?"

"But I thought you two joined a new klarn."

"Oh, that's over," Karrol replied.

"Right." One side of Brinda's mouth twisted up. "Karrol couldn't get along with Tallvis the leader. We split with them after just one hunt."

"He was always barking at me." Karrol waved a hand dismissively. "And if you questioned his decisions the slightest little bit, he took it as an insult. Highly unreasonable. It was all I could do to not throw him out of the boat."

Eben was laughing again. "That is something I can easily imagine."

Karrol shook her head. "Lonn never acted that way. I miss our old klarn. We were all good mates."

"That we were," Eben agreed.

"I miss it too," Brinda admitted.

"And I *do* think the klarn-soul led us to find you tonight," Karrol added. "It draws us together. Maybe it's because of Glyssa. Maybe it's due to Amlina's magic, or all the adventures we shared. But I can't imagine another bond ever being so strong."

The three of them sat quietly in the rising steam.

Perhaps Karrol was right about the klarn-soul, Eben thought. Certainly, sitting with these two former mates, he felt happier and more relaxed than he had in months.

"So what are your plans now?" he asked.

Brinda answered, "We thought of going up to the farmstead, to visit with Glyssa and Lonn."

"They're still up there, aren't they?" Karrol said.

"Yes, I believe so."

"We, uh," Karrol hesitated. "We thought they might want to form a klarn with us again. You'd be welcome too, of course."

"Oh, I don't know if that would work. Draven and Glyssa at least will want to stay with Amlina."

"Amlina hasn't sailed back to Larthang yet?" Karrol asked.

"I'm nearly certain she hasn't."

"Why not?" Karrol said. "What is she waiting for?"

"She's been ... indisposed."

"Well, fine." Karrol frowned. After a moment, she peered at Brinda. "Maybe we could reform the klarn and sail with her."

Brinda shrugged. "I wouldn't mind."

Eben stared at them both, a quiver of excitement moving in him. Maybe it was the klarn-soul after all. They had sailed to the Tathian Islands and Gwales in the north, to Near and Far Nyssan in the east. Larthang on the western continent was the only remote part of the world they had not visited together.

"You know," he said. "I have to admit, that idea sounds both ridiculous and appealing."

"Ha!" Karrol playfully poked his ribs. "You'll need to regain some muscle if you're coming with us. Honestly, you're a scrawny mess."

Four

As the winged creature drifted down from the ceiling, Amlina jumped to her feet. So did Lonn and Draven, who rushed to grab spears and hunting swords from a rack by the front door. They were back in a moment, weapons ready.

"No!" Glyssa raised a hand to ward off any attack. "She means no harm, I think."

In her time studying under Amlina, Glyssa's witchsight had grown keen. But Amlina herself was not so sure.

The intruder, now clearly revealed as a woman with insect wings, wore a sheer white gown, leggings, and slippers. Her hair was long and black, her face thin and angular with a bronze tone, not much different from the Iruk skin color. Hovering in the air, glancing from face to face, she spoke in Low-Tathian in a soft, unsteady voice.

"These are Iruks. And this one"— she gestured toward Kizier—"is a man of the Tathian Isles, perhaps? But you, lady"—staring now at Amlina—"I do believe are Larthangan?"

"That is so." Amlina stood rigid. "And you are a *drell*."

She had seen the winged people before, of course, when she lived in Minhang and studied at the Academy of the Deepmind. Always it was from a distance, at public events and ceremonies. A small delegation of drells lived at the court of the Tuan, and others made occasional visits to the capital. The drells were among the sentient races spawned in the Age of the World's Madness, a time of chaos brought on by the unrestrained use of magic. Now the drells lived in a forest of giant trees that formed the border between Larthang and the southern land of Zindu.

A smile spread on the winged lady's mouth "Indeed. I am a drell." Her wings grew still and she settled onto the floor, bells tinkling on the pointed toes of her slippers.

"What a lovely creature," Glyssa said, then asked Amlina. "What is a drell?"

Draven and Lonn had lowered their weapons, but still watched the winged woman suspiciously. Kizier's expression was one of intent, thoughtful curiosity.

The drell's eyes were on Amlina. "I am named Trippany. May we speak?" she asked in Larthangan.

Amlina relaxed into her chair and gestured to the bench beside her. "Of course. Be seated if you wish. But speak in Tathian please, so the others will understand."

Trippany frowned and remained standing. "Better if we talk privately."

Amlina shook her head. "There is nothing you cannot say in front of my *mates*."

She used the Iruk word meaning "members of my klarn." The drell's expression was puzzled as she glanced at the others.

"Very well," she said, returning to the Tathian tongue. "I am an envoy from the House of the Deepmind in the city of Minhang. I seek the Cloak of the Two Winds. Do you know where it might be found?"

Now everyone stared at Amlina, faces tense. She forced a calm smile. "I do indeed. The Cloak is in my possession."

"Oh, at last!" Trippany's body slumped with relief, to the point where her balance faltered. Her wings fluttered briefly to restore her footing. "Then you are the witch who confiscated the Cloak from the Archimage of Tallyba. And these are your Iruk crew, as the stories told."

"Some of the crew," Amlina answered.

Trippany's eyes shifted again, resting on the weapons still held by Draven and Lonn. Her nerve seemed to falter, but she set her shoulders and spoke with what firmness she could gather.

"I have been charged to return the Cloak of the Two Winds to the House of the Deepmind, from whence it was stolen long ago. Will you give it to me, so I may restore it to its rightful owners?"

Amlina pressed her lips. "It has always been my intention to return the Cloak to Minhang. In fact, we were discussing this very matter when you made your uninvited entrance."

"Forgive me," Trippany replied. "I know my appearance was ... abrupt. But I have been searching for so long and returning the Cloak is urgent."

"Why is it urgent?" Kizier inquired.

"Because others are searching. It must not fall into their hands."

"Others from Larthang?" Amlina probed.

Suddenly Trippany seemed exhausted. She put a hand on the table, then reluctantly settled herself down on the bench. "Yes. Naval squadrons have been dispatched. They are searching everywhere— including the Polar Sea. There is a war faction in Larthang, a group of nobles seeking to conquer the Tathian Islands. They hope to use the Cloak as a weapon."

Amlina considered. The story seemed all too plausible—and confirmed her suspicions that her hiding place might soon be discovered.

"Which faction do you represent?" she challenged.

Trippany straightened her spine. "I was sent by Drusdegarde the Archimage. As Chief of the House of the Deepmind, it is her duty to maintain the balance of magical forces in the world. That is why the Cloak must go to her and no other."

Amlina saw wisdom in that as well. The Cloak was one of the most powerful instruments in existence. Fashioned by the great mage Eglemarde, it embodied the forces of freezewind and meltwind, which Eglemarde created to vent excess magical energies from the Deepmind. Wielding the Cloak's power excessively—as one likely would in a war—might conceivably upset the age-old balance, might even bring on a new Age of Madness. Were such a disaster to happen, Amlina reflected, she could blame no one but herself. Foolishly, selfishly, she had delayed returning the Cloak to Minhang.

She peered at the drell, frowning. "So you are asking that I turn the Cloak over to you. How do you propose to deliver it to the Archimage?"

Trippany gripped the edge of the table. "I can fly there at once. I have the gift of *second flight*, you see?"

Amlina nodded. "I suspected as much. That is a rare gift among your people, I believe."

"Yes. That is why I was sent to study in Minhang. To learn to master this gift. And that is why the Archimage sent me on this quest."

Amlina's companions watched her intently. The decision was hers. But there were so many factors to consider. The drell's story rang true, but Amlina had no proof the winged lady could be trusted. And if she did hand over the Cloak now, could she still hope to return to Larthang and find help for her sickness? She would still have the Scrolls of Eglemarde to offer, but they were ceremonial artifacts, of historical interest at best. Amlina's position would be much stronger if she were the one delivering the Cloak.

She stared at the drell. "It has always been my intention to return the Cloak to the House of the Deepmind. And I do realize others are searching for it, and may be closing in. I have sensed this in my deepseeing. Now I must decide if the rightful course is to hand the Cloak over to you or to sail to Larthang myself to return it."

Trippany rose slowly to her feet. "Perhaps you do not trust me? What proof might I bring you, that I speak the truth?"

"None," Amlina said. "Any token or document you showed might be forged by witchery. For all I know, the Archimage herself might be corrupt and allied with this war faction. No. My duty as a witch of Larthang is to seek the guidance of the Deepmind. I need only a little time, a night and a day. I will give you my decision by tomorrow evening."

Trippany's face evinced frustration and disappointment. She compressed her lips, but nodded. "Very well. I shall await your answer." Her wings fluttered and she rose into the air.

"Wait," Amlina said. "You appear tired. I know that spaceless travel is taxing, even for one such as you. Will you accept our hospitality until tomorrow night?"

Trippany seemed to consider it, then flew higher. "Thank you, but no. Even as you cannot trust me, so I cannot trust you. If one of you will open the door, I will await your answer in the forest outside."

"As you wish," Amlina said. "But it will be very cold overnight, and you hardly seem dressed for this climate. At least accept a sleeping fur, to keep yourself warm."

When the drell had flown out the front door, Amlina went immediately upstairs to her bedroom. The bed-closet where she slept had built-in drawers for storage. Amlina made sure the window shutters were closed, then bent and opened one of the drawers. Inside, beneath clothes and boxes of her jewelry and trinkets, lay the black and silver cloak.

Amlina knelt and set her hands on the smooth fabric, sensing the vast magical energy at rest within. Calling upon the art of pure shaping, she placed protection over the Cloak. When the work was finished, she turned to find Draven standing in the doorway, watching her quietly.

"You do not trust the winged lady," he said.

Amlina closed the drawer. "No. How can I? Her story *appears* plausible, but the arts of deception are highly developed in Larthang. And she has the power of second flight. She could materialize in this room, snatch the Cloak, and be gone before we even suspected. That is what I'm guarding against. A little mind-trick, so even if she searches here, she will, I hope, fail to see the Cloak."

Draven approached her. "So you will not give her the Cloak. Will you sail to Larthang yourself to return it?"

Amlina bit her lip. "I don't know. I was truthful when I told her I would seek the counsel of the Deepmind. But I do feel time is running short. I will seek guidance in my dreams tonight, then meditate on the problem all day tomorrow if necessary."

A slight nod was his only reaction. Amlina sensed his worry for her, and below that, his wild love and devotion. She smiled fondly and placed a hand on his cheek.

"My dear one. How much trouble I have caused you."

Draven laughed and clasped her tightly in his arms. "We Iruks are made for trouble. But your sort of trouble? I admit, that is uncommon."

Embracing him, Amlina shook from a mixture of laughter, exhaustion, and tears.

"And if I sail to Larthang, you will come with me?"

"Of course," he murmured. "So will Glyssa and Lonn and Kizier, I am sure." He kissed her neck, then her earlobe.

Amlina sighed. "And will you take me to bed now? I know I will sleep better with you beside me."

Still holding her tightly, Draven grinned, then kissed her on the mouth.

In the hills above Fleevanport, farms and open meadows gradually gave way to pine forest. From the upper slopes, a traveler could sometimes look down on a broad view of the town and the bay.

Today, of course, Eben could see nothing—because of the scarf tied over his eyes.

Bent at the waist, he marched with his gear strapped to his back—a bed fur, weapons, a small water skin filled with mead. He followed the tug of a rope tied to his belt, and walked with a careful flat-footed gait. Still, he stumbled sometimes. Whenever that happened, Karrol complained.

"This is so stupid! Eben can't see where he's going because he's blindfolded. Why is he blindfolded? Because he dreamed of seeing a lady with bee's wings and now is afraid she might spy on him. Honestly, Brinda, I think all the mead has finally addled his brain."

"I may be overcautious," Eben allowed. "But if the bee lady *was* real, she was looking for Amlina. And if she can appear and disappear in a ball of light, it's just as possible she can read my thoughts. I won't have her finding the way to our mates' hideout because I was afraid of appearing foolish."

Actually, he was rather enjoying walking blindfolded—an interesting mental challenge, both to keep his footing and to try to gauge the distance they had traveled. Hearing Karrol gripe was just an added amusement.

It was mid-afternoon when the three companions approached the farmhouse, after ascending several miles through deep woods. Only then did Eben consent to untie the scarf.

The place looked the same as he remembered—a spacious, two-story house of dark wood with sloping roofs, a barn of equal size, a smaller woodshed, fenced pens for keeping sheep and woolgoats, now empty. In front of the barn, two men were chopping firewood. Spotting the newcomers, they stopped their work.

"Hallo!" Lonn called, waving an arm. He and Draven dropped their axes and ran toward the road.

Laughing, Brinda, Karrol, and Eben discarded their bundles and embraced their friends.

"What brings you here?" Lonn asked.

"We missed you all," Karrol said.

"Also, we left our klarn," Brinda added. "So we're free."

"Your visit is timely," Draven said. "I think we may leave very soon."

He explained how Amlina would decide this very night whether she would quit Fleevan and sail to Larthang.

"We were all trying to convince her to make this decision," Lonn said. "Then this winged lady forced her hand."

Eben's eyes widened. "Did you say *winged lady*?"

"Yes. You missed some excitement last night." Draven related how the drell had appeared in a flash of light, and described her conversation with Amlina.

"So." Eben looked smugly at Karrol and Brinda. "A lady with bee wings, searching for the Cloak of the Two Winds. Who could have dreamed up such a wild story?"

Brinda laughed. Karrol shook her head with lips clamped, but a smile tugging at the corners.

"Mates! Mates!" Glyssa came running from the front door of the house.

Another round of laughter and joyful greetings ensued, Glyssa hugging each of the newcomers in turn.

"I am so happy to see you," Glyssa cried.

"We are always happy to see you." Brinda embraced her a second time and kissed her forehead.

"I don't think this is chance." Glyssa spoke with a distant look in her eyes, a look that told Eben her thoughts were spun up by witchsight. "I think we will be leaving soon, and I feel the klarn-soul may have drawn us back together."

They contemplated this in silence for a moment, then Karrol burst out.

"The klarn-soul drawing us all back together! Who could have dreamed up such a wild idea?"

Five

They carried their luggage inside and set it down in the foyer. Glyssa and Draven put the kettle on for tea and fetched bread, butter, and cheese. Kizier emerged from his room on the first floor and greeted the new arrivals.

Soon they were warming themselves at the fire, eating and drinking and talking in the manner of close friends. Kizier and Glyssa spoke of Amlina's illness and how they hoped she would return to Larthang to seek a cure. Karrol related her and Brinda's experiences with the klarn of Tallvis and why they had left. Lonn and Draven talked about hunting lamnocc in the woods.

After finishing his tea, Eben grew restless. He alone had no worthy news to recount, having mostly passed Second and Third Winter dawdling in Fleevanport. His mates voiced no disapproval, but he sensed—or imagined—they worried about his idling and excessive drinking.

Leaving them to their chatting and laughter, Eben went out for a walk. Lonn had told him the drell spent the night high in the branches of a tree behind the barn. Eben wanted to see if she was still there.

Circling the house, he walked along the back lane where once sheep and woolgoats had been driven toward the pens. Eyes squinting in the daylight, he scanned the upper branches of the tall conifers.

Suddenly he spotted her high overhead—a small figure wrapped in a gray fur, sitting with her back to a tree trunk. Even at this distance, he could see her eyes watching him. Hesitantly, he raised a hand in greeting.

The lady shrugged the fur from her shoulders, stood and then stepped from the branch. Wings fluttering, she floated down toward him. She stopped three yards above his head.

"That cannot be a comfortable resting place," he said.

Her lips curved in a faint smile. "My people are used to sleeping in trees. We are wild creatures." The wings slowed and she settled on the ground in front of him. "I remember you, Iruk-man from the alley. So you knew where the Cloak was. It seems you are an even greater liar than you pretended."

He grinned, abashed. "True, I can be a very great liar when necessary. In this case it *was* necessary. I was sworn not to reveal the hiding place of my friends. You can understand that, surely?"

The lady's eyes were solemn. "I understand. There is no blame. We must keep our word, and we must always be loyal to friends."

They watched each other silently, the drell still floating in the air. Eben felt a mad attraction to her—so small and fragile-looking, yet full of strange power. He wondered if she might have bewitched him.

"Did you find this place through me?" he asked. "By reading my mind?"

The question surprised her. "No, indeed. Your lying worked well. I serve the Archimage in Minhang. She and her adepts have searched for some time and were finally able to locate the Cloak. They directed me here."

"It seems odd to me," he observed, "that the great witches of Larthang should send you alone. I do not know all your powers, it's true, but it seems they could have mustered a larger force."

Stilling her wings, she settled to the forest floor. "Others are searching, in other places. This time of year it is difficult to find ships whose captains are willing to sail. For me of course, that is no problem, since I can fly outside of normal distance."

"A strange power to be sure. Amlina tells me you can appear and disappear at will, almost anywhere."

A half-smile tugged the corners of her mouth. "That is my gift, but it is not so simple. Second flight extracts a price; it drains my strength. That is why I stayed in this forest overnight, awaiting Amlina's decision. Do you know if she will surrender the Cloak to me?"

Eben shrugged, back on his guard. "I have no way to know. Amlina will do what she thinks best. As her mates, the rest of us will support her."

Her face expressed disappointment. "If she promises to bring the Cloak to Larthang, will she keep her word?"

"I believe so. That is what she always meant to do."

"I hope so," the drell said. "If the Cloak falls into the wrong hands, the consequences could be terrible."

Amlina sat in a chair, facing the door, eyes shut in meditation. Her dreams last night had given her no message. Indeed, she recalled no dreams at all, only a deep calm sleep, feeling utterly safe with Draven beside her. Turning her mind within, she sensed the stain of sorcery still present in her, but quiet, dormant—not the terrible raging hunger it had been yesterday.

She focused her mind on the question at hand: surrender the Cloak to the drell, or sail with it herself to Larthang? Which was the rightful path? If she had more time, she would have asked the question in deep trance, or even tried the *Bowing to the Sky* rite once more. But both of those might take several days, and she had promised to decide by this evening.

Because time was running out.

Amlina dismissed the distracting thoughts, sought again to still her mind so that an answer might arise.

For a time, she sat in stillness, aware only of the slow currents of the *ogo*—that Larthangan name for the Deepmind which meant "the drift of things." Within the drift, she sensed another mind, a familiar and beloved soul.

Glyssa. It has been some time since you joined me in trance.

In their early months at the farmstead, Amlina had meditated with Glyssa often, as part of the Iruk woman's training.

I hesitated to form the link, Glyssa admitted. *The dark power inside you, and your pain—they are hard to bear.*

And now?

Not so bad now. Today you seem better.

You are right, Glyssa. Not cured, certainly, but the pain is lessened. I'm not sure why.

That is the way you are, Amlina. I have said this to our mates. In times of waiting, when you are uncertain, you worry and doubt yourself. But once you have set your course, and the time arrives for action, then you are the toughest and bravest of us all.

But have I set my course?

I feel you have.

A vision rippled in Amlina's mind. She stood on the prow of an Iruk boat, sailing on soft water. In her arms she held the black and silver Cloak. In the distance lay a harbor, spread at the mouth of a great river. On either bank of the river stood a giant tower of white and yellow stone. Amlina recognized the city, Randoon of the Onyx Gates—the Larthangan port she had sailed from more than ten years ago.

Perhaps you are right, Glyssa. Perhaps I have my answer.

Full of many thoughts, Eben wandered up the trail. Soon the trees thinned and the path turned off to the left. Walking straight ahead, Eben ascended a slope of bare, rocky ground and came to the edge of a cliff.

Below him spread the sea, or rather an inlet, bordered by a narrow beach of black shale. A meltwind had blown in the early morning, and soft water tossed and surged, rippling with witchlight under a gray, cloudy sky. The wind now was a steady breeze from the south. Another freeze might come at any time.

Eben sat on a boulder and stared at the choppy waves. A chant rose in his mind:

Old winds, blow for us
Wide seas flow for us
Give us your fishes
Give us your treasures
We Iruks sing to you

How simple life had been once, before the voyages to unknown lands. Now he had witches and winged ladies to think about. And too much drinking and idleness, he had to admit. Soon the last of his coin would be gone—then what?

Perhaps Lonn would re-form the klarn, and they would sail on another wild adventure. Eben found the idea appealing. Larthang was a land of legendary wealth and wonders. No doubt there would be plenty there to satisfy his curious mind. He might even see Trippany again ...

Soft footfalls sounded behind him. He turned to see the witch Amlina coming up the hill. As she approached, Eben examined her, wrapped in a heavy coat with a fur hood, leaning forward as she climbed the slope. But it was her face that alarmed him. Amlina had always appeared a pale, fragile woman, but now she looked sunken-eyed, almost starving.

"Hello," she said. "May I join you."

"Of course." He gestured to the ground nearby.

Amlina sat down, feet tucked at her hips. She stared out over the sea.

"I am glad you and Karrol and Brinda have come. I think we will be leaving very soon."

Eben nodded. "Then you have decided to sail to Larthang—and not give the Cloak to the winged lady?"

"You heard about the drell then?"

"Oh, yes. To be honest, she came upon me in Fleevanport. I worried that she might have read my mind and that was how she found you here. But she told me this afternoon it was not so."

"You spoke with her today?" Amlina asked.

"Yes. I went looking for her in the woods."

"And what do you think of her?"

"A strange and beautiful creature, to be sure. I find it hard to understand how she can fly, even with the speed of her wings."

"The bones of her people are said to be hollow, like those of birds," the witch answered. "And of course their wings tap some magical current of the Deepmind. But I meant, what is your impression of her character. Can she be trusted?"

"Oh." Eben laughed. "I've not much experience judging the characters of witches. But, since you ask, she reminds me of you, Amlina, when the klarn first joined up with you: unsure of herself, feeling over her head, but determined nonetheless. Do you think her trustworthy?"

Amlina sighed. "I don't *distrust* her. Her heart seems pure, to my reading. But I do not think I will give her the Cloak. Delivering it to Larthang feels like a thing I must do myself."

Eben grinned. For all her physical weakness, and whatever the doubts she might be suffering, Amlina had spoken with the same stubborn determination he had noticed in Trippany.

"So. Are you looking for a crew?"

The witch bowed her head with a smile. "You would be most welcome. I know Glyssa and Draven and Lonn would feel the same. Especially Glyssa. She misses her absent mates very much."

"All of us love Glyssa."

"Yes. But for her it is more than that. When she had the psychic wound from being enthralled, she healed herself by the spiritual disciplines of magic. But it was not the love of magic or power that filled the void in her heart, it was love of her klarnmates."

Eben stared at the sea, reflecting. When he turned back, Amlina was gazing at him with round eyes—reading him with deepsight.

"Now," she said, "I think both you and I have holes in our hearts that we must fill. For me, it is a raging void, an evil hunger brought on by the blood magic. For you ... I am not sure."

Eben shrugged. "Nor am I. Perhaps just a lack of purpose. Or maybe, like the others, I miss the old klarn."

His eyes drifted to the beach thirty yards below. That was the place where they had disbanded and set the klarn-soul to rest. The sea had looked much like it did this afternoon, soft water tossed by a chill wind. It was a few days after they settled in at the farmstead. Their Gwales raiding ship was anchored in the inlet. They burned the vessel to make a proper funeral for Meghild, the pirate queen who had sacrificed herself to allow the witch to forge the Mirror Against All Mishap. Meghild's body was already gone of course. But they had taken the cloak she wore and spread it out on the deck with a Gwales-forged sword and spear and the queen's share of the treasure won on the voyage. After bidding Meghild farewell, they had raised the sail and put the ship to the torch. As it drifted out to sea, Wilhaven the bard sang a dirge to honor the queen he served. A few days later, he sailed from Fleevanport, bound for the north to fulfill his vow to sing Meghild's saga in all the halls of Gwales.

Amlina, it seemed, was remembering that day too. "In retrospect, it might have been a mistake to burn our ship," she murmured.

"There are other boats," Eben answered. "We can acquire a dojuk in Fleevanport."

Amlina's eyes kindled. "You have decided to sail with us then?"

"I am leaning that way, to be sure."

"I am glad. But it would be unfair not to warn you: finding a boat will be just the start of our problems. This voyage figures to be dangerous, with many powerful people chasing us. How it will end, I cannot even guess."

Eben grinned. "Now you are trying to tempt me."

Six

At sunset they walked back toward the farmhouse. As they reached the trees, Amlina spotted Trippany, swooping among the high branches as though searching. When the drell spotted them, she darted down.

"Hurry!" she cried, flying near. "Hurry! They are coming."

Amlina halted, rigid. "Who are coming?"

"Larthangan troops, marching up the road. They have found you! They have come for the Cloak!"

Amlina broke into a run, Eben on her heels, Trippany overhead. The witch did not doubt the drell's report. For days now she had sensed the powers seeking the Cloak were drawing near. Now they were upon her. She ran past the farmhouse and up a wooded hill. From the ridge at the summit, one could see a long way down the road.

Stopping there, she peered down the slope. A column of warriors moved up the trail—Larthangans for certain, judging by their banners, armor, and long coats. A few in the front of the party wore the brightly-colored robes of witches. No pipes or drums were beating, but otherwise the intruders made no attempt to conceal their approach. They would reach the farmhouse in a few minutes.

Amlina whirled and hurried down the hill, Eben and Trippany following behind. They burst into the house through the front door—to find Glyssa and the others in the great room, preparing dinner or else resting by the fire.

"My friends, we must leave," Amlina told them. "Soldiers are coming."

The Iruks looked at one another for just an instant, then scrambled to grab weapons.

Trippany dropped down, landing directly in front of the witch. "Will you give me the Cloak? It must go back to Larthang."

Amlina hesitated, then emphatically shook her head. "I will take it there myself."

She shouted to her mates. "I suggest we go out the back and down the cliff, then along the beach to Fleevanport. Eben says we can find a boat there. I intend to sail to Larthang. If you'll come with me, then hurry. Pack only what you can carry."

Glyssa, Draven, and Lonn were already charging up the stairs to fetch their gear. Kizier hastened to the door of his room on the first floor. Karrol and Brinda had armed themselves but now stood by the fireplace, uncertain.

"Will you two come with us?" Amlina asked.

The sisters exchanged glances, then both nodded. "We will," Karrol answered, "at least as far as the port."

Trippany, wings beating furiously, bounded up and down in front of the witch. "This is madness. You cannot escape! There is no time. And there are too many for you to fight."

"We shall see." Amlina ran for the stairs.

In their bedroom, Draven was tying bed furs and clothing into a bundle. Amlina dragged a hinged wicker basket from the closet. From the drawers under the bed she took a gown, her witch's robes, jewelry, trinkets, tools, small sacks of gold. No time to pack much, but there were certain things she would not part with.

Trippany had followed her and now flew about the room in agitation. "Amlina, you must know this is senseless. They are already here. They will surround the house."

"I know that," Amlina said, picking up the black and silver Cloak.

Trippany settled onto the floor. For a moment, Amlina feared the drell might attack her and try to snatch the Cloak away.

"These men will certainly deliver the Cloak to the Iron Bloc," Trippany said quietly. "They must not take it."

Amlina gripped the fabric. "They will not take it from me, but neither will you."

Trippany winced, wings quivering. "I have not the power to take it from you. So I must ask: if you escape, do you swear on your honor as a witch to deliver this Cloak to the House of the Deepmind?"

"Yes," Amlina replied. "I see this as my rightful path, as counseled by the Deepmind. It is my duty, and I will follow it as best I am able."

"Then we are allies," the drell said. "I will delay them as long as I can." With a humming of wings, she swooped from the room.

The farmhouse loomed dark and silent in the twilight. Smoke rose from the chimney and lamps burned behind some of the slatted window shutters. Admiral Pheng scanned the outbuildings and fences and the woods beyond, but detected no sound or movement.

"You are certain?" he murmured to Arkasha.

Beside him, the witch nodded, jaw tight, eyes narrow. "The emanations are strong. The Cloak is very near."

Dressed in a quilted coat of orange and gold, Arkasha held a black silk cord in her fist. The cord was tied around the waist of the thrall girl, who stood beside her mute and dull.

The flotilla had entered the harbor of Fleevanport that morning, a growing atmosphere of excitement and urgency apparent among the witches. Traces of the Cloak had grown stronger as they crossed the sea from the Iruk Isles, according to the reports channeled from Minhang through the thrall. Arkasha was certain the prize was near.

Wasting no time, Pheng lowered boats and landed on the docks with a detachment of a hundred troops, armed with pikes, swords, and crossbows. Marching through the city, the landing party was challenged, first by town watchmen, then by Tathian guardsmen in steel armor, carrying truncheons and swords. Pheng judged his troops more than a match for the Tathians, but a battle would have cost both lives and time. Besides, his orders were to make war on the natives only as a last resort. Instead, Pheng and his lieutenants attended a hastily arranged meeting with the colonial governor, a tall gray-beard with a cautious, wily demeanor. The admiral claimed that he sought the arrest of a certain renegade Larthangan witch believed to reside in these parts. Pledging a peaceful withdrawal whether they found this witch or not—along with a not insignificant bribe of Larthangan gold—was enough to secure the governor's cooperation.

By noon, Pheng and his party were on the march. The young girl, black cord around her waist, walked in the lead, her mind a blank, her steps directed by the powerful circle of witches far away in Minhang. Past the outskirts of the city, they climbed into hills and thickening forest. Pheng kept a sharp eye out for possible ambush, but the only people they passed were native Fleevaners—stout folk wrapped in heavy furs, riding in sleds pulled by the large deer they called lamnoccs.

Pheng had put aside his doubts and feelings of futility about the mission. He was obeying the Duke's orders, following where the witches led. He could not be faulted. Besides, he had to admit to a certain incipient excitement at the thought that they might actually win the precious Cloak at last.

Now, out of the shadows, a soldier hurried up to the Admiral and bowed low. Pheng had sent him to scout the edges of the property. He reported seeing no one about, but hearing noises within the main house. The door facing the road and another at the back were the only exits.

Pheng deployed his troops, sending ten archers to cover the back door, ten more to station themselves along each sides of the farmhouse. The remaining men he ordered to spread out along the road, facing the front door. He waited as the crossbows were drawn with levers, arrows slipped into place. Beside him, Arkasha and her apprentices watched with eager, greedy expressions. The thrall stood with shoulders slumped, the cord still fastened to her waist.

When the troops were in position, Pheng waved a hand. He and his men moved forward quietly. He planned to come within a few paces, then shout out an order that those inside surrender.

Suddenly the door creaked open. Pheng gestured and his men dropped to their knees, bows pointed.

In a blur of motion, a figure appeared in the doorway.

"Do not shoot!" A female voice called in Larthangan.

Pheng rose to his feet. "Hold fire," he commanded.

The drell flew to within several yards and sank to the ground. She stood erect in her silk gown, leggings and slippers—a remarkable sight in this barbaric land, even aside from the insect wings.

The Admiral was not surprised to see her. Arkasha had mentioned the likelihood that the winged woman would be here. The fact that she had come out to parlay was a reassurance that she had not yet taken the Cloak.

On seeing her, Arkasha and the other witches hastened forward to stand beside the Admiral.

"Greetings to you, sister," Arkasha called.

She and the others bowed ceremoniously to the drell, who returned the gesture. Arkasha then lifted her hands, moving them about with some fingers stretched and others bending. The drell observed this, and began a like series of gestures. *Witch signs*, but to Pheng they were gibberish.

"Speak aloud, if you please," he called gruffly. "I am in command here."

The mouth of the winged lady pulled back with disdain. But she answered. "Very well, my lord. I am Trippany, envoy from the Archimage of Larthang. I greet you and ask your mission here."

"You know it well enough. Do not try to dissemble. Your very presence is proof that the Cloak is here."

The drell looked puzzled. "How is that so?"

At Pheng's shoulder, Arkasha spoke: "We know of your mission. Indeed, our superiors in Minhang were able to trace your movements. That is part of what led us to this place."

This disclosure seemed to trouble the drell. "Then you know my orders come from the Archimage herself. If you oppose me, then you and your superiors must be deemed renegades."

"Enough!" The Admiral barked. "We will not debate the politics of the House of Witches."

The lady's wings vibrated, and she lifted from the ground. "Indeed, the Cloak is here. But the situation is in hand. Your assistance is not needed and your incursion unwelcome. The Cloak will be returned to Larthang. I state this on my honor."

"Not good enough!" Pheng shouted, losing his temper. "I am under orders to return to Larthang with this Cloak . I will not be thwarted by one unarmed witch, who might or might not have true authority."

Hovering, the drell answered icily. "My mission is from the Archimage. In this matter, she is supreme. Not even the Tuan can overrule her."

Pheng grabbed a bow from the man beside him, and pointed it at the drell. The archers in line followed his lead.

"With all respect due to the Archimage, I tell you to surrender the Cloak to me. If you refuse, I will treat you as an enemy."

The drell rose higher, hovering now above the level of Pheng's head. "And I tell you, with all due respect, that I cannot allow you to have the Cloak, and will prevent it by any means in my power."

Admiral Pheng waited no longer. "Shoot!" He yelled, and triggered the bolt.

Caught by surprise, her eyes wild, Trippany thrust up her arms. A ball of white light appeared and swallowed her. At least one arrow pierced the sphere, and Pheng might have heard a cry of pain from within. The rest of the bolts clattered and rattled as they struck the farmhouse wall. By then the drell had vanished.

"Reload," Pheng commanded, and handed the bow back to the soldier he had taken it from.

Along the line, his men placed their bows on their thighs, fitted iron levers in place, pulled back and locked the powerful bowstrings. Looking up from observing their actions, Pheng's eyes were drawn back to the open doorway of the farmhouse.

A pale-haired woman emerged, dressed in a quilted gown and open, fur-trimmed coat of Larthangan design. Behind her came five warriors in leather and furs—barbarians, grim-faced and armed with throwing-spears.

Amlina walked a short way from the doorstep, just enough for the Iruks to fan out beside her. Draven, Lonn, Eben, Karrol, and Brinda held swords and spears at the ready.

Peering through the open doorway, Amlina had observed the last moments of Trippany's confrontation with the troops. The drell had bought Amlina and her mates the time they needed. She only hoped Trippany had not been wounded or killed before escaping through the spaceless portal.

Straightening her shoulders, she called aloud to the intruders.

"I am Amlina, witch of Larthang. I charge you now to leave this place in peace."

The crossbow men had finished reloading. The troop commander stared at her belligerently.

"I am Admiral Shay-Ni Pheng. I charge you to surrender the Cloak of the Two Winds."

"I have the Cloak and will return it soon to Minhang," Amlina answered. "Your aid is neither needed nor wanted. I give you one last warning. Go in peace or risk all of your lives."

"I will dally no longer!" the Admiral shouted. "Give me the Cloak, or you and your companions will be slain." He lifted a hand and the row of crossbows rose up.

"Wait!" Amlina lifted both her arms, then shouted. "Now, Glyssa!"

At a darkened window upstairs, a silver light appeared. In the pulsing glow, Glyssa could be seen, standing with right arm raised high and left hand pointed. She wore the black and silver Cloak.

On instinct, Amlina had entrusted her with the task. Glyssa had wielded the Cloak before and Amlina judged that, by emerging from the house without it, she might put the troops off-guard.

"Shoot!" the Admiral ordered.

Bolts flew. Amlina and the Iruks dove for the ground. Blinding light burst from the window above as Glyssa summoned the freezewind. The air sang, then shrieked with abysmal cold. A glittering curtain blew across the yard and into the woods. Caught in mid-flight, arrows froze and fell pattering to the ground.

Cries of pain and dismay erupted as the wind engulfed the Larthangans. It blew over them for the duration of seven heartbeats, the noise fading as it passed into the forest.

In the dimming witchlight, Amlina spied the troops in retreat, running or staggering, some fallen to the ground. A few, who had caught the full force of the magic wind, crouched or stood rigid, transformed into lifeless statues of ice.

Seven

Crouching low, Lonn and Karrol led the way through the back door. They knew soldiers had been stationed on all sides of the house, and might still be lurking. Peering past Lonn's shoulder, Eben scanned the corral and the woods beyond, but spotted no enemies. He surmised the Larthangans had responded to the shouts of alarm at the front of the house, had run to join the battle and then the general retreat.

Still, he kept careful watch in all directions as the party hurried away from the farm and up the trail. The Iruks carried bundles on their shoulders and held spears in their free hands. They had strapped on their leather harnesses, and swords and long knives hung from their belts. Amlina now wore the Cloak, ready to summon its power if necessary. Draven had Amlina's wicker basket tied on his back, and Kizier struggled under the weight of two heavy satchels.

"I hope you all remembered to bring your gold," Eben muttered when they had reached the woods.

"Of course," Lonn said.

Karrol and Brinda stopped in their tracks. Just like Eben, they had kept their share of the loot from Tallyba at the farmhouse for safekeeping.

"In the excitement, we forgot." Brinda said.

"We'll have to go back," Karrol declared. "I'm not leaving my loot behind ..:"

"Don't worry," Glyssa answered. "I cleaned out the strong box under the floor. All of the gold is in my pack and Lonn's."

"Oh, what a relief," Karrol said. "Good work, Glyssa."

"Of course," Lonn said.

"I do wish we'd had more time to pack," Kizier puffed. "I tried to gather all of my writings, but I fear I left some behind. And of course, I couldn't begin to carry my reference volumes."

"What about the talking book?" Eben asked.

"Yes, I have him," Kizier replied. "For all his surly temper Buroof is often most helpful."

With Eben and Brinda guarding the rear, the party came to the top of the cliff. Night had fallen and the sky was overcast. Pale blue witchlight from the seawater below cast a misty illumination. Cautiously, the mates picked their way down the steep, narrow path. In some places they had to stop and pass their bundles down by hand.

At last they stepped onto the beach. Waves lapping on the black shale churned up gleaming bands of blue light. After tossing down his bundle and jumping to the ground, Eben took a deep breath of the salt air—exhilarated by the danger of this mad adventure with his old mates.

Here, at the base of the path, was the place they had laid the klarn to rest, marking the spot with a small circle of stones. Glyssa stopped and faced the others.

"Should we raise the klarn? Do we have time?"

Amlina shook her head. "We'd better not stop. Our enemies will regroup and likely come after us."

Lonn grunted. "Let's pause for a moment then, so those who wish can call the klarn-soul into themselves. We can have a proper ceremony on the boat." He cast a meaningful glance at Eben, Brinda, and Karrol. "Once everyone has decided whether or not they *want* to re-form as a klarn."

He spread out his hands. Glyssa and Draven moved immediately to join him. Eben stepped up, clasped Draven's hand and extended his own toward Karrol and Brinda. To his surprise, the sisters hesitated, glancing at one another, before walking up to place themselves next to him. Amlina came last of all—reluctantly, it seemed to Eben. Her back to the sea, her face shadowed, the witch marched over and took hold of Glyssa's hand. Kizier, not a warrior and never a member of the klarn, waited in silence, glancing nervously at the cliffs above.

The mates stood with heads bowed. Eben felt the stirring of the klarn-soul rising in him, a spirit that all of them shared. But he also sensed uncertainty, inner conflicts. This was not the firm, living bond he remembered.

Without further words, the mates picked up their bundles and headed up the beach in the direction of Fleevanport. They marched deliberately, making as much speed as their burdens allowed, watching warily for any pursuit. After a time, Eben fell back to where Karrol and Brinda walked a little behind the rest of the group.

"What are you thinking, mates?" he asked. "You both hesitated back there."

Brinda gave a shrug.

"I'm not sure."Karrol said. "I know I suggested we might sail with Amlina to Larthang. But now I've had time to think about it. It would mean leaving our village and our mother. We might never return. This is all happening too fast ... I'm just not sure."

"What do you think, Eben?" Brinda asked him.

He walked a little lighter on his feet. "Oh, I'm in, if they'll have me. I've enjoyed myself today more than I have in months."

Brinda and Karrol trudged on, making no reply.

"At least come with us on the boat," Eben said. "We'll need to stop for supplies, and the Iruk Isles are on the way. We will leave you on Ilga if that's what you decide."

"You make everything sound so simple," Karrol grumbled. "We haven't even got a boat."

"Oh, don't worry about that," Eben laughed. "There will be dojuks in the harbor. And I already know the one I want to take."

Harful woke with a knife point pricking the bridge of his nose. His eyes popped open in alarm. Eben smiled.

"Remember me? No, don't move! I would hate to accidentally split your nose." He pulled the knife back an inch. "Nod if you agree with that."

Harful nodded, mouth tight.

About two hours before dawn, Amlina and her party had reached the edge of town. Hurrying along the waterfront, they came to a stretch where Iruk boats were tied at the quay or rode in the shallows. Eben had spotted Harful's boat by the carved figure of a tusk-bear on the bone prow and the extra-long outriggers. Just two seasons old and large for a dojuk, it was considered one of the prize hunting boats on Ilga.

The one sleepy warrior standing watch had quickly been overcome. Lonn in the lead, the Iruks had crept aboard. A large sleeping tent was rigged on deck between the mast and prow. Brinda and Draven cut the tent's lines and then yanked up one whole side. In the faint witchlight from the harbor, the mates had jumped over the five warriors who had been sleeping within, spear tips holding them down even as they woke up startled.

"We have an offer for you and your klarn," Eben whispered to Harful. "We want to buy your dojuk."

Brows lowered, Harful shook his head furiously.

"Oh, but reconsider." Pressing the point close again, Eben reached into his shirt and removed a purse. He bounced it in his hand, jingling the coins. "Forty Nyssanian gold pieces—enough for you and your klarn to loaf in Fleevanport for a year if you choose."

The greedy gleam in Harful's eyes said one thing, the grim set of his mouth another. Again, his head shook. "I cannot sell the boat without holding a klarn meeting."

"Oh, you can't expect me to believe that." Eben smiled dangerously. "It's well known the boat belonged to your kinsmen, and also well known how you bully your mates. None of them would dare gainsay you."

"Has he agreed?" Amlina asked impatiently, her boots appearing at the edge of Eben's vision.

"We have you at a disadvantage," Eben told Harful. "We could just take the dojuk, and either leave you and your mates standing on the dock, or spear you and dump your sorry carcasses into the harbor. Or worse, we could let the witch of Larthang deal with you..."

Harful gaped up at the witch.

"So." Eben poked the knife. "Forty gold pieces. This offer will last till I can count to three. One ... Two ..."

"Very well," Harful grunted. "You have a deal."

Harful's crew was given time to collect their clothing and other belongings—but not their weapons. Instead, Eben and his mates gathered up the spears, swords and knives and carried them as they escorted Harful's klarn from the boat. To forestall any change of heart, the dispossessed Iruks were marched several streets from the waterfront to an inn. There, pounding on the door roused the morning staff, who were already at work baking the day's bread and cooking porridge. Eben made sure that Harful's klarn was settled comfortably around the fireplace and served tankards of mead before he paid Harful the promised gold.

Dawn was breaking over Fleevanport by the time the mates returned to the waterfront. Amlina stood with Kizier in the bow of the dojuk, anxiously watching for them. The Iruks set to work at once stowing their gear, checking rations, making the boat ready to sail.

At forty-five feet from prow to stern, Harful's dojuk was larger than most. Like all Iruk hunting boats, it was fashioned of thick yulugg hide stretched over a bone frame—light, agile, and impermeable to sea water. Twin outriggers provided stability on soft water and served as runners when sailing on ice. In the stern, beside the bone tiller, two dark green fern-like *bostulls* stood in pails of sea water. Also called *windbringers*, the one-eyed bostulls were sentient creatures whose magical talent for calling winds endeared them to mariners of all nations. For a dojuk to carry two was an extra benefit.

The Iruks unwrapped the soft water sail and fitted it to the yardarm. Draven stepped forward and announced to Amlina that the boat appeared to be in prime condition. His grin confirmed the excitement that the witch sensed in the Iruks. They were happy to be together again and happy to be setting out to sea. While they had seemed content enough living at the farmstead, sailing and hunting in a boat such as this was the life they were raised for.

Amlina wished she could share their enthusiasm. Much as she tried to suppress her feelings, she was undeniably frightened. During the long night's march along the shoreline, the exhilaration from the battle with the Larthangan troops had vanished, leaving her tense and fretful. Now, in the rising daylight, she scanned the sweep of the waterfront, wary of danger. She had no doubt Admiral Pheng would regroup and lead his troops back to Fleevanport, no doubt that the witches under his command could continue to trace the Cloak's emanations. Amlina only hoped she and her friends could be away before the Larthangans reached their ships.

"I'd like to find a place to sleep. Where do you think I'll be most out of the way?"

Kizier's question had been directed at Amlina, since Draven had returned amidships where he was helping his mates raise the sail. Distractedly, Amlina looked back over the length of the boat. She had not even thought about sleeping arrangements, or food, or how the eight of them would manage for months on this crowded vessel. The voyage from Gwales on the *Phoenix Queen* had been uncomfortable enough. But that craft was half again the length of this one, and at least Amlina had a small crawlspace under the foredeck where she could sleep and do her magic.

"I'm not sure," she answered. "Best check with Lonn or Draven."

Disconsolately, the scholar lifted his heavy satchels and carried them toward the mast. He walked unsteadily, and almost fell as the deck below his feet shifted with a wave.

Amlina turned away, leaning on the bone carving on the prow—the image of a bear with tusks, she believed it to be. Nameless dread loomed up in her chest. It was not just exhaustion, worry over the voyage. Undeniably, it was the blood magic. Suppressed for a time by her meditations, her acceptance of her duty, and belief that it was rightful, the power had been reawakened by the fight with the Larthangans. She desired to feel that power again, longed for it. She might need to cut herself this morning, however much it horrified her friends.

As this thought settled in her mind, her eyes detected a new movement across the harbor. A quarter-mile west, boats were pulling away from the docks. Even at this distance, Amlina recognized by the dark coats, glints of armor, and banners on poles that they were Admiral Pheng's men.

"Boats rowing across the harbor," Eben sang out from the masthead, where he had climbed to keep lookout. "Might be our crossbow friends from the hills."

Lonn had just stationed himself at the tiller as the Iruks prepared to depart. Now he and the others ran forward to stand beside Amlina.

"Larthangan troops for sure," Lonn said. "Are they the same we faced at the farmstead?"

"The same," Amlina answered.

"They don't seem to have spotted us," Draven said.

"But they will, as soon as we set sail." Lonn scanned the harbor from end to end.

The boats were rowing toward the three Larthangan warships anchored midway across the bay. Two Tathian galleons also rode at anchor, closer to shore, with a dozen more beyond the Larthangan vessels.

Lonn glanced at the sky, judging the wind which blew steadily from the south. "We might be able to keep out of the range of their arrows," he told the witch. "But it will be easier sailing on ice."

He stared meaningfully at the Cloak, which Amlina still wore.

Amlina caught her breath. "Let's try it on soft water," she said. "I'll only use the Cloak if all else fails."

Lonn nodded once then ran off, calling orders to the mates to push off and stand by the lines. Amlina clutched the bone carving and stared at the distant boats.

In truth, she feared attempting to summon the Cloak's power. The raging energies inside her were so strong, so unbalanced, she could not say how her psyche would handle such vast magic. Perhaps that was the true reason she had asked Glyssa to call the freezewind last night at the farmstead. Perhaps she should ask Glyssa to wear the Cloak again.

No. Something prevented that course, some unappeasable urge that told her that wielding the Cloak was her responsibility, her fate. Perhaps it was the taint of the blood magic, the ravenous hunger for power. If so, at this moment it was too strong for her to resist.

Glyssa and Brinda pushed off from the quay with poles. With the sail raised, Draven and Karrol hauled on the sheets. The yard swung around the mast and caught the south wind. The dojuk heeled as it slipped out over the water.

Amlina watched the Larthangan boats, which were drawing near their ships. Suddenly a man stood in the foremost boat, pointed toward the dojuk. The man held a spyglass. Now he took a megaphone in his other hand and shouted orders. The rowboats paused in the water, then came about, heading to intersect the dojuk's course.

"They've spotted us." Eben called the warning from the masthead.

Lonn adjusted the tiller, swinging as far from the pursuing boats as possible. Bending low, he called out an entreaty to the two windbringers to lend their aid.

Amlina stared at the on-coming Larthangans. All the oars were manned, stroking hard, churning up the glowing sea water. Soldiers stood amid the rowers, cranking crossbows and knocking arrows. On the ships beyond, sailors were scrambling, raising anchors and unfurling sails.

Anxiously, Amlina stared at the mouth of the harbor. At present speeds, the Larthangan craft would not intercept the dojuk before it reached the sea—but they would draw well within range of their crossbows.

A giant bolt streaked through the sky, splashing in the water yards from the dojuk's bow. The Larthangan warships were armed with arbalests, and the nearest ship had already swung into position and fired.

"Amlina!" Lonn shouted from the stern. "A freezewind would be most helpful right now."

She had no choice. Heart pounding, she leaned her back against the prow. She steadied herself by placing her right arm on the carving, then pointed her left arm beyond the dojuk's stern.

In her mind she called the freezewind, envisioning the frosty curtain dancing into life. Sparks glittered before her eyes—and a terrible pain burst inside her skull.

No wind came. She tried again. The pain snaked down from her head, coiling around her heart. Gasping, she dropped to her knees.

"Are you truly so weak?" Beryl's voice hissed in her brain. "No! You just won't accept what you are—a ruthless witch full of lust and rage and murder."

The deck lurched. Another arbalest bolt had landed in the water nearby, it's wave shifting the dojuk's course. Amlina trembled on hands and knees, blinded by pain and glittering light.

Glyssa and Kizier reached her, lifted her arms to help her stand.

"Amlina," Glyssa said. "Do you want me to try?"

"No!" A scream of rage tore itself from her throat. Her arms flailed, pushing her friends away.

The power was inside her, irresistible, demanding release. Amlina whirled and faced the Larthangan boats drawing near, the ships beyond. Her left arm shot up high and she screamed.

The gray sky above split open with a clap of thunder. Blue light and ice appeared through the fissure. The freezewind howled across the water, engulfing the oncoming boats, capsizing them. Men bawled as they were tossed overboard, their bodies skidding on the gleaming ice even as it formed below them. The wind streaked over the ships, tilting them back, encasing their hulls in ice that crackled as it formed.

Eyes wild, Amlina turned, pointing one finger at the sky to stern. A milder freezewind shimmered into existence, blowing over the dojuk, lifting its hull as the ice formed. Then the boat was streaming forward, flying over smooth ice with a swoosh of runners.

"Keep those lines tight." Lonn called, as the soft water sail billowed and bowed. "We'll change sails as soon as we clear the harbor."

Amlina slipped to her knees again, shoulders slumping. This time Glyssa and Kizier did not rush to assist her. They both stood clutching the rail, gaping wide-eyed at the witch.

The rest of that day, as the dojuk sailed from Fleevan, Amlina sat alone in the prow, wrapped in the Cloak of the Two Winds. Whenever Draven or Glyssa came and inquired if she were well, she made no response, only stared dully.

Only in the evening did Draven come, wrap her in a thick bed fur, and carry her to the sleeping tent that the mates had raised before the mast. By then, the witch had fallen into an exhausted sleep.

Eight

Their second night out from Fleevanport, Eben stood the watch with Glyssa. While the rest of the crew slept, Brinda handled the tiller, the boat skidding over wind-smoothed ice. The mates had deemed it wise to sail both night and day until reaching the Iruk Isles—putting as much distance as possible between their dojuk and the likely pursuit.

Given the catastrophic freezewind summoned by the witch, Eben had figured it would take a day at least for the Larthangan crews to chop their ships free from the ice. But Kizier had suggested their opponents might have some witchery to melt the ice and free their vessels sooner. Amlina had offered no opinion on the matter. Indeed, the witch had said almost nothing since she screamed the freezewind into being in the harbor. She either sat meditating in the sleeping tent, or stood in the prow, staring solemnly over the luminous ice. At night, she slept fitfully, moaning, sometimes bolting upright with a shriek that woke the mates resting beside her.

Standing at the rail near the mast, Eben scanned the ice ahead and the sky full of stars. Rog, the red moon was waxing and hung half-full in the north. In Iruk lore Rog was the hunter moon, blood red, ever chasing swiftly across the sky.

Rog the red one
Scarlet knife
Leads us to game
Sustain our life

The chant rolled through Eben's mind with the swish of the ice-runners. A footfall nearby made him turn. Glyssa paced near him.

She was assigned the sheet on the opposite rail, but on these long tacks it was seldom necessary to adjust the ice-sail.

She took a deep breath of the frosty air and smiled. "I have missed sailing." She spoke softly, so as not to wake the klarnmates asleep under the fur canopy. "I am glad we are all together again."

"I've missed it too," Eben admitted, "although, at the moment, my body aches so much it might prefer to be missing it still."

"Too much slack living," Glyssa whispered. "You'll soon get used to the work again."

"I hope so."

"You *are* coming on to Larthang with us?" she asked, suddenly earnest.

"Oh yes, assuming you'll have me."

Her smile was heartfelt. "Indeed, we will." She tilted her head back toward the tiller, where Brinda stood. "Do you think the sisters will come also?"

"That I cannot say," Eben muttered. "Brinda, I think, will do whatever Karrol wishes. Her strongest urge seems to be keeping watch on her little sister. As to Karrol, she might decide one thing and then the opposite, as you well know. What she will decide when the moment comes when there's no more chance to change her mind—that is anyone's guess."

Glyssa leaned her elbows on the rail. "I hope they will sail with us. It comforts my heart to have us all together again."

Eben gave a fond smile but made no other reply.

Out of the silence, they heard Amlina moaning. For a moment, Eben thought she might cry out, but then she subsided into sleep again.

"The witch seems greatly troubled," Eben murmured. "She was like her old self when we faced the Larthangans at the farmstead, but since then ..."

"Her sickness seems worse," Glyssa agreed. "If one can call it a sickness."

"Power from the blood magic eating her up inside?" Eben said. "I don't understand it. But then I've never claimed much understanding of shamans and witches."

"I don't really understand it either. It feels as though she is haunted. But the ghost is herself." Glyssa shook her head. "I only hope she can find healing in Larthang. If not, I fear this ghost will destroy her."

Brinda called the order to come about. With a nod, Glyssa hurried back across the deck. As soon as she untied her sheet, Eben loosed his line and strained his back to pull the yard about. By the time the ice-sail was set on the new course and the sheet retied, his back and shoulders were screaming.

Under the tent, Amlina cried out, murmured, then groaned as she sank back to sleep.

Eben stared into the sky. In his restless longing for new adventure, he had foolishly forgotten the hardships and the fears. Rog hung among the stars like a bloody, half-shut eye. Grizna, the larger moon, was waning and had yet to rise. While Rog was the hunter, Grizna was the mother moon, strong and stable, believed to be the home of the Great Mother. Eben recalled another chant:

Grizna mother moon
Watch over and protect
Your children on the sea
Guide us safely home.

Blue flames sputtered and flickered on the surface of the oil. Amlina stared at liquid swirls of color below the flames. Wrapped in a bear-fur, she sat with shoulders hunched at the edge of a round stone hearth. Overhead, the dome of the lodge house curved upward, hide walls stretched over the ribs of a giant sea beast. Daylight shone at the circular opening in the roof where the smoke escaped.

Despite the fire and fur wrapping, Amlina shivered. By Kizier's calculation, it was the fourth day of First Summer. In the mid-latitudes of the world, temperatures were rising. But here in the Iruk Isles, close to the South Pole, the weather remained frigid.

For five days and nights the party had sailed from Fleevanport. The freezewind Amlina had raised in the harbor had spread out from shore. No doubt it had merged with a seasonal front blowing from the South Pole. In any case, the whole voyage the seas had stayed frozen, so the journey was swift. With wind blowing steady from the south, the boat had tacked along the edges of reefs and jutting rocks that Draven said formed the edge of the Iruk archipelago. Half a day later they had landed on Ilga, the home island to Draven and his mates.

The isle was low and rocky, sedges and stunted conifers the only vegetation. Hunting klarns lived in round lodge houses built along the beaches. Those who did not hunt—elders, young children, and "village women"—lived in a settlement at the center of the island. As was the custom, people had hurried down to the shore to greet the arriving boat. Amlina and Kizier were introduced to the Iruks' kinfolk, including Draven's mother and the mother of Karrol and Brinda. Amlina and her friends presented the elders with gold, a gift that was most prized for the oil, metal, and luxury items it could purchase in the Tathian ports. The party was greeted with a hospitality close to reverence. Strangers visiting from the sea, Draven had explained, were sacred to the Iruks. This lodge house, near the center of the village, was immediately vacated for their stay. In the evening a feast of welcome was held in the Long House, a wide structure in the center of the village where the elders lived.

Now, the day after their arrival, Amlina sat alone and attempted to meditate. The Iruks had gone out at first light to visit with kinfolk and trade for provisions for the long voyage ahead. Kizier, carrying pens and a writing book, had followed the mates, anxious to learn all he could about the Iruk culture.

Amlina welcomed the solitude. Since the flight from Fleevanport, she had existed like one in a dream, eating little, staring listlessly into space, constantly seeking the peace of meditation—and often failing to find it. What had happened in the harbor terrified her: first her failure to summon her magic, then the rage tearing free, inciting her to turn the Cloak's power on her adversaries.

"Admit it," Beryl's voice rose like a vapor, taunting. "You enjoyed casting that freezewind, wrecking those boats, drowning your enemies. There is no pleasure so delicious as venting the rage, bringing forth terror and death."

"I am not like you," Amlina whispered. "Not so much as that."

Beryl's laugh mocked her. "You continue to deny your true self. But the denials grow weaker, Amlina. This long voyage on that pitiful little boat? Have you thought it through? Before it is over you will be killing your friends, feasting on their blood. You will have to be strong then, very strong, or they will kill you instead. What a sad ending that would make for a promising little witch ..."

Amlina's finger moved violently, tracing a warding sign in the air. "I am not you. I will not become you!"

Shaking, she stood and paced around the fire, rubbing her arms to restore circulation. When her mind had cleared she sat down again, tucking feet at her hips. She breathed slowly and deliberately, seeking to cast her awareness into the peaceful layers of the Deepmind. It was difficult, with no desmets or hanging mirrored balls to help her focus.

But at last her spirit began to settle ...

In her vision, she pulled opened a door flap and crept into a lodge house. This dome was smaller than the one where her body sat. The air was dark and smoky. Two figures sat by the gray stone hearth. One of them smiled warmly and held out her hand.

"Glyssa ..."

"Yes. I want you to meet someone. This is Belach. As you are my teacher, so also is he."

The bearded Iruk stood and bowed. Amlina thought she had seen him last night at the feast, an unassuming little man who kept to the shadows. Now he wore a black feathered cloak, a beaked mask over his forehead—and he seemed to shine with power.

He said something in Iruk, which Glyssa translated.

"Belach greets you and bids you welcome."

Amlina bowed. The shaman gestured for her to sit, then resumed his seat beside Glyssa.

"I thank him for his welcome," Amlina said. "And I thank him for caring for you, Glyssa. He has taught you well, much better, I think, than I have. You are my dear friend."

Glyssa interpreted her words. Belach spoke again, and Glyssa blushed.

"Belach says you also have taught me well. That with your help, I have recovered from my wound and become a true woman of power." He added something, and Glyssa said. "But he sees that now you, Amlina, are wounded."

Amlina glanced down at her chest. Crimson worms writhed there, gnawing at her heart. She shivered. "Can I be healed?" she asked.

Before Glyssa could speak the question, Belach lifted his arms in their feathered sleeves. His body floated into the air and flew three times around the fire, his mouth making loud, clacking noises. Finally, he settled back on his feet.

He spoke and Glyssa translated, her tone hollow.

"Belach says it is difficult. He says you are tormented by ... by nothing." Glyssa faltered, questioned the shaman in his own tongue, then continued. "This is hard to understand. Belach says it is nothing, but it is a nothing you must let go of. He sees a long journey before you, a walk in dark places, before you can—before you let yourself—be free of this nothing."

Amlina opened her eyes. With a shudder, she recalled the worms wriggling at her heart. She winced as the tightness and pain returned.

But the shaman's words made her thoughtful. The thing that tormented her was nothing—what did that mean? From the highest perspective, of course, everything manifest in this world was nothing, merely waves of thought passing through the Deepmind. But how could she release this nothing that had seized upon her, this stain of blood magic? A long journey, a walk in dark places. Was that a vision of her sailing to Larthang, finding purification in the House of the Deepmind?

Amlina grasped at that notion as a faint ember of hope.

In the middle of the afternoon, Eben entered the guest house, accompanied by Draven and Lonn. They had finished loading the boat with supplies: frozen meat and fish, barrels of water and oil, tea and herbs and other sundries. They figured to be at sea two small-months at least before they could make landing on the Tathian Island of Xinner and restock.

Inside the lodge house they found Amlina, sitting alone, staring at the hearth. She had allowed the fire to go out. Draven glanced at the witch unhappily and knelt to light it again.

"Time to hold the meeting," Lonn said to Eben. "You want to round up the others, or shall I?"

"Let's both go," Eben said, thinking it would be good to leave Draven and the witch some time in private.

Parting the door flap, they ambled outside, soft snow crunching under their boots. The village consisted of some twenty houses, a mixture of large and small domes, their size determined by the size of the yulugg whose ribs made up their frames.

The mates went first to the Long House. There they found Glyssa talking quietly with Belach, while Kizier sat furiously scratching words on paper. Lonn and Eben bowed respectfully to the shaman, who gave his blessing and wished them all a safe voyage.

In a lodge house at the far end of the village, they found Brinda and Karrol sitting over a fire with Oalasha, their mother. Oalasha was a stout old woman with a beaked nose and leathery face. A fierce warrior in her day, she had passed that characteristic down to both of her daughters. Eben knew that Brinda and Karrol both loved the old woman dearly—although Karrol had often complained of disagreements and conflicts, claiming that her mother was stern and cold. More than anything, Eben thought, it was the sisters' attachment to Oalasha that had drawn them back to Ilga, and which might now cause them to decide against sailing with the klarn. Indeed, they seemed reluctant to leave the woman now, until Oalasha waved dismissively and grumbled they should go and have their meeting.

In silence, the Iruks walked back across the village to the guest house. The air was crisp, the breeze from the south, the sky a clear and whitish blue. Good weather for sailing, Eben thought, and that only added to the urgency to get underway. Good sailing weather would also help the ships hunting them.

Inside the dome Draven had gotten the fire going again. The mates sat down in a circle, Glyssa ladling out cups of water. Eben noticed that Amlina shook her head, refusing the offered cup. Kizier sat down at the edge of the circle. He requested that the Iruks conduct the meeting in Tathian, that he might understand their words.

"Very well," Lonn said and rose to his feet. "The matter before us is simple. We are sailing the dojuk north, to bring Amlina to her homeland. I and Glyssa and Draven will sail—and Kizier of course. The only question is who else will come with us? Eben, Brinda, Karrol—I know I speak for the others when I say you are most heartily welcome. But, should you decide to not sail with us, there will be no hard feelings."

Eben glanced at Brinda and Karrol, who both were looking down at their laps. With a sigh, he climbed to his feet.

"I may be, as Karrol recently commented, a scrawny mess. But I've missed our adventures, mates. We've seen a good part of the world together, and won some lovely treasure. But we have not seen Larthang, and who knows what treasure this voyage may bring. I certainly will sail with you."

Glyssa, Draven, Lonn, and even Amlina smiled at him as he sat down.

Now all eyes turned to Brinda and Karrol. The two sisters regarded each other uncomfortably. Finally, Brinda stood.

"For my part, mates. I would like to go with you. But I cannot, for my heart, sail without Karrol. And the last I heard, she was still undecided."

She sat down, everyone gazing now at Karrol. She grimaced, raised a hand and let it flop down. Finally, reluctantly, she stood.

"I am sorry. I *want* to sail with you. You are the best klarn I could ask for, and I love you all. But you're talking about leaving our home, our kinfolk, our whole way of life—perhaps never to return. I'm simply not ready to do that. I only wish I had more time to decide."

Frustrated, she sat down, leaving all of the mates quiet and grim. Then, to Eben's surprise, Amlina stood.

"Karrol and Brinda, I understand. As Lonn said, we bear you no ill will. I wish we could give you more time to decide, but as you know, we are likely being pursued and must sail as soon as we can." The witch turned to Lonn. "Will we be able to sail with so small a crew? I fear Kizier and I will be little help."

"Hah, don't underestimate Kizier," Lonn smiled. "We will make a crewman of him yet. But anyway, the answer is yes. We'll not be able to sail both night and day shifts, but we'll surely manage."

"Then there is just one other thing," Amlina said. "I know you intend to reform the klarn before we sail. This time, I cannot take part in the ritual. Please know that I loved the closeness I felt with all of you when I joined the klarn before. But now my spirit is too out of balance—the klarn-soul might impair me further, or more likely, I might damage some of you. I dare not risk it."

She was gazing at Glyssa and Lonn, whose faces showed surprise and perhaps hurt. Draven stood up beside the witch.

"Amlina has told me this already. I assured her that we would still sail with her. That we would not abandon her. I hope I spoke for the rest of you?"

"Of course." Glyssa said. "Amlina, you have been klarn with us. That spirit will support and protect you still, whether you join us this time or not."

The witch bowed her head and murmured. "I am grateful dear friends ... to all of you."

After a few moments of silence, Lonn rose to his feet. "I believe there is nothing more to be said. I suggest we pack our gear and head for the boat."

Karrol and Brinda stood and watched as the others gathered up their belongings. Before leaving the lodge house, Glyssa came over and embraced them both.

"I will miss you, mates."

Eben spotted moisture in her eyes as she turned away. She hurried to follow the others outside. Eben stayed behind, staring at Karrol and Brinda who were both holding back tears.

"You are fools if you don't change your minds," he said bluntly. "Have you thought about what it will be like when we are gone? Joining another klarn like that of Tallvis? It will end the same, and you know it. You'll not find another klarn like this one. And you'll be missing what could be the best adventure of your lives."

"How can you agree to leave home and never return?" Karrol demanded.

Eben hoisted his bundle onto his shoulder. "This island is not home to me anymore. My home is with my mates."

The dojuk lay on the beach, stakes and mooring lines holding it just above the shoreline. After stowing their gear on board, the four Iruks took spears and a water cup and walked a few paces up the snow-covered slope. Amlina and Kizier stood on the dojuk, watching them in respectful silence.

Standing in a circle, the mates thrust their spears into the snow. Lonn took the water cup from Glyssa's hand and poured a libation over his spear.

"Now the hunt begins. We summon the klarn-soul, into our bodies and into our hearts. We pledge to share food and water and warmth, to tend our mates' wounds before our own, to live for each other and, if need be, die for each other. So we all swear."

He took a sip, then passed the cup to Glyssa. She repeated the oath and the libation, and passed the cup to Draven.

Eben had just received the cup when a voice called out at his back. He whirled to spy two Iruks in fur capes, struggling through the deep snow on the upper slope, carrying packs and weapons on their shoulders.

"Wait!" Karrol cried. "We are coming with you!"

Part Two

To Randoon
of the Onyx Gates

Nine

I t is regrettable your force failed to acquire the Cloak."

The Duke's words seemed all the more threatening coming through the subdued voice of the young woman thrall. Seated at the table in the incense-scented cabin, surrounded by Arkasha and her party, Admiral Shay-Ni Pheng pulled back the corners of this mouth and struggled to hold back his temper. He would offer no defense of his command, no assertions about the overwhelming force unleashed by this accursed Cloak. Such assertions, however true, would sound like excuses and doubtless be greeted by his uncle with disdain. Instead, the Admiral kept his tone carefully neutral as he reported on the current situation.

"We were able to free our ships within a day and have resumed the chase. Now we are following the trail, north of the Iruk Isles. Assuming our quarry is still sailing an Iruk boat, their progress over ice will be very swift. Until they lay in for supplies, it is doubtful we'll be able to overtake them."

"That is irrelevant now," the Duke answered. "Our latest report has this renegade witch—Amlina by name—sailing for Larthang, supposedly to deliver the Cloak to the Archimage. The Inner Council accepts this report as true. For the time being, so do I since the trail of the Cloak's emanations aligns with a course for Larthang. Your orders now are to continue to follow the Cloak, but *not* try to intercept it. I do not wish another embarrassing debacle in which our warships are scattered by a single witch in a primitive boat. Is that clear, nephew?"

The Admiral swallowed. "Yes, my lord uncle, perfectly clear."

"Excellent. We will reassess these orders only if the route of the Cloak alters. Meanwhile, a flotilla under the command of Squadron Leader Tong has been dispatched from Gon Fu. When you reach the waters off the coast of Xinner, they will take over the task of following the Cloak. Your flotilla will then sail for Hanjapore. On landing, you personally will take a launch upriver to join me as soon as possible in Minhang."

"If that is your order, my lord."

"It is."

So, Shay-Ni was being called back to the capital to answer for his failure. No matter how unjust, the Admiral had no choice but to face this false dishonor. How heavily would the blame fall upon his head? His uncle's next words made the answer painfully clear.

"It is unfortunate you chose to attack the drell witch."

The Admiral's stoical mien broke. He burst out in a mixture of fear and fury. "You ordered me to use force if necessary. She was obstructing our objective."

"Yes. It is even more unfortunate that you failed to kill her. She returned to Minhang to report your assault. The Archimage has filed a formal complaint with the Tuan."

With an effort, Shay-Ni regained his composure. "I see. And of course, I will bear the blame."

Around the table, Arkasha and the younger witches stared at him aghast, plainly fearful they might share some part of his guilt.

"Most regrettable," the Duke said. "But I would not be overly concerned, nephew. I will testify that you acted under orders to obtain the Cloak. We will insist your actions were justified, albeit rash. Still, you must come to Minhang as soon as possible to answer these charges in person."

Eight days out from Ilga, the ice changed to soft water. No meltwind blew. Instead, the frozen surface on which the dojuk sailed broke apart as it merged with warm seasonal currents flowing from the north. The conditions were hazardous, as giant slabs of ice floated and bobbed around the dojuk. All hands were needed on duty as the boat frequently had to change tacks, and the mates used iron-hooked poles to shove aside glimmering, frozen blocks that drifted too near the hull.

"Why doesn't the witch just call a freezewind and keep us sailing on ice?" Karrol grumbled as they worked.

"She has her reasons," Glyssa replied.

Eben knew that to be true. He had heard the witch say more than once that she would invoke the magic of the Cloak only when she had no other option. Amlina had emerged from the tent that morning and observed the thinning ice. After drinking hot tea, she had crawled back among the sleeping furs and had not come out again. Indeed, it had become her habit to spend little time in the open and to eat and drink almost nothing. To Eben, she appeared ever more emaciated and frail. He had begun to wonder how she would even survive the voyage.

"Well, I can't say I understand what her reasons might be." Karrol grunted as she shoved hard on a mound of ice floating near the prow.

Eben nearly laughed. He was happy to have Karrol and Brinda along, and not just because their strong bodies were needed for crewing the boat. No, he admitted to himself, just like Glyssa he was gratified to have the klarn whole again.

Karrol wouldn't say what had changed her mind back on Ilga. But from a private conversation with Brinda, Eben had gathered that the sisters were walking back across the village when they encountered their mother. Karrol had gotten into some minor argument with Oalasha, and both of them grew angry. Suddenly a startled look came over Karrol's face. Turning, she bid her mother goodbye and rushed back to the guest house to collect her gear. Brinda had to run hard to keep up with her.

After a few hours, the ice flows disappeared and so did Karrol's grumbling. The dojuk tacked into a brisk north wind, the air warm and smelling of salt. Except for two mates to handle the sheets and Lonn at the tiller, the Iruks were able to stand down. Draven and Karrol crawled into the sleeping tent to nap.

Eben, restless and sore, leaned on the bow for a time, staring at the sea. He wished he had some mead to drink, but the little he had brought on board was long gone. Instead, he fetched his sword and a spear. Bracing his feet wide on the swaying deck, he stretched his arms and shoulders. Then he began a series of training exercises, ducking, pivoting, cutting, parrying imagined attacks and stabbing the air in response. As Karrol had said back in that bathhouse in Fleevanport, if he meant to be good klarnmate, he would need to regain some muscle, to shape himself into a warrior again.

In the middle of the night, Amlina crawled from the tent. The dojuk rode on gentle waves, the sea luminous with witchlight. The sky was cloudy and Grizna, the peach-colored moon, drifted nearly full high above—a beacon shining in a fog. Most of the mates were asleep. Only Brinda stood watch at the tiller. At dusk, the anchor stone had been lowered overboard to prevent the boat from drifting far off-course.

Amlina crept forward to where her wicker basket was stowed. She untied the canvas covering and opened the lid. Sorting through her belongings, she found the neatly folded magic Cloak. Her fingers brushed over the smooth fabric, caressing its power. Standing up, she slipped the Cloak on over her shoulders.

A figure moved toward her on the deck. Recognizing Draven, Amlina smiled and embraced him.

"Are you well?" he asked.

She clung to him. "Not well, my dear. But improving, I think."

It was true. The hideous fear that Beryl's voice had engendered—that the insane hunger would grow out of control, make her turn on her friends—had not come true, not so far at least. Pain and rage still possessed her at times, still ate at her heart like the scarlet worms of her vision. But with meditation and visioning exercises, Amlina was keeping her mind under control.

"Why do you wear the magic Cloak?" Draven asked, holding her now at arm's length.

Amlina smiled, allowed her hand to caress the silvery sleeve. "I'm not sure. It comforts me somehow. In my dreams, I see myself wearing it. Back on the island, I had a vision in which I spoke with Glyssa and your shaman, Belach. He told me there was an emptiness in my heart—a *nothing*. That is the evil hunger, the taint of the blood magic I have spoken of. I have been seeking guidance on how to fill the nothingness. I think the Cloak might be part of the answer."

"You can cure yourself by its magic, you mean?"

Amlina gazed off at the shimmering sea. "No. Not exactly. By tradition in Larthang, the great magical treasures are held in keeping by a single accomplished witch. Once the Cloak has been returned, a new Keeper of the Cloak will have to be appointed. It's mad to think they might appoint me—I have not even attained the rank of adept. And yet, aspiring to become the Keeper of the Cloak seems to be what the Deepmind is guiding me toward." She laughed at how absurd the words sounded spoken aloud. *And yet*— "Do you think I'm mad? Or might such a thing be possible?"

Draven grunted. "As long as I've known you, Amlina, I've known you able to accomplish anything you set your mind to—no matter how impossible you thought it might be."

She laughed again, and hugged him. "Yes, I supposed I have accomplished much, with the help of you and your mates."

"And so you will again. But only if you care for yourself. My arms tell me you've grown woefully skinny."

"I know. I will start eating more. I promise."

"Ha," Draven said. "You can start now. I will get you something."

Amlina did not resist as he led her aft by the hand. Kneeling, he opened the food locker and handed her a piece of dried fish wrapped in a *kiia* leaf. Amlina stared at it, then hesitantly took a bite. At first, her stomach recoiled, but under his stern glance, she continued chewing.

Draven poured oil into the fire bowl and lit it from a lantern's wick. He filled the kettle with water. By the time the tea was ready, Amlina had eaten a second portion of rations.

Lady with wings
Lady with wings
Does she still live
The bright lady?

The chant passed repeatedly though Eben's mind as he leaned and stretched, preparing for his weapons practice. Twice in the past few days, he thought he might have glimpsed the drell flying high in the wake of the dojuk. Then last night he had dreamed of her. She conversed with him in her endearingly hesitant Low-Tathian, then started teaching him phrases of her own language.

He was being silly, he knew. What he had seen in the sky were no doubt terns or gulls. Seabirds were becoming more frequent now that the dojuk had passed the Shoals of Sarn and was tracking along the southwest coast of Xinner. They had also encountered fleets of fishing boats, but so far no patrolling warships—neither Larthangan nor Tathian. In another day or two they planned to put in at a town along the coast to restock their supplies—before striking west across the sea to Larthang.

Kizier the scholar approached the prow, walking unsteadily on the tilting deck.

"Still trying to find your sea legs, Kizier?" Eben teased him.

"Yes, I fear so." The scholar smiled wryly and gripped the rail. "I confess, this voyage has been tiresome. I think we'll all be happy to go ashore for a bit."

"That's certain," Eben said. "We Iruks are accustomed to dojuks, of course. But we seldom sail so many days without landfall. I believe we're all looking forward to a bath and a few tankards of mead."

"A bath in particular sounds wonderful." Kizier stared dreamily at the low, rocky coast. "I remember when I was a windbringer, warm salt water washing over my roots was most pleasant."

When the klarn first met him, Kizier had a been a bostull, transformed to that fern-like creature by the evil magic of the Archimage of the East. When Beryl was slain and her designs overthrown, he had reverted to his human form. Surprisingly, he had found the return to human shape a difficult adjustment. During the voyage from Tallyba to Fleevan, he had spent much time seated near the windbringers, seeking to regain the harmony he had lost.

"Do you still miss being a windbringer?" Eben asked.

The scholar sighed. "Not so much as I did at first. But yes, if I am honest. The mentality of the windbringers offers a certain peace, an easy attunement to the Deepmind. Of course I enjoy my present life too. I am fascinated with all I am learning from you Iruks and from Amlina. But, when this voyage is over, and I have finished writing my memoirs of our adventures, I think I may retire to a hermitage or monastery in Larthang and devote myself to peaceful meditation."

Eben pondered the idea, thinking how his heart longed for excitement and new knowledge. The last thing in the world he could imagine himself doing was retiring to a monastery. He thought again of the winged lady and his dream of conversing with her.

"How well do you speak Larthangan?" he asked.

"Oh, well enough to get by, I hope. It has been some years, so my knowledge is a bit stale. Why do you ask?"

"Because my mates and I know almost none at all. I'd like to learn as much as I can before we arrive there. Can you teach me?"

"Well, I can certainly drill you in the basics. You might also want to consult Buroof. His fluency is superior to mine, if somewhat archaic."

Eben liked that idea and asked if they might consult the talking book at once. They stepped aft to where Kizier's satchels were stored under a waterproof cover. Unwrapping the book, the scholar carried it to the stern. He and Eben sat down near the windbringers' pails.

"Why do you summon me?" Buroof's voice was more irritable than usual. "Where are we? I sense a confusing sway in the environment."

"We are on a dojuk, an Iruk hunting boat." Kizier told him.

"I know what a *dojuk* is! They have been recorded for over 1400 years you know. Similar boats are used by the Skeddlanders and the islanders off the south coast of Zindu."

"Never mind," Eben said. "The reason we've summoned you is, I need you to teach me the Larthangan tongue. Can you do it?"

"Well, of course I can do it. I am probably the world's foremost authority on the ancient dialects."

"We are more concerned with the modern, spoken language," Kizier said.

"Naturally—Wait, we are on an Iruk boat and this Iruk wishes to be schooled in the Larthangan tongue? Does that mean we are sailing for Larthang?"

"Indeed, it does," Kizier said.

"Well, that is a relief. Does Amlina intend to present me as a gift to the House of the Deepmind, as I requested?"

"That will be for Amlina to decide," the scholar said. "For now, the question is can you provide language lessons to Eben, and perhaps the other Iruks?"

"Didn't I just say that I can? For a supposed scholar, Kizier, you are sometimes rather a blockhead."

"Fine," Eben said. "Let's begin at once. But first, tell me everything you know about the drells."

Ten

Departing from the coast of Xinner, they struck off across open sea. These waters were new to the Iruks, but Buroof the talking book displayed a chart that allowed them to plot a course west by northwest. They steered by the sun and the moons.

The weather was fair, except for occasional rain squalls that danced over the sky like gray curtains, fluttering away as suddenly as they appeared. With steadily warming weather, the seas remained melted. The Iruks packed away their fur garments and wore deerskin shirts and trousers. At night they slept atop the bed furs.

After six days, the wind slackened. At first, the two windbringers were able to summon enough breeze to keep the boat on course. But bostulls' powers were known to be weakest in periods of calm. On the afternoon of the seventh day, the air grew still and the soft-water sail hung flat against the mast. The sky was a clear, deep blue, and the mates worried they might drift becalmed for days. They were all surprised when Amlina emerged from the tent and put on the magic Cloak. Standing with her right arm raised, she summoned a staunch, warm wind that lasted into the night. From then on she repeated this magic whenever the winds died, so their progress across the sea remained steady.

Their destination was Randoon of the Onyx Gates, one of three major ports on the Larthangan coast, each built at the mouth of a river. Kizier described the city one evening, as he and Eben sat in the stern beside the windbringers. It had become their custom to spend an hour or two there each day reviewing and practicing Eben's language lessons.

In ancient times, the scholar said, the three rivers had flowed free and wild from their sources in the west and north. But during the first centuries of the current era, when the Dynasty of the Tuans was established and the great witches of Larthang practiced their arts, the rivers had been tamed. Now levees and dams controlled the floods and maintained irrigation of the farmlands. Inland, a grand canal linked the three rivers at Minhang, the Celestial Capital.

"But why is it called Randoon *of the Onyx Gates*?" Eben inquired.

"This you will see when we arrive," Kizier answered. "On each side of the river stands a mighty tower fashioned of smooth, precious stone. These towers control a magical force that can be raised from the riverbed like gates of onyx to prevent ships from passing in or out of the channel. This witchery guards Larthang from invasion by sea."

"So? Do the other ports also have such defenses?" Eben asked.

"Indeed," Kizier said. "Hanjapore of the Jade Gates to the south, and Haji-Chan of the Moonstone Gates in the north."

"The history is all very interesting," Lonn grumbled, speaking Low-Tathian. Standing at the helm, he had listened to their talks in Larthangan for days now and was understanding much of what they said. "But I am more concerned with the greeting we're likely to get when we land."

"Yes, and with good reason." Kizier shifted to Low-Tathian himself.

"This war faction that the drell described," Eben said. "They tried to take the Cloak once. We haven't spotted any naval vessels since Fleevanport, but once we near the coast of Larthang, what then? Will Amlina wield the Cloak against their ships again? If not, how will she keep them from taking it? But if she does, it's hard to imagine we'll be received as friends when we do reach Larthang."

"All true," Kizier allowed. "But there are other powers in Larthang."

"You mean the witches at the House of the Deepmind," Eben said. "They who sent the drell."

"They, yes. And still others, I am sure. It's many years since I studied in Larthang, and no doubt the political situation has evolved. But I can tell you this for certain: by tradition there are three powers in the Golden Land, known as the Three Pillars of the Throne. The Witches, who practice the arts of the Deepmind; Warriors, who practice the arts of war; and Magistrates, who administer the laws and maintain the civil government. Within these three orders, or *estates*, there are always factions and sub-factions, and constantly shifting alliances. Above all sits the hereditary ruler, the Tuan. In name, the Tuan is supreme, but in practice he or she must balance the contending forces of the three estates."

"Are the witches always women?" Eben asked. "We know that elsewhere in the Three Nations, mages and sorcerers might be men as well. Is this not true in Larthang?"

"No and yes." Kizier seemed to relish conveying the complexity of these matters. "The House of the Deepmind, known as Ting Ta Roo, is the supreme magical power and home to the Five Revered Arts. It trains only women and only they may properly be called 'Witches of Larthang.' But there are other, lesser traditions of deepshaping and deepseeing that teach both males and females. These schools train prognosticators, alchemists, and conjurers, as well as scholars and sages who may include mysticism as part of their studies. Any of these practitioners might be called mages, but never Witches of Larthang."

"Sounds very complicated," Lonn grumbled. "So, assuming we manage to land, Amlina will need to seek out her fellow witches, since she plans to surrender the Cloak to the House of the Deepmind."

"Yes, but perhaps not just any witches," Kizier said. "Some witches are allied to the so-called Iron Bloc. This we have seen already. No doubt there are other factions in the three estates who would love to possess the Cloak and the power it brings. Amlina has chosen to surrender the Cloak to the Archimage in Minhang—but how we will get there is an open question. Indeed, what will happen when we land in Randoon? That I cannot even guess."

The harbor of Randoon shimmered like a liquid opal. Centuries ago in Minhang, the legendary Archimage Eglemarde had cast her First Great Ensorcellment, engendering the witchlight that streamed down the river and out to all the seas of Glimnodd. Here, along the coast of Larthang, the magic light was strongest, a clear blue-green color. Amlina had forgotten how beautiful it looked.

Wearing the Cloak of the Two Winds, she rested one hand on the carved bone prow as the boat sailed a reach into the harbor. In the distance, the city stretched above the bright water, a sprawling mosaic of white, silver and scarlet—hazy now, but growing sharper as the distance dwindled.

The distance between Amlina and her homeland.

Three days out, they had spotted the first navy ships. Patrolling the coast, the warships had not changed course to pursue the dojuk. This morning, beyond the headland that formed one arm of the harbor, a flotilla of three galleons had raised sail. But again they kept their distance, as if escorting the dojuk into port.

"This is eerie," Glyssa said, standing beside the witch. "It reminds me of our approach into Tallyba—when the queen allowed her forces to lure us in so she could trap us."

"I was thinking the same thing," Amlina answered. "Let us hope our welcome today is not so hostile."

Truly, she did not know what to expect. The authorities in Randoon would certainly know she was coming. Given what had happened in Fleevanport, and the actions of the naval vessels that shadowed them off the coast, there could be little doubt. More than one coterie of witches and mages would be tracing the emanations of the Cloak. Its approach to Randoon would be no secret.

"Sure, we will hope for a friendly welcome," Karrol said at Glyssa's shoulder. "But we will keep our weapons handy too."

Amlina smiled at that—the combativeness and irrepressible courage of the Iruks. But her amusement was tempered by the knowledge of how useless all their courage and weapons would be against even a single company of Larthangan troops.

Passing galleons and coasters lying anchored in the shallows, the dojuk tacked in toward shore. Red sandstone walls reared above long stretches of piers and quays, with vessels of many types riding at the moorings. Tall gates stood at intervals along the walls, carved tigers and phoenixes decorating the arches.

Amlina went to join Lonn at the helm. She directed him toward a gate near the center of the city. The docks before it were clear of boats, and a large crowd was gathering. People congregated dressed in plain garb or bright-colored robes, some holding staffs or waving banners. Ranks of soldiers in helmets and bronze armor carried spears and rectangular shields.

"I believe they are gathered to welcome us," the witch said.

"Or else arrest us," Kizier answered nervously.

Amlina quoted a deepshaper's adage. "We will go forth expecting the best."

Lonn steered the boat toward the quay and shouted the order to take down the sail. As the dojuk drifted the last few yards, brass trumpets blew a flourish and the crowd erupted in cheers. The Iruks cast bow and stern lines to men on the quay, who quickly secured them to bollards. Since the outriggers on the Iruk boat prevented a snug mooring, a gangplank was hastily fetched and placed atop the rail to allow the party to disembark. The Iruks, with swords at their belts and spears in hand, all glanced at Amlina—leaving it to her to lead them ashore.

As the witch climbed onto the gangplank, the crowd cheered again and another flourish sounded. A stout man in gold-embroidered robes and a square silk hat was assisted from a carriage. He stepped before the crowd and raised his arms for quiet. Beside him, a servant produced a rolled parchment, which the stout man read from in a booming voice.

"Amlina, Lady of Larthang. In the name of the August Tuan, I, Count Sinn Oran-T'say, Prefect of Randoon, greet you and welcome you to the Golden Land."

Nervously, Amlina scanned the cheering throng, which now numbered in the hundreds—dignitaries and officials with their entourages, merchants and dock workers, squadrons of soldiers. She had hoped for a favorable welcome, but never expected this. She swallowed and struggled to make her voice clear and loud.

"My lord Prefect, I am honored by your welcome, and most grateful. My companions and I have been many days at sea, and we would welcome a chance to rest, before continuing our journey to Minhang."

The Prefect nodded, smiling behind his thin, long-hanging mustache. "Of course. If you will do me the honor, my humble palace is at the disposal of you and your esteemed party."

He bowed slightly, and gestured toward his carriage.

Amlina spoke over her shoulder, explaining the invitation in the Tathian tongue. Lonn and Eben expressed concerns about leaving the dojuk unattended. Amlina relayed this question to the Prefect, who immediately ordered a squadron of his troops to stand guard by the boat.

Satisfied, the Iruks finished securing the lines and rigging, and packed the gear they would take ashore. Amlina and Kizier proceeded to the quay and held polite conversation with the Prefect and his secretaries. By the time the dojuk had been secured, a second carriage had arrived. Like the first, it was drawn not by the six-legged *aklors* the Iruks were familiar with from other lands, but by *tali—*

huge cat-like creatures with striped fur and long twitching tails. Frowning suspiciously at the tali, the klarnmates declared they actually preferred to walk, having spent so many days at sea. Amlina and Kizier accepted Count Oran-Tsay's offer to ride in his carriage.

Flanked by troops, accompanied by the beat of cymbals and drums, the strange parade set off. With the Iruks marching directly behind the Prefect's carriage, they passed through the phoenix gates and into the city. Crowds of citizens lined the route, waving, cheering, and staring with curiosity at the fierce barbarians from the far South Pole.

The Prefect's palace was a fortified compound of courtyards and pagodas located at the center of the city. Arriving there, Amlina and her crew were conducted to a feast hall, a pavilion with wall panels painted with scenes of seacoasts and ships. In the garden outside, birds chirped in flowering mulberry trees. Servants at the entrance offered to relieve the travelers of their luggage. But Amlina shook her head, and the Iruks held on to their bundles and weapons. The witch declined to remove the Cloak of the Two Winds.

This choice was not lost on Count Oran-T'say. But he refrained from any comment until the travelers were relaxing on cushions and had been served silver goblets of chilled berry wine. The gentle plucking of a lute mingled in the air with the bird song from the garden.

Setting down his cup, the Prefect cleared his throat. "We are most honored to host you in our humble home, Amlina—the famous witch who defeated the heinous Archimage of the East and has brought one of the great magical treasure home to Larthang."

"I am humbled by your generous reception, my lord." Amlina had let the chilled wine touch her lips, but deliberately not swallowed. Unsure of the Prefect's intentions, she remained on her guard.

"And if I may ask," her host continued, "now that you have delivered the Cloak, what are your plans? I believe you mentioned travelling on to Minhang. I am sure the reception you receive there would far exceed what Randoon has been able to offer. Of course, you are welcome to linger here and rest for as long as you wish. If you choose to travel to the Celestial Capital, I will of course place a riverboat at your disposal."

Amlina set down her goblet. She had carefully parsed the Prefect's words. "My lord is most affable and generous. And the use of a boat to go upriver may suit me very well. But if I might make one small correction: I have not as yet *delivered* the Cloak. That duty will not be discharged until I place it in the hands of the Archimage at the House of the Deepmind."

The lute's descending notes seemed timed to punctuate her statement. The Count lifted his chin slightly. "It was not lost upon me that you have chosen to wear the magical garment, even here in the hall of refreshment. But might I suggest that your wisest and most proper course would be to place the Cloak into my keeping—as I am the representative of the Tuan in this instance."

Across the table, Eben shifted, staring at the Prefect. Amlina surmised the Iruk understood the conversation well enough. Sensing his tension, the other Iruks set down their cups and sat up straight.

Amlina smiled as she replied. "I do appreciate this most generous offer, your eminence. But delivering the Cloak in person to the Archimage is a duty laid upon me by the Deepmind. As a Witch of Larthang, I can view no other course as rightful for me."

The Prefect's lips twitched minutely. "Even though I speak with the mandate of the Tuan?"

"Even so," Amlina said. "In matters of high magic, the Archimage, not the Tuan is supreme."

Count Oran-T'say measured her with a glance. Presently, his facial muscles relaxed into a smile. He settled down, reclining on an elbow. "No doubt, we will speak of the matter again. For now, let us not spoil the mood of celebration. I have given orders that apartments be prepared, that you and your company may rest here at least for the night. And of course, you will join my household at a banquet this evening."

Amlina nodded, and again pretended to sip from her goblet. The lute music resumed with a lighter melody. At the couches along the table, the Iruks once again relaxed.

But Amlina's mind was in ferment. The Iruks still had their weapons, and she still wore the Cloak. But using force to resist the Prefect's authority would make them outlaws throughout Larthang. And there was also the matter of arranging for the Onyx Gates to be opened and a boat to take them up river.

Amlina was wondering how she could extricate herself from this impasse when a gong sounded at the entrance to the pavilion. All heads turned in that direction. A steward bowed to the company and called out:

"It is my honor to announce Melevarry Lo-Song, Mage of Randoon."

Everyone rose from their couches and bowed. Melevarry strode toward the open space before the Prefect's table. She was a tall, strongly-built woman of late middle-age, dressed in witch's robes of yellow and gray brocade. Her face was long, with pointy nose and chin and sharp, narrow eyes. Her glance lingered briefly on Amlina and her company, then turned to the Prefect.

"Your eminence." Her head dipped in a slight nod.

"My lady." The Prefect's expression made it clear he had not expected the Mage's appearance—and was not pleased by it.

"Lord Prefect, I thank you for taking the trouble to welcome Amlina and her entourage to our city. Rest assured that I am now at leisure to take them into my charge and offer them the hospitality of my house."

The Prefect's lips thinned. He seemed to be weighing his options.

Amlina was also measuring hers. While she did not know Melevarry, the Mage's office made her subordinate to the House of the Deepmind. She was therefore more likely than the Prefect to honor Amlina's desire to deliver the Cloak in person to the Archimage.

Suddenly she stood. "My Lady Mage is most generous, and I will be honored to accept your kind offer." She bowed first to Melevarry, then to Oran-T'say. "Lord Prefect, I thank you again for your generous welcome. We shall take our leave of you."

Seeing no option but to acquiesce, the Prefect bowed courteously, first to Amlina, then to the Mage. "You are most welcome, esteemed Amlina. And to you, Honored Mage, my humble office is always here to assist you."

Amlina backed from the table and signaled her party to follow. "Come, my friends," she told them in Low-Tathian. "Tonight we shall enjoy the hospitality of this esteemed lady, the Mage of Randoon."

They followed the Mage out of the feast hall. Melevarry had entered without attendants, and she walked beside Amlina in silence, hands folded in her sleeves. Passing through the gardens and halls of the Prefect's palace, they arrived at length outside the main gate. There, at the edge of the grand ceremonial square, a single vehicle waited, a chariot of twisted wicker drawn by two tali. A half-dozen warriors guarded the chariot, dressed in scaled blue-green armor with short, peculiar capes. These Amlina recognized as members of the *alatee*, the so-called Warriors of the Chrysalis, who served as guards at the House of the Deepmind and the homes of some high witches.

"I entered without my guard," Melevarry explained, "so as not to alarm the poor Prefect. Amlina, if you would do me the honor of riding with me? My mansion is not far. I hope you do not mind if your servants follow on foot?"

"They are not servants, but my friends," Amlina replied. "So long as we drive slowly, I am sure they will not mind walking."

She conveyed the arrangement to the Iruks and Kizier, then stepped up onto the chariot next to the Mage. Melevarry picked up the reins and spoke a few words in an archaic dialect. The tali, who appeared to be sleeping, lifted themselves to their feet, arched their backs, then padded off slowly across the plaza.

The Mage surveyed Amlina with a sidewise glance. Amlina gripped the chariot rail and gazed straight ahead, setting her face in an impassive mask.

But after a few moments, it was Amlina who broke the silence.

"I find myself perplexed, my lady, as to why you did not appear at the dock, or at least send representatives. If the Prefect of Randoon was aware of my arrival, was not the Mage also?"

A hint of a smile appeared on the older woman's face. "Oh, I was aware. I simply considered it better to let the Prefect make his welcome first, then arrive in person and take you off his hands. A theatrical ploy perhaps, but effective in reminding everyone of the proper order of things."

"By which you mean who has rightful authority to receive the Cloak of the Two Winds."

"Precisely."

"And who, in your view, has that authority?"

The Mage's smile broadened. "Not the Prefect, nor the magistrates, and certainly not the military. No, the proper answer should be obvious to you: only the House of the Deepmind and the Archimage, whom I serve."

Amlina's grip on the rail relaxed. "I am relieved to hear you say that."

Eleven

M arching behind the chariot with his mates, Eben stared in all directions at the strange and wonderful city. The streets were paved with pink brick, the buildings a mixture of gray and white, with gilded portals and upturned, red tile roofs. The air was soft and balmy, scented with the fragrance of flowering trees and shrubs that grew along the curbs or behind the walls of courtyards.

People of all descriptions—merchants, officials, soldiers, servants—hurried along on the thoroughfare. Those who spotted the Mage in her chariot paused and bowed their heads respectfully—before frowning in confusion at the Iruks in their deerskin garb and sword-belts.

"Can someone tell me what's going on?" Karrol demanded after they had walked a short distance. "First we're met at the docks by a cheering mob, then we're marched to the house of the fat official dressed in silks, then just as we're getting a chance to rest, this witch in the gray robes shows up, and now we're marching again."

"I think there was a dispute as to which arm of the government gets to claim us," Eben said, "by which I mean, claim the Cloak."

"You are correct." Kizier panted, struggling with the weight of his luggage. "The Prefect wanted to confiscate the Cloak. He claimed the authority of the Tuan, but as to whom he might ultimately deliver it, that was uncertain. The Mage, the witch we follow now, claims the authority of the House of the Deepmind. That she intervened is actually a hopeful sign."

"I agree," Glyssa said. "I sensed Amlina relax as soon as the Mage appeared."

"That is fine," Karrol answered. "I am hopeful. I'm especially hopeful that we get a chance to bathe soon and then some dinner."

The avenue sloped down to the river, which flowed gently and shone with witchlight under the overcast sky. To the west stood a tall onyx tower, with its mate looming across the water on the opposite bank—the magical Onyx Gates. The party followed a winding path through a park on the riverside. At length, they arrived at a mansion with pink walls, bronze parapets, and high pagoda roofs beyond. Gates embossed with gold emblems of the sun and moons swung open as the chariot approached.

Entering a brick courtyard, they were welcomed by servants and attendants and observed by a detachment of the blue-armored guards. Grooms took charge of the chariot, and Melevarry ushered her guests inside. She offered them the choice of taking refreshments or going immediately to apartments where they could rest. Amlina conveyed her thanks. Knowing the Iruks' fondness for bathing, she asked if a visit to the mansion's bathhouse might be arranged as the first stop. Melevarry gave the order to her steward then withdrew, promising to dine with Amlina and her party in the early evening.

Presently, the travelers were relaxing in tubs of warm, scented water. Servants took their clothing to be laundered. The Iruks insisted on keeping their weapons close at hand, as Amlina did with the Cloak. They enjoyed the baths for nearly an hour, sipping tea and munching on rice cakes spread with honey. After toweling off, they dressed in fresh garments that the steward provided—silk shirts, quilted jackets and trousers, along with soft slippers. The Iruks laughed and joked about the unfamiliar, luxurious costumes. Eben and his mates were now enjoying themselves.

Amlina was dressed in a clean witch's robe, and a maidservant combed and pinned up her hair. From her solemn expression and the dark circles under her eyes, Eben realized how tired and strained Amlina must be.

From the bathhouse, they were conducted across a garden to the main building of the mansion. This was a huge square structure with balconies at many levels. They climbed a grand staircase and then a series of smaller stairs, arriving finally at their quarters. The apartment was spacious, carpeted, and hung with tapestries. A furnished hall and library room gave access to six bed chambers with large featherbeds. A terrace afforded a splendid view of the river and the vast city stretching far below.

Amlina shut herself in one of the bedrooms and spent the rest of the daylight hours in meditation. Eben, Kizier, and the others occupied themselves with enjoying the luxurious accommodations and discussing what might happen next.

At sunset a servant came and summoned them to dinner. Amlina appeared, having put on the silver and black Cloak. But on her word, the Iruks left their weapons behind. They followed the attendant up another set of stairs to a banquet chamber near the top of the mansion.

The room shone with tinted yellow lanterns and a crystal chandelier suspended from the ceiling. Aromas of roasted fowl and spices floated on the air. The Mage of Randoon sat in a high-backed chair, flanked by three other women. Scanning these seated guests, Eben nearly stumbled as he recognized Trippany, the winged lady.

He had thought of her often since last seeing her in the hills beyond Fleevanport, wondering if she had been wounded or slain by the Larthangan crossbows before she could disappear in her flash of light. Now, as her eyes met his startled gaze, her narrow lips bent up in an amused smile.

Melevarry was welcoming Amlina's party and gesturing to the empty chairs. She introduced the two witches as her apprentices, Yensia Meltai and Wenpheenae Chon. "And I believe you have already met Trippany Besu Keli, of the drell people."

Eben had maneuvered his way to the seat facing the drell. Her gaze remained locked on his as he sat down.

"I am happy to see you have arrived safely," she said in Tathian.

Eben grinned and replied carefully in Larthangan. "I am pleased that you are ... safe—not injured."

Her face evinced delight. "You are learning Larthangan! How lovely. Yes, I am well now. I *was* wounded, but the healers at the House of the Deepmind restored me."

"That is fine—good," Eben said, wishing his command of the language was better. Encountering the drell was so unexpected, in a pleasant way. She looked so lovely in her silver and blue witch's robe, the delicate wings rising behind her shoulders.

In the corner, a young man sat on a tall stool and strummed gently on a lute.

"How is it that we find you here?" Eben asked the drell. "I thought I might have seen you, once or twice, flying behind our boat as we crossed the sea."

Her smile showed small, pointed teeth. "Why yes, I tracked your crossing. Once I had been cured of my wounds, I was assigned to find and keep watch on Amlina. I was stationed here with the Mage of Randoon, to make my flights shorter, do you see?"

"Yes, I see."

Waiters appeared carrying trays and covered dishes. The party dined on roast duckling and rice and platters of sweet fruits Eben had never seen before. The Iruks devoured large portions with relish, and downed many cups of the sweet plum and berry wines. Amlina and the other witches ate abstemiously, and exchanged conversations that, so far as Eben could tell, amounted to little of importance.

When the dishes had been cleared away, Melevarry rose and made a formal speech. She welcomed Amlina and her party and praised them for returning the Cloak of the Two Winds to Larthang.

She said something Eben did not quite follow about arrangements for transporting the Cloak up the river.

More fruit and wine were served. Melevarry asked all the guests to relax and enjoy themselves, then invited Amlina to walk with her out to the balcony. Glyssa talked with two of the Mage's assistant witches, with Kizier joining the conversation and acting as interpreter. The rest of the Iruks helped themselves to more wine.

Eben, who had drunk four cups already, felt both lightheaded and emboldened. He stepped around the table and touched Trippany on the arm.

"I wanted to say again how happy ... I am very happy to see you," he said, starting in his minimal Larthangan and ending up in Tathian.

The drell looked surprised, her dark eyes kindling. "I am also happy to see you, Eben," she ventured in Tathian. "You and your people ... I find interesting."

"Do you indeed? Well, we have no wings but ..." He trailed off, embarrassed by how stupid that sounded.

She laughed. "No. You have no wings. You are not like my people, nor at all like the Larthangans. But you are strong and brave, and have been honorable friends to Amlina, I think."

"Oh yes. She is klarn—I mean, one of our crew. We are very loyal to our friends."

Her eyes were staring into his.

"I would like to be your friend," he added.

Smiling, she bowed her head, then surprised him by allowing her finger to caress his hand.

"I think I might like that as well. But for now, I will bid you good night." Her wings hummed to life, and she rose into the air. Then she surprised him again, bending near and kissing his cheek before fluttering from the room with a merry laugh.

Grizna the peach-colored moon hung nearly full, rising over the sea. From the high balcony Amlina observed the city, sprawling to her left, lit by moonlight and sealight nearly bright as day. The Onyx Towers stood guard on each shore of the river, the gates protecting the Golden Land.

"A lovely view, is it not?" Melevarry said.

"Very lovely. But you did not ask me out here to admire the scenery."

The Mage of Randoon scrutinized her for some time before replying. "That is correct. Now that you are rested and fed, I need to discuss matters with you."

This time Amlina allowed the silence to linger.

Melevarry showed a half-smile. "I must confess, Amlina. I really did not know what to expect of you. And now that I've observed you for half a day, I am still not sure what to think. You deport yourself as a schooled witch of Larthang, to be sure. But there is also a wildness about you—almost akin to the spirit of your barbarian friends. And yet, again, you lack their obvious vigor, your physicality is almost fragile ..."

"Is there something in particular I can answer, my lady?"

"Ah, but can I believe anything you say? You see my dilemma."

"No, not exactly."

"Well, let me review what we know of you. A young witch from a western province studies at the Academy. She shows promise both as a pure shaper and especially at the art of trinketing. However, she fails her fourth-year examinations. Rather than stay for more study and to try again, she leaves Minhang, goes into exile. The next anyone hears of her is eight years later, on the far side of the world. She has reportedly become apprenticed to the self-proclaimed Archimage of the East, the most reviled renegade witch of our age— one who is known to practice evil arts and forbidden sorceries. However, this apprentice somehow slays the Archimage and recovers treasures she stole from Larthang a century ago. Then, rather than returning them to Minhang, the apprentice goes into hiding ... "

"I always meant to return the Cloak and the scrolls to Minhang," Amlina said. "I was delayed by illness."

Melevarry appraised her through narrowed eyes. "We shall leave that for the moment. Our envoy reported that, once cornered, you swore on your honor to bring the Cloak to the House of the Deepmind, and now, indeed, you have come back to Larthang. The Scrolls of Eglemarde, as you may know, are valuable mainly for historical purposes. Most believe their magic has long been duplicated by other means. The Cloak, in contrast, is vitally important. Because it was woven at the time of the casting of Eglemarde's Second Ensorcellment, the power it contains can never be matched."

"So I understand."

"Yes. As I was saying, you have indeed brought the Cloak back to Larthang. Now you claim your intention is to present it to the Archimage. What will you demand in return?"

Amlina let her gaze wander to the high, pale circle of the moon. "Once I deliver the Cloak and the scrolls, I will be in no position to demand anything. But there are two boons I will request. One is for magical help to heal my illness—which I have not been able to overcome."

"I see. And the other?"

Amlina swallowed, knowing her second request would sound outrageous, but forcing herself to go on. "Assuming my health can be fully restored, I would ask to be considered for the post of Keeper of the Cloak."

Melevarry's eyes widened slightly. "Well, you are certainly not without ambition."

Amlina compressed her lips. "Indeed, I have often thought I am prone to exaggerated ideas about myself. But, exaggerated or not, they have driven me to ... meaningful accomplishments." She lifted her arms indicating the Cloak that she wore.

"So they have." The Mage of Randoon considered. She set back her shoulders and placed her hands in her sleeves. "Tomorrow, I will make arrangements for my personal barge to take you and your friends up the river. You will be greeted in Minhang with great ceremony, I am sure. There you can present the treasures into the hands of our greatly honored Archimage, and make your requests to her in person."

Amlina nodded. "I thank you, my lady. I could ask for no more."

"Then I bid you good night, Amlina, and consign you to a deep and restful sleep."

Twelve

S he floated in darkness, lost, an ache at the back of her skull ...

How long? Had she placed herself in deep trance, the dark immersion? She could not remember ...

Something tugged at her shoulder. The shaking became more insistent. Her eyes sprang open, vision blurry. She was staring into faces ... Lonn, Glyssa.

"Amlina, you must wake up," Glyssa said. "We're in trouble."

They helped her to sit up. She had been lying on a stone floor. Looking around, she saw Kizier and the other Iruks. They stood or knelt in near-darkness. Shafts of dim light slanted though the grate of a prison cell door.

Amlina clutched her aching head, pulling at her memory. After leaving the feast hall, they had returned to their apartment. The Iruks, having brought pitchers of wine, sat drinking and talking in the outer hall. Exhausted, Amlina had crept off to bed. She recalled feeling dizzy, nauseous. She had shrugged off the Cloak and collapsed on the bed, still wearing her other garments ...

Had she been drugged, or simply succumbed to an enchantment?

"Amlina, wake up!" Lonn shook her shoulder. "We are imprisoned."

"The Mage betrayed us," Draven said. "We were drugged or else witched. We woke up here."

"And without our weapons!" Karrol growled. "We have to get out of here."

Lonn and Draven took Amlina's arms and helped her to stand. As her eyes adjusted, she could just see the extent of the cell, a dozen feet square—a dungeon somewhere underground. The chilly air smelled wet and moldy.

"We found this beside the door." Eben handed her a parchment. "It looks to have writing on it, but it's too dark for Kizier to make it out."

As soon as Amlina's fingers touched the sheet, the writing kindled into tiny flames—Larthangan ideograms, intended for her alone.

Honored Amlina

I am sorry that I must incarcerate you and your companions. While I perceive nobility in you, in my judgment you are too unstable to entrust with so powerful an object as the Cloak. These are unsettled times in Larthang, and my duty compels me to ensure that the Cloak reaches the Archimage. Once it is safely on its way upriver, you and your friends will be released.

- Melevarry, Mage of Randoon

Amlina sank to her knees, the parchment slipping from her grasp. Scarlet rage swelled inside her—directed not at Melevarry, but at herself. She had failed, utterly failed to foresee the trap. How stupid and naïve she had been, to fall for the Mage's pretence of friendship, to believe that the Witches of Larthang would welcome her back, honor her for what she had accomplished. From far away she heard a strangled moan and realized it was herself. Her whole body was convulsing.

"Amlina." Glyssa gently pressed her shoulder.

Draven was holding her other arm. "Amlina, you must stop this! We need your help."

Sobbing, she flung herself into Draven's arms, shuddering now not with rage but hopeless weeping.

"Well, this is a fine time for her to come unstrung," Karrol grumbled.

"Be quiet," Draven barked.

"Stop it," Lonn said. "Let's not fight among ourselves."

"It's all right." Draven stroked the witch's hair. "Your mates are here with you."

Amlina's chest heaved. "I am sorry. I have led you into danger and treachery, and it's all been for nothing. Nothing."

"You have to help us get out of here," Draven said.

The witch blinked, shook her head. "No. It doesn't matter. The Mage's letter says we'll be released as soon as she sends the Cloak on to Minhang."

"But how can you trust her?" Lonn said.

"I'm afraid he is right," Kizier added. "The Mage has demonstrated that she cannot be trusted."

Amlina had not even considered that. Melevarry had lied to her once, perhaps she was lying still. Perhaps Melevarry was secretly allied with the Iron Bloc or some other cabal and meant to hand the Cloak over to them. If that were the case, Amlina and her friends might be imprisoned indefinitely—perhaps even executed.

Her mates needed her help to get out of here. Amlina sniffled and climbed to her feet. By her own vanity and weakness, she had led them into this trap. She would not fail them again—not if she could help it.

"You are right," she said. "We have to find a way out."

She felt inside her robes, touched her hair. No dagger, no rings or trinkets. Even her moonstone fillet had been taken. She walked over and examined the door: solid iron, no handle on the inside, thick iron grate at eye-level, small trap door near the floor to allow food to be passed inside.

The Iruks hovered behind her. Amlina sighed, shut her eyes, probed with her deepsight. Strong hinges on the outside allowed the door to swing outward. Across from the hinges, three iron bolts, old and slightly rusted ...

"Glyssa, come help me." Amlina held out her hand. Glyssa stepped beside her, and their fingers intertwined.

"I perceive three bolts on the right side."

Glyssa shut her eyes. Presently, she replied: "Yes, I see them."

"We will move the top one first," Amlina said.

Amlina lifted her free hand, two fingers pointing. She envisioned the top bolt and sent force to move it. She perceived the stream of Glyssa's thought, moving in concert with her own. The bolt resisted their efforts.

Then suddenly it gave and slid aside. Amlina and Glyssa nodded to each other and went to work on the middle bolt.

Within a few minutes, they had pried all three bolts lose. At the witch's word, Lonn and Karrol set their shoulders to the door and shoved. With a loud groan, it pushed open.

Amlina followed them out of the cell. They stood in a stone passageway, utterly quiet except for their breathing. Widely spaced lanterns in iron brackets cast the only light. The passage extended some distance in both directions, ending in corridors set at right angles.

"Which way?" Draven asked.

Amlina shook her head. Closing her eyes, she consulted her intuition. The indication was plain. She set off to the left, Kizier and the Iruks following on her heels.

After only a few steps, the witch jerked to a halt in response to a violent, shrieking noise. At first, she thought a cell door was crashing open. Then she realized that below the lamp directly ahead of her, the wall itself had broken. A figure stepped from the fracture, an iron warrior, seven feet tall and armed with a truncheon. Raising its weapon, it turned and stalked toward them, moving with a slow, menacing grace.

The dim corridor shook and screeched. More of the metal guards stepped from the walls behind the first. Amlina whirled and spotted still more of them, approaching from the opposite direction.

"Without weapons we have no chance," Lonn muttered at the witch's ear.

"Yes," she answered. "Back inside. Quick!"

The mates retreated to the cell they had vacated. As the monstrous figures drew near, Draven and Lonn shoved the door closed and braced it with their shoulders.

"Are they drogs?" Kizier asked.

Amlina nodded. "Activated by the dungeon itself, I think, whenever it senses a prisoner escaping—doubtless an ancient design woven into the stone foundation."

"So now what do we do?" Karrol asked.

Amlina lifted her chin. "We think of something ..."

A quarter-hour passed, Amlina pondering their dilemma. She wondered if she could create a formulation to blind or paralyze the drog guards just long enough to move past them. But without trinkets to help her focus and store power, it was difficult. The Iruks talked about whether they could tackle one of the drogs, bowl it over and steal its weapon. Dangerous, they agreed, but with one truncheon they might have a chance to win more.

In the midst of their sober discussions, a sizzling light burst in a corner of the cell. Amlina shaded her eyes at the sudden flash. Next moment, Trippany materialized, her wings fluttering in the dank air.

She settled to the floor, stared at the witch and the Iruks.

"I did not know," she said in Larthangan. "I did not know what the Mage intended. I swear this on my honor."

"Why are you here now?" Amlina demanded.

The drell lowered her gaze. "I-I wish to help you. I am going against Melevarry in this, but I do not agree with her judgment of you—and certainly not with casting you into a dungeon." She stared frankly at the witch, then her glance shifted briefly to Eben.

"How can you help us?" Amlina asked.

"I can reappear outside the cell and open the door. Then I can show you the way out of the dungeon."

"We've already opened the door," Amlina told her. "The passage is guarded by iron drogs."

Trippany put a hand to her lips. "Oh. I did not know. They are not there now."

"They will reappear if we try to escape," Amlina told her.

"Can you bring us our weapons?" Eben asked. "Then we can fight our way out."

The drell considered. "Yes ... I suppose they are still in your quarters? I will find them and bring what I can."

Her wings sputtered to life and she lifted. In a moment, she vanished in a burst of sparkling silver.

"I wonder if we can trust her," Kizier murmured. "Or is this another elaborate ruse?"

"If she returns with our swords," Eben said. "We'll be happy to take our chances."

A short time later Trippany reappeared. Her arms were laden with six sword belts and a quiver of Iruk throwing spears hung on a strap from her elbow. She landed on the dungeon floor and staggered, dropping the weapons and then collapsing to her knees.

Eben rushed to her side. "Are you all right?"

"Yes. A bit dizzy I'm afraid." She smiled. "Invoking second flight three times in so short a period—and your weapons are heavy."

The witch lifted the drell's arm and helped her to stand. "You have taken a risk, defying the Mage to help us."

Trippany nodded soberly. "I know. No doubt I will face censure. But the Lady Melevarry is not my mentor, and my heart tells me she was wrong to imprison you."

Eagerly, the Iruks strapped on their sword belts and picked out spears.

"Now, we will give those metal soldiers a surprise," Karrol exulted.

"You said you could show us the way out of here," Amlina said to the drell.

"Yes. I had to examine the dungeons from *beyond* to locate you. We are three levels down." She pointed in the direction they had tried before. "The stairs are that way. One turn to the left, then two the right."

Moments later, the Iruks were ready. Lonn and Karrol pushed open the door. Eben and the rest of the klarn followed them out of the cell, with Amlina, Kizier, and Trippany coming last. At the moment, the passageway looked empty. But as they headed up the corridor, the floor rumbled and the clang of metal sounded in front and behind them.

Once again, the drog guards tore themselves from the stones. The Iruks drew their swords and lifted spears. They arranged themselves at the front and back of the group, shielding Amlina, Kizier and Trippany who clustered together at the center.

The drogs approached—hulking iron forms like men, with long arms and squat bodies. Their domed heads showed no mouths, noses, or ears, only eyes that glinted like red embers. Spying the Iruks' weapons, the creatures dropped their truncheons. The clatter of the weapons on the floor was followed by the loud noise of scraping metal—from the fists of each drog grew two long swords.

"Well, that will change things," Eben muttered. He glanced back to where drogs with swords now approached the rear guard of Draven, Glyssa, and Brinda.

With a wordless roar, Lonn charged, Eben and Karrol right behind him. The Iruks had an advantage: the passage was so narrow and the drogs so large they could not fight two abreast. The ones in the rear could only cluster behind the first drog, poking with their sword points without making strong thrusts.

The mates attacked the first drog, Lonn and Karrol parrying while Eben searched for an opening. They had fought drog warriors in the past. They were always supposed to have a weak point—a conduit for the magical power that animated the lifeless bodies. But these creatures appeared to be cast of solid metal—even the tiny eyes looked hard. The Iruks' sword and spear points slipped harmlessly over the metal hides.

Eben saw his mates being forced back from both directions. If the drogs had a vulnerable point, it must be on their backs. Eben took a reckless chance. Squeezing along the wall, he slipped into the crevice where the first guard had broken through the wall. He had a brief moment to scan the drog from the rear. At first he saw nothing, but then he spied slivers of pulsing light behind each knee.

One of the rear drogs had spotted him and thrust with both swords. Eben just managed to duck under the attack. He lunged and swung his blade, cutting his attacker behind the knee. The drog straightened up with a loud creaking noise and dropped one of its swords. Eben shoved his spear tip into the back of the creature's other knee.

The drog collapsed across the passageway, falling into the one behind it.

"Cut behind the knees, mates!" Eben shouted.

He glanced up to see the next drog looming over him. Eben flinched and raised an arm to protect himself. A blade struck the top of his skull.

He lay dazed for several moments, blood running over his face, excruciating pain pounding his head. Distantly, he heard the shouts of battle, the clang of weapons, and what he hoped was the crash of metal guards falling onto stone.

Next thing he knew, Glyssa and Trippany knelt over him. The drell used the edge of her gown to wipe the blood from his eyes. Beyond them, a glance showed metal bodies lying askew on the floor. At the end of the passage, the mates were surrounding the last two drogs.

"We've nothing to bandage you with," Glyssa said. "Can you walk, mate?"

Eben braced his hands on the floor and managed to stand. He wiped a sleeve across his forehead, glanced at the red stain on the fine silk of the Larthangan jacket.

"I can try."

With Glyssa holding his elbow, Eben staggered to the end of the corridor. Karrol and Lonn dueled with the last of the drogs, while Brinda and Draven pivoted behind them and cut at their knees.

"Glad you managed to find their weak point," Glyssa said.

"You were brave." Trippany hovered at his shoulder.

Dizzy, eyesight swimming, Eben laughed. "Yes. A shame I wasn't also quick."

With the last of the guards disabled, the party turned and hurried down the side passage. Lamps shone along the walls, but no more drogs emerged to attack them. Two more turns and corridors brought them to the base of a narrow stairway leading upward—just as Trippany had said.

Lonn and Karrol led the way up the steps, the witch and the rest climbing behind them. The blood from Eben's wound had slowed to a trickle, but still he had to clutch Glyssa's arm now and then to steady himself. Up two flights they passed an arched corridor. Still, they encountered no drogs or human jailers. Except for their footsteps, all was silent.

At the top of the next flight Lonn held up his hand. Everyone halted. Above was one more stairway, ending in a wide iron door. In front of the door, equally wide, squatted another drog—a legless, blue-skinned human torso with eight muscular arms. Four of the arms ended in sword blades, four others in battle-axes. The face was broad and glaring, a sapphire set in the forehead.

"We can't topple that thing. It has no legs," Lonn observed.

"Well I don't see how we can go around it," Karrol answered.

"Where is the weak spot?" Glyssa asked the witch. "That gem in its forehead?"

Amlina shook her head. "That would be too obvious." After probing with her mind, she answered: "The throat is soft. We must get it to raise its head."

The witch laid her hands on their spear tips, investing them with power.

With Lonn in the lead, the Iruks advanced up the steps, spears held ready to cast. The drog watched them in silence, chin sunk to its shiny blue chest, weapons raised to strike.

"Wait," Trippany called. "I will distract the drog."

She flew from behind the Iruks, hands raised, silver wings beating. Her shimmering form rose to the ceiling, and the drog followed with its eyes. When she dove toward the creature, it lifted two arms and the chin tilted up—revealing a pulsing white throat.

"Now!" Lonn yelled and flung his spear.

While the drog swiped at the looping drell, four spears lanced through the air. Two struck the chest and clattered away. A third slid past the shoulder. But one spear found the mark, puncturing the white flesh of the throat.

The drog's mouth gaped wide, emitting a strangled cry. The arms flailed wildly, and black ichor flowed from the wound. The head lolled sideways and the shoulders sagged, arms and weapons drooping. A hissing noise erupted, and the giant torso collapsed like a water skin torn open and spilling its contents.

The Iruks looked inquiringly at Amlina. She nodded, and they started up to the landing.

"I will open the door!" Trippany's form burst into a dazzling light and she vanished.

Seconds later, the party stood over the ruined body of the drog, their noses wrinkling at the stench. They heard bolts sliding on the far side of the door and then Trippany's muffled voice calling them to push.

Thirteen

Amlina and her companions emerged in a broad corridor outside the gate to the dungeons. Daylight, shining through small windows near the ceiling, disclosed that they stood in a basement of the mansion. Storage rooms bordered the right and left of the corridor. At the end a stone stairway led up.

The Iruks and Kizier stood clustered behind the witch. Trippany settled to the floor beside her.

"Now what?" Lonn asked.

Amlina gave a faint laugh and looked around at her companions. Eben had a bad gash on his scalp, and Brinda a puncture wound in her shoulder that prevented her raising her arm. The others appeared unhurt.

"I leave it to you, mates," Amlina said. "Do we try for the boat and sail away, or do we go and have words with Melevarry?"

Lonn and Karrol grunted angrily. "I think we'd like to confront the treacherous lady," Draven said. The others nodded vigorously, except for Kizier who merely rolled his eyes.

Amlina turned to the drell. "Where are we most likely to find the Mage this time of day?"

Trippany's mouth bent in a smile. "I left her in her study. There is only one stair. I will show you."

She flew off and Amlina and her friends hurried after. They ran to the end of the passage and up the steps. At the top, they pushed open wide doors and entered a well-lit hallway at the rear of the mansion. They followed the drell past storerooms, pantries, and a kitchen. Servants spotted them, gaped for a moment, then turned and fled. To

Amlina's surprise, the party did not encounter any of the Mage's household guard.

They arrived in the main foyer of the mansion, a high-domed chamber with a curling ceremonial staircase. Across from these stairs, the drell landed before a wall panel painted with a stylized image of a phoenix. Trippany placed two fingers into the eyes of the bird and pushed. Her action triggered a mechanism and the panel slid aside.

Beyond was a narrow staircase leading up. Amlina went first, Trippany and the others following. Higher and higher they climbed, past numerous landings and hidden doors. Nearing the top at last, Amlina held up a hand to signal for quiet. She crept to the top landing, the Iruks moving silently behind.

Amlina bent and peered through a peephole. She spied a round, finely-furnished chamber with daylight streaming in from an open balcony. Melevarry sat at a mahogany writing table, working with pen and parchment. She wore the Cloak of the Two Winds.

Amlina took a deep breath, slid aside the panel and stepped into the room. Melevarry looked up calmly, as the Iruks and the rest of the party sidled into her study.

"Hello, Amlina." The Mage gestured toward a globe of amber glass. "I followed your progress in this looking-lamp. Your escape from the dungeon was quite remarkable—" Her eyes shifted to Trippany—"albeit, accomplished with unexpected assistance."

Behind Amlina, Karrol lifted a spear, ready to throw.

Lonn held out an arm to restrain her, but also lifted his own spear, as did Draven and Glyssa. He spoke to Amlina: "This witch offered us hospitality and then betrayed us. By our law, we have the right to kill her. What do you say, Amlina?"

"Wait a moment," she answered.

They had spoken in Tathian, but Melevarry clearly understood well enough. Her eyes widened, but she did not flinch. "Your warriors seem eager to kill me. Perhaps you wondered why none of my *alatee* guards intercepted you on the way up here."

"The question did occur."

"When I saw you would escape the dungeon, I ordered them outside—to prevent needless bloodshed." She lifted an arm, showing the black and silver sleeve. "As you see, I am not unprotected. And while I am inexperienced, I judge the Cloak's operation is simple enough that I could quite possibly freeze all of you in an instant. We seem to be at an impasse. Shall we fight or talk peace?"

The Iruks still awaited Amlina's word. She locked eyes with the elder witch, probing, seeking to read her. Finally, Amlina held up her hand.

"Stay your weapons, my friends. Please. Let me speak with her."

The Iruks kept the throwing spears raised, but let them rest on their shoulders.

Melevarry smiled, setting down her pen. "Good. We shall talk peace. Will you propose terms, or shall I?"

"First," Amlina answered, "you must swear on your honor to deliver the Cloak to the Archimage, and no other."

Melevarry seemed surprised. "Certainly. I swear it."

"Next, you must swear to free my companions without retribution. Restore their property, including their boat, and let them sail from Randoon in peace. Also, Trippany must not be punished for helping us."

Melevarry gave a shrug. "Trippany is not my responsibility. I am sure she will discuss this morning's events with her mentor, and they will sort it out."

"Yes," Trippany replied evenly. "So I shall."

"Well enough," the Mage said. "I did not foresee Trippany helping you, Amlina. And I doubt you could have escaped without her help— or that of your stout warriors. Still, the capacity to attract worthy allies is itself a significant talent. You mention freeing your companions, but what of you? Do you not intend to sail away with them?"

Amlina swallowed. "No. The affliction that I spoke of yesterday prevents that. I wish to present myself to the House of the Deepmind, request help to be healed. I will accept whatever judgment they make on me."

Again, Melevarry registered surprise. She stared hard for the space of a few heartbeats. "Very good. I agree to your terms."

Amlina let her shoulders sagged. "Put up your weapons, my friends," she said in Tathian. "All is well."

The Mage stood, took off the Cloak, and laid it on the table. "In fact, I not only accept your terms, but I give you back the Cloak. I will accompany you to Minhang and stand at your side as you present it to the Archimage."

Amlina eyed the Cloak mistrustfully, fighting the urge to step forward and snatch it. "Why the change of heart, my lady?"

The Mage's expression evinced amusement. "Because your actions have proved you worthy."

Amlina sank into a chair, suddenly weak and light-headed. Behind her, the Iruks watched suspiciously.

"I do not understand you," Amlina said.

"Then I'll explain. When I met you yesterday, I discovered an enigma, a trained witch, quite powerful, yet also frail and—frankly—damaged. Different stories of how you obtained the Cloak have reached these shores, but one in particular came to mind. It seems there is a certain bard in Gwales reciting a saga of how his queen joined with Amlina the witch of Larthang in a rite of blood magic. By the power thus released, Amlina killed the Archimage of the East. Of course, troubadours make up many tales, but this one corresponded with what I saw in you. In the afternoon, I consulted old texts about the effects of blood magic, and they supported my suspicions. Then last night, you told me you aspired to become Keeper of the Cloak. I decided then I must test you—to find out how badly you were damaged. By escaping the dungeon, you showed talent and resilience. By deciding not to kill me in revenge, you showed virtue and good judgment. So, I conclude you are both capable and honorable, and I can with confidence give you back the Cloak."

Amlina stared at her levelly. She rose from the chair, crossed to the table, and picked up the black and silver garment. "I accept your explanation and your offer. We will travel together to Minhang. But know this: I will instruct my warriors to keep their weapons ready, and I will watch keenly for any further treachery."

The Mage grinned. "I would hope so. Anything less, and I would think you lacking in prudence. Larthang is a land of deceptions, Amlina. A witch who treads the ways of high power must always remain on her guard."

Amlina and her companions were conducted downstairs to their apartment, where a breakfast of hot tea, boiled eggs, and rice cakes was served to them. A physician was summoned to tend to Eben and Brinda's wounds. The doctor appeared within the hour—a raw-boned old woman with a leathery face and brusque demeanor, followed by two assistants. She fussed and grunted over Eben's head, squeezing the scalp with her fingers. She insisted on shaving the area, then smeared it with an ointment before stitching up the skin. Although the ointment had a numbing effect, the pain was terrible. Eben gritted his teeth and uttered curses under his breath in Iruk. When the surgery was over, he gratefully accepted a sleeping draught and crawled off to his bed.

Early next morning, with Eben wearing a cap over his sore and conspicuously-shaven head, and with Brinda's arm in a sling, the mates returned to their dojuk in the harbor. Melevarry had provided a coach and draymen, and Kizier came along as interpreter. The Iruks collected all of the remaining luggage from the boat—furs and spare clothing, water skins and extra spears. They also brought the witch's wicker basket, which contained her garments, trinkets, and magical tools, as well as Buroof the talking book.

At Amlina's request, the Mage had arranged with the harbor master for the dojuk to be placed in dry dock. After loading their baggage onto the coach, the Iruks watched as lines were attached and their boat towed away. The harbor official handed Lonn a paper with a red seal, which Kizier explained was a receipt that would allow them to reclaim the craft at a later time, upon payment of the storage fees.

"There goes our boat, and all we have is this sheet of paper," Karrol remarked. "I wonder if we'll ever see it again."

They rode the coach back through the city. But instead of the Mage's mansion, they were driven beyond the Onyx Gates to a dock on the river. There at anchor lay a boat nearly as big as a galleon, with three stacked decks and a paddle wheel in the stern. The wheel, Eben learned from Kizier, was powered by rowers in a cabin on the lower deck. These crewmen worked hand cranks and foot pedals—an ingenious system that magnified their muscle power and could drive the craft upriver at surprising speed.

When the Iruks arrived, bundles and satchels were already being carried up the gangplanks. Melevarry stood on the dock supervising. With her was a group of guards and servants and her two apprentice witches, who would also make the journey. Nearby Amlina and Trippany waited. After they had unloaded the carriage, Eben took the opportunity to practice his Larthangan by conversing with the drell.

"Will you travel with us ... on the boat?"

She smiled and shook her head. "No. I fly ahead. I must report to my superiors at the House of the Deepmind."

"Oh." Eben stared at the ground and her tiny belled slippers. "I hope you will not have trouble because you helped us out of the dungeon."

She lifted a thin shoulder. "I may face a reprimand. But I do not worry. Let the winds blow so they will."

"What does that mean?" Eben was confused by the phrase.

She gave a quiet laugh."A line from a ballad sung by my people. It means 'things will be what they will be'—things we cannot change. Is your head all right?"

"Oh, yes." He pulled off the cap and showed her the wound.

Trippany winced.

"It is not so bad," he laughed. "I have seen much worse."

"But you are a warrior. To me it looks terrible." She touched him gently on the hand. "It will heal, I hope."

"Oh yes. I will see you again, in Minhang, I hope?"

"I hope so too," she said, then added. "Let the winds blow so they will."

Part Three

In Minhang the Beautiful

Fourteen

Precious Stone Fortress stood on the Ling Va Troo River, just downstream from Minhang. Guarding the eastern approach to the city, the fortress loomed dark and forbidding, an enormous castle with high turrets, ramparts and a towering keep.

Admiral Shay-Ni Pheng arrived in a chariot at the landside gate in the middle of a sunny afternoon. The breeze was warm and smelled of tea flowers from the nearby hills. It was the 27th day of the second month of First Summer, the warmest of seasons in Larthang.

Shay-Ni's mind prickled with apprehension. Two months ago, he had received orders from his uncle the Duke to return to the Celestial Capital. He had traveled in his flagship across the sea to the southern port of Hanjapore of the Jade Gates, then by boat up the river and across the canals to Minhang. Weary from travel, angry at being summoned home to what he expected would be some degree of disgrace, he had reached the city that morning. Going at once to the family's mansion, he had been told that the Duke awaited him at Precious Stone Fortress, that he should hasten there without delay. Further irritated, Shay-Ni had ordered a chariot and driver and rode here at once.

Now, having identified himself to the sentries at the outer gate, he marched across courtyards and parade grounds, passing low-roofed barracks and stables. His inner garments were damp and soiled from travel. But he had deliberately stopped at the mansion long enough to don a fresh coat, sword, and the medallions of his naval rank. If he was marching into disgrace, he would do so as a warrior.

Past the rampart of an inner wall, he came at last to the main keep. At the gate, a lieutenant bowed and led him up a broad staircase. Even the fortress interior featured defensible parapets, with carvings in the shape of fire turtles that could be employed to spew burning oil down on attacking troops.

Finally, Shay-Ni reached the apartment at the very summit of the keep. Duke Trem-Dou Pheng, supreme commander of Larthang's armed forces, used these chambers as his sanctuary. Having been informed of his nephew's arrival by a courier, the Duke waited in a spacious study hung with tapestries depicting ancient battles. He stood with his back to the door, hands clasped behind his back, at the edge of a wide terrace that afforded a spectacular view of the land downriver. When Shay-Ni was announced, the Duke did not turn around.

Gritting his teeth, the Admiral strode across the tiled floor toward his uncle. A maiden, one of his uncle's concubines, sat in one corner beside a lute. She did not play, only stared with an impassive, white-powdered face. Another woman sat at a long table, middle-aged and scrawny, wearing the black and red robes of a seer. Beside her a copper brazier burned charcoal and incense resins.

When Shay-Ni had approached within two yards, his uncle finally faced him. The Duke displayed an amiable smile.

"Ah, nephew. Good of you to meet me here."

Shay-Ni made a proper but not obsequious bow. "I came as summoned, uncle." His words were chosen to imply that he always strictly obeyed orders.

The Duke touched his lightly-bearded chin with a fingertip. "Yes … Some wine?"

Shay-Ni nodded politely. Tired, angry, and worried, he would have preferred to dispense with the fencing and proceed to business. But, of course, he would not say so.

The Duke poured pinkish cherry wine from a crystal decanter into two goblets. He gestured Shay-Ni to the long table. They sat at the opposite end from the seer, who waited in solemn silence. On the table lay a game board with 44 squares and 16 jade and onyx pieces representing different ranks of warriors. The strategy game *xingpoa* was a favored pastime of the Duke.

"What news of the engagements at Gon Fu?" Shay-Ni asked as soon as he was seated.

Gon Fu was a large island midway between Larthang and the Tathian Islands. With sizable populations from both nations, it had been disputed territory for centuries. Winning the island back from the Tathians was the first step in the Duke's ambitious plans for conquest.

"Stalemate," Trem-Dou answered. "Our positions in the west and north are held, but under siege. All our attempts to blockade the island have failed."

Shay-Ni stared at the dark, polished tabletop. He nurtured a frail hope that his uncle might still send him to join the fighting.

Trem-Dou took a sip, set down his goblet, and changed the subject with a sigh. "Most unfortunate, this business at Fleevanport."

Shay-Ni evinced fitting embarrassment. "Yes."

"However, we must move on with the game. This witch Amlina has, as we expected, brought the famous Cloak back to Larthang. She arrived in Randoon ten days ago. Yesterday, I received a missive from the Prefect there, a man with some loyalty to our cause. He tried to intercept the Cloak and claims he had it in hand until the Mage of Randoon appeared. The Prefect writes he was forced by law to surrender it to her, which I imagine he felt was true."

"So the Cloak is lost to us?"

"Oh, not at all. We can no longer prevent its reaching the House of the Deepmind. But we are not without our allies there, Lady Clorodice chief among them. I have consulted the oracle." The Duke lifted his chin in the direction of the seer. "Now it appears all depends on who will be appointed Keeper of the Cloak. We must strive to ensure the Keeper is a witch sympathetic to us, who will vouchsafe using the Cloak for the military."

Shay-Ni pondered, staring at the game board. His uncle's shrewdness and patience always impressed. "How can I be of help?"

"Ah." Trem-Dou lifted a finger. "You will recall the regrettable complaint lodged against you for launching arrows at the drell woman—the Archimage's envoy."

Shay-Ni forced down his resentment. "Yes. To my shame, uncle."

"Lady Clorodice reports that the matter has been discussed by the Inner Council, but no decision yet reached. Likely, they will wait until the Cloak is safely in their hands to either make a move or drop the issue. Clorodice is quietly using her influence to quash the complaint." He gestured toward the far end of the table. "This is why the esteemed prognosticator, Lady Belnorra, attends us now. I have asked her to consult the oracle as to our best course of action."

He rose with a gesture and Shay-Ni followed him to the opposite end of the long table. When the men were again seated, the Duke lifted a hand toward the seer.

"Pray proceed, my lady."

Belnorra nodded and rose. From a satchel at her feet she took a slim iron poker, a set of tongs, and a gray scaly object—the shell of one of the miniature breeds of fire turtle. She used the poker to stir the brazier, until the flames rolled high, then placed the shell on the fire.

While Shay-Ni waited impatiently and the Duke watched with a serene expression, Lady Belnorra chanted and waved hands. The turtle shell crinkled and blackened. When it finally cracked from the heat, the witch picked up the tongs and removed it from the fire. Holding it near her face, she stared for some moments, reading the oracle's message in the pattern of fracture lines.

Finally, she spoke in a thin, cackling voice. "Patience. Regathering of strength. The wise general retreats. In winter, the beaver seeks his lair." She set the blackened shell down beside the brazier and turned her eyes on the Duke. "The oracle has spoken. Patience is counseled. Withdrawal until conditions are more favorable."

Trem-Dou Pheng nodded sagely. Shay-Ni pulled back the corners of his mouth.

The Duke thanked the prognosticator and handed her a silver coin. She placed the burnt shell and tools into her satchel and, with bent back, shuffled from the room. When she had gone, Trem-Dou stared at his nephew.

"The oracle confirms my feelings of the wisest course. You had best keep out of sight until this witch's complaint is resolved."

Shay-Ni saw a faint glimpse of hope. "Might I suggest, uncle, that I would be well out of sight if sent to command a flotilla at Gon Fu."

The Duke frowned.

"... Or perhaps, farther west?"

The Duke's expression darkened. He held up a hand. "No, nephew. That is not what I meant at all. If charges are brought, you cannot appear to be avoiding them. No, you must remain in Minhang—but out of sight of the Court. I've arranged an apartment here in the Keep."

Shay-Ni slumped in his chair. Disgrace and now imprisonment. It occurred to him that the shadow play with the prognosticator had been a sham. His uncle had already decided this outcome.

"For how long?" he asked.

"That will depend. A month or two, at least. If Lady Clorodice succeeds in getting the matter dismissed, that would be the end of it. But, if the complaint goes forward and a lawsuit is filed ..." The Duke showed a regretful shrug. "That would likely take many months. I would of course do all in my power to ensure the case went before a magistrate sympathetic to our cause. Meanwhile, you must remain out of sight."

The Duke stood with a benevolent smile. "It will not be so bad. Your quarters are luxurious. You may send to the mansion for anything you wish—books, servants. Practice your swordsmanship, read up on strategy. I will provide a concubine or two to amuse you."

Controlling his inner rage, Shay-Ni bowed. "My uncle is most generous and gracious."

Fifteen

O ver the course of fair and balmy days, the paddleboat travelled up the River *Ling Va Troo*. This name, Eben learned, meant 'River of Turquoise Light'—well-chosen, since the witchlight that illumined all the seas and oceans of Glimnodd, but not usually the fresh water, glowed here as brightly as he had ever seen. Nights shone nearly as clear as days, so the stars and moons appeared hazy.

Along the shores stretched endless farmlands, irrigated by canals, planted with orchards, terraced rice paddies, and fields of wheat that glowed golden in these last days of First Summer. Spying the paddleboat, farmers would pause in their work to wave and shout greetings, wishing long life to the Mage and her party. Twice the boat pulled in at landings to restock provisions. Then the travelers were greeted by town officials and elders. But when it was learned that the party included the witch Amlina and her warrior band, who had wrested the Cloak of the Two Winds from the evil witch of Tallyba, then feasts were arranged, songs and puppet plays performed, and gifts of gratitude offered—flower wreathes, tinctures, perfumes, and sweets. Eben had never eaten so well, not even in the Tathian Islands or Queen Meghild's castle in Gwales. He was cautious, however, to avoid excessive drinking—limiting himself to two cups of the sweet and varied Larthangan wines at each dinner.

Otherwise, he spent his time aboard the boat in rigorous training with his mates, practicing with sword, spear, and knife. His physique had grown sleek and strong again, and he disciplined himself to keep it that way. The rest of his waking hours he studied, working with Kizier and Buroof to hone his command of the Larthangan tongue.

Often the lessons were shared with the rest of the klarn. With Glyssa's encouragement, the Iruks took to speaking Larthangan as much as possible when conversing among themselves. At first, Karrol and even Lonn balked at this idea, but Glyssa argued that they had all learned to speak Tathian readily enough, so this should be no harder.

As Amlina had advised, the mates kept a wary eye on the Mage and her servants, and slept with their weapons near and one of them always awake to keep watch. These precautions seemed increasingly unnecessary, as Melevarry and her people treated Amlina's party with all friendliness and courtesy. Kizier suggested that the Mage was probably satisfied with the deal she had struck with Amlina. Looking at the matter with her witchsight, Glyssa pronounced a similar opinion. That was when Karrol muttered that Glyssa always thought well of everyone and that she, Karrol, thought they should still be wary of the Mage.

The mates' other concern was Amlina. Once they left Randoon and settled on the boat, the witch's energy drained. She appeared on deck infrequently, looking pale and exhausted. Mostly she stayed in her cabin, and did not invite Draven to share her bed. She claimed to be meditating and weaving designs to help ensure their success in Minhang. But Draven fretted that his love had lost herself again in fear and brooding, struggling against the tainted power that had ravaged her on and off now for many months. He suggested she might be cutting herself again, drawing her own blood to relieve the terrible pressure. Glyssa went and talked with the witch each day. She tried to reassure Draven and the others that Amlina was coping well with her burdens, all things considered. But Eben sensed Glyssa was more worried than she pretended.

When the craft was eight or nine days from their destination, Amlina entered the dark immersion. Witches of Larthang usually invoked this ritual once a month, in alignment with the cycle of Grizna. The moon was now at its dark phase, and for Amlina the timing was propitious. She would lie in deep trance for several days, but waken well before their arrival in Minhang.

That same evening, Karrol called a klarn meeting. The Iruks assembled on the platform of the upper deck. Grizna hung like a pale, curved blade in the fading twilight of the eastern sky. The Iruks sat in a circle, wearing their deerskin garb as they had most of the voyage—in preference to the Larthangan costumes given them by the Mage. To ensure secrecy, they spoke in Iruk.

"Karrol requested the meeting," Lonn said. "It is for her to begin."

Karrol climbed to her feet. "I'm troubled, mates. Ever since I watched our dojuk being towed away, I've been worried. We don't know what we'll do after we reach this inland city. On our past voyages with Amlina, at least we had a clear purpose."

"Our purpose," Glyssa said, "is to help Amlina deliver the Cloak and the scrolls, and to heal her inner wound."

"I know that, but what happens then? What happens to us? We've not talked about that at all. *What happens to us*?"

Eben had to admit he had not given the matter much thought. After Karrol sat down, the mates looked at each other. It was Glyssa who stood.

"I have spoken with Amlina about this a little. After she is healed, she hopes to be appointed Keeper of the Cloak. If that fails, she expects she may receive some other post from the House of Witches. As a high-ranking witch, she will need warriors to guard her house and accompany her on journeys. That could be a good life for all of us, and the klarn could stay together. That is what I hope will happen."

"I don't know," Karrol muttered without rising. "I'm not sure we'd be happy in such a life."

As Glyssa sat down, Eben bolted to his feet. "Well I, for one, think we would be happy. Anyway, how can we know until we try?"

"Because it is not a fit life for Iruks," Karrol answered. "Far from the sea, from our own people, and with this blasted hot weather!"

"Were you happy in the Iruk seas?" Eben shot back. "No! Wherever you are you want to be someplace else."

"Stop it!" Lonn jumped up and raised his hands. "This is a klarn meeting. Let's keep order. If Eben has finished, I will speak next."

Eben clenched his mouth and sat down.

Lonn said: "For myself, I find Larthang a pleasant enough land. If things turn out well for Amlina, I think I might like staying here. Of course much would depend on what Glyssa wants to do. Wherever she is happy, I expect I will be happy."

Glyssa smiled at him fondly and placed a hand on his knee when he was seated.

Draven stood next, his expression somber. "These past seasons, I assumed that I would stay with Amlina no matter what. But lately, I am not sure. I still love her dearly. But I see how she suffers and it tortures me—because there is nothing I can do to help. I hope she is able to find healing, but I'm not sure how long I can wait. Also, I know that if she is cured and then satisfies her ambitions, she may change into a different person. Will I still love that person, or she love me? I don't know. So, like Karrol, I can see myself leaving Larthang and going back to the Iruk seas."

A gloomy silence hovered over the group. None of them had expected these sentiments from Draven.

As often happened, Brinda was the last to speak. Her words too, Eben found surprising. "Plainly, it's too early to know what will happen with Amlina, or what other options the klarn may have. If we are given the opportunity to stay in Larthang with the witch, then we will each need to choose for ourselves. As to what I will choose, I honestly don't know. I left this klarn once before, because Karrol insisted. I joined the klarn of Tallvis with her and then left that one too. I came on this voyage because Karrol agreed—at the very last moment. At some point, mates, I think I must stop chasing Karrol because I feel the need to protect her, and decide my course for myself."

She sat down, looking at her sister with an expression that was both apologetic and determined. For once, Karrol was speechless.

Presently, Lonn stood and extended his hand to the center of the circle. "As Brinda stated so well, we must wait and see what happens with Amlina and what options we might have, before we can choose what the klarn will do. So, for now our decision must be to revisit this question after the witch's course is set. Agreed?"

After getting to their feet, the mates placed their hands over his.

"Agreed," they all said.

Karrol grumbled: "Well, this was unhelpful. I am now more confused than ever."

When Amlina emerged from deep trance, a steward informed her that the paddleboat was now three days from Minhang. After dinner that evening, she attended Melevarry in her chambers. The Mage occupied a spacious cabin on the upper deck, at the square bow of the riverboat. Couches arranged in front of glass doors afforded a view of the broad, shining water and the shores drifting by on either side.

Melevarry sat in company with her two apprentices, dressed in witch's robes of varied colors. Yensia Meltai, the elder, was a small, solemn woman with a sharp chin, clad in blue and silver. Wenpheenae Chon, the younger was tall and slim, her garments brown and pale yellow. She watched Melevarry with a quiet deference.

"Good evening, Amlina." The Mage waved to the seat beside her own. "I trust you found the dark immersion replenishing."

Amlina declined a proffered cup of wine. "Yes, my lady. I am well enough."

In truth, she struggled to keep her anxiety and apprehension under control. The long journey up the river had worn on her nerves and allowed the unnatural rage inside her to fester. Melevarry scrutinized her, peering past Amlina's pretence and likely discerning the truth.

"I wanted to prepare you for what will happen when we reach the capital," the Mage said. "Runners have been dispatched ahead, and we are expected. Yesterday, I received word that arrangements have been made for a representative of the Inner Council to meet us when we dock. Doubtless, news of our impending arrival has also reached the Tuan's court and from there the civil service and military. They almost certainly will also send envoys to the landing. This will probably include Wu Tong, the Tuan's Primary Minister, as well as one or more high-ranking magistrates and generals."

Amlina nodded, digesting all this.

"You will have to be presented to these envoys. When we leave the boat, I will walk with you and make introductions as necessary. They will insist on making speeches and offering you gifts. My aim will be to make these ceremonies as brief as possible and get you away to the House of the Deepmind."

Amlina nodded again. Melevarry's expression darkened.

"You should definitely wear the Cloak when we land. Also, instruct your entourage to follow immediately behind you. The envoy from the House of the Deepmind will be accompanied by a large detachment of Chrysalis Warriors. They should be sufficient to forestall any trouble."

Amlina cringed inwardly. "What sort of trouble do you mean?"

The Mage frowned and shook her head. "Difficult to say. I do not think the Iron Bloc would try to seize you or take the Cloak in the midst of a public ceremony, but these are turbulent times and nothing can be ruled out."

Amlina was astonished. "That would mean openly defying the House of the Deepmind. Would they dare such a step?"

Melevarry made a fatalistic gesture. "They have dared much these past few years, driven by ambition and the lust for conquest. If they appear on the dock with a large body of troops, or if Duke Pheng himself is present, that might be a warning sign."

"Duke Pheng?" Amlina frowned as a memory stirred. "The commander who tried to seize the Cloak in Fleevanport ...?"

"His nephew," Melevarry said. "Duke Pheng is supreme commander of all the Tuan's forces, and the leader of the Iron Bloc. A dangerous and unpredictable man."

"I see."

The Mage stood and stretched. "We must both be on our guard, Amlina—until the Cloak is safely handed over to the Archimage at the gates of Ting Ta Roo."

Amlina retired to her cabin a short time later. In spite of her deep trance, she felt frightened and inexpressibly weary. The taint left in her by the blood magic had grown active again, gnawing at her without respite. Now, as she neared the goal of her journey, she did not know if the healing she sought would be found—or if it was even possible.

For a long while she sat on her bed, breathing slowly, staring out the open window at the flow of glimmering water. Eventually, she slipped into meditation, and then into a vision.

The currents of the Deepmind flowed and broke like waves against a looming solid form. A towering rock formation? No, a structure black as obsidian sprinkled with flakes of light.

The House of the Deepmind, Amlina realized. *Drawing ever nearer.*

Would she find an end to her torment there?

The vision shifted and a figure appeared—a small child dressed in rich regalia, with a round and laughing face. The child would assist her, Amlina thought. *And glimpsed another, a tall witch in a silver robe, guiding her by the hand. Was it Melevarry?*

A new vision rippled into being. Amlina saw herself as a child, wandering long ago on the moors of Shen Tong, the western province that was her home. She often traipsed the moors well into

—133—

the dusk. Cold and lonely, it was still more pleasant than the home
she shared with her mother—an angry, unforgiving woman whose
approval she could never win.

"Oh, poor Amlina." A voice dripping with cruel sarcasm. "Your
mama never loved you."

Amlina opened her eyes and traced a banishing sign. It had been
many days since Beryl's presence tormented her. "Begone," she
whispered.

"I am not really Beryl, you know. I am yourself, your own hatred
of yourself. You can never make me go away."

"I will make an end to you," Amlina promised.

"Do you really think so? You think the witches in Minhang will
help you? You remember how they treated you before. Oh, they will
receive the treasures, gladly. They might even promise help, but they
will be laughing at you in secret. They will send you away somewhere
and leave you there to die. Because that is really what you deserve.
You know it, and they will know it."

Amlina sighed and repeated the warding gesture. "If that will be,
then I will let it be. I will make an end of you, even if it means ending
myself."

Sixteen

As the paddleboat neared Minhang, the shores of the gleaming river began to change. Irrigated flatlands gave way to gently rising hills marked by watchtowers, docks, and towns. On a warm cloudy morning, the boat passed the imposing castle known as Precious Stone Fortress. Beyond, the majestic city came into view under a silvery sky. It was the tenth day of Second Summer, twenty-one days since leaving Randoon.

At first sighting, the Celestial Capital appeared to stand at the end of the Ling Va Troo, rising in tiers of crenellated walls and curved rooflines as far as one could see. But as the paddleboat approached, it became clear that the channel split into canals running off north and south. Amlina knew from her days here as a fledgling witch that the canals circled Minhang like a moat, ending upstream in the eternally-glowing Perfect Light Lake.

The quay facing the river was wide and long, and this morning mobbed with people. A fanfare of trumpets arose when the paddleboat was still some distance from the city. The music and noise of the crowd only increased as the craft worked its way toward the docks.

Amlina stood on the lower deck, hands hidden in sleeves, nervously clutching her forearms. She was dressed in her finest robe, an embroidered belt with her dagger, rings and bracelets, her moonstone fillet, and the Cloak of the Two Winds over all. In a satchel near her feet lay the Nine Scrolls of Eglemarde that she had taken from Beryl's lair in Tallyba.

Beside her stood Melevarry and her apprentices, arrayed in ceremonial finery. On Amlina's other side, the Iruks and Kizier stared at the vast city. The Iruks had stubbornly refused Larthangan dress, wearing instead their hunting garb, light deerskin shirts and trousers, boots and their leather harnesses and sword belts. Melevarry had looked askance at their attire but made no remark.

The Mage had counseled Amlina on what to expect when they reached the capital. Still, the spectacle of the city and the huge crowd overwhelmed and unnerved her. Her wildest dream had been to return to Minhang and receive such acclamation. Now, weak and frazzled, she only wished the day over.

A boisterous cheer erupted as the paddleboat sidled up to the dock. Lines were thrown and secured and a gangplank lowered. Melevarry took Amlina's arm and led her to the edge of the railed gangplank. They faced a throng numbering in the thousands, far larger than the one that met them on the quay at Randoon.

Raising her arms and lifting Amlina's wrist to conspicuously display the Cloak, Melevarry proclaimed: "Greetings, Minhang! I am Melevarry, Mage of Randoon. It is my honor to present to you Amlina Len Tai, noble witch of the House of the Deepmind, who has brought the Cloak of the Two Winds and other treasures back from distant shores. All hail Amlina!"

The multitude shouted out the words of praise and welcome. Amlina trembled, her legs weak as the Mage led her down the gangplank. Kizier and the Iruks came after, followed by the Mage's party.

"Stay close to me, my friends," Amlina pleaded over her shoulder.

"Don't worry," Draven laughed. "You won't lose us now."

In the front ranks of the crowd was a party of witches in colorful robes backed by a battalion of male and female *alatee* warriors in scaled armor and feathered helmets. In the center stood a stern-faced witch in bronze-colored robes and a high, squared headpiece. She stepped forward as Melevarry and Amlina set foot ashore. Hands folded in sleeves, the witch bowed slightly at the waist. Taking her cue from Melevarry, Amlina returned the gesture.

"Greetings, Melevarry, my sister, and to you, Amlina. I am Clorodice, Keeper of the Keys. It is my honor today to represent our esteemed Lady Drusdegarde and to conduct you to her presence."

"I thank you," Amlina murmured, noticing the medallion of office Clorodice wore, a necklace fashioned of tiny copper and silver keys.

At a hand wave from Clorodice, the warriors behind her separated, forming two ranks. Beyond them, a wide path was cleared through the crowd, leading to a gate in the city wall. Along the path stood more delegations—officials in rich robes grouped with assistants, body guards with spears and shields, musicians carrying horns, pipes, and gongs.

"I see there are other welcoming parties," Melevarry remarked dryly.

Clorodice lifted an eyebrow. "Indeed. It could hardly be avoided."

They led Amlina forward at a slow march. She glanced about nervously, assuring herself that Draven and his mates still followed close at her heels.

First she was introduced to the Harbor Master, and then the City Mayor, both portly men with small entourages who presented gifts and made brief speeches of welcome. But when they came to the third delegation, Melevarry stood rigid and instinctively grabbed Amlina's wrist.

A broad-shouldered warrior stepped forward, clad in grandiose armor and headpiece, a long curved sword in his belt. Behind him stood officers similarly dressed, and behind them, rank on rank of troops stood at attention, the tips of their long spears conspicuous over their heads. Amlina noticed an almost imperceptible tension come over the Chrysalis warriors as the commander of these troops stepped forward. Lady Clorodice gave an affable smile and courtly bow.

"Greetings to you, Duke Pheng. You honor us with your presence."

The Duke had a wide face and tan, weathered complexion. His neat mustache and beard were flecked with gray. He showed a thin smile as he returned the bow.

"It is my privilege, Lady Clorodice." His eyes shifted to Amlina.

Clorodice lifted a hand in introduction: "Lady Melevarry, Mage of Randoon, and Amlina, noble witch of Larthang, it is my honor to present Duke Trem-Dou Pheng, supreme commander of the Tuan's armies. "

"I know the esteemed Mage of Randoon, of course," the Duke said. "And this is the heroic Amlina. Indeed, it is a pleasure. A witch of such renown, I had not expected to find so young."

Awkwardly, Amlina gave a second bow. The Duke's hand reached out, his fingers closing on her sleeve.

"And this is the mighty Cloak?" He caressed the fabric. "Such an unpretentious garment. Unless one knew its power, one would scarcely guess."

Abruptly, Amlina yanked her arm away. "Yes," she answered coldly. "Unless one knows its power."

A look of malice kindled in the Duke's eyes. In Amlina's mind, that look confirmed him as an enemy. She suddenly feared he would signal to his troops to charge forward and seize her. Incipient rage quivered deep in her soul, a wild impulse to draw her dagger and strike him.

Melevarry interrupted the tension with a cheery smile. "My Lord Duke does us great honor to come here in person. Will you also accompany us to the House of the Deepmind—where Amlina will formally present the Cloak to the Archimage?"

Duke Pheng seemed perplexed for an instant, but quickly resumed his courteous mien. He was about to answer when a trumpet blast erupted at the far end of the plaza.

A moan of surprise and awe swept over the crowd. Through the gates came a giant palanquin, three stories high and carried by forty bearers. Enthroned at the top sat a tiny figure in glittering robes of gold and white.

"Who is the little man in the big chair?" Karrol asked.

She stood with her mates at Amlina's back, surrounded by the Mage's entourage and the warriors in blue-green armor.

"That is the Tuan." Kizier bent at the waist. "Everyone must bow."

Indeed, Eben saw that across the plaza the entire crowd was bowing, some prostrating themselves on the pavement, others simply leaning well forward.

"Bow, mates," Glyssa ordered. "We must be courteous to our hosts."

Awkwardly, Eben and the others followed her lead. Gongs tolled at the front of the Tuan's procession and everyone resumed standing.

"The Tuan looks to be only a child." Eben spoke to Kizier out of the side of his mouth.

"Indeed," Kizier replied. "I had not realized that the old Tuan had passed. This one must be his son or other relative. I believe that makes him the 154th in the line. The Tuan is rarely seen outside the Celestial Palace. His appearance makes this an even more momentous occasion."

"But you have said," Eben muttered, "that the Tuan is the supreme ruler of the land. How can that be if he is a child?"

"Well," Kizier answered with a shrug. "It is rather complex—like so many things in Larthang."

Amlina stared as the bearers placed the giant throne down on the pavement. She had not realized that the new Tuan was a child, and she certainly had not expected the Ruler of the Golden Land to appear here on the docks.

In the hushed plaza, the Tuan rose from his seat and nimbly descended the stairs. A troop of officials and ministers who had followed his procession now came forward and arranged themselves at the foot of the palanquin. Three steps from the ground, the child ruler lifted his arms in his splendid robes. His high-pitched voice rang out strong and clear.

"People of Minhang, I and my ministers have ventured from the palace on this auspicious morning to celebrate with you the restoration of our national treasures. Where is the honored Amlina?"

"She is here, August Ruler." Clorodice called out.

She tugged Amlina's sleeve and ushered her forward. While the multitude stood in reverent silence, Amlina, Clorodice, and the Mage marched across the plaza, followed by their respective entourages. The Tuan watched with a serene smile as they drew near. Amlina followed Melevarry's lead and bowed deeply.

"August Ruler," Clorodice said. "It is my privilege to present to you Amlina, who has returned to us from afar."

The Tuan's smile was warm and genuine. "Honored Amlina, I welcome you to our city. Is that the magical Cloak that you wear?"

Throat tight, Amlina managed: "Yes, August Ruler. Your greeting honors me."

"On the contrary, it is you who have done me great service. Your restoration of our national treasures marks a most auspicious day in this, the morning time of my reign." The Tuan craned his neck, then pointed to the space behind her. "And, might I ask if these are your companions—the formidable Iruk warriors I have heard such wondrous stories of?"

Amlina cast a nervous look behind her, and gestured for the Iruks to step forward. As they moved beside her, a calm entered her spirit. *The klarn-soul,* she thought. *Even here, I draw strength from Draven and his mates.*

Her voice now was steady and strong. "It is my honor to present them to you, Lord Tuan." She named each of them and Kizier as well, and called them the bravest and noblest of friends.

The Tuan displayed a boyish grin. "Marvelous! I do so look forward to speaking with all of you and hearing the stories of your adventures. Apartments are being prepared for you at my palace, where I hope you will honor me as my guests."

Amlina bowed, nervous again. "Of course. We are greatly honored."

"But it seems I have interrupted your arrival," the Tuan said. "Pray forgive me. I know you must proceed to the House of the Deepmind to present the magical treasures to the Archimage. My party shall accompany you there. Then, this evening, we shall meet again at the palace, at a feast in your honor."

With an amiable smile he turned and ascended the steps. All present bowed as he reached the summit and resumed his seat. Gongs sounded and the crowd made way as the palanquin was lifted and turned. The Tuan's entourage moved off to the stately beat of cymbals and drums.

Clorodice and Melevarry stood beside Amlina as chariots wheeled near, pulled by teams of tali.

"Come," Clorodice ordered brusquely. "The Archimage awaits."

Amlina complied, thinking how her long, stressful day had now grown even longer.

The Tuan's dining hall was illuminated by paper lanterns—white globes suspended from the high ceiling on tiny threads so they appeared to float in the air. The floor rose in concentric, half-circle tiers to a high dais where the Tuan's party sat at the royal table. Behind the dais, wall panels were open, revealing a splendid view of gardens, groves, and lawns, ending at the gleaming water of Perfect Light Lake. The gentle splash of fountains sounded as a contrast to the clatter and babbling conviviality of the feast. The soft air of twilight drifted in, carrying the scent of jasmine and orchids to mingle with the delicious smells of roasted meats, soups, and spices.

The royal table was occupied by the Tuan, high officials of his court, and the guests of honor, Melevarry the Mage of Randoon and Amlina, the honored witch on this the day of her triumphant return. Curving tables on the tiers below were crowded with courtiers, magistrates, ambassadors, and their guests—all arranged according to their rank and honors on this evening.

In a state of dreamy weariness, Amlina gazed at the crowded hall and the floating globes of light. Earlier in the day, she had been paraded through streets lined by cheering throngs, riding in a chariot with Clorodice, the Keeper of the Keys. Arriving at last at the huge, shiny black edifice known as Ting Ta Roo, the House of the Deepmind, she had climbed the steps to the obsidian portico and delivered the Cloak of the Two Winds and the scrolls of Eglemarde into the hands of Drusdegarde, the Archimage—thus completing the return of the magical treasures that Beryl had stolen over a century ago. The moment the last scroll left her hands, a sense of enormous relief descended, her heart fluttering. It was all she could do to stand erect and grasp the hands of the Archimage, a gaunt elderly witch, who regarded her with a mixture of admiration and uncertain suspicion. Already informed about Amlina's wish to seek healing for her affliction, the Archimage had promised to welcome her into the House of the Deepmind in a few days time, after Amlina had had a chance to rest. Then the Inner Council would receive her and hear any petitions she cared to make.

With the Cloak and the scrolls safely within the walls of Ting Ta Roo, Amlina and her friends had been driven east across the city to the Tuan's Celestial Palace. Conducted to spacious apartments overlooking a garden of floss silk and bougainvillea, they'd been given food and drink, offered baths and fresh clothing, and allowed to rest ahead of the evening's banquet.

Now, Amlina had to force herself to make polite conversation with Melevarry and the Tuan's ministers. The relief of delivering the Cloak still comforted her. But already a gnawing fear constricted her stomach. She recalled the malice in the eyes of Duke Pheng, the instinctive recognition of a dangerous enemy. And she remembered the mistrust she had seen in the face of Drusdegarde—understandable, certainly. For although Amlina had defeated Beryl and brought back what she had stolen, Amlina was herself a renegade witch, one damaged by forbidden sorcery. Would the Archimage and the Council take steps to help her, or would they send her back into exile? Even if they did decide to offer her aid, would it be enough to cure her affliction? She had this day achieved her great goal, yet her fate seemed uncertain as ever.

One level below the royal dais, Eben was seated with his mates and Kizier and Melevarry's apprentice witches. Between bites of roast fowl and fish and sips of chilled wine, his eyes scanned the crowd, which numbered in the hundreds. He had hoped to see Trippany here tonight, but so far she had not appeared. On the far side of the hall he did spot several of the winged people, seated together on a lower tier. Inquiring of one of Melevarry's group, he learned that this was the party of Prince Spegis Besu Keli, the ambassador from the Drell Forest. Given the distance, Eben had peered closely before satisfying himself that Trippany was not with the party.

"This is what I call a feast," Karrol said, sticking her knife into a crispy roasted bird to retrieve it from a serving platter.

"Yes, and a beautiful palace," Lonn opined. "I think we will like being guests here, however long it lasts."

"Amlina looks tired," Glyssa said.

Eben followed her eyes to the high dais, where the witch was seated in a place of honor beside the young Tuan.

"Of course she is," Draven said. "This whole journey has been hard for her."

Having eaten all he wanted, Eben prodded Kizier who sat beside him. "I wanted to learn more about the Tuan," he said. "He is a but a boy, and yet the supreme ruler of the land. This is hard for me to understand."

"Well, as I said, it is complicated." The scholar set down his goblet. "And I can only speak as a foreigner, so some of the nuances are no doubt lost on me. But firstly, the Tuan's primary and most important duties are ceremonial—to perform and participate in rituals meant to ensure the prosperity of the realm and the um ... continuation of the *Sacred Mandate*."

"The Sacred Mandate. What is that?"

"Essentially, it is the blessings of the ancestors, particularly all previous Tuans. The Larthangans place great importance on the unbroken succession of the dynasty. Indeed—and this is difficult for foreigners to grasp—it is believed that every Tuan takes on the consciousness of all their predecessors, that the Tuan, in a kind of trance state, can confer with any of these ancestors and acquire their knowledge and wisdom."

"A strange idea, do you think?" A brash, boyish voice spoke behind them.

Eben turned his head to find the Tuan, standing at his elbow, backed by two solemn-faced attendants.

"Ha ha! Forgive me. I did not mean to startle you!"

Everyone at Eben's table rose and bowed stiffly.

"No, no, my friends." The Tuan flapped his hands, signaling them down. "Please, no excessive courtesies. This is your festivity. I am an interloper."

"You speak Tathian," Eben observed.

The Tuan grinned. "Yes. I have been tutored in the tongue. May I join you?"

"Of course," Glyssa said. "We would be honored."

The boy signed to a servant who stepped forward with a high royal chair. Around the table, the Mage's apprentices looked flustered, rose once more, and bowed. The Iruks, still seated, watched in bemusement. The chair was set down and the Tuan climbed into it, sitting on his heels. His large attendants stood behind him, arms crossed, faces set in sober frowns.

He gestured with a folded fan he carried. "Pray go on with your dining." Turning to Eben and Kizier, he said: "You were discussing the Sacred Mandate, and how I can speak with my ancestors. It is true. I can call their voices to me—like wandering through a library and selecting a book from the shelves. Most unusual, wouldn't you say?"

"Quite remarkable," Kizier answered. "Can you summon these experiences at will, or does it require ritual actions?"

"Ha ha! I can usually just shut my eyes and ask. Sometimes they even come without invitation! I have had this ability ever since I ascended the throne. Do you know my name?"

"No, August Ruler," Kizier replied. "Only your title."

"Of course! Only titles are used at ceremonial functions. And my full name is seldom spoken at all. This is because it includes the names of all of my ancestor Tuans, and takes more than an hour to say! Can you imagine? In shortened form, it is Me Lo Lee. I hope you will all address me as Me Lo, and that we shall be friends." He looked eagerly around the table. Behind him, one of the tall attendants cleared his throat.

Me Lo smiled. "Sometimes my noble elders opine that I am too frivolous and should adopt a more solemn mien on all occasions. But then one or other of my ancestors will speak in my mind and remind me that I am just a boy, and there is no harm if I enjoy myself a little."

Eben had to laugh. "I agree with your ancestors. One should enjoy oneself as much as possible, especially when a child."

"So we agree!" the Tuan cried. "I expected it would be so. I long to hear all about your adventures, and to learn about the Iruk people. For, though I have consulted with the vast number of my ancestors, we know very little of your folk."

"We are at your service, sir," Lonn said.

"I thank you." The Tuan smiled. "I tried to speak with the esteemed Amlina about your travels, but she had little to say. I fear she is tired tonight, which of course is understandable. I must say, she surprises me. Given her mighty deeds, I expected a powerful and robust woman, but I find her thin and fragile, almost a child herself."

"She has been ill," Glyssa disclosed.

"Oh, I did not know. I am so sorry to hear this. I shall place my royal physicians at her disposal."

"That is very generous," Kizier said. "But the illness is ... metaphysical. Amlina hopes to find healing at the House of the Deepmind. But she is not certain it will be offered."

The boy's face showed puzzlement. "Why should it not be offered? And to so worthy a witch?"

Kizier's expression was guarded. "I am uncertain, August Ruler, but I believe the matter is complex."

"Oh, yes?" Me Lo sighed. "The affairs of witches are often abstruse." After pondering this a moment, his face brightened. "You know, as the avatar of all the Tuans, I have a seat on the Inner Council. Perhaps I can exert some influence ..."

Seventeen

The floor of the council chamber was wide, circular, and invisible. Walking over it with Melevarry at her side, Amlina seemed to be treading on air. Below her shoes lay a shifting image—white clouds floating in a deep cerulean sky.

In shade cast by the brilliance of the floor, a semi-circle of figures faced her from a dais, seated behind high podiums, each with two or more attendants. The witches of the Inner Council wore elaborate hats above faces painted with white and red ceremonial makeup. At the center was Drusdegarde, the gaunt Archimage, with her sloping shoulders and flinty eyes. Beside her sat Clorodice, Keeper of the Keys, and on her other side the Tuan, his gold robes and bright, child's face an incongruous sight. Flanking these sat an array of high witches whose official posts, Amlina knew, included Keeper of the Books, Keeper of the Forge, Mage of the Academy, and four of the nine provincial Mages currently visiting Minhang. Melevarry's own podium stood empty as she had chosen to stand with Amlina and advocate for her. Amlina was not entirely sure why.

A coach had awaited her at the palace gates and driven her through a gray, rainy morning to the House of the Deepmind. Amlina was grateful as she had spent a sleepless night, struggling with the angry power inside her, the obsessive hunger and rage that had become almost a creature with a will of its own. For the first time in many days, Amlina had cut herself to quiet the beast, and numbly watched as the blood dripped down her arm.

Awaiting her under the portico of Ting Ta Roo, the Mage of Randoon had remarked on how drawn and haggard Amlina looked and inquired if she was well enough to face the Inner Council.

Unwilling to delay the confrontation, Amlina had offered what assurances she could. With Melevarry leading the way, they had passed the main gates and marched through corridors and pillared halls, arriving here at last.

Now they stopped at the center of the floor, the brightest spot in the chamber. The faces of the Councilors, lit from below by the sky image, regarded Amlina with shadowed expressions.

"Honored Amlina," Drusdegarde began in her wheezing voice. "You have done a great service to the Land. You are invited now to present petitions. What recompense do you seek for your service?"

Coached by Melevarry, Amlina had prepared her words. "I returned the Cloak and the Scrolls to their true owners. I ask no rewards for following this rightful course. But I do seek succor from the House of the Deepmind. First, I am afflicted with an illness of spirit, and I believe my best hope for healing lies within these walls. I request healing rites be performed on my behalf. Second, should this healing prove successful and I am made fit again, I request that I be granted the gray mantle of an adept, which I believe my accomplishments now merit. Third and lastly, assuming I attain these first two gifts, I request that I be considered as candidate for the post of Keeper of the Cloak, which has been vacant since the Cloak was stolen long ago."

Her last appeal brought an intake of breath from the figures on the dais. Below her feet, the floor shifted, clouds now colliding. Amlina fought down the feeling of vertigo and stared levelly at Drusdegarde.

But it was Clorodice who spoke: "She is certainly not lacking ambition." Her statement brought nods and grunts of agreement from several of the podiums.

Amlina drew in a breath to reply, but Melevarry touched her arm. "Obviously, ambition is a key element of her character. Else she could never have accomplished what she has in winning back the stolen treasures."

"That is so," the Archimage said. "But we have much to consider here. First, Amlina, you must tell us all about your illness, its causes and effects on you. Rumors have circulated on the matter, and I have spoken in private with Lady Melevarry. But the entire Council must hear it, and from your lips."

Amlina swallowed. She had known this would be necessary. "The illness is the result of forbidden practice, an ancient ensorcellment that I performed."

"We have heard that the rite involved blood magic," said the Mage of the Academy, a witch named Linskarra.

"It is true," Amlina replied, as a murmur crept around the dais. "I do not deny it. But I will tell you what led me to take that course."

Her voice quavering at times, she related her tale. She had left Larthang after studying four years at the Academy of the Deepmind, but failing to advance to the rank of adept. She had gone first to the Tathian lands and lived there for a time, seeking to build her knowledge—especially of trinketing, the art of constructing magical objects. Beryl, the renegade Archimage of the East, was said to be the greatest trinketer of the age, and eventually Amlina had decided to go to Tallyba. She had disregarded the stories of Beryl's pernicious sorcery, and learned too late that those stories were true. First confined to a dungeon, then serving as a kitchen slave, Amlina had eventually been taken on as Beryl's apprentice. She lived for seven years in the Archimage's court, and in that time learned some inklings of the powerful, ancient arts that Beryl practiced. But, she swore, she herself had never engaged in either blood magic or Nyssanian sorcery. Eventually, sensing that Beryl was turning against her, Amlina had stolen the Cloak of the Two Winds and fled, intending to restore the Cloak to Larthang. When the prize was stolen from her in turn, she followed its trail to the Tathian port of Kadavel. There, she managed to rescue the Cloak from a serd sorcerer who was bent on destroying it. But Beryl too had followed the trail. She appeared and snatched the Cloak. Amlina would have died then but that her Iruk warriors forced the already-wounded Beryl to retreat.

Amlina and her crew also fled Kadavel, taking refuge in the far northern land of Gwales. They wintered in the Castle of Meghild, queen of one of the Gwales tribes. Amlina pondered her next move. From a magical book she had stolen from the serd's lair, she learned of an ensorcellment called The Mirror Against All Mishap—which, the book suggested, would provide her the power she needed to defeat Beryl and win back the Cloak. Repelled by the idea of using blood magic, Amlina had invoked the trance ritual known as *Bowing to the Sky*, vowing to take whatever course the Deepmind chose for her. That rite seemed to indicate that using blood magic was indeed what she ought to do. Still, Amlina had resisted until a conversation with Queen Meghild. Old and crippled, the queen vowed that she would willingly give her life in exchange for one last voyage of adventure.

"I took the queen at her word," she said. "That she had uttered those words seemed beyond chance or accident. Because, by its nature, the Mirror required a sacrifice commensurate with its goal—in this case, the death of a queen in exchange for the death of a queen."

The chamber stood hushed, the faces of the Councilors at rapt attention. Below her feet, the panorama of the sky had grown still.

"I knew that I was invoking evil power," Amlina confessed. "But the rightfulness of the goal seemed to outweigh that price. And in achieving that goal I was successful. With the aid of my friends and by the noble queen's sacrifice, I was able to rid the world of a bloodthirsty tyrant, as well as return the treasures she stole from Larthang."

Her eyes rested on Drusdegarde. The Archimage spoke after a moment's silence.

"We are thankful for both of those achievements," she said. "Though officially we cannot condone how they were achieved. But let me ask you this, Amlina. Do you feel it was worth the cost?"

Amlina's gazed dropped to the floor, where the clouds were drifting again. "I do not regret my choice. I do not feel I could have done otherwise. And yet, the cost has been high. I was prepared to give my life in the attempt to overthrow the tyrant. I did not expect that long after, I would be twisted, ravaged inside, possessed by the evil I had invoked." Tears misted her eyes. "I have told my story. You nobles must judge what should be done with me. I will accept your decision without complaint."

Another silence came. Once again, it was the Archmage who presently spoke.

"These are weighty matters. My Lord Tuan, sisters of the Council, what are your thoughts on Amlina's petitions? First, on her request that we endeavor to heal the affliction she suffers?"

"That seems a small and rightful request," said Crandora, Keeper of the Books. "Surely, we would grant the same to any honorable witch who suffered sickness of the soul."

"True, but this sickness results from abominable practices," Clorodice pointed out. "Strictly from the laws of this House, it could be argued that punishment rather than reward should be our proper response."

Clorodice, Amlina knew, belonged to a faction known as *The Thread of Virtue*, which favored the strictest interpretations of laws and the harshest punishment for offenders.

"That is debatable," Melevarry said. "Surely punishment rather than healing would be merited only by the most blatant disregard of moral precepts. That is not the case with Amlina."

"I agree with the Mage of Randoon," the Tuan spoke up for the first time. "*I am informed that*, even in times when the interpretation of law has been most strict, wisdom has always required exceptions be made for extenuating circumstances."

Drusdegarde made a slight frown, perhaps annoyed at the Tuan's unusual appearance at the Council. Also, by using the ritual phrase "I am informed," the boy was citing his mystic authority as avatar for all preceding Tuans.

Kanshilia, Mage from the province of Dai-Shan said: "I also agree on that point. But the question is: What healing we can offer? There may be designs or rites in the ancient texts for curing afflictions caused by blood magic. But such have not been practiced here in centuries."

"If I may," Melevarry replied, "there are records of a purification rite used for exactly that purpose. I have been consulting with my sister, Keeper of the Books. It will take some study, but I see no reason why I cannot perform the rite in accord with the tradition. That is, if Amlina will agree to the necessary preparations and to my guiding her and working the designs."

"I will," Amlina said with surprise. "Gladly and most gratefully."

Drusdegarde looked around at the Councilors. "Since the Mage of Randoon has kindly volunteered this service, and the Keeper of the Books lends her aid, I see no reason for the Council to deny Amlina's first petition."

Heads nodded, some grudgingly Amlina thought. She bowed and uttered her thanks.

"As to the second petition," the Archimage continued, "if the purification is successful and Amlina is proven free of contamination, I again see no reason why she should not be granted the opportunity to stand for examination and—if successful—be given her gray mantle. She has certainly proven her capabilities . Do any of the Councilors disagree?"

Amlina scanned the semi-circle of podiums. She was heartened to find no opposition.

"Good." Drusdegarde was also pleased. "Now, as to the third petition—"

"There I must object," Clorodice announced. "Amlina is plainly talented, and if she can be purified she deserves the rank of adept. But that is a long, long way from earning the right to hold one of the great treasures of the Land and to sit on this Council. Certainly, there are many witches in this House who must be considered more worthy."

"I dispute that," Amlina answered with an anger that surprised her. "I - I do not make this petition lightly. But I have possessed the Cloak, and used it—"

"Used it without authorization," Clorodice snapped.

"Used it by necessity and with success," Amlina answered more calmly. "I have come to know its power. In deep trance, I have felt that power knitting itself into my being. I have developed an affinity for the Cloak, and that is why I aspire to be Keeper."

Now the silence was profound, as the Councilors seemed to weigh her words.

"Affinity or not, I cannot support such an improper idea," Clorodice declared.

Two of the Councilors echoed her sentiments.

"If I may make a suggestion," the Tuan said. "Of old, I am informed that when there was competition for appointment to specific posts in the House of the Deepmind, the matter was often settled by the Tournament of Witches, the post in question going to the tournament champion. Perhaps that venerable custom would serve now."

The witches on the dais frowned and shrugged, plainly caught off-guard by this suggestion. The sky image in the floor had grown gray and threatening, as before a looming storm

Drusdegarde harrumphed to clear her throat. "That is an interesting solution, August Ruler, and perhaps one we ought to consider. At this time, I believe we can postpone the decision. Amlina and Lady Melevarry have much work and preparations ahead, and I am sure arduous workings to perform. If, as we all hope, these workings succeed and Amlina finds healing, she will then have to pass her examinations for the grade of adept. Should those two goals be accomplished, we can consider her third petition at that time. Is that agreeable to the Council?"

"That will mean serious delay in appointing a Keeper of the Cloak," Clorodice pointed out.

"True, but I see no need for haste," the Archimage said. "The requirements for the post will need to be reviewed, and any candidates would need time to understand them and prepare." She turned to Melevarry. "How long will the purification likely take you?"

Melevarry considered. "The ritual requires one full cycle of Grizna for preparation. Then I think four or five days to complete the work." She eyed Amlina, who nodded. "Forty days total should be more than enough."

Drusdegarde pursed her lips. "The Tournament of Witches is nearly three months away. That should give Amlina ample time to take her examinations as well. Therefore, I propose this in regard to the post of Keeper of the Cloak: My Lady Keeper of the Books will research and publish the requirements and duties by the end of this month. Any witch aspiring to the post will solicit a member of the Council to act as her sponsor. The Council will consider all sponsored candidates. Whether we decide to use the Tournament or other means of selection, we will be able to name the new Keeper by the start of First Winter."

She looked down at Melevarry and Amlina. "Does this decision satisfy your petition, Amlina?"

"It does, My Lady." I am most grateful."

"Then unless there are any other objections ...?" Drusdegarde scanned the podiums right and left. "No? Then I declare the Inner Council adjourned."

In a mood of elation amounting almost to disbelief, Amlina walked with Melevarry down the long, polished corridor outside the council chamber.

"Well. That went about as well as we could have hoped," the Mage said quietly. "Are you pleased?"

"It is all I could have asked," Amlina said. "I am most thankful. And I am also curious as to why you chose to go so far in helping me."

A half-smile creased the Mage's face. "As I told you in Randoon, I have found you worthy."

"No. There must be more to it."

The smile broadened. "You are perceptive. Let us say then it is because you are both worthy and *unusual*."

"So?"

"You insist that I explain myself? Very well. If I am to lead you in the purification rites, you must trust me absolutely, and so I will explain." She stopped and looked around to make sure no one was in earshot. Then she stepped close to the wall and gestured for Amlina to follow.

"You are unusual for a witch of Larthang because of your experience in other lands and with other magical traditions. That is obvious enough. But there is also a wildness about you. Perhaps it comes from association with your barbarian friends, but I suspect it was there already, a deep element of your character that drove you to leave the Academy in the first place and seek your fortunes abroad."

Lips parted, Amlina nodded. "I must agree with that assessment. But none of this sounds like reasons you would want to help me."

"Oh, that is where you are wrong." Melevarry again scanned the corridor to be sure no one listened. Now she whispered. "There is a certain, dare I say, *stagnation* in the Land. It thrives in all three of the estates—the Magistrates, of course, and the Military. And here in the House of Witches, as exemplified by Lady Clorodice and her legalist faction. Now, do not mistake me, I would never advocate disorder or immorality. But too strict adherence to order and law lead to their own kind of evil. The way of the ogo is constant change and rebalancing. That is why I find you—shall I say—*refreshing*? I have meditated on the matter, and my guidance suggests that your very wildness may serve the House of the Deepmind well."

These words struck a chord in Amlina's heart. No witch of power had ever treated her with such confidence—or kindness. She swallowed a lump in her throat and answered.

"You do me great honor, Lady. I will do my utmost to prove worthy of your confidence, I promise."

Eighteen

Departing from Ting Ta Roo, Lady Clorodice rode in a carriage northwest across the city. From the central district of the capital, she was conveyed through commercial and residential warrens, which grew more crowded and less prosperous as she neared the canal. Clorodice kept the shutters closed to avoid the sights, but could not escape the bustling noise and unpleasing smells as the carriage jostled down narrow, crowded streets.

A solemn frown gripped her face and grim thoughts occupied her mind. The Council had not gone at all as she would have liked. Clorodice had developed an intense antipathy for the disreputable Amlina, the more so after learning that the renegade had actually performed blood magic. But Drusdegarde, the weak old fool, had shown the outcast every courtesy—even to the point of entertaining the possibility of appointing her Keeper of the Cloak. That notion was an outrage! Worse, it could make it all the more difficult for Clorodice to add the Cloak to her own power base.

Contemplating these unhappy thoughts, Clorodice arrived at last at her ancestral home, a four-story mansion on the bank of the north canal. Descending from the carriage, she walked through the front gates to find more irritation. She had intended to pass the rest of the afternoon in meditation and reading the *Adages of Law*. But as she entered the foyer, her chief steward informed her of a visitor.

"I wish to see no one for the rest of the day," she told the man.

"Pardon, my lady, but it is the esteemed Duke Pheng who awaits you in your study."

The Keeper of the Keys sighed, regretting her standing order that Trem-Dou Pheng should have access to her house at any time. No doubt, the Duke wanted to hear the outcome of the Council, and if the matter of the Keeper of the Cloak had been discussed. He would not be happy with the news.

Mentally preparing herself for the encounter, Clorodice stepped onto an elevation platform. Two servants hastened from the back apartments to work the device, bending their backs to turn brass-handled wheels. From their efforts, the platform rose up the narrow shaft, saving the witch the exertion of climbing the stairs.

The ivory platform stopped at the top floor of the mansion and Clorodice stepped into her study. Duke Pheng stood with his back to the room, staring out the wide terrace to the city below. Feet wide apart, hands behind his back, he was dressed in plain apparel, the long coat, trousers, and boots of a merchant or gentleman of leisure. He visited the mansion in secret and avoided any dress indicating his identity. On hearing steps, he turned.

"My lady, how went the Council?"

When they met in private, Trem-Dou never wasted time on polite conversation. That suited Clorodice. The sooner she could end this conference, the better.

Still, she would not give the appearance of feeling rushed. She strolled across the study to a table with a pitcher and glasses.

"Would you care for wine, my Lord Duke?"

He brushed the offer aside. "Thank you, no. What news?"

Declining to pour a drink for herself, she settled into a wide chair. "The news is not of the best, I fear. For the most part, the Council approved Amlina's petitions."

"She is to be given charge of the Cloak, then?"

"No. At least not yet." She lifted a calming hand. "The Council granted permission for healing rites to be performed, to purify Amlina. Should this work succeed, she will stand for examination to receive her gray mantle as an adept. Only if both of these obstacles are cleared will she be considered a candidate for Keeper.

Frowning, Trem-Dou began to pace. "This is ill news. Will Amlina likely pass these two hurdles?"

Clorodice shrugged. "The examination will likely not be difficult for her to pass. As for the purification, I have no knowledge. Such rites have not been performed for centuries."

"But the way is open for her. This troubles me." The Duke paused, a finger to his lips. "She is a threat to us, a danger to all our plans. My instincts have told me this ever since I learned how she fought off our flotilla in the harbor of Fleevanport. And the tortoise shell oracle consistently validates my concerns."

"She is a long way from being named Keeper of the Cloak, I assure you. I have been grooming my own assistant, Elani Vo T'ang for the post. Certainly, other Councilors will also put forth protégés."

"That is not good enough," the Duke snapped. "I warn you, Amlina is a formidable enemy. If it appears likely she will succeed in this purification process, you must be ready to take decisive action."

Clorodice sat up straight. "What exactly do you mean, Lord Duke?"

Trem-Dou's glance shifted. He resumed pacing. "I think you understand me well enough. When it became apparent that the old Tuan could not be convinced to support the worthy military goals of the Iron Bloc, fortune smiled upon us ..."

Clorodice gulped. His meaning was frighteningly clear. The old Tuan had resisted the programs of the militarist faction as well as the more hard-line legalists. His sudden illness and death three years ago had taken the nation by surprise. When a six-year-old child was designated to replace him on the throne, it had opened the way for many abrupt changes. The magistrates of the Thread of Virtue had enacted strict new laws, and the warriors of the Iron Bloc had moved forward with their campaign against the Tathians. The Duke had just informed Clorodice, in plain but indirect language, that she must be ready to assassinate Amlina if necessary.

Clorodice rose to her feet. "Is there anything else you wish to discuss?"

The Duke scowled at her. "Yes. Any developments concerning the complaint against my nephew, Shay-Ni?"

Clorodice walked over to her desk. With the unsettling events of the past few days, she had almost forgotten the complaint against the Admiral. "There at least I have good news. It seems this Trippany, the drell witch who brought the charges, made a misstep in Randoon. Without authorization, she helped Amlina and her band escape from the dungeon where the Mage had confined them. Trippany is under reprimand and serving a penance in the House of the Deepmind. The incident raises serious doubts about the drell's judgment, if not her character. Doubts which I and my allies made sure to promulgate. I am now confident the complaint against your nephew will not reach a full hearing by the Council."

"Good." The Duke stroked his chin. "I shall have to find a new posting for Shay-Ni. Unfortunately, his debacle at the South Pole has undermined his reputation among his fellow officers, so it will not be easy. But that is my problem, not yours." He started for the door. "I bid you good afternoon, Lady Clorodice. Remember what I advised regarding decisive action."

When he had gone, Clorodice breathed a sigh of relief. Attempting to settle her agitated mind, she walked to the bookshelf and removed an expensive volume bound in leather and gold leaf— *The Pronouncements of the Sage Lo Tang Ho*, one of the founders of Legalist thought. But after reading a few pages, her concentration wavered. She closed the book and stepped out on the balcony. The rain had started again, a bleak drizzle. She gazed down at the canal and the barges and hovels along the shore.

Decades of overcrowding in the city had reduced the once elegant neighborhood to impoverishment. Worse, the area along the waterfront had descended into vice. Taverns, puppet theaters, and music halls occupied the once-fine houses, while gambling barges and floating brothels lay anchored to the wharf. Crime was rampant.

All her life, Clorodice had worked to promote virtue and order. Now the manor house of her ancient family was surrounded by despicable slums. Plainly, she and those of like mind who followed the Thread of Virtue had not been successful enough. Perhaps she needed to take a harder line, to invoke stronger powers.

That thought turned her mind back to Amlina—the unrepentant renegade who cavorted with barbarians, who shamelessly admitted practicing foreign arts. The Duke saw Amlina as a dangerous enemy. Looking at the matter with her witchsight, Clorodice suddenly agreed. The renegade was more than a petty annoyance, she might actually win the Cloak, crushing all of Clorodice's hopes.

The Duke was right: She would need a plan to eliminate Amlina.

"I understand this is what you must do," Glyssa said. "Still, I had not expected we would be separated for so long."

Amlina would leave tomorrow for the House of the Deepmind to begin the month-long preparations for her purification. She had disclosed the news to her friends that afternoon on returning to the palace. Now she dined with them in the central chamber of the apartment they shared. Pink glass lamps decorated the long table with a hazy glow. An alabaster fountain in the shape of a phoenix bubbled nearby. Beyond the open wall panels, a terrace lit by braziers overlooked the formal garden. Below the terrace, at the edge of the footpath, stood a circle of Iruk spears. This was the spot where the mates had set the klarn-spirit to rest on the day Amlina surrendered the Cloak. By tradition, they performed this ritual at the end of every hunt, the klarn-soul residing as a protective presence at the doorway of their abode.

"We will miss you," Glyssa added.

"And if you should need us," Draven said, "we will not be there to help you."

Amlina took hold of his hand and Glyssa's. "My dear friends, you all have helped me already more than I can ever express, or thank you for. I have drawn strength from you all, but this time I must stand on my own. Well, not entirely alone, I will have Lady Melevarry's guidance. I am very lucky she has agreed to help me." She squeezed the two hands firmly. "I don't know where I would be without my friends."

"I still don't like it," Draven said, brow lowered. "More than a month without speaking with you or knowing how you are."

"I know, my dear," Amlina said. "I would not take this course, were it not my best hope of growing strong again."

"And what should we be doing all this time?" Karrol wondered aloud.

Amlina had spoken with Lord Sim, the Tuan's Chief Steward, and received assurances that her companions could remain guests of the palace for as long as they wished. Still, after doing nothing for four days but feasting and touring the gardens, the Iruks were growing restless.

Eben raised his goblet with a laugh. "I for one intend to keep enjoying the Tuan's excellent hospitality."

"That's a fine answer," Karrol grumbled. "We feast and grow fat for three or four small-months?"

"Well," Eben spread an arm expressively. "I'm also learning the language, which you should as well."

"Karrol makes a good point," Lonn said. "We should practice with spear and sword every day."

Up and down the table, the Iruks nodded their agreement.

"For my part," Kizier said, "I plan on spending many hours exploring the volumes in the palace library. As long as I am a guest here, this is an opportunity I should not miss."

"Oh, you must take me along," Eben said. "I need to resume learning the characters." While studying the Larthangan language with the aid of Buroof, the talking book, he had also made a start at learning to read.

"Perhaps I will try that as well," Glyssa said. "If I can learn the characters, I can study the *Canon of the Deepmind* on my own."

"That would be excellent for your training," Amlina agreed.

"Hmm. What about the talking book?" Eben asked. "Are you going to give him as a gift to the House of the Deepmind as he requested. Or will you leave him with us?"

That question had occurred to Amlina in the afternoon, as she packed the few belongings she would take with her. "Actually," she said, "I had a different thought about Buroof."

"Thank you for granting us this audience, August Ruler."

Amlina carried the heavy, leather-bound book into the Tuan's private apartment. With Kizier at her side, she stepped up to the inlaid table where Me Lo Lee sat eating rice cereal, surrounded by his personal entourage.

"Oh, it is my pleasure to see you, Honored Amlina, and you, revered scholar." The boy waved his gold spoon in the air. "Pardon my taking breakfast while we talk. My schedule today is over-crowded with ceremonial appointments."

"It is we who ask pardon for interrupting you."

Amlina rose from her deep bow, and cast a quick glance at the Tuan's attendants. These included Lord Han Sim, the palace steward, responsible for all household affairs; Mosavan Quo Tom, the chief tutor; and the governess, Sheil Na Quee, responsible for the Tuan's dress and deportment. All three returned her look with carefully neutral expressions.

"As you may know, August Ruler, tomorrow I depart the palace to enter the House of the Deepmind in preparation for the rites I must perform."

"Indeed?" The boy held the spoonful of cereal before his mouth. "I knew the day must be approaching. I most sincerely wish you success."

"Thank you. I wanted to see you in person to express my gratitude for your speaking on my behalf to the Council."

Chewing, Me Lo gestured to indicate the matter was of no consequence.

"And of course," Amlina said, "I wish to thank you for all of your generous hospitality to myself and my friends this past small-month."

"Oh, it is both my duty and my pleasure," he replied. "You are a hero of the nation, Amlina. And I find your Iruk warriors most interesting company."

"They are indeed noble," she said. "So, I possess little of value in worldly terms, certainly nothing worthy of your kindnesses. But, as you are a scholar of wide interests, I thought this might at least provide you some amusement." She set the heavy volume on the table. "This is a talking book, which I acquired from the lair of the serd sorcerer in Kadavel. For more than three thousand years it has passed from hand to hand and acquired much recondite knowledge of magic and witchery."

The faces of the chief tutor and governess evinced both curiosity and reservation. But the Tuan bolted to his feet, eyes full of excitement.

"Indeed, it is a talking book? I have heard of such books, but never seen one. They are very rare in this age, I believe?"

He had directed the remark to Kizier, who replied: "Definitely so. This is the only one either Amlina or I have ever come across."

"Wonderful!" the boy cried. "Can you demonstrate?"

"Yes, of course." Amlina opened the front cover. Immediately, a haze of light appeared over the parchment leaf. "Buroof, I Amlina summon you."

"I am here." The book answered, inciting a delighted grin from the Tuan.

"As I said I would, I am presenting you to the Tuan, Me Lo Lee, August Ruler of Larthang. He is now your owner."

For once, Buroof sounded not proud and impatient, but humble. "This is indeed an honor, August Ruler. I had asked Amlina to offer me as a gift to the House of the Deepmind, as I was frankly rather bored with her and the low company she keeps. But I never expected to greet so glorious and magnificent a master."

"Ha ha!" the boy was exultant. "He is wonderful! Buroof is your name?"

"Yes, majestic one. I have absorbed knowledge into my pages for thousands of years. And I know, of course, that you are gifted with the wisdom of your esteemed ancestors. I think we may have a great many interesting conversations."

"Oh, yes! I am sure we shall," the boy cried.

"August Ruler," the steward said. "I'm afraid the time of your first appointment draws near."

"Please finish your breakfast, August Ruler," the governess added.

"Yes, yes!" the boy said. "Thank you, Amlina, for this wonderful present! I wish you all success at the House of the Deepmind, and look forward to your return. In the meantime, this worthy scholar and your Iruks will of course remain my honored guests."

Nineteen

N ext morning, Amlina met Melevarry once again at the gates of Ting Ta Roo. This time she was conducted along a side corridor and down several flights of steps lit by flickering lamps. The Mage of Randoon showed her to a small, windowless apartment. It consisted of a bedroom, a washroom, and a tiny chamber for meditation. The furnishings were sparse: narrow bed and nightstand, reading table, lamps, an hour glass to keep the time, a floor mat in the meditation room. The walls were plain gray stone.

"This basement level is seldom used in these times," Melevarry told her. "The rooms are insulated by thickness of stone and by ancient designs to keep out mental influences. You must keep strictly to these chambers for the next month. Solitude is essential for your preparatory work." The Mage set a scroll down on the table, black ink written in her own hand. "Here is a recommended daily schedule of activities. I will visit you here every morning and evening to see how you are getting on."

Amlina stared down at the scroll. "I am very grateful to you. I realize this is keeping you here in the city and away from your normal duties in Randoon."

"True. I will stay now through the end of Third Summer. I have dispatched my apprentice Yensia to manage affairs in Randoon. It will be good training for her. I trust my sojourn here will also be of value."

"I will do all I can to make it so," Amlina promised.

"I know you will, Amlina." The elder witch laid a hand on her shoulder. "From all I can discern, what lies ahead will be harrowing. But I will do my best to help you through it."

The Mage departed, leaving Amlina to unpack the clothing and jewelry she had brought, along with her worn copy of the *Canon of the Deepmind*. She reviewed the schedule Melevarry had written, then settled down to begin.

In the days that followed, her time was strictly regimented. She woke early, meditated for two turns of the hour glass. By then, her breakfast had arrived: rice cakes and tea. Morning tea was the only stimulant she was allowed, the rest of the time she drank water.

Her other meals were more robust and varied: apples, green salads, rice, almonds. On Melevarry's insistence, she ate everything provided. She also drank potions that the Mage brought in tiny vials: purgative medicines in the daytime, sedatives at night.

Afternoons were divided between more meditation and physical exercise. In the center of her bedroom, Amlina practiced the movements of *weng-lei*, magical combat. This art involved drawing energy into the body and directing it out as mental force. The basic routines were designed to energize and strengthen the physical form.

As promised, Melevarry visited twice daily without fail. Each time she examined Amlina with witchsight, holding her wrists and staring into her eyes. She brought with her ancient texts to study, passages explaining what was known of the lingering effects of blood magic and the processes for purification.

Reading these made Amlina quail inside. The dark spirit that had seized a part of her soul would rise up, angry and seething with hate. Sometimes Amlina paced the small chamber like one driven mad, sweating, grunting, pounding with her fists on the door jambs. If Melevarry had not taken away her dagger, she would certainly have cut herself.

Slowly, over many days, the rage began to subside—isolation, physical rigors, and constant meditation having their desired effects.

Noting this change, Melevarry introduced new elements. Some days, a young witch came with a lute. Sitting on a cushion, she plucked notes which Amlina sought to match with her inner vibrations. Other days, a Chrysalis Warrior appeared. She would stand in the center of the floor and strike poses with a heavy, curved sword while inwardly Amlina attempted to mirror her strength and poise.

After perhaps twenty days, the Mage instituted another stage of the process. Seated in the meditation room with Amlina, she projected images onto the wall. These looked exactly like the colorful shadows cast in puppet theater, except they were purely mental castings. Still, like figures in a play, they acted out the tales and trials of ancient witches, those who had succumbed to evil practices and others who had overcome them and found redemption.

After she had seen a few of these performances, Amlina found that her own mind began casting images on the walls while she sat in meditation. These shadows recounted incidents from her past, her dismal childhood, her time at the Academy, her strange and frightening journeys to foreign lands. Eyes wide open, Amlina watched the events of her life streaming by, her mind detached, her heart numb and serene.

Each morning the Iruks marched out to a lawn at the edge of Perfect Light Lake and drilled with swords and spears. After stretching their muscles and practicing leaps and lunges, they performed intricate movements that resembled a dance—ritual exercises they had learned as children when they first took up the warrior path. The sessions would finish with mock combats, where the mates tested each other's reflexes and honed their skills.

Before long, these activities drew spectators—first gardeners and servants, then courtiers and members of the Imperial Guard. Occasionally, a guardsman or noble would participate in the drills, studying the foreign Iruk swordsmanship and demonstrating skills of their own.

These sessions became a daily entertainment for the Tuan's household. Ministers and ladies of the court came to watch, accompanied by servants carrying lawn chairs and parasols. The courtiers applauded politely, gasped at violent moments, chatted among themselves, and sipped tea from delicate porcelain cups.

Following the combat training, the mates adjourned to the bathhouse. Of all the luxuries of life in the palace, soaking each day in perfumed water was easily their favorite. After, they would take a midday meal, then spend time learning the language and customs of the Larthangans. In this, they were assisted by Kizier and by a tutor, a gentleman named Ting Fo, who was assigned by the Tuan to accompany the Iruks everywhere and assist them in any way needed.

Sometimes, Eben went with Kizier to the Tuan's library, a huge complex of rooms stuffed with scrolls and bound volumes on shelves and populated by a host of scribes and scholars. Kizier read books on Larthangan history and philosophy, and worked on composing his own accounts of Amlina's voyages and on the culture of the Iruks. Eben meantime was learning to read. Coached by Ting Fo, he studied basic texts, matching the pictographs to the words in his growing Larthangan vocabulary.

A few times, Kizier was summoned to attend the Tuan and Eben went with him. At these meetings, the boy ruler would open Buroof the talking book and question him and Kizier both about foreign lands, their peoples and customs. Clearly, in the little leisure time he was allowed, Mo Lee was having wonderful fun with Buroof.

In the evenings, the Iruks sometimes dined with the Tuan, either at large banquets or with a few honored guests. Following dinner, they would be entertained by concerts, puppet plays, or poetry recitals. Eben found the poetry especially interesting.

The mates started to receive invitations to private banquets and tea parties. They attended a few of these, in the company of Ting Fo who guided them on the intricacies of polite etiquette. The Iruks were a novelty in Minhang, and the fact that they enjoyed the Tuan's favor increased their notoriety. In the refined and affected court, their barbarian appearance and manners were viewed as refreshing. Court dandies began to trim their mustaches to match those of the Iruk men. Some ladies affected to braid their hair like that of the Iruk women. Silk trousers and jackets tailored in the shape of Iruk deerskins suddenly became a fashion.

But as First Summer moved into its second month, the mates were growing restless. Karrol and Brinda said little, but Eben noticed they sometimes appeared gloomy and bored. Glyssa and Draven both expressed worries about Amlina. The witch had been in the House of the Deepmind more than twenty days but because of her deliberate isolation, they had received no word of her. Outwardly, Lonn maintained his stoic, imperturbable demeanor.

More than the others, Eben definitely enjoyed the life of a palace guest. Still, he began to feel something missing. Increasingly, his thoughts found their way to Trippany. He had neither seen nor heard from her since their departure from Randoon. One day, he questioned Ting Fo about the drell witch. She had helped Amlina bring the Cloak to Larthang and Eben reasoned she ought to have garnered some acclaim. After asking among the palace servants, Ting Fo reported a rumor gleaned from the mansion of the drell ambassador, to the effect that Trippany was undergoing some sort of penance in the House of the Deepmind. But that was all he could say.

Eben fretted over the matter, concerned that she might be unduly punished for helping Amlina and the klarn. In odd moments, he found himself composing verses about the drell, praising her courage, grace, and beauty. He saw this as a way to hone his mastery of the Larthangan language, and he sought to match the rhythms used by some of the Minhang poets he had heard.

One night, when Amlina's month of preparation was nearly over, the Iruks dined at a poetry festival in a garden of the palace. After eating, most of the mates grew bored and returned to their apartment. But Eben lingered, enjoying both the recitals and the varied and delicious assortment of wines.

Immersed in listening, and mildly inebriated, he did not notice her approach. Suddenly there was a flutter of air and a trickling laugh. Startled, he looked up to see Trippany settling to the ground beside his bench.

"I thought that was you!" She laughed.

Earlier, Eben had noticed a party of the winged people on the far side of the audience—the drell ambassador's entourage. It had not occurred to him Trippany might be with them.

He bolted to his feet, delighted. "What are you doing here?"

"Celebrating," she cried. "For three small-months I've been confined in Ting Ta Roo, atoning for my misdeeds. Now I am free again!"

On the stage, the poet was still intoning and plucking his lute. Audience members turned to cast dour looks and wave for the pair to be quiet.

"Let us go where we can talk," Eben whispered.

They wound their way to the rear of the garden, where a fountain of green marble splashed and paper lanterns hung on strings.

"Will you take some wine with me?" Trippany asked.

"Gladly."

The drell flew off and presently returned holding two goblets. Fluttering to the ground, she handed him one. With an enticing smile, she touched her cup to his and they drank.

"That is lovely," she said. "I have not tasted wine since the night before we parted in Randoon. Perhaps tonight I have tasted too much."

"Your punishment was not harsh, I hope," Eben said.

"Oh, no. Tedious rather. I spent thirty days scrubbing floors and reading in a cell, reviewing the adages of 'proper respect and obedience to senior witches.' My mentor understood why I disobeyed the Mage. And Lady Melevarry, I believe, did not ask for severe punishment."

"I am glad," Eben said. "You deserved reward rather than punishment. We might not have gotten out of that dungeon without your help."

She lowered her eyes, smiling. "And how is your wound?"

"Oh, mostly healed." The hair had grown back, though it was still shorter where the scalp had been shaved. To hide the conspicuous scar, Eben had taken to wearing the sort of cap favored by court musicians. His klarnmates liked to tease him with the Larthangan word for 'dandy.' Timidly, he pulled off the cap to show her.

Trippany winced, then hurried to offer a sympathetic smile. "I am glad it is healing. Where are your companions tonight?"

Eben smoothed the cap back in place. "Gone to bed early. They do not enjoy poetry so much as I."

"You are a lover of poetry? You continue to surprise me, Eben. You are both wild and civilized—rather like my people."

"Well, I don't know how civilized. But I do find the poetry is helping me polish my language skill."

"Yes!" She seemed to suddenly recall that on earlier meetings they had spoken only Tathian. "You speak now very well. I am impressed."

He waved the compliment aside. They gazed into each other's eyes.

Presently, Trippany put down her goblet and took hold of his wrist. "Shall we walk?"

Like one in a dream, Eben allowed her to lead him. They strolled under a flowering arch and into a maze of hedges. Grizna was a rose-colored shape at the peak of the sky, a face wearing a mysterious smile.

Holding his hand, Trippany stopped beside a jade statue of a graceful crane bending over to drink. "I have thought about you often," she said.

"I have thought of you very often," Eben confessed.

Staring at her shiny black eyes, he saw amusement, perhaps desire. He leaned close to kiss her. She pressed a finger to his lips, giggled, then flew away.

"Wait!" Eben stumbled as he tried to follow.

Laughing, she swooped down the path. As she turned a corner, she glanced over her shoulder. Eben ran after her. When he got to the corner, she was gone.

He looked around, called her name. She answered with laughter, and he looked up. She floated down near him. He reached up a hand and she darted out of reach.

She continued the game and Eben continued to chase her. Twice more she disappeared, only to show herself when he thought she was lost. Finally, when they were deep in the maze and far from anyone, she settled to the ground. As he walked near, she held out her arms in their gauzy sleeves.

Eben kissed her. Their lips opened and his tongue slipped over her pointy teeth.

Breathing hard, he stared at her shiny eyes. "I have often wondered, " he said, "with your wings and delicate bodies, how your people make love."

"Oh, much like your people, I should say." She touched a fingertip to his chin. "Of course, there are differences."

"I would be very interested to learn," Eben avowed. "If you might show me some time?"

She grinned, unabashed. "Why not now?"

Twenty

At dawn on the appointed day, Melevarry came to Amlina's cell. The Mage was clothed in silver ceremonial robes and headpiece and carried a staff topped by a black onyx the size of her fist.

Amlina had already risen, bathed, and dressed. She wore her best witch's robe and all of her bangles and rings—trinkets with magical properties she had fashioned over the years. On her head was the moonstone fillet, imbued with protective power.

Melevarry scrutinized her and nodded approval. From within her sleeve she removed something—Amlina's dagger in its scabbard, which the Mage had taken away when Amlina first came here. "You will need this as well."

Amlina took the dagger and attached it to her belt.

"If you are ready," the Mage said, "we shall begin."

Amlina followed into the corridor, crossing the threshold for the first time in more than a month. During that time, the strict routines of diet and physical and mental exercises had nourished and strengthened her. She felt more alert and calm than she had for a long time—ready to face the trials ahead and whatever future the Deepmind might decree.

Melevarry walked in silence to the stairs at the end of the passage. They had used these same stairs to descend to this level. Now they went down farther, the air stale and humid, their shuffling footsteps the only sound. When the lamplight from the passage above was lost, the stone in the Mage's staff flickered to life—casting a faint, golden witchlight.

Down and down they walked, till Amlina lost count of the number of floors they had passed. She understood there were crypts at some of these levels, tombs of witches from ages past, as well as vaults and chambers where magic ceremonies were practiced in earliest times.

Finally, the Mage halted on a landing before an arched portal. There still seemed to be many flights of steps below, and this landing looked no different than many others. Beyond the arch lay an alcove and an iron door. Melevarry took a key from within her robe and turned it in the keyhole. The door moved sideways, creaking on metal wheels as it slid into the wall.

"This is the way to the Labyrinth of Gar Tuo," Melevarry said. "In ancient times, neophyte witches entered here for trials of initiation. It was also used to purify ones who had strayed from the rightful path—as we shall use it today. Come."

She reached out her hand. Amlina grasped it, and they stepped across the threshold. They moved in silence down the passageway. From what Amlina could see, both walls and floor were made of plain black stone.

Presently, they came to an alcove. Melevarry stopped and directed Amlina to look. A shimmer of light appeared. Within floated a face like an ancient mask. The mask spoke in a soft and hollow tone.

"Why are you here?"

The language was Old Larthangan. Melevarry answered: "This one must be purified."

"What is her stain?"

"Answer, Amlina," Melevarry prompted.

She had not been prepared for this. The exact details of the rite had deliberately been kept from her. She struggled to frame a reply and to call up her command of the old language.

"I am tainted, stained by blood magic."

"Are you still wed to these practices?"

"No."

"Are you certain?"

"Yes. I wish to be healed."

"Surrender something, and move on."

Unsure, she turned to the Mage.

"Leave some of your jewelry," Melevarry said. "Eventually, you will need to surrender all."

Amlina removed her bracelets and set them on the floor.

Melevarry nodded to show her approval. She took Amlina's hand and led on. They reached a corner, turned, and traversed another passage. At the end, they found another alcove. A curtain of light rippled inside and once more the mask appeared.

How much of this magic came from designs cast by Melevarry and how much from the ancient labyrinth itself, Amlina could not say. She guessed it was some combination of both.

"What has the stain done to you?" the voice asked her.

She cast a helpless glance at Melevarry, whose look indicated that she must answer for herself.

"It has ... Sometimes it fills me with rage and power. Other times it ... *eats* me inside. It hungers for more and more power, and when I deny it, it ... feasts on my heart."

A mind seemed to probe at her, an ancient presence reading her spirit.

"You know the truth of it. Surrender something and pass on."

Amlina placed her dagger on the floor. Melevarry led her away.

They walked down a side corridor. The air grew warmer and wetter, tingling on Amlina's face. Or was that a perception caused by increased sensitivity?

They stopped before another alcove and again the mask appeared. "What do you love?"

A completely unexpected question. Amlina contemplated, asking herself. Draven came to mind, and Glyssa and the rest of her crew. "A certain man. My friends."

"What else?"

She examined her heart. "Witchery. Constructing trinkets, weaving designs. I love the energy I feel, and the power to make effects in the world."

The mask scrutinized her. "Surrender these and move on."

That was the point, Amlina realized with a pang. To be purified she must surrender everything, including her love and her power. As a token of this, she removed her rings and set them carefully down.

"Come." Melevarry touched her arm.

Amlina walked on, fearful and tingling, as if layers of her skin were being peeled away.

Passing through two more corridors, they came to another alcove. This time the floating mask said: "To what do you aspire?"

"Peace," Amlina answered. Then, pondering, she had to admit there was more. "Achievement, recognition ... to be of service to the Land." The last surprised her. Yet that aspiration had grown the more she used the Cloak. Larthang was her home, and the kingdom was troubled. She felt called to help.

"Surrender these and move on."

Amlina removed her moonstone fillet, her last and most loved piece of jewelry. She set it on the floor.

"Come." Melevarry was already moving down the passage.

Amlina followed, numb inside. Now it almost seemed that her skin was gone, her flesh fading away.

At the end of a long corridor they came to a door of ribbed iron. They stepped close and Amlina spied blue light fluctuating on the metal surface. This time no mask appeared, only the voice.

"What do you fear?"

The question struck a note of terror at her heart. "The dark power, the rage that is inside me."

An image appeared in the blue light, looming large as it seemed to flow toward her—Beryl, the Archimage.

"What else?" Beryl's voice cried.

"That I will be destroyed."

Beryl vanished, and other forms drew near: witches in the robes of the Academy, the shades of teachers who had treated her with contempt. "What else? What else?" they cried.

Amlina searched her mind. She shuddered at the answer: "That I deserve to be destroyed, because I am unworthy."

"What else?" Another face joined the witches: Amlina's mother. The vision of this ghost terrified her—a haughty, angry woman who had ruled their home like a tyrant, who had never loved her.

"What else?" she screamed.

"That I am worthless. That I am nothing."

The blue light vanished, leaving her staring at the bare black iron.

"What does the *Canon* say that we are?" Melevarry asked gently.

Amlina stared up at the tip of the Mage's staff, which now cast the only light. Her own voice seemed to come from far away.

"We are only thoughts of the Deepmind, waves on the surface that rise and disappear."

"What else?"

"That we have purpose."

The iron door rumbled open. The Mage smiled. "Surrender all and move on."

Amlina gazed down at her empty hands. "But I have nothing left."

"Haven't you?"

"Oh, I see." Amlina said. *All must be surrendered.*

She bent and removed her shoes, then straightened and pulled the heavy robe up over her head. After stripping off her shift, she stared uncertainly at the Mage.

"Go ahead," Melevarry said. "You are ready now."

Naked, Amlina stepped through the doorway. Gray light emanated from the walls, enough for her to discern that she stood in a square chamber some thirty paces across. A square arrangement of steps led down to a square opening in the floor—an inky blackness. Not knowing what else to do, Amlina walked down the steps.

All must be surrendered. She was nothing. With these thoughts, the dark rage crawled to life inside her. Pain writhed in her chest. Looking down, she envisioned the scarlet worms eating at her heart. But they seemed weaker now, their power diminished by the month-long solitude and preparations, by her passing through the labyrinth and sacrificing everything.

She was nothing. She recalled what the Iruk shaman had said, that at bottom, her affliction was nothing, a void she must allow herself to release.

She reached the bottom of the steps and peered down into the dark. It seemed bottomless, silent as death.

She stepped off the edge.

As she fell, terror blazed inside her. She surrendered to it. It did not matter. She was only a thought. Red sparks rushed up past her eyes. Detached from her heart, the worms flew away into the void.

Her body faded to nothing ...

In a vision, she marched into a grand rectangular hall with redwood pillars and white, opalescent floor. On a dais at the far end of the chamber sat a throne, black but swirling with iridescent colors. A man in multicolored robes detached himself from the throne and walked toward her. As he moved, he seemed to fracture, splitting into more and more persons—like an infinity of images seen in two facing mirrors. Drawing near, the figures coalesced into one—a man of noble mien, broad-shouldered, ageless. Amlina gasped as she spotted scarlet worms writhing around his heart.

"Who are you?" she asked.

"I am the Land." The words reverberated as though spoken by countless voices. "As you see, I am infested. Lust for power has corrupted many. The world is out of balance."

"That is why you have been called here." Amlina's shoulders jumped as a woman strode up beside her—a tall witch, of solemn countenance, dressed in ancient fashion. Amlina peered hard. She had seen this woman before.

"*Throughout time, the Sacred Balance is established, then lost. The current problems began a century ago, when Beryl stole the Cloak of the Two Winds. Since then, the world has been disrupted, drifting toward chaos.*"

Now Amlina recognized the woman, from images she had seen on statues and paintings. Eglemarde, the Weaver of the Winds.

"*You have returned the Cloak to Larthang,*" Eglemarde said. "*But now others seek to possess it, to feed their ambitions and cravings for power. You, Amlina, are charged with keeping the Cloak from them, and to use it only as it was meant to be used—to heal the Land and maintain the Sacred Balance.*"

Amlina felt the truth of these words in her deepest soul. All the twists and turns of her strange, wandering life had led her to this. To serve the Land as Keeper of the Cloak: this was her purpose.

Staring at the visage of Eglemarde, she gave a shaky laugh. "When I leave here and return to the surface world, I will likely have a hard time believing this. I always think I have too high an idea of my own importance."

"Ha!" Eglemarde answered. "So too did I."

The bright hall faded. Amlina's body floated motionless in darkness.

Blue witchlight flickered below her feet.

She began to rise. The witchlight was a power that both lifted her body and filled its every fiber. Riding the power, she floated up out of the pit, above the level of the steps, high toward the vaulted ceiling. The entire chamber pulsed with blue light.

All the rage and fear were gone.

Naked, full of power, she willed her body to drift to the floor. Her bare feet settled easily on the stone.

At the doorway she met Melevarry, who scrutinized her.

"You are purified," the Mage said.

"Yes. And I know my purpose."

Dressed in her robe and shoes again, Amlina followed Melevarry back through the tunnels of the labyrinth. Her steps came with an easy balance, her spirit calm and poised. *Had she ever felt so strong and certain?*

Stopping at each alcove, she retrieved her fillet, rings, and dagger. Reaching the first alcove, she bent to pick up her bracelets.

A voice cried out in her mind. *"Look up!"*

Even as she recognized the voice, Amlina flicked up her eyes, spotted a shadow in the darkness. She flung her body aside just in time.

A tiny feathered dart clattered as it struck the wall beside the alcove. Amlina leaped up and summoned her power. She swept out her hand in time to deflect a second dart. Instinct told her they were poisoned.

"Halt!" Melevarry commanded, raising her staff and casting its light toward the attacker.

The witchlight shone on a slim man dressed in the scale armor of the Warriors of the Chrysalis. Instead of the usual pike or sword, he held a bamboo tube. The light showed him inserting another dart.

"Halt, I say!" Melevarry's voice conveyed her power.

The assassin's hands fell to his sides, the bamboo dropping from his fingers. His eyes were wide and blank—the eyes of a thrall, a mind-slave.

"Down on your knees!" The Mage strode toward the man. "Tell me who sent you."

For an instant, the thrall hesitated, unsure. Then instead of kneeling he whirled and fled into the darkness.

The Mage lowered her staff, but kept it's light at high intensity. She knelt to pick up the discarded tube. "A blowgun," she muttered. "Used for hunting in the jungles of Zindu. Not a Larthangan weapon, but useful for assassins." She slipped it into her robe.

"Your instincts are keen," she told Amlina. "You sensed the attacker before I did—and just in time."

"A voice warned me," Amlina murmured, thinking back.

"Whose voice?"

"Glyssa—the Iruk woman. I have trained her, and we have often linked minds in meditation. Apparently she was watching over me."

"Effectively, it seems. Congratulate her when you see her. And thank her for me. No doubt the assassin meant to kill us both. Now, walk behind me and be watchful. There may be others lurking."

The two witches traversed the final passageways without encountering further attack. At the entrance of the labyrinth, they found the thrall lying dead in a widening puddle of blood, a knife still gripped in his hand. The man had stabbed himself through the throat.

Twenty-One

Seated in meditation on a floor cushion, Clorodice heard footsteps approaching in the corridor outside. She opened her eyes, staring at a single red glass lamp on the floor. Its light flickered on mirrored balls and feathered desmets that hung at different levels, suspended from the low ceiling. The vault was located underground, in one of the numerous levels below the House of the Deepmind. As Keeper of the Keys, Clorodice had access to many seldom-used corridors and forgotten chambers.

Her eyes settled on the iron door as the footsteps stopped just outside. "Enter," she called, before the person had time to knock.

The door swung open, and her apprentice, Elani Vo T'ang, slipped inside.

"You were not observed," Clorodice said.

"No, my lady." Cautiously, Elani closed the door. "I was very careful."

She hurried over, bowed deeply, then sat down on her heels with knees pressed together. She appeared flushed and nervous.

"I came as soon as I received your summons. What news from the Council?"

Clorodice cast her eyes at the lamp flame. "We are safe, for now."

That morning, she had attended an emergency meeting of the Inner Council, called in response to the attempted assassination of Melevarry and Amlina. The high witches had discussed and debated, going so far as to cast a circle and probe with their group mind to discover the source of the nefarious act. Fortunately, Clorodice's concealments had held.

After deciding to take the bold step of eliminating Amlina, Clorodice had plotted with deliberate care. With the aid of her circle of adherents, Elani among them, the Keeper of the Keys had selected a Warrior of the Chrysalis who was a foreigner, a native of Zindu, skilled in the use of the blowgun. After enthralling the man over many days, she had arranged for him to be waiting in the labyrinth, ready to slay Amlina—and Melevarry too, as a precaution. As a final touch, they had placed a ring in the thrall's pocket, a signet of the *Way of the Wise Serpent*. That sect was a favorite of alchemists, dissidents, and foreigners, and had no known associates in the House of the Deepmind.

"We were wise to plant that ring on the thrall," Clorodice murmured. "It helped to muddy the waters."

"So the assumption that foreign mages must be behind the attack was accepted?" Elani asked.

"Only as one possibility. Some guessed that the attack was aimed at Amlina, to remove her as a candidate for Keeper of the Cloak. The suspicion was raised that mages allied with the Iron Bloc might be involved in such a plot. But our own connection with Duke Pheng remains unknown."

"That is good, at least."

A note of fear in the young woman's voice made Clorodice stare sharply. "Keep your nerve, young witch."

Like the others of Clorodice's circle, Elani had been carefully chosen because of both her talent and her strict dedication to the Thread of Virtue. She and the other subalterns had shown no qualms when the circle first began to explore enthrallment—along with certain other ancient arts. But when Clorodice had revealed the purpose of *this* thrall, some of the circle had grown squeamish.

Elani blanched. "I am sorry, my lady."

"You know we are playing for extremely high stakes—to preserve morality and virtue in the Land."

"Of course."

"I have chosen you, of all my students, for a singular honor, to become the Keeper of the Cloak. But if you are not up to meeting the price required, another must be selected."

"I know. I—My dedication remains firm, my lady."

"Good." Clorodice nodded, satisfied. Elani's fear of her mentor must be kept stronger than her fear of the tasks required of her—especially as those tasks grew more demanding.

"What ... what will we do, now that the thrall has failed?" the apprentice asked.

Clorodice's stare returned to the flame. "There are other methods, requiring greater power. I had hoped to avoid such steps, but I *will not* be thwarted in my duty."

"How may I assist?"

"For now, keep your head. Communicate to the others that they must say nothing and think no more about this, until they hear from me. Thoughts must be concealed, for there will be probings. Also, we must not meet again in the House of the Deepmind. I will arrange another place, and will let you all know when it is ready."

On Perfect Light Lake, the pleasure boats had peculiar qualities. For one, they were shaped like swans, with broad, rounded hulls and gracefully carved prows. For another, they required no oars or paddles, gliding neatly over the water at the whim of their occupants.

Amlina relaxed in the stern of the boat, directing it smoothly with her thoughts. She rested in Draven's arms, her back against him, leaning on his strong chest. Kizier and the Iruks reclined on cushions as the boat drifted on the gleaming water. In the east, the pink circle of Grizna had risen, full and ripe over the beautiful city.

"So Glyssa saved your life?" Eben asked.

"Indeed," Amlina replied. "I heard her warning in my mind, and threw myself down just in time."

"The vision came out of nowhere," Glyssa said. "We were walking back from our arms practice when I suddenly saw you in danger. So I called out with my mind."

Amlina reached over to touch Glyssa's hand. "The bond between us is strong, dear friend."

"You feel much stronger to me," Glyssa answered. "And I can sense you are more at peace."

Amlina smiled dreamily. "Yes, I am much improved."

"Tell us more about the preparations for the purification rite." Kizier sat upright, with the pens and writing book he had brought on board to take notes. He was keenly interested in adding an account of the rite to his book.

"Later for that," Draven said. "Tell us what you know about the assassin."

"Not much," the witch answered. "Melevarry tells me the Council reached no conclusions. Of course, they do intend to investigate thoroughly. No one has been murdered in the House of the Deepmind for almost two hundred years."

"Happy to know that streak is unbroken." Eben spoke in Larthangan as he poured another cup of plum wine from a bottle with a stopper.

"So are we all," Glyssa said, switching back to Low-Tathian for the sake of the other Iruks—who were nowhere near so adept at the Larthangan tongue as Eben had become. "And we are so glad to have you back with us, Amlina. We missed you."

Draven wrapped his arms tighter around her waist. "I missed you the most."

"So what happens next?" Karrol asked, holding her cup out for Eben to fill.

Amlina pointed at the bow to shift the boat's direction. Boating on the lake was especially popular when Grizna was full, and their craft had drifted close to a clustered group near the northern shore.

"Next ..." the witch said. "Next, I must study for my examination. If I am to be considered a candidate for Keeper of the Cloak, I must first win my gray mantle, signifying the grade of adept. I have only a small-month to prepare."

"Why so soon?" Kizier asked.

"Well, by tradition, examinations are conducted only on the first day of a month. Melevarry suggested I do not wait. She believes I will have no trouble passing."

"I would expect that to be true," Kizier agreed. "You are certainly more knowledgeable and experienced than most who attain the grade."

"True." Amlina showed a self-deprecating smile. "I am ten years older than most witches who stand for the exam. Of course, I failed when I was their age. That is why I must study with all diligence. This time I cannot fail."

"Then why be in such a hurry?" Glyssa asked. "Why not take more time?"

"Because," Amlina said, "afterward, I must prepare my candidacy to become Keeper of the Cloak. From speaking with others on the Inner Council, Melevarry thinks they might follow the Tuan's suggestion and use the Tournament of Witches to select the Keeper. Whether or not this turns out to be true, the selection process will certainly be rigorous and demanding. I will need all of my focus and strength to win."

Glyssa nodded, taking this in. She was about to say something else when Karrol spoke up.

"That all sounds sensible. But actually, when I asked what comes next, I was thinking about the klarn."

"Oh," Amlina laughed. "Forgive me."

"That's all right." Karrol lifted her hands. "I am just wondering. The last time we talked about this, we were on the boat coming up the river. We said we needed to wait until Amlina had delivered the treasures and had a chance to heal herself. It seems we have come to that time, so I'm asking again: What happens next?"

Lonn sat up straight. "Are you asking for a formal meeting?"

"Not here and now," Karrol replied. "No one needs to answer if they don't want to. But we will need to decide soon, and I'm wondering what you all think."

"Fair enough." Lonn settled down, leaning on an elbow. "My first thought is this: we had talked about staying with Amlina, if she wanted us to, as warriors of her household."

The Iruk's all turned their eyes inquiringly on the witch. Amlina's heart grew warm and she smiled.

"Dear friends, nothing would make me happier than to have you stay with me. I truly believe I will be made Keeper of the Cloak. That is my path, as revealed to me during the purification rite—and I must hold to that belief, whatever doubts may come. But, even if that does not happen, I expect I will be given some post by the House of the Deepmind. That will allow me to keep a household and maintain a retinue. And there are no warriors in the world I would rather have as guards and companions." She squeezed Draven's wrist where it rested at her side.

"Would that mean you might rejoin the klarn?" Glyssa asked.

Amlina hesitated. She was aware how Glyssa missed having her as part of the klarn. Sometimes Amlina missed it too. The group soul had given her comfort and strength. But its wild influence was alien to the prescribed practices of Larthangan witchery.

"I will have to wait and sort that out," she said, "after I have met these other challenges. But let me ask you a question, Glyssa: I know you are continuing your magical practices, despite my woeful neglect as teacher. But here in Minhang you could get proper schooling. With just a word from the Tuan or Melevarry, you could be admitted as a student at the Academy."

Glyssa smiled. "I have thought of that, and I will not rule it out for the future. But I would have to spend so much time away from the klarn. My mates are most important to me."

With a moment of deepsight, Amlina glimpsed many paths open to Glyssa: witch, shaman, warrior; but also klarnmate and lover, perhaps wife and mother. All of the Iruks had different personalities and strengths and might choose different paths.

"You each must decide what life will suit you best," she told them. "The Tuan and the Archimage both have offered generous stipends of money as reward for returning the Cloak. That is a reward you all have earned. It will allow you to stay in Larthang or leave and go anywhere you wish."

"I am glad you said that." Karrol stared moodily into her wine. "Because I don't believe I will stay in Larthang, whatever the rest of the klarn might choose."

"She's been saying that for a while," Glyssa told Amlina. "I am still hoping we can change her mind."

"Well, staying in Larthang sounds fine to me." Eben's voice was slightly slurred. "I am finding this land most agreeable to my spirit."

"Yes, and not just his spirit," Lonn laughed.

"What do you mean?" Amlina asked.

"Well, he won't say much about it," Lonn answered. "But it's plain to us Eben has found a lady friend."

"Yes," Draven added. "He came in drunk several nights ago from a poetry reading—but with more than poetry on his mind."

"Is this true?" Kizier asked him.

Eben held up a hand with solemnity. "As I understand the etiquette of this lovely country, a gentleman is discreet and does not discuss such things openly."

The swan boat rocked with the group's laughter.

"I am glad, Eben," Amlina said, "that you seem to be enjoying yourself."

Brinda changed the subject: "As I understand things, the witches of the House of the Deepmind have special guards—the *alatee* or Warriors of the Chrysalis."

"Yes, warriors of that sect guard Ting Ta Roo," Amlina replied. "And a high witch can request a retinue of alatee as a household guard. But it is not required. I would be free to keep you as my guards, or simply as guests in my residence."

Brinda still seemed curious. "Kizier has told us that these Chrysalis Warriors undergo special training, and also some kind of magical transformation."

"That is so," Amlina affirmed. "First there is an evaluation for warriors who would join the order, just as there is for witches. Candidates then undergo a period of training, both in spiritual disciplines and techniques of combat. Finally, there is the Chrysalis process itself, in which the warriors experience a sort of magical regeneration."

"They are literally cocooned like bugs," Eben said. "And can emerge with their bodies completely changed."

"Not just their bodies," Amlina said. "Supposedly, both bodies and minds are transformed into a conformation more aligned with their true ideal. At least, that is the theory. If you are curious, I could arrange for you to visit the order's academy. As you enjoy the friendship of the Tuan, I am sure you would be welcomed."

"That sounds like a good idea," Lonn asserted. "It is always worthwhile to learn new techniques of arms."

"Agreed," Draven put in. "Especially since this assassin was a Chrysalis warrior. If more of them come after Amlina, knowing how they fight would be helpful."

Twenty-Two

Within Duke Pheng's private apartments in Precious Stone Fortress was a wide, low ceilinged hall. Though located high in the castle, the chamber had no windows. Indeed, the stone walls were extra thick and the door solid iron. The hall was sealed with magical designs to ensure the secrecy of what passed within.

At the center of the spacious floor, the Duke sat at a round mahogany table, dressed in armor and a headpiece indicative of his high rank. His fingers were steepled, his elbows propped on the table. The expression on his broad, bearded face was gloomy.

At the table sat twenty of the Duke's closest allies, the most stalwart men of his faction, the Iron Bloc. Two were his sons, Ting Le Pheng and Shan Pheng. Two others, the only civilians, were powerful ministers at the Tuan's court. All the rest were military men, high-ranking officers in the army and navy. These included Admiral Shay-Ni Pheng, the Duke's nephew.

But it was another Admiral, Tavee K'un, whose droning report had the masters of the Iron Bloc in such low spirits. Tavee had just returned from the waters off Gon Fu where he commanded the fleet. His account made it dismally clear that, after fifteen months of war, the Larthangan forces were no closer to conquering the island.

The campaign had started with high hopes. At the start of First Summer, eight squadrons of warships and a large expeditionary force had been dispatched in a surprise attack. This occurred soon after the death of the old Tuan, before the current successor had ascended the throne. The Duke had taken advantage of the unsettled conditions in the capital to move without imperial authorization. Gon Fu was an enviable prize, a rich island with a mixed population of Larthangan and Tathian descent. More, its strategic location made it an ideal launching point for future campaigns against the Tathian Isles.

But the islanders had shown stout resistance to the initial attack and, within a month, reinforcements arrived from the Tathian city states. The expeditionary force was soon bogged down in the beachhead they established on the western coast. Larthangan attempts to blockade the island were met with stiff resistance by Tathian warships. The resulting stalemate had lasted now for over a year.

A gigantic miscalculation, the Duke thought sourly. The Larthangan commanders had blithely overestimated the divisions among the Tathians. The assault on Gon Fu had spurred the city states to set aside their differences and band together into a formidable alliance. The Tathian princes seemed determined to spend whatever lives and treasure were necessary to prevent a Larthangan victory.

"And so, my lords," K'un was saying, "I must express the opinion that the mission as currently formulated is untenable. I can only recommend that it be terminated."

"You advise withdrawal to our own waters?" one of his fellow naval commanders asked.

"Regrettably, I do."

"To be followed by what?" asked Shin Fo, one of the Tuan's high ministers.

K'un made a slight shrug. "That is for the war council—and of course the Tuan's government—to decide. I would suggest we plan further campaigns, using what we have learned."

"A worthy suggestion," the Duke allowed. "The game is long. Strategic setbacks must be viewed as lessons."

Around the table, several men nodded with somber agreement.

"If I may voice a different opinion." Shay-Ni Pheng spoke up.

The Duke suppressed a frown. His nephew, he knew, was anxious that the campaign continue. Shay-Ni had been in the capital for over two months. As soon as it became clear that the witches of the House of the Deepmind would not bring charges against him, the Admiral had requested a new command. The Duke had held back, not wanting to undermine Admiral K'un's position. His nephew was known as a firebrand. Worse, his debacle in the South Polar Sea had damaged his reputation among his fellow officers. Giving him a new command so soon would certainly have been unwise. Predictably, Shay-Ni had fretted, bridling against the enforced inactivity, venting his frustration with whoring and drinking. The Duke had warned him more than once that excessive vulgarity would only mar his reputation further.

"Of course, Admiral Pheng." The Duke saw no choice but to let the man speak. "All comments are welcome."

The Admiral thrust himself to his feet. "I believe that, instead of retreating, we must enlarge the campaign. In the shipyards of Hanjapore, seven new warships are nearing completion ..."

"Respectfully," Admiral K'un interrupted, "speaking as one just returned from Gon Fu, seven new ships will not alter the balance."

"Not if we continue the same failed tactics," Shay-Ni retorted. "No. My suggestion is to confront the Tathians at sea: sink their freighters, attack their war squadrons, even launch surprise attacks on their naval bases."

"All with seven galleons?" another navy commander asked.

"Those seven, plus others peeled off from the blockade," Shay Ni said. "I propose a new flotilla be formed to take the fight to the Tathian princes."

"Under your command, no doubt," K'un remarked.

Shay-Ni grew furious. "And why not under my command? Who has a better right? Or do you question my *fitness* for command?"

"Enough!" Standing, the Duke slapped the table with both hands. "This council is no place for emotional outbursts. Sit down, Admiral Pheng."

Reluctantly, Shay-Ni sank into his chair, his complexion flushed and bitter. Around the table, faces regarded him grimly.

"My nephew has voiced a proposal for revising the campaign," the Duke said quietly. "We will hear discussion of its merits."

The debate did not last long, and Shay-Ni's suggestion found little favor. This was due in large part, the Duke saw, to the loss of face Shay-Ni had suffered—both because of the events at the South Pole and his behavior since returning to Minhang. Now he listened with a surly expression, fighting back the urge to argue as his proposal sank into obscurity.

The Duke sighed. More and more, Shay-Ni was becoming a problem—one the Duke had neither the time nor patience for dealing with.

In the end, the warlords agreed to end the blockade of Gon Fu but to continue to supply the expeditionary force—leaving the small piece of the island they had conquered in Larthangan hands. Duke Pheng favored this as both a face-saving solution and a means of holding a launching point for future, better-planned campaigns.

After the group adjourned, the Duke climbed the stairs to his study at the top of the keep. His mind weighed down by many concerns, he looked forward to an hour or two of contemplation and perhaps summoning his seer to read the oracle.

So, when a steward informed him of a visitor, the surprise was unwelcome. But on hearing the identity of the visitor, the Duke agreed to the audience. After all, he must be kept informed about events in the House of the Deepmind.

Clorodice awaited him on the threshold of the terrace, staring down at the long view of the river below Minhang. She seemed lost in reverie, and when he approached she turned, a startled look on her face.

"Good afternoon, my lady. Will you sit." He gestured at a chair.

"No, thank you. I prefer to stand. But please sit if you wish." She stared at him with wide, alert eyes. Her manner impressed him as both excited and ill-at-ease.

"The attempt to eliminate Amlina failed," she said.

"Yes." The Duke settled himself into a seat. "Word reached me this morning. The news, it seems, is much discussed at the palace."

"Of course. All attempts to keep such news within the walls of Ting Ta Roo were bound to fail." She began to pace in front of his writing table. "However, my circle's involvement is not suspected. So, for the moment, we are safe."

"That is well." The Duke waited for her to disclose the reason for this unexpected visit. The silence lasted while the witch paced back and forth twice more.

"I have not given up on my resolve that Amlina be thwarted, that my apprentice Elani should win the Keepership of the Cloak. But for now I must move with more deliberation, lest I risk suspicions turning upon me."

Duke Pheng pursed his lips. "You indicated that Amlina's next hurdle would be to attain the rank of the gray mantle."

"Yes, but that is almost a foregone conclusion." Clorodice waved a dismissive hand. "In any case, that will be decided by the Academy, where I have little influence."

"So then. Amlina will likely qualify as a candidate. And there will surely be others. Do you have any further word on how the Inner Council will decide the matter?"

Clorodice shook her head. "Nothing has been decided. But from my reading of the currents, I expect the Tournament of Witches will be used to select the winner. This will please the Tuan, since it was his suggestion. More importantly, it will avoid a vote that would likely divide the Council. Lady Drusdegarde likes to avert such conflicts."

"So. Then what is your plan?"

Clorodice responded to the blunt question by stopping, setting both hands on the table, and leaning toward his face.

"I must summon more power."

Pheng was taken aback: a strange statement for a high witch to bring to him. He turned up both hands in a shrug. "How can I assist you in this?"

Clorodice paced again. "First, I wish you to understand I do not take this path lightly. It is purely because of my dedication to virtue, to the moral order necessary for the good of the Land."

"Of course. That is the driving force for both of us, and the reason we are allies."

"Indeed. My alliance with you has ... convinced me to take certain steps, to invoke elder arts that I would never have otherwise considered. But now I contemplate going even farther ..."

Again, Pheng deemed it wise to listen patiently until the witch arrived at her point.

"Of old, those who practiced these arts augmented their power by seducing other minds, using them as sources and conduits."

"You speak of thralls?"

"That is one type of servant that these arts can procure. But now I speak of something more potent by far. A thrall is simply one whose mind is disabled and the body controlled by another. But the old books describe another kind of servant, sometimes called an anti-self, sometimes a *phingarr*."

"Phingarr? Isn't that an archaic term for 'ogre'?" The Duke was a man of considerable learning.

"Indeed. I believe that connotation came later. *Anti-self* is the more meaningful term. Such a creature is derived from a human. This human is carefully selected because it is a complete psychic opposite of the mage who will fabricate the anti-self. Through this very opposition, this *imbalance*, enormous power can be drawn."

The Duke's mouth went slack. He was not often intimated by the workings of witches, but this discussion had taken a morbid, rather appalling turn.

"These practices have their risks," Clorodice said. "Because an ongoing opposition is necessary, the human's mind must remain intact, even as their souls are sliced open to allow vast energies to rise up from the Deepmind. And since some part of the will survives, such creatures can be difficult to control. But to the degree I can keep this anti-self confined and under my control, I will gain tremendous power—power I will use to further our mutual goals, the first of which being to defeat Amlina and assure my apprentice is awarded the Cloak of the Two Winds."

She ended, leaning close to the Duke again. Trem-Dou swallowed and stroked his neat beard.

"My lady, I congratulate you, on both your scholarship and your willingness to take bold action. And I thank you for keeping me informed of your admirable plans. Is there any way in which I can assist."

A grim smile spread over the witch's face. "There is indeed, Lord Duke. I need you to supply the human whom I will transform."

Pheng shifted uncomfortably in his seat. "I am more than happy to help, of course. But surely, you have it in your power to acquire any number of ... persons."

"Ah, but not just any person will do." Clorodice's expression was alight with eagerness. "Remember, the anti-self must be my precise opposite. Where I am female, it must be a male. Where I am strict, self-controlled, abstemious, *he* must be the opposite. I have already done preparatory work on this project, including searching in the Deepmind for a likely candidate. That is why I come to you today."

Duke Pheng leaned back, now actually frightened. Clorodice's smile grew wide and feral.

"No, I do not mean you, my lord. But … perhaps another man comes to mind? Someone reckless, impulsive, rapacious in his appetites? Someone who might have proven *troublesome* lately?"

The realization made Pheng's belly freeze. He stared at the witch for a long moment, taking hold of his feelings, pondering the repercussions. To deliver his nephew Shay-Ni into the hands of these witches to be murdered—No, rather *transformed* into some sort of ogre …? A heinous act, to be sure, to betray a member of one's own family. Still, sometimes the game required the sacrifice of favored pieces. And Shay-Ni *had* grown more and more bothersome.

"I will need to think it over," he finally said. "I might have someone for you."

Twenty-Three

When the day came for the Iruks to visit the Chrysalis warriors, Eben was disappointed to learn that their headquarters was not within the House of the Deepmind. Instead, the Castle of the Chrysalis stood on the outskirts of Minhang, across the northern canal.

Eben had been hoping he might catch a glimpse of Trippany. He had not seen the winged lady since their enchanting night in the garden when he had seduced her—or she had seduced him—he scarcely knew which. She hadn't said anything after their lovemaking, only rearranged her clothing, kissed him tenderly, and flown away. That was twelve days ago, more than a small-month. Eben had attended palace parties and performances in the interim, but though he had spotted the Drell ambassador on two occasions, Trippany had not been in the Prince's entourage. Eben had no access to the House of the Deepmind, and so there was no way to get in touch with the lady. He considered it indiscrete to mention the drell to Amlina. In any case, the witch was much absorbed in her studies— dividing her time between the Academy and the study halls of the House of the Deepmind.

Still, memories of his night with Trippany occupied him constantly. Eben consoled himself with planning what he might say when next he saw her, with composing poems to her in his mind, and with drinking an excess of wine to ease the melancholy.

It was a fine, warm morning as the Iruks rode a ferry across the choppy water of the canal. They were accompanied by Ting Fo, the tutor who still attended them as guide— and as interpreter when needed, although all of the Iruks now spoke enough Larthangan for most occasions. Also in the party was Kizier who, as always, brought a writing book, pens, and ink to make notes.

The mates wore their leather harnesses, with swords and knives in their belts, and they had brought along one quiver of throwing spears in order to demonstrate Iruk fighting techniques. Below the harnesses, most of the klarn wore linen shirts and trousers cut and sewn for them by palace tailors. Only Karrol had resisted adopting Larthangan clothing and still wore her deerskins.

Disembarking from the ferry, Ting Fo dispatched a runner to inform the Castle of their imminent arrival. The group marched for another quarter mile up an avenue bordered by walled houses and gardens. The Castle of the Chrysalis was a wide enclosure set behind walls of yellow and gold. The figure of a broad-winged butterfly adorned the archway over the entrance.

The visitors arrived to find a squadron of warriors in the familiar blue-scaled armor waiting before open gates. Most carried pikes hung with streaming pennons. A tall, broad-shouldered woman with a curved sword in her belt stepped forward as the Iruks drew near.

She gave a stiff bow. "Esteemed warriors and guests of the Tuan, it is my great honor to welcome you to the Castle of the Chrysalis."

Ting Fo, who carried a parasol for shade, returned the bow. He introduced the woman as Shen Volana, Mistress Warrior and Commander of the Order. Ting Fo then introduced Kizier and the Iruks by name. The mates offered bows as they had been schooled to do in polite Larthangan company.

The Mistress Warrior led the way into the compound. For the next several hours the visitors toured the castle. They strolled through barracks, classrooms, and meditation chambers, and visited a sacred chapel high in the castle keep.

Then, in a broad tiled courtyard, they watched drills and combat practice. Duels were conducted with swords and shields, pikes and axes. Archers stood in rows and showed their skill with the crossbow by downing feathered targets at fifty paces.

Afterward, by invitation, the Iruks demonstrated their own fighting techniques. They fenced with swords and knives, first in pairs and then three against three. Next, they flung their hunting spears at the same small targets the bowmen had used. Though their accuracy was far from perfect, they did score several hits. All the while, Kizier sat in the shade writing notes, while Ting Fo sipped fruit punch.

The Iruks found Shen Volana a most amiable hostess. When they had finished with their weapons exhibition, Eben ventured to ask her if anything more had been learned about the assassin who attacked Amlina at the House of the Deepmind.

The face of the Warrior Mistress grew somber. "I fear not. The man in question was a member of our order for nine years, and in all that time his record was without blemish. True, he hailed from outside the borders of Larthang, but that is not uncommon. The alatee have always welcomed worthy candidates from foreign lands. Our order has served the Witches of Larthang since the Reign of the Eleventh Tuan, over 2500 years. Such incidents as this are extremely rare, and we take them very seriously."

"But the warrior was enthralled," Kizier pointed out. "Surely no blame can fall on your order in such a case."

"Nevertheless, it is a stain on our honor. Rest assured, we are carefully examining all of our warriors for any hint of unwarranted influence, as well as conducting our own investigation into the affair."

"Your order is most noble, from all we have seen today," Glyssa said. "And your hospitality to us has been most gracious."

"Indeed, your warriors are impressive," Lonn added.

"Still, there is one thing we have not learned about," Eben said, prompted by curiosity. "The Chrysalis process itself—this transformation that your warriors experience—is most intriguing to an outsider. Is it permitted for you to tell us more of how that works?"

The lady answered with a ready smile. "Of course. I can show you, if you like."

She led them back inside the keep, explaining as she went. "The Chrysalis transformation was devised by witches under the 19th Tuan, and has been revised and improved over the centuries. When a candidate has completed their training and made the final decision to commit to our order, the initiation can begin. For one small-month, they fast and meditate, and chant certain verses to invoke power from the Deepmind. All of these activities are focused on a single goal: to call into being the individual warrior's highest ideal."

They filed down a stairway and entered a long, lamp-lit passage. Every few paces, doors gave access to side chambers.

"Within these cells," Shen Volana said, "you can observe the actual cocoons. After the small-month of preparation, the warrior enters a cell and the cocoon is spun around their body. This ritual takes many hours and involves secret magical formulations. The warrior then sleeps within the cocoon as their ideal takes shape."

She directed the visitors to look through the opening in one of the doors. Within, a single man-sized cocoon hung from a beam, a dark shape like a shroud blanketing the warrior within.

"How long do they sleep?" Draven asked in a whisper.

"That varies with the amount of change. Normally one to two months, longer in some cases."

"And when the warrior emerges, they are changed," Brinda remarked.

"Oh, indeed. Sometimes the changes are small—sleeker bodies, or stronger and more muscular forms. Sometimes the changes are more pronounced. Changes in gender are not uncommon. I myself was a man before my cocooning."

"Most remarkable," Eben said, glancing at the faces of his mates to gauge their reactions.

Later, as the party walked back to the ferry, the Iruks discussed their experience.

"It was worthwhile, I think," Lonn suggested, "to see the Chrysalis warriors in action."

"Agreed," Draven said. "I picked up a trick or two from their sword craft."

"They are skillful," Karrol allowed. "But I was not intimidated. We have faced tougher foes."

"True enough," Lonn said. "The one advantage they might have in a fight would be the crossbows. At distance, they would be hard to match."

"Perhaps we should take up the weapon," Draven replied. "Something to consider if we are to stay in Larthang as Amlina's retainers."

They discussed this for a bit. When the talk ran out without reaching a consensus, Brinda changed the subject.

"What did you think of the cocoons?" she asked. "Would any of you ever consider undertaking such a change?"

"Not I," Eben laughed.

"Why not?" Karrol said. "It might make you into a better warrior."

Eben scoffed. "Well, I know they say one is changed into a form closer to their ideal, but what does that really mean? I, for one, cannot imagine myself changing into a woman."

This brought a round of laughter from his klarnmates.

"Women make the best warriors," Karrol declared. "Besides, you might feel different about it if you weren't infatuated with your mystery lady."

"Hmm." Eben shrugged. "That might be a fair point."

On the first day of the following month, the first month of Third Summer, Amlina entered the Academy of the Deepmind for her examination. The Academy, known as Col Sang, was a long white building adjacent to the compound of the House of the Deepmind. Identifying herself to a porter in the outer lobby, Amlina was conducted up a central stair and through a series of corridors, passing offices, classrooms, and scriptoriums. After waiting a quarter-hour in an anteroom, she was summoned to the examination chamber.

The room looked exactly as she remembered from thirteen years ago: circular, with a high dome and a floor of gray flagstones flecked with silver. In the center of the floor was a round fountain filled with bubbling water, the basin of mosaic tiles. In the center of the basin stood a broad pillar, obsidian black. Water gushed from the mouths of carved faces on the pillar. In the center, between the faces, hung a simple cloak, the gray mantle Amlina sought to claim.

Enthroned on the pillar, above the level of Amlina's head, sat three witches, Faculty of the Academy. Two of these examiners she did not recognize but upon scrutinizing the woman in the center, Amlina clenched her teeth.

She looked older than Amlina remembered, and even more stern and sour, if such a thing were possible. But there was no doubt that it was Arulanna Li Tow, one of Amlina's former teachers. In her days as a student, Arulanna had taken a dislike to her, deemed her careless and rebellious. Her treatment of Amlina bordered on persecution, and Amlina believed it had undermined her studies, leading to her failing this very examination.

"Let the candidate step forward." Arulanna said.

Steeling herself, Amlina walked to the edge of the fountain. She stared up at the three examiners and took a deep breath. Over the past small-month she had studied with earnest dedication. She was well-prepared for the examination and had walked in to the Academy this morning confident she would pass. Now, suddenly, she had doubts.

"You are Amlina Len Tai, from Shen Tong province?" Arulanna asked.

"Yes." Amlina seldom thought of her family name or the place of her birth.

"And you are here to be examined for advance to the grade of adept."

"I am."

On her high seat, Arulanna leaned forward. "This committee is also well aware that you are the *famous* Amlina, who spent years overseas and has lately returned bringing treasures from foreign places. But those accomplishments have no bearing here. Any deepshaping tricks or foreign sorceries you may have learned will not help you. This committee will examine you purely on the Five Revered Arts and their Thirty-Five Respected Applications."

Calmly, Amlina returned the belligerent stare. "I expect nothing else."

"Very well then." Her former teacher sat back. "Let the examination begin."

The witches took turns asking questions in rapid succession. They began with the most basic. Amlina answered just as readily.

"What are the Five Revered Arts of the Deepmind?"

"Wei-shen, the deepseeing; quon-xing, pure shaping; jai-dah, that is formulation or weaving; barang-xing, trinketing; and weng-lei, magical combat."

"How does formulation differ from pure shaping?"

"Formulation is the creation of mental constructs that are then released through incantation and casting. Pure shaping is the instant use of mental power to manifest effects."

"Name the seven respected applications of deepseeing."

"The first is summoning dreams; the second, evoking visions; the third, peering into a moment; fourth, peering into a soul; fifth, seeing outside of time; sixth, seeing through another's eyes; and the seventh, bowing to the sky."

The questions rolled on, gradually growing more difficult. Amlina answered nearly by rote. She had studied thoroughly.

There followed demonstrations. Amlina was asked to read one of the witch's minds and describe a certain color held in the woman's thoughts. Next, all three examiners focused on deepseeing in the moment a specific place—the harbor in faraway Haji-Chan of the Moonstone Gates, and Amlina was required to look there also and describe the scene. For magical combat, Amlina demonstrated fighting poses, then drew her dagger and cast it looping and flying in the air by mental control. She had prepared a formulation and when asked, summoned it by gesture and chant. Remembering the fountain in this chamber, she had chosen to create a design that stopped the water in first one spigot, then the next. Her success in this seemed to impress the committee favorably.

But when they tested her on trinketing, Amlina's luck turned. She handed over her moonstone fillet, her favorite piece. It floated through the air to Arulanna who examined it, frowning, and then passed it to the others. The three witches muttered back and forth. Arulanna then turned on Amlina with a wry expression.

"We suggest that this piece was constructed using techniques outside the approved *Canon of Assemblage*."

Amlina's heart sank. She had fashioned the fillet while studying in the city of Kadavel, where she had learned some Tathian alchemy. "There may have been some small influence from foreign sources," she allowed in a guarded voice.

"Obviously this must count against you." With a dismissive wave, Arulanna sent the trinket drifting back over the water.

After more than two hours, the committee had exhausted all of their questions and requested performances. Amlina waited with a gnawing pain in her stomach while the three faculty members discussed her application using hand-signs. She noted what appeared to be some disagreement between Arulanna and the others. Finally, the three sat back in their chairs. As they did so, the gushing from the spigots ceased, and the water in the basin changed to ice.

Arulanna cleared her throat. "Amlina Len Tai, this committee has reached a decision. We find your knowledge of the arts of witchery adequate, in some cases commendable. Your demonstrations, though less exemplary, are nonetheless deemed adequate. Also, I must say that, due to your notoriety, the Academy has been placed under political pressure to pass your application. But, be that as it may, you may proceed to claim your gray mantle."

She pointed her chin down at the ice. Amlina nodded and put her hands on the rim of the basin, forcing herself not to shake. This was the final test. Based on the pure shaping of the committee members, the ice had appeared in the fountain. How thick and strong would depend on their degree of approval for the candidate.

Now she must walk across and reach the mantle without falling through. The ice must either be solid enough to bear her weight or—should it begin to break—she must summon the power to lighten her body and step softly enough to reach the prize. At her first attempt, thirteen years ago, Amlina had made it less than halfway before falling through, soaking herself to the waist with freezing water. Utterly humiliated, she had left the Academy soon after.

Now, under the stern eyes of the examiners, she stepped into the basin. The ice appeared firm, though streams of tiny bubbles moved beneath the surface. Cautiously watching her feet, Amlina took a step, then another.

She had reached the midway point when she heard the first crunch. Tiny cracks spread out from her foot and suddenly the ice grew slippery. Fear surged into her heart, and with it the devastating memory of her first failure.

"No," she whispered. "I will not fail this time."

With the courage of that thought, something else rose within her. The power she had felt in the labyrinth, when she had brought her body out of the pit and risen high into the air. Immediately, she directed the power. Almost without realizing it, she was lifting off the ice, levitating her body.

Reaching out her hand, she touched the gray mantle. Grasping it, she turned in the air and flowed back across the fountain.

Her feet came to rest softly on the flagstone floor. Amlina wrapped the mantle over her shoulders. She caressed the heavy silk for just a moment, then turned to the committee. After a curt bow, she left the chamber without speaking a word.

Twenty-Four

Admiral Shay-Ni Pheng was surprised by the invitation to join his uncle for an early evening conference. More surprising was the location: not the Pheng mansion in the center of Minhang, where Shay-Ni had been living these past two months and where the Duke held the main apartments; and not Precious Stone Fortress, where Shay-Ni had been confined when first returning to the city and where the Duke resided most of the time. No, this meeting would take place at the house of a certain Colonel Nenn, one of the Duke's lesser retainers.

Nenn's residence stood in a peripheral warren near the mouth of the north canal. Across the canal stood the outermost walls of the Tuan's celestial palace and the shores of Perfect Light Lake. The remote location hinted at a clandestine gathering to discuss secret matters. Shay-Ni hoped the affair might at last lead to some new assignment for him—although Colonel Nenn had no connection with the navy, only a career commanding border outposts. Still, there was no telling what plans the crafty Duke might be hatching and, of course, Shay-Ni would not have refused the invitation in any case. Anything that promised relief from the tedium of his present existence was welcome.

On arrival, he found the manor house as modest and unimposing as expected. But when a serving girl ushered him to a small dining room at the rear of the house, Shay-Ni was met by another surprise. Along with the Duke and the Colonel, two others occupied the low-set table: the Duke's sons, Commander Ting Le and General Shan. Their greetings were subdued, and they regarded Shay-Ni's with hooded expressions that made him uneasy. Colonel Nenn likewise appeared nervous, his eyes downcast. Only the Duke smiled with his usual aplomb as he waved Shay-Ni to the cushion next to his own.

Shay-Ni moved the sword on his belt and sat down cross-legged. He preferred chairs and waist-high tables to this archaic manner of dining. But many considered the low table style more "military."

"I am grateful for the invitation, esteemed uncle," Shay-Ni said.

"I am appreciative of your promptness, dear nephew. We have important matters to discuss, which may result in new and important duties for you—assuming you are willing."

"My only wish is to serve the Land to the best of my ability," he answered, excitement kindling.

"Well said. We are waiting for one other to begin the conference. Meantime, take some refreshment." Duke Pheng crooked a finger to summon the serving girl, who stepped forward with a goblet on a silver tray.

Shay-Ni smiled at her as he took the cup. She was a small, pretty thing, and he wondered if he might have an opportunity to enjoy her later.

"Who is the other officer we are waiting for?" he asked.

"Someone you do not know." The Duke raised his hand, encouraging Shay-Ni to drink up.

The wine proved slightly acidic, and Shay-Ni wondered if this was the best Colonel Nenn could afford. Still, after the first sip he scarcely noticed the taste. Soon he had drained his cup and held it up for a refill.

The talk was low and subdued, a review of troop placements in the northern border regions, mention of a certain Duke Khin of Tongvann Province who had failed this year to provide the called-for troop requisitions. Was Khin an incipient threat to raise a rebellion in the northwest? Shay-Ni wondered if this might be the purpose of the conference.

As he sipped the wine a strange warmth crept through his veins. He began to feel light-headed. His cousins eyed him from time to time, and he wondered at the meaning of their glances. Perhaps he should contribute to the conversation, but even understanding their words was becoming difficult.

What was happening to him? He glanced into the near empty cup with sudden panic. The cup shook violently in his hand as he tried to set it down. His arm twitched, and the wine spilled over the table.

With a groan he thrust himself off the cushion. He tried to stand but his knees buckled. He fell over sideways, collapsing against the Duke. His uncle wrapped arms around his benumbed body and laid it gently on the floor.

Paralyzed, mouth fallen open, Shay-Ni stared at the ceiling. Faces appeared, peering down at him. He heard his uncle's voice.

"Summon the witches."

Nerves thrumming with anticipation, Clorodice waited in the dark parlor of Colonel Nenn's manor. On the couch beside her sat Arkasha, her most-trusted subaltern. It had been Arkasha who had accompanied Admiral Pheng on his ill-fated voyage to the South Polar Sea. Tonight, she would meet him again—under far different circumstances.

The two witches had heard the Admiral's arrival and listened in acute silence to the muted discussions coming from the dining room. When she heard a muffled crash and a flurry of movement, Clorodice knew the moment had come. She and Arkasha were already on their feet when the Colonel appeared in the doorway. They followed him to the dining room, where the Duke and his sons bent over the supine, inert body of Shay-Ni Pheng.

Clorodice brushed past the men and knelt. She felt the pulse at the neck, then moved her hand in front of the unblinking eyes.

"Yes. This will do nicely."

"Is he conscious?" Duke Pheng asked.

"I believe so." Clorodice turned to her assistant. "Bring the sheets," she said, and then to the Colonel: "Get the cart ready, if you please."

The Duke leaned over his fallen nephew. "I regret any discomfort you may be feeling, Shay-Ni. Rest assured, I did not select this course without due consideration. The oracle advised that this was the most auspicious way for you to serve the Land, and you *will* now have new duties as I promised—though not ones you would likely have chosen."

When the body was carefully wrapped in a burial sheet, the Duke's sons lifted it on their shoulders and carried it out to the street where a dray cart was waiting. After thanking Nenn for his assistance, the Duke dismissed him. Duke Pheng and his sons climbed onto the cart along with the two witches. Ting Le, the elder son, took the reins. Arkasha sat beside him to give directions.

The pink moon had already set and the red moon not yet risen. With a soft veil of clouds, the night was as dark as it ever appeared in Minhang—illumined only by the ghostly ambient witchlight that rose from the nearby canal and the more-distant lake. The cart rolled up a narrow lane and turned onto a back street. Traveling away from the canal, they crossed the western edge of the city. Clorodice spotted no one as the cart made its way through a suburb of rolling fields with widely spaced houses and barns. The trail led over an antique bridge that spanned a dry gulley. Beyond the bridge, they passed through a gate in a crumbling wall of stone blocks.

Inside lay the City of Tombs, an immense necropolis of monoliths, obelisks, and domed pavilions spread over low, rounded hills. For more than five thousand years, the highest ranking nobles of Larthang had been buried here. Clorodice noted with wry satisfaction how the Duke and his sons attempted to mask their superstitious dread. The high witch herself felt no such scruples. Oh, the ghosts were real enough. Clorodice could summon any number of them if she so desired. But that was not why she had chosen this place for her sanctuary. The tombs offered several advantages. Fear and reverence for the dead would keep away the curious, while the immanent spiritual power of the place could be tapped to hide her activities from the deepsight of her fellow witches. As Keeper of the Keys, Clorodice could open the magical locks that sealed many of the underground vaults.

The cart rolled to a stop between two shallow hills. Below a fallen obelisk lay a pit with stairs leading down. Figures in black, hooded robes stood waiting—nine witches of Clorodice's circle, all of them loyal to the Thread of Virtue. They gathered at the back of the cart. The Duke and his son handed down the rigid body.

"Thank you, Lord Duke," Clorodice said. "My people will take over from here."

"You will keep me informed of your progress," Duke Pheng said.

"Naturally."

Her assistants were already carrying the wrapped body toward the stairs. Arms folded in their sleeves, Clorodice and Arkasha followed. The Duke and his sons climbed back onto the cart and drove away into the darkness.

Clorodice descended the stairs and lowered her head to enter the tomb. The file of her subordinates preceded her, moving slowly down the passage. Removing a key ring from her pocket, she selected an old, tarnished key and pointed it at the entrance. As she turned the key in the air, a metal door rose up from below, sealing the portal.

Lanterns carried by a few of the subalterns now gave the only light. Initially narrow, the tunnel soon broadened into a brick passageway twelve paces across with a vaulted ceiling and painted walls. Faded murals depicted the funeral procession of an emperor from the days before the Tuans. The air hung damp and smelled of mold.

At the end of the tunnel, Clorodice and her followers emerged into a wide, circular chamber carved in the rock below the hill. The curving walls were lined with shelves holding dusty urns of brass and gold. Statues of ancient gods and sages stood in alcoves, and open doorways led off to smaller rooms. Lamps and dozens of candles burned in the close air. Furniture had recently been added: carpets and chairs, trunks containing ritual implements. In the middle of the floor sat a heavy table. The comatose body of Admiral Pheng was set down there and carefully unwrapped.

Clorodice stepped into a side chamber, removed her robe, and washed her face and hands in a basin. Assisted by her apprentice, Elani Vo T'ang, she donned a ritual gown of white linen and a necklace of amber beads.

By the time she joined the others, Pheng's body had been stripped and sponged. Three of the witches were rubbing the skin with a spicy, numbing gel. Stepping near, Clorodice scrutinized the glistening, rigid form. The man was full-chested and broad-shouldered, with a thick beard and considerable tufts of hair on the chest and belly. He had strong legs and a large male member—a robust specimen. He should do very well.

She gave the order, and the body was carried to a rack formed by two cross-beams in the shape of an X. The arms were stretched, the wrists and ankles strapped in place. Clorodice examined the restraints and stepped back, satisfied. She spoke an order and one of her acolytes brought forward a glass bottle filled with milky liquid. A long, flexible tube was sealed to the bottle's top. The acolyte threaded the tube into Pheng's open mouth. The man gave a soft, gagging sound as the instrument was pushed down his throat. Clorodice watched as the bottle was inverted, the drugged liquid emptied into Pheng's stomach. His eyes widened slightly.

When the bottle was drained, the tube was quickly removed. Clorodice gestured and two of the witches bent their backs and lifted. The rack pivoted on hinges until the body's position was nearly vertical, then the cross-beams were locked in place.

Clorodice scanned the faces of her subordinates. The witches gazed with parted lips, some eager and excited, others pale and frightened at what they were about to do.

But their fear of Clorodice was greater. She had made sure of that.

Forcing down a moment of inner reluctance, she issued the command for the ritual to begin.

At a carpeted space before the cross-beams, the witches formed a circle. Nine in black robes stood holding hands, with Clorodice in the center in her pure white gown. The tenth woman, Arkasha, sat on a podium nearby, a stack of parchment sheets near her hand.

The witches chanted, raising power. Sometimes they moved, circling. Occasionally, Arkasha prompted them with a new verse. Clorodice raised her arms, lifted her head, felt the energy rotating and growing. The man on the rack let out soft moans.

The ritual went on for hours and hours, the invocations rising louder, the sobs of the victim coming more frequently, but always soft and feeble. At one point, Arkasha left the podium and marched over to the rack. With a razor she slit the man's arm and let the blood run into an alabaster bowl. She carried the bowl to the circle and smeared the blood on each witch's forehead. Clorodice received the libation last, the bowl inverted, the remaining blood spilling over her hair and face.

The chanting and circling resumed. Some of the candles burned out, Arkasha left the podium to replace them. She added more oil to the lamps.

Finally, after many hours, the ritual reached its climax. Clorodice stripped off her gown. The circle parted, though the chanting went on. Naked except for the amber beads, Clorodice approached the rack.

It seemed the man's body had already changed, thickening, growing more hairy, the jaw more pronounced. This was only the beginning.

From a silver tray held by her apprentice, Clorodice picked up a knife with a long, curved blade. In a state of keen awareness, she stepped close to the bound form. Whispering the ultimate words of the design, she carefully sliced into the man—two cuts from shoulder to breastbone, then a single cut down the belly. His eyes bulged and his mouth moved—looking like a fish plucked from water and straining to breathe the air.

Behind her, the chanting changed into roaring and shrieking. Clorodice stepped back and flung up her arms. She raised her head in exaltation. Power flowed like fire into her belly.

Twenty-Five

O n the day of the next new moon, Amlina waited outside the chamber of the Inner Council at the House of the Deepmind. The tall, columned hallway was crowded with witches, servants, and guards. Many of these were attendants, waiting for the high witches to emerge. Others, like Amlina, were anxious to hear of the Council's decision on a singular matter: how would the appointment be decided for Keeper of the Cloak?

After more than two hours of deliberations, the brass doors swung open. The high witches and their assistants in their varicolored robes filed out, chatting among themselves, mingling with the entourages who awaited them in the hallway.

Amlina spotted Melevarry, the Mage of Randoon walking alone and hastened over.

"What news, my lady?"

The Mage eyed Amlina with a half-smile. Her gaze roved over the crowd, and she gestured with a finger. "The day is warm and pleasant. Let's take a stroll in the gardens."

Amlina fell into step beside her. Midway down the corridor, they exited the building, crossed a portico, and descended into a courtyard formed of towering walls of pure white marble.

"The Council has agreed," Melevarry said, "to allow the benevolence of the Deepmind to select the new Keeper."

"It will be the winner of the Tournament then?" Amlina's voice pitched high with eagerness.

"Yes. And before you ask, you *have* been approved as one of the contestants. Given the fact that you returned the Cloak to Larthang, and with the Tuan's strong endorsement, it could hardly have been otherwise."

"I am so relieved." Amlina stared straight ahead, eyes widening. "Yet, now there is a great challenge before me."

"Indeed." Melevarry chuckled.

They strolled beneath a tall arch into a garden. Immediately, the environment changed. Dense palm fronds lined the curving path and black branches leaned above, hung with jungle flowers. The air, dry and balmy a moment ago, now settled warm and humid, infused with the faint perfume of orchids.

"Who are the other contestants?" Amlina asked.

"There will most likely be seven," Melevarry responded. "So far, three have been named. Tolanga of Gon Fu, a warrior witch who is protégé of Wicksa, our Keeper of Swords; Elani Vo T'ang, favored by Clorodice, Keeper of the Keys; and Shen Tra Lo, known to be a skilled trinket-maker and apprentice to Kanshi, Keeper of the Forge. No doubt other high witches will nominate their favorites. By tradition, the maximum number is seven, so you can expect three more to be approved."

Amlina watched the ground as she walked, but her mind was perusing the many facets of the Tournament. "So far the field includes one warrior and one trinket-maker. Does Elani Vo T'ang have a specialty?"

"I know little about her, except that, like her mentor, she is an adherent to the legalist sect, the Thread of Virtue. In any case, I would not spend much thought on specialties. All entrants must compete in all of the disciplines."

Amlina was well aware of how the Tournament worked. On four successive days, the witches would compete in contests based on the first four of the Five Revered Arts. The contestants who achieved the highest combined scores would then meet in the final event, a contest of pure shaping.

"Still," she murmured, "knowing the relative strengths of my rivals might be of some use."

They walked under another arch and again their surroundings changed. Now they paced along the side of a high mountain, with a stunning view of cliffs and valleys stretching away into a blue distance. The cold air smelled crisp and clean. Each of the many gardens of the House of the Deepmind cast an ever-changing panorama of illusions, generated by age-old witchery.

Melevarry folded her hands in her sleeves in response to the sudden chill. "If I may offer you advice: I would give no thought whatsoever to your rivals. Rather, give all of your attention to perfecting your own efforts."

Amlina considered this. For the deepseeing and magical combat events, she could only hone her skills with practice. But for both the trinketing and formulation events, she would have to make presentation pieces—the one a magical object, the other a mental construction. No doubt, her rivals had already prepared, perhaps even constructed, their designs. It was now the sixth day of Third Summer. Amlina had less than two months to prepare. Suddenly, her task felt overwhelming.

"No doubt, you are right," she said in a subdued tone.

"Do not sound so downcast," the Mage of Randoon chided. "If you plan well and work hard, I firmly believe you'll have as good a chance as anyone."

"Do not go expecting disaster." Amlina quoted a witch's maxim.

They walked on, discussing ideas for the trinket and formulation Amlina should make for the Tournament.

Presently, they entered another garden. Now they strolled through a fragrant orchard in the weather of First Summer. Cherry trees lined the curving path, with bursts of white flowers adorning the black branches. Among the petals fluttering to the ground came a larger shape—a lady with bee wings.

In a gauzy white gown and belled slippers, Trippany settled before them and made a hasty bow.

"My lady Mage, esteemed Amlina, please pardon my interrupting you."

Melevarry nodded pleasantly to the drell, and Amlina smiled.

"My friend, it is good to see you."

"I searched you out as soon as I heard," Trippany spoke breathlessly. "I mean that the Council had decided about Keeper of the Cloak."

"Yes," the Mage answered. "As many expected, we chose to allow the Tournament to decide."

"And will you, Amlina, be allowed to compete?"

"I will. We were just discussing strategies."

"Oh!" Trippany's grin showed pointy teeth. "I am so glad. I confess, I had hoped it would be so."

Amlina reached out and clasped the drell's hand. "Your friendship is most welcome, Trippany. But how are you doing? I've scarcely seen you since we left Randoon."

"I have been deeply involved in my studies. My mission for the Archimage, as you know, and then my subsequent period of penance, cost me time and progress that I dearly wish to make up."

Trippany, Amlina knew, already ranked as an adept. But for witches who chose to continue in Ting Ta Roo, there were many grades and levels of achievement that could take years to accomplish.

"Your devotion to our arts is commendable," Amlina said. "I will soon need to apply myself with similar diligence."

Trippany still held her hand. "If I can assist in any way, please call upon me."

"Thank you, I shall. If you decide you can spare a little time from your studies, perhaps we can dine together some evening? By the kindness of the Tuan, I still reside at the palace, along with my friends. I know they would enjoy seeing you as well—Eben in particular. It seems he is composing songs about a lovely lady with wings."

Trippany cast down her eyes, seeming embarrassed. As she flew off, Amlina wondered if Eben's infatuation might in fact be mutual.

The one who had been Shay-Ni Pheng stared out past the bars of light that formed his cage. The beams emanated from disks on the floor, arranged in a semi-circle that arced out from the masonry walls—imprisoning him most effectively in an area five paces wide.

For the bars were no ordinary witchlight, such as shone on the sea. The few times he had tested them, he had pulled back a clawed finger, howling in excruciating pain.

How they burned, those razor sharp beams of light. Burned in a different way from the insatiable hunger forever coiling in his belly. Burned more like the hate he felt for those who had betrayed him and cast him into this prison.

How long had he been here? Days and days, for certain. At first, his mind had been befuddled. Only gradually did his wits return— and with them, his memories of that night he had come here, betrayed by his uncle and cousins, paralyzed, then tortured by the black-robed witches.

His body had changed terribly. He wished for a mirror so he could see all the changes. Coarse white hair now covered his legs and torso. His hips, he was certain had widened, legs bowed. His arms seemed longer, and they naturally swung when he walked, his spine bent forward. His lower jaw protruded, and when he felt with clawed fingers he could touch fangs pushed over his upper lip.

They had made him into a monster. They called him phingarr—as good a name as any. For he was no longer Shay-Ni Pheng, a puny and miserable man. Now he would call himself Phingarr. Phingarr Pheng—a name to be feared.

Vile witches! Their leader he knew all too well—Lady Clorodice, the Keeper of the Keys and his uncle's ally. She was the one who had sliced open his chest at the climax of the rite, summoning unimaginable power that burst into being and filled them both.

Frequently now, she came to the tomb to stand before his cage and draw that same power. How it flashed in the air and blazed through every fiber and sinew of his body. Then Clorodice would leave, looking dazed, drunk with the power. Somehow, she needed this monster he had become to call up this wild magic. What she did not seem to suspect was that a portion of the power stayed with him.

Shay-Ni Pheng, miserable human, had always shunned the ways of witchery. But Phingarr Pheng reveled in the power. He sensed it working in him, building in his soul. Already he perceived how he could use it. Use it, for example, to turn off the magic disks on the floor that kept him imprisoned. And then ...

"Agh!" He growled, the hunger suddenly an agony writhing in his stomach.

Across the chamber, two witches seated at a writing table looked over at him. At least two of Clorodice's subordinates were always here to keep watch on him.

"Agh!" He growled again, pointing to his open mouth.

With a grimace of disgust, one of the witches put down her book. This one he also knew—the Lady Arkasha. Someday, for certain, he would pay her back for her betrayal.

Arkasha walked to a pen near the entry tunnel, where four piglets were confined, feeding themselves from a trough of mash. A dozen of the swine were brought to the tomb every few days. The witch picked up a piglet by its hind legs. The struggling creature was heavy for her to carry, and she had to hold it close and lean her back as she trudged over to the cage. Stopping within a yard, she swung the animal behind her and then flung it through the bars.

The pig squealed in pain as the witch light burned it, sizzling holes appearing on its back and side. Pheng snatched it up immediately in his huge hands. With a growl, he bit into the throat, sucking up blood as the piglet shrieked and shuddered.

When the creature ceased struggling, he brought the carcass over to the wall. He sat down on the pile of straw that served as his bed and devoured the body greedily.

Soon, he thought, he would gather enough power to turn off the disks that kept him imprisoned. Then he would feed on more than pigs.

In the twilight, cool jasmine-scented air drifted in from the garden, carrying the trill of songbirds. Amlina listened in a contemplative mood as she packed her trunk. Tomorrow she would leave the palace again, move back to the House of the Deepmind so she could focus all of her attention on the upcoming Tournament of Witches.

She paused before an open drawer, staring down at the trinketing tools folded in with her garments. A jeweler's hammer, thin steel files, a saw—implements she had acquired long ago in Kadavel and carried on all her journeys since. Strange how one grew attached to certain things—insignificant things really—yet she could not bear to part with them.

Draven walked in, his shoulders tense, face solemn.

"How did the klarn meeting turn out?" she asked.

At Karrol's insistence, the Iruks had convened a formal meeting. They were to discuss how much longer to stay in Minhang and whether to dissolve the klarn. They had resided in the capital for almost two months. Karrol, and perhaps others, were growing restless. Absorbed in her own challenges, Amlina had not paid as much attention to the Iruks as she otherwise would.

Draven's mouth was tight at the corners. "The decision is to wait until after the Tournament, to see how that turns out for you."

"Oh, I am glad." She turned back to her packing.

Draven gripped her shoulders, making her face him again. "Don't you want to hear what was said? Or what we plan to do after your course is settled?"

Amlina showed an apologetic smile. "Forgive me, my dear. I am so distracted. Of course I do." She led him over to sit on the bed. "Tell me all."

The Iruk frowned. "We each have different ideas. Glyssa definitely wants to stay with you. Lonn likes Larthang well enough. Besides, he is content to be wherever Glyssa is happy. Eben is quite satisfied with the life here. He says he will stay whatever the rest of us decide. Karrol, of course, is not happy—though she's been complaining about it less. Brinda just said she will wait and see. I don't know if she will leave with Karrol—and I suspect Karrol might be reluctant to leave alone."

Lips pursed, Amlina nodded. "That is about the outcome I expected."

She started to rise but Draven's strong hands pressed her down. "You haven't heard what I had to say."

"Oh." She stared at him, taken aback. "I just thought—"

"You thought I would be happy to stay with you whatever the others decided." Draven stood up. "That's not how I feel, Amlina. I'm sorry."

She gazed at him, shocked. "Why-What *are* you feeling?"

He threw up his hands, let them flap at his sides. "I don't know anymore. I used to feel you would be my woman no matter what. But I no longer think so. You have found healing for your sickness, and I am glad of it. But now you are changing so much, becoming a great witch of Larthang. This land is strange to me, and you are becoming more like the people here. I am just an Iruk, a barbarian to your people."

"I still love you."

"Perhaps you do. I'm no longer sure." He laid a hand on her shoulder, gently this time. "I hope you win your victory, Amlina, and fulfill the fate you desire. When the Tournament is over, you must decide then how you feel about me. And I will decide how I feel, and choose my own course as best I can."

He flicked a sad smile and walked from the room.

A turmoil of emotion swirled in her: regret that she had not done better to show him her love; fear that she might actually lose him; anger that he should distract her with this problem now, when she needed to prepare for the Tournament.

Her thoughts revolved back to the purification rite. Walking the labyrinth had required her to surrender everything. The vision after made her believe her purpose was to become Keeper of the Cloak.

Was that really her calling—or just her ambition? And would it really mean she'd have to sacrifice everything—even her love?

"That cannot be," she whispered. "It must not be."

Twenty-Six

C lorodice woke before down, possessed by a horrible vision. She dressed at once and roused Elani and the two other apprentices who presently occupied guest rooms in her mansion. Clorodice ordered a team harnessed to her carriage, and the four witches rode along the canal as the sun rose over the city. Leaving the carriage at a gate of the necropolis, they hurried on foot to the hidden sanctuary. What greeted them at the entrance there confirmed Clorodice's worst fears.

Caspia, another witch of the circle, was supposed to be on watch duty below. Instead, she sat on the ground before the stairs, shuddering, her face buried in her hands. Bending beside her, Clorodice used a charm to calm the young witch and make her speak.

"Horrible. Horrible. It is free. I just barely managed to seal the door. But it—he said he would not eat me. He said he will speak to you, my lady."

"So be it." Clorodice straightened.

Setting her face to a grim mask, she started down the steps.

"But, my lady!" Elani cried. "The danger …"

Clorodice glanced over her shoulder, considering. The other two apprentices, warrior witches, carried swords as well as daggers in their belts. Their hands were on the hilts, ready to draw.

"No," she decided. "This is for me to face alone. Stay here, I command you."

Hands folded in sleeves, she descended the steps and marched down the processional tunnel. A key lay on the floor where the panicked Caspia had left it. Clorodice picked it up and turned it in the air. The iron door groaned as it sank into the earth.

The carnage inside made bile rise from her stomach. Clorodice had sensed the phingarr growing stronger, but had never expected he could break out of the light-cage. The second apprentice on duty had paid for this mistake with her life. A torn robe and bloody undergarments littered the floor—along with crushed and splintered bones. The skull, with bits of hair and flesh still attached, was perched on the top of the writing table where the phingarr sat. Calmly, the monster used a talon to turn the page of an ancient book.

He spoke without looking up, the voice hoarse and soft, something between a growl and a hiss. "Lady Clorodice. We must have words."

The former Admiral Pheng was now fully transfigured: broad sloping head with fanged, ape-like lower jaw; massive shoulders; long arms ending in huge, clawed hands. The legs appeared short only in relation to the elongated, furry torso. Standing erect, the creature was nearly seven feet tall.

Visiting here almost every day, Clorodice had watched the changes, reveled in the increasing power she could draw from the being. But now the project had unraveled disastrously.

She raised her hands in a warding gesture. "I am listening."

The yellow eyes came up to gaze at her. "*Now* you are listening. You never thought it would be necessary. You have enjoyed sucking the power through me. But you never imagined I was keeping part of it, that I could use this vile magic myself."

"True. You have surprised me. What is it you want now?"

"Revenge."

Her spine straightened, "You do not frighten me. Whatever force you may be able to summon is nothing to the power I now possess."

"Perhaps. But you also need me, as a source of that power—even as I need you. So for now, at least, we must reach an accord. I want revenge on the others, my uncle and cousins who betrayed me, and on that witch Amlina and her allies, who humiliated me in Fleevanport and led to my disgrace."

Clorodice let out her breath through clenched teeth. "Duke Pheng and his sons are my allies. I need them to accomplish my goals—at least for now. As for Amlina, she is the very reason I was tempted to create your present shape. But the protections around her are strong. The best way to revenge yourself is to defeat her claim to win the Cloak of the Two Winds. Once the contest for the Cloak is over and she is beaten, she will be weaker, more easily taken."

The ogre showed a grimace. "There are also others, her friends— the drell witch, the Iruk girl who used the Cloak against my troops."

She touched her chin, considering. "Those may be more easily slain, if that is your desire."

"Not just slain, *devoured!* I wish to eat them alive and feel their pain and terror. That is the revenge I seek."

Clorodice suppressed a gasp.

"Meantime, I must have other food." The phingarr sneered. "And not just suckling pigs. My hunger for human flesh is insatiable!"

Something had gone wrong with the ensorcellment. By now, as Clorodice understood the process, the phase of needing meat and blood should have ended, the creature, once transformed, living purely on the energies flowing up from the Deepmind. But the archaic texts were cryptic, and in ancient times human life was cheap. Perhaps slaves were used as a perpetual source of nourishment.

"I cannot have you devouring my apprentices," she told him.

"Then find me another source!"

The Keeper of the Keys sighed. It would be dangerous, but there was certainly an abundance of available human flesh in Minhang. The city was overcrowded with commoners—worthless people polluting the place with their indolence and vice. To kidnap and murder even such people as those was a crime, to be sure. But perhaps it was a sacrifice she must make for the higher good.

The phingarr must remain her tool, at least until her new power was solidified and her worthy goals accomplished. After that, she could dispose of the ogre—unless of course she had found a way to make him a compliant slave.

Third Summer in Minhang the days were sunny, the weather as warm as the Iruks had ever known. When the mates finished their morning arms training their garments were drenched in sweat. They would march immediately to the bathhouse to soak themselves in cold water.

In the afternoons, they typically went separate ways. Karrol and Brinda might hike along the shores of Perfect Light Lake, sometimes marching all the way to the lower slopes of Noble Grandfather Mountain. This land was an imperial game preserve, although hunting there was forbidden. Sometimes Lonn and Draven went with them, but more often they would just relax in the shade, lying in hammocks in the garden or on lounge chairs by the lakeside.

When not with Lonn, Glyssa spent much of her time indoors, practicing the meditations and spiritual exercise she had learned from Amlina. For the most part, these helped her maintain a patient and serene demeanor. Still, at times she seemed disturbed by vague premonitions. She spoke little of this, claiming that her witchsight had disclosed no definite visions, only uneasy feeling that might amount to nothing.

Like Eben, Glyssa also spent hours with Kizier, either conversing about the history and society of Larthang, or visiting the reading room in the Tuan's library. Glyssa was slowly learning to read, with the aid of Kizier and Ting Fo, who was still assigned to the Iruks as interpreter and guide. But while Glyssa labored over simple texts, Eben was now reading books of poetry and the writings of Larthangan sages. For him, both the language and the philosophy of Larthang had become a passion.

In the evenings, the mates might attend a concert or party, or take a swan boat out on the lake. When these diversions began to bore them, the Iruks took to wandering beyond the palace walls, visiting the entertainment district on the north canal. After taking supper in a tavern, they would enjoy the entertainments: puppet plays, street musicians, acrobats, and jugglers.

On occasion, Eben, Karrol, and Draven visited one of the floating brothels to enjoy the attentions of perfumed "flower women." Brinda had no interest in physical love, and Lonn and Glyssa were bonded together and shared their bed. Draven claimed these visits were simply a diversion, but Eben wondered if he might also be using them to distance himself from Amlina. As to Karrol, she professed to enjoy herself well enough, though she found the flower women generally a little too soft and cloying for her tastes. Eben, cheerfully drunk, felt no such qualms.

Still, afterward he always experienced an odd sadness. Much as he hated to admit it, he still nursed an infatuation for Trippany the drell. He had not seen her since their one brief encounter in the palace garden. But the more he tried to forget her, the more he longed for her. Although Eben scorned himself for such feeble sentimentality, he came to believe the winged lady had captured his heart.

One evening he stood in the crowd with his mates on a street across from the canal watching a puppet play. Back lit by a lantern, the shadows of the puppets moved across a silken screen. One character, a fat magistrate and adherent to the Thread of Virtue, scolded the audience for their vices—especially the vice of attending puppet plays. Meanwhile, to the crowd's delight, his young wife was being seduced in the next room by a roguish young scholar.

After the show, the klarnmates were ready to return home. Eben, in a melancholy mood, tried to convince Karrol and Draven to visit a nearby brothel, the House of Butterfly Delights. When they declined, he told the mates to go on without him.

"Are you sure we should separate?" Glyssa asked with concern.

"Of course." Eben threw out a hand. "I am a full-fledged warrior, mate."

"You are also on the verge of stupidly drunk," Karrol pointed out.

Eben scoffed. "Oh, I will be fine! I have my knife, and I'll make it a quick visit. The evening is still early. I promise to come home before the thieves and ruffians come out."

Reluctantly, the mates left him. He purchased a small jug of berry wine and strolled down to the canal. But as he neared the flower-festooned barge that was the House of Butterfly Delights, he had second thoughts. The lights, music, and laughter emanating from the brothel suddenly felt less than inviting.

With a dismal sigh, he plopped down on the barrier wall, letting his feet dangle over the gleaming water. As he swigged the wine, he thought back to the puppet play. The puppets were made of colored paper, moved by bamboo rods. But it was only their shadows projected on the screen that the audience saw. Eben recalled a centuries-old poem, wherein the poet compared human life to the puppet plays, the world of appearances nothing but fleeting projections, while that which truly moved the images remained hidden behind some fathomless screen.

Another drink, and Eben's thoughts revolved inevitably onto Trippany. He muttered one of his unfinished verses:

Bright lady with wings,
If you be but a shadow:
More lovely, more fleeting than most ...

A new, vivid light reflected on the water. Eben's head swung to the side and he nearly spilled the jug. A ball of blue radiance had appeared behind his shoulder. As he watched, it expanded and Trippany stepped onto the pavement. Her wings stilled and she grinned at him.

"Hello, my friend."

"Where have you been?" Eben's tone was more surly than he'd meant.

Frowning, she sat down beside him, her slim legs extending over the water. "At the House of the Deepmind. Working hard, you know."

Eben's glance traveled from her face to her belled slippers, then to the wine jug in his hand. "I have missed you," he confessed.

She laid a hand gently on his shoulder. "Ah, my dear. You are my hearty warrior. Who would have guessed you are also so sensitive?"

"I never have been before." Eben took a generous swallow of the sweet wine.

When he lowered the jug, Trippany was smiling at him, her black eyes sparkling. "I enjoyed our dalliance—although it was perhaps reckless of me. You must understand, Eben, that I am a deepshaper and dedicated to my training and duty."

Eben glowered down at the water. "I understand little of Larthang," he admitted. "And you least of all, lovely lady with wings."

She giggled and leaned close, placing her arm around his back. "I have heard some of your poems about me."

"How can that be?" He often ran verses through his mind, but only spoke them aloud when he was alone.

Trippany blushed. "It may be wrong of me, but I have listened to you from the spaceless place. I never intended to spy, but I hear you sometimes in my mind and then I follow the thread. This is easy because we have bonded in physical love, you see?"

Eben's mouth hung slack as he tried to ponder the implications.

"When I hear your poems about me, it is hard not to listen. I hope you are not angry?"

"No. How could I be?" He set down the wine jug and put his arm around her waist. The sensation of her closeness filled him with contentment. She leaned her head on his shoulder.

"I hope ..." he said. "Well, I wish ... Might we have another *dalliance* some time?"

Her delicate body quivered with laughter. "Perhaps, when I am reckless again. But not tonight. It is getting late, and you are inebriated. Shall I walk you home?"

"Very well," Eben sighed. "But let's make it a long, slow walk."

Twenty-Seven

As Third Summer moved into its second month, Amlina was deeply immersed in her preparations for the Tournament. She rose at dawn each morning and spent the first two hours of the day in her austere cell, practicing *wei-shen*, the art of deepseeing. Gazing into a mirrored paper globe suspended from the ceiling, she would empty her mind and let impressions flow in from the Deepmind. After a time, she would summon specific visions—faraway places, faces she knew, events remote from her in space and time.

After breakfast, she moved on to *weng-lei*, the art of magical combat. In an exercise yard adjacent to one of the many wings of the House of the Deepmind, she would practice in duels with other witches—sending a blunt wooden dagger flying through the air, dodging and casting aside missiles sent toward her body from many angles at once, thrusting with her mind to weaken the strength and will of an opponent.

Afternoons she worked on *barang-xing*, the trinketing art, and *jai-dah*, the art of formulation. For her trinket, she fabricated a necklace of chased silver inset with garnets. Into each garnet she poured a design so that, as she touched each stone with her fingertip, a song vibrated in the air—ancient Larthangan music of harp, flute, and drum. The trinket's concept was simple, but after her experience at the examination, when her moonstone fillet was downgraded because it was fashioned using Tathian techniques, Amlina wanted to be scrupulously certain to avoid any suggestion of foreign influence.

She hoped her formulation would prove more spectacular. For many hours she fashioned this design, decided upon after consultation with Melevarry. Built up as a mental construct, the formulation would be released at the Tournament, creating a vision the entire crowd would see—a vast flight of birds moving across the sky.

Finally, at the end of each day, back in her cell, she practiced for the Tournament's final event *quon-xing*, the pure shaping. This art involved casting mental force to create effects in a moment. What effects might be demanded in the contest was not disclosed in advance. Amlina could only prepare by building her mental powers. For hours before sleeping, she moved objects through the air. Mirrored balls, feathered desmets, tiny beads: she arranged them in patterns, set them looping or spinning. Before going to sleep, she would cast a final thought to extinguish her bedside lamp.

Absorbed by this constant routine of witchery, she felt her powers magnified as never before. Yet, as the Tournament neared, a restless anxiety gnawed at the back of her mind. Her confidence, so high after her vision at the purification rite, began to ebb. Frightening dreams troubled her sleep. At times, it reminded her of the dark void, the rapacious despair that she thought she had vanquished. Yet this felt different too—as though it were not her inner mind but some external forces deliberately sapping her confidence. Probing for the source of these impressions, Amlina perceived only impenetrable darkness.

Then, four days before the start of the Tournament, her routine was interrupted. A courier had come from the palace—summoning Amlina to appear before the Tuan at once.

Wondering what this could mean, Amlina changed into fresh garments and followed the messenger through the gates of Ting Ta Roo. A chariot waited at the base of the steps, drawn by a pair of tali. As soon as Amlina climbed aboard, the courier snapped the reins and the giant, cat-like creatures bounded forward. Amlina had to grip the rail tightly to keep her balance as the vehicle careened up the broad streets.

In the late afternoon, the chariot drove through the gates of the Celestial Palace. Down a wide processional avenue, at the far side of a grand plaza, the chariot rolled to a stop in front of the Castle of the Golden Land. A four-story edifice of ancient redwood inlaid with gold and jade, this was the Tuan's most sacred hall—regarded as the ritual center of Larthang. For all the time she had spent in the palace, Amlina had only seen the castle from a distance. *What could it mean that the Tuan had ordered her here?*

Forcing herself to walk with steady dignity, she followed the courier up the steps and past tall, gold-plated doors guarded by imperial soldiers. The courier stopped and pointed her through a vestibule. Amlina marched into an airy hall—and was jolted by a flash of recognition.

She had been here before, but not in her physical body. By the tall red pillars and shiny, white floor, she recognized the hall from her vision—the place she had met the Spirit of the Land and the ancient witch Eglemarde.

On a dais at the far end of the chamber, a cluster of attendants surrounded a tall seat. This was the famous Dark Bright Throne, whose shiny black surface displayed an ever-shifting flow of iridescent colors. The throne was aligned to the exact center of the hall, the palace, and the city. Behind it, in the shadowed light of late afternoon, a perfectly-straight perspective showed a view of courts and gardens culminating in Perfect Light Lake and the distant peak of Noble Grandfather Mountain.

Looking tiny on the huge throne, the Tuan was dressed in white raiment. He and his attendants cast sober glances as Amlina approached.

"Greetings, esteemed Amlina, I regret the necessity of interrupting your preparations for the Tournament of Witches. There is a grave matter we must discuss." The Tuan's voice and demeanor were far from the cheerful child Amlina had come to know. Rather, he spoke with solemn dignity, the avatar of all the Tuans before him.

At the base of the steps, Amlina bowed. "August Ruler, I am of course at your service."

He gestured for her to approach.

Amlina climbed the seven steps of the dais. The attendants watched her with grim expressions, perhaps with suspicion. Amlina recognized a few of them: Wu Tong the Primary Minister, Lord Han Sim, the palace steward, other high magistrates and city officials. One woman wore the red robe of a seer. To her surprise, Amlina also spied a podium holding a large volume with shimmering pages—Buroof the talking book.

The Tuan read her glance. "We sit in the presence of our most trusted advisors, as well as of Buroof, who has given us much useful knowledge."

Amlina bowed her head. "How may I assist?"

The Tuan's gaze was wide and unfocused. "Signs and omens are inauspicious. We had hoped, Amlina, that your arrival in the Land and the return of our lost treasures might mark the beginning of new, good fortune for our reign. But the opposite has occurred."

He spoke as if channeling an oracle. Amlina listened with parted lips.

"The military campaign against Gon Fu has failed. Perhaps a Tuan who was older, not a child, could have been more forceful in averting this disaster."

The statement was questionable, from what Amlina knew. The Iron Bloc was powerful and determined. They had started the war even before the young Tuan was crowned.

"Following on the military debacle, the summer harvest has been poor. There will likely be shortages and rationing. Granaries must be guarded to avoid riots ... These are our concerns not yours, Amlina. But another evil portend has lately appeared, within the confines of Minhang itself. In the past month, five murders have occurred in the northwest warrens. Both adults and children have been killed, seized on the streets or abducted from their homes. Worse, remains that were found were partially eaten. Have you heard anything of these atrocities?"

"Nothing, August Ruler." Absorbed in preparing for the Tournament, she had deliberately avoided news from beyond the walls of Ting Ta Roo.

"Of course, you have been sequestered." After a moment, the boy continued. "In regard to these murders, witnesses have been scarce— indicating the likely use of magical concealments. The two accounts that have surfaced are most bizarre: a shambling beast was seen, accompanied by figures dressed in black, hooded capes. The latter might be sorcerers or even renegade witches from some hidden cabal in Ting Ta Roo. As for the creature, we have consulted our ancestor Tuans and antique books, as well as the tortoise shell oracle. Buroof has been a welcome source of additional information. From all of the evidence, we are led to suspect that this monstrous being is a *phingarr* or anti-self. Accounts of such a creature date back to the centuries of dangerous magic that precipitated the Age of the World's Madness. In those times, Larthangan witchery, the alchemy of the Tathians, and the sorceries of Nyssan were often mixed—sometimes with disastrous results. One reason we have asked you here, Amlina, is that you have familiarity with foreign practices. Do you know anything of formulations that might produce such a creature?"

Amlina swallowed, scanning the faces of the Tuan's advisors. Did they suspect her of creating this abomination? Had some enemy contrived to cast the blame on her?

"I learned small bits of alchemy in the Tathian lands, and I have studied some threads of Nyssanian sorcery. Beryl, the former queen of Tallyba, cast ensorcellments that transformed humans into sometimes hideous shapes. But she kept this knowledge to herself. In any case, on my honor, I would never have pursued such abhorrent magic."

The Tuan peered at her intently. Suddenly, in Amlina's mind, the chamber seemed to fracture. She found herself standing in another hall—like this, but enormously long. From an endless series of redwood pillars, faces peered down at her, reading her depths.

Next instant, she was back on the dais. The boy Tuan watched her with a half-smile.

"The second reason we summoned you, Amlina, is because certain signs and prognostications indicated that you were connected to these murders. By the wisdom of my ancestors, I perceive that you are certainly not the author of the evil. And yet, I still discern a link. The nature of that link is hidden by powerful agencies. One may guess that, since you are not the source, you might somehow be the target. We are aware there has already been one attempt to assassinate you. We counsel you to be careful, and to examine all forces that come into your ken for any sign of malevolence."

"Thank you, August Ruler. I will certainly stay on my guard."

"Thank you for attending me here. The chariot will return you to Ting Ta Roo."

Amlina bowed to the Tuan and then to the courtiers. She backed cautiously down the steps.

"Oh, one thing more." The Tuan had slid from his seat. His manner was once again that of the amiable boy. "I wish you all success in the Tournament!"

As she arrived back at the House of the Deepmind, Amlina's spirit was in turmoil. Intuition told her the Tuan was correct—somehow she was a target of this heinous sorcery loose in the city. Further, these designs somehow connected to her fearful dreams and the forces that seemed intent on sapping her confidence for the Tournament.

Night had fallen as she climbed the steps of Ting Ta Roo. Only three more days till the Tournament's first event. Amlina had missed her scheduled time to work on the formulation. She wondered if she should apply herself to that task before bedtime, in lieu of pure shaping practice. Either way, she decided she would skip supper. She had lost all appetite for food.

Passing through the tall bronze doors, she met with a new interruption. The porter informed her that Drusdegarde, the Archimage, had left word that she wished to see Amlina immediately on her return from the palace.

A neophyte witch was summoned and conducted Amlina down long corridors and through spacious high-vaulted chambers. At the far end of the complex, Amlina trudged up a seemingly-endless spiral stair inside a slender minaret. At the very top, she entered a bare, round chamber walled in gleaming onyx. Drusdegarde sat in the center on a cushion, her body still in meditation.

Without opening her eyes, the Archimage ordered Amlina to shut the door and sit down on the cushion in front of her. Drusdegarde was a slim, vibrant woman, with loose white hair and wrinkled complexion. Her age was unknown, but she had been Archimage for over forty years—meaning she was at least in her nineties.

Eyes still shut, she spoke as soon as Amlina was seated. "Why did the Tuan wish to see you?"

Frowning with annoyance, Amlina launched into an abbreviated account of her meeting.

"Yes, we are deeply concerned by these cannibalistic murders," Drusdegarde interrupted. "Sorcery, no doubt. There are even hints that the origins of this evil lie within Ting Ta Roo itself. As to whom is responsible: we have not yet identified the culprits. But rest assured, we shall. And the Tuan's information suggests a *phingarr*? I shall have to consult the old books on that ..."

"May I go now?" Amlina asked.

"No. You may not. Did the Tuan suggest at all that you yourself might be suspected?"

"He did," Amlina answered, thrusting our her chin. "He examined me and found me blameless. 'By the wisdom of my ancestors' were his exact words."

"Were they indeed? I am happy that he shows such confidence in you. I, myself, must reserve judgment. Like the Tuan, I perceive the influence of barbaric magic. And of all the witches currently residing in Ting Ta Roo, you alone are known to be schooled in foreign arts. It has even been suggested that the assassination attempted on your person was actually a blind to divert suspicion."

Amlina was losing patience. "Is that what you believe?"

The elder witch pursed her lips. "I am not certain. You are favored by the Tuan, and he enjoys the Mandate of the Ancestors. I must respect his judgment—up to a point. My main concern is this: Should you win the Tournament and earn the right to wield the Cloak of the Two Winds, that you will use that great power honorably, in service to the Land, and according to the age-old traditions of this House."

"Had I not wished it so, I would never have delivered the Cloak here."

"Indeed, that too argues in your favor. You have my blessing to compete in the Tournament. But be assured, I and my Councilors will be watching you for any sign of treachery or malign magic."

Amlina thrust herself to her feet. The movement caused Drusdegarde to at last open her eyes.

"You will also be watching the other competitors, I hope," Amlina said.

The Archimage regarded levelly. "You can rely on it."

Part Four

At the Tournament of Witches

Twenty-Eight

T he Tournament of Witches was held each year in Minhang as part of the harvest celebration known as First Winter Festival. In the days prior to the festival, flotillas of paddle boats streamed up the river loaded with grain, swine, and fowl. From north and south came barges bearing cargoes of apples, plums, and pears. From the vineyards of the southwest, casks of new wine arrived at the city docks. The fact that the grain harvest had been poor did little to dampen enthusiasm for the festival—at least in Minhang. From all over Larthang, and as far away as Gon Fu and Zindu, officials, nobles, and wealthy commoners arrived in the city riding in trains of carriages or on pleasure boats.

The walls of the city were decked in flowers. The streets and plazas swarmed with an endless, colorful parade of festival-goers both rich and poor. Scents of smoke and incense flowed on warm breezes from the temples, mixed with the savory aromas of countless cook stalls and the smells of the human crowd and their beasts of burden.

On the first day of First Winter, throngs gathered to watch the Pageant of Witches. To the music of pipes and gongs, the women of the House of the Deepmind paraded to the Celestial Palace. High witches of the Council rode in tali-drawn chariots. Behind them, acolytes and apprentices marched along in their colored robes and hats. Many made signs of benediction to the crowd, or tossed them flakes of glitter or beaded trinkets with magical properties.

The seven competitors in the Tournament of Witches rode in chariots, each standing beside their sponsor. First came Shen Tra Lo, a proficient trinket-maker and apprentice to Kanshi, Keeper of the

Forge. Next followed Von Lui-Tong and her sponsor, the Mage of Long Mountain; Tolanga of Gon Fu, famed warrior witch accompanied by Wicksa, Keeper of Swords; Elani Vo T'ang, apprentice to Clorodice, Keeper of the Keys. In the next chariot stood Liska Quenn of Hanjapore, sponsored by the Mage of that City, and behind her came Ulleena Tuvari, a scholar witch sponsored by Crandora, Keeper of the Books.

Last in the procession, and drawing the loudest acclamation, came Amlina, the returned exile who had slain the Archimage of the West and brought the Cloak of the Two Winds home to Larthang. She was accompanied by her sponsor, Melevarry the Mage of Randoon. To many of the crowd, this was their first sighting of the famous Amlina. Although she stood still and straight and deported herself like a trained deepshaper, spectators remarked how small and frail she appeared—not at all the redoubtable warrior witch they had expected.

Many in the crowd had thought Amlina would be favored to win the Tournament. Instead, the gambling houses in the pleasure district favored Ulleena Tuvari, the scholar, and also Tolanga, the redoubtable warrior of Gon Fu. Amlina's capabilities were too uncertain. The oddsmakers considered her a sleeper and ranked her with the secondary favorites Elani Vo T'ang and Shen Tra Lo the trinket-maker. The other two contestants, unknown witches from the provinces, drew the longest odds.

Staring at the crowd, Amlina herself was contemplating her chances of success. The Mage of Randoon read her thoughts.

"I counseled you before against analyzing the skills of your rivals."

"I know." Amlina showed a wan smile.

Her confidence, already dwindling as the Tournament approached, had suffered twin blows the night she was summoned first by the Tuan then by the Archimage. Those interviews had confirmed her impression of potent, malevolent forces converging on the Tournament and, it seemed, aimed at destroying her chances.

"Do not lose focus, Amlina," Melevarry told her. "All this pomp and fanfare mean nothing. The capabilities of your opponents, the rival factions lending them power—these are beyond your control. All that matters is that you bring your best effort to every event."

Amlina shook her head. "I fear my best may be inadequate."

"Then listen to me," Melevarry replied sternly. "I said in Randoon that I sensed a wildness in you. What I did not express then is my belief that this wildness instills in you extraordinary potential. In these past months, I have seen you work very hard to bring your power under control and align it with rightful principles. I have known many deepshapers in my time Amlina. If you show your best these next five days, I not only believe that you can win but that you *will* win."

Amlina stared straight ahead, affected by the Mage's words and the power in her voice. "My Lady, I am humbled by your confidence in me."

"Don't be humbled," the Mage of Randoon answered. "Be bold!"

That evening the Tuan and the Archimage together presided over the Witches' Ball. The seven contestants for the Tournament were formally introduced at a banquet in an airy feast hall of the Celestial Palace. The contestants and their sponsors dined on the dais with the Tuan, the Archimage, and the highest-ranking witches and officials of the Land.

As soon as courtesy allowed, Amlina excused herself from the high table. She crossed to the far end of the circular hall, where the Iruks and Kizier were seated among other guests. The mates jumped up and embraced her. They had not seen her for nearly two months.

"You feel wonderfully strong," Glyssa told her. "I think you will win!"

Amlina only smiled, wishing she felt remotely so confident of her chances as others seemed.

"We were sizing up your opponents," Eben said. "We hear there's a lot of wagering."

"Indeed." Amlina sat on the bench between Draven and Kizier. "I hope you have not been so foolish as to adopt *that* Larthangan custom."

"Certainly not," Lonn declared. "Iruks are too wise to risk hard-won wealth on matters of chance."

"No," Karrol laughed, "we only squander it on too much feasting and drinking."

"Why do you look at me when you say that?" Eben cried, setting down an empty wine cup.

Amlina joined in the klarnmates' laughter.

"Oh, but he has an excuse tonight," Draven said. "He's performing later, on the poetry stage. He must be a little nervous."

"Not in the least," Eben asserted, reaching again for the pitcher.

"You are reading one of your poems?" Amlina asked with surprise. "In Larthangan?"

"It's not the first time," Eben said.

"Indeed," Kizier confirmed. "Eben has become quite adept with the language. His recitals have drawn some acclaim in literary circles."

"I had no idea," Amlina said. "My congratulations."

"Will you come and listen to the reading?" Glyssa asked.

Amlina hesitated. "Not this time. I'm sorry. I really must return to the House of the Deepmind and prepare for tomorrow."

"We understand." Eben smiled. "You also must perform."

Amlina nodded absently.

"We were talking about how the Tournament works," Brinda said. "I mean, how the winner is decided. Kizier has explained it, and Eben has his own version, but some of us are still confused."

"It can seem rather involved," Amlina admitted. She described how, over the next four days, the seven witches would compete in contests based on four of the Revered Arts: deepseeing, formulation, trinketing, and magical combat. The witch placing first in an event would receive seven points, the second-place finisher six points, and so on down to one point for the witch who finished last.

"Exactly," Eben said. "Imagine seven hunting boats racing each other during ice-fishing season. The first boat to arrive at the first hole gets seven fish, the next boat to arrive, six fish, and so it goes. Then everyone gets back in their boats and they race to the next hole. At the seventh hole, everyone counts their take. The crews with the most fish fight it out, and the winner goes home with all the fish."

Amlina laughed. "That is not at all a bad analogy. After the first four days, the three competitors with the highest scores meet in the final event, pure shaping. The winner of that contest wins the Tournament.

"But what happens if there are more than three?" Brinda asked. "If the scores end up tied?"

"That is why the fourth event is magical combat," Amlina explained. "If two or more witches tie for third place, they duel until only one is left."

The mates looked at one another and nodded.

"As Iruks, we find that a sensible way to settle things," Lonn declared.

Amlina stayed a while longer, enjoying the companionship, feeling how sorely she had missed these friends, their warmth and humor, their brave and loving spirits. But when the banquet was ending and the guests wandering off to other festivities, she decided she had best retire. Draven volunteered to escort her to the outer gates where carriages waited to convey the witches back to Ting Ta Roo.

As they walked together down a long, pillared corridor, Amlina hesitantly reached out and gripped his hand. He had declared that after the Tournament he would decide whether he would stay with her, or leave Larthang. She desperately hoped he would stay.

Suddenly, Draven pulled her aside and hugged her fiercely.

"Oh, my dear one," she whispered. "How I have missed you."

"Yes." His voice was thick.

Amlina leaned back, peered into his eyes. "You have given me so much, and I have returned so little."

His response was direct, befitting an Iruk. "I still want you."

Amlina nearly wept, her emotion so strong. She had nearly lost him once, on the plateau outside the ruined city of Valgool. He had been wounded, near to death. She had journeyed into the spirit world to call him back. She had known then that whatever else she longed for in this world, nothing mattered more than her love. How had she let herself forget? First the taint of the blood magic and her long struggle to heal, then lately her belief in her duty to Larthang— or was it rather her inflated delusions about herself?

"Dear Draven, I have sacrificed some of our time together. Perhaps it was all for foolishness. But in a few more days it will be over. Whatever happens with the Tournament, whatever rank or position Larthang offers me, I want to be with you again. And I will do all I can to make you happy."

A grin spread over his face. "If that's how it is, then I will wait."

Amlina kissed him once, avidly. "Till then, my love." She broke away and ran up the hallway toward the palace gates.

A grand and extravagant celebration, the Witches' Ball spread out through the halls and grounds of the Celestial Palace. Pavilions, terraces, and gardens abounded with music, dancing, puppet plays, and entertainments of every type. The performances began early in the evening and would continue past midnight.

At a late hour, the Iruks and Kizier strolled into a broad garden with chairs arranged on the lawn and lanterns strung in the hedges. A stage at one end held a podium where the poets read, accompanied by musicians playing lute and drum. Grizna, waxing, hung past zenith, while Rog the red moon had risen in the east.

Eben had stopped back at their apartment to retrieve his fur cape. He always wore it on stage, along with the musician's cap, the costume of his poet's identity. While his mates took their seats, Eben walked up to join the line of readers. His step was a bit rocky, and a pleasant thrumming filled his ears. Still, he considered himself far from drunk. He was certainly not the only poet who indulged in wine before and after performing.

When his turn came he bounded up the steps and scanned the audience with a confident smirk. He had thought he might see Trippany tonight, either here or earlier at the banquet, but those hopes had again met with disappointment. He had not seen her at all since that night on the canal, nearly a month ago.

Well, he thought, if she could hear him from the "spaceless place," then let her hear this. He recited:

This land Larthang is rich and ripe,
Rivers shine, warm wind sings,
But of all the folk of the Golden Land,
Loveliest is a lady with wings.

Witches are keen, warriors bold,
But a lady with wings is hard to hold.
Women might love and lovely girls may.
O Lady with wings, will you not stay?

The Iruks erupted with a loud ovation. The rest of the audience gave moderate applause. Kizier had somewhat exaggerated the positive reputation Eben's poetry had garnered. While some courtiers were fervent in their appreciation, citing the Iruk's plain diction and 'forceful barbarian simplicity', more sophisticated critics found these same qualities 'childish' and 'dull.' Eben cared not at all. He viewed poetry as a way to polish his language skills and a pleasant outlet for his feelings.

Walking back to join his mates, he encountered the source of much of those feelings. Trippany the drell stood waiting beside the seated Iruks.

She grinned, her little hands applauding. "I like your poem."

He bowed with a flourish. "The work is appreciated by its inspiration."

"Ha! A nice turn of phrase, that!" Draven declared amid the Iruks' laughter.

"Oh, please!" Karrol cried.

The party adjourned to a nearby grove where music played and cakes and wine were being served. Trippany visited with the group for a while, talking with Glyssa and Kizier about her magical studies, and discussing with all the mates the prospects of the different competitors at the Tournament.

Eventually, Eben managed to convince Trippany to take a stroll with him alone. He picked up a fresh jug of wine and they wandered through the groves and terraced gardens, moving away from the crowds and noise, toward the gleaming waters of Perfect Light Lake.

Trippany wore a sly smile. At times her wings fluttered and she hopped above the path. Eben strode with his customary stalking gait. They spoke not at all.

Finally, they paused at the base of a statue, an ancient water goddess. The pink moon hung overhead. Beyond the path, a broad lawn sloped down to the lake. Eben took a swig of wine and handed her the jug.

"It's nice to be alone with you," he muttered as she drank. "You must be feeling reckless again."

Trippany showed her pointy teeth. "I confess that I am. I've been working very hard, and the Witches' Ball is a night for celebrations." She set the jug on the pedestal, as though making an offering. "Or perhaps it was your poem. I have never felt so flattered."

She leaned in, and her lips brushed his. Eben reached and twined his fingers in her hair, holding the back of her head so the kiss went on and on. Presently, they undressed. Eben spread out his fur cape, and they lay side by side, kissing, stroking each other. Then Trippany pushed him down on his back and sat astride his loins. As they coupled, her wings would flutter suddenly. Eben held tight to her hips and was lifted part way off the ground.

After, they cuddled together, wrapped in the fur. Eben fell asleep to the soft sound of her breathing ...

He woke with a shock as Trippany cried out.

Shadowy figures surrounded them, dressed in hooded capes. Two of them had grabbed Trippany. Their arms held her wings so she couldn't move them. A third pressed a hand over her mouth. Eben scrambled halfway to his feet.

A giant figure loomed above him. A staff thrust down, the point striking below his collar bone. With the pain of the blow, a freezing cold surged into his chest. The staff punched his belly and he doubled over.

Helpless, unable to stand, Eben glimpsed the drell held by three of the attackers. Ropes were being lashed around her ankles, more around her arms and chest. Her wings were pinned to her back so she could not escape by flight. Eben looked up at the figure standing over him, a giant hulking form with long arms and massive chest like some monstrous drog.

Struggling, Trippany let out a muffled scream.

"Cover her face, but do not freeze her," the giant growled. "I want her alive and undamaged."

A staff jabbed Eben between the eyes. Freezing blackness filled his brain.

He who called himself Phingarr Pheng stared eagerly past the bars of the light-cage. The drell maiden, naked except for the ropes binding her, hung by her wrists. Pheng had just removed the sack from her head, and now he watched as her eyes adjusted to the dim light.

Seeing the phingarr's face inches from hers, she gasped. Her shoulders tensed as she tried to beat her wings. Her body writhed, struggling frantically.

Pheng inhaled, savoring her terror with a satisfied smile. "Oh, no, my little insect girl. You're not getting away. You probably don't know me in my present shape, but I remember you well. That cursed back-country off the Polar Sea. You cleverly delayed my forces while the witch Amlina prepared her trap. Not so clever now though, are you?"

The drell shut her eyes and slowed her breathing, trying to calm herself. Pheng felt the intensity of her fear settle slightly.

A woman approached and stood at his shoulder, one of the three witches who had helped him capture the drell. They were Clorodice's followers, ordered to serve him. They had hunted with him during the past month as he captured and devoured his victims in the city. This was the compromise he had reached with Clorodice. She had wanted her followers to kidnap the commoners and bring them to the tomb. Pheng had insisted on going himself to hunt at night, to personally select his human meals. The acolytes, two warrior witches and the one called Arkasha, had been assigned to go with him, to weave concealments as they stalked the streets.

Tonight was the first time they had hunted within the palace compound. With his growing ability of deepsight, Pheng had glimpsed that the drell would lie there, enjoying a tryst with her Iruk lover. He had wanted to take the Iruk too, but Arkasha had balked. Too dangerous, she insisted, too difficult for their concealments to hide them carrying two victims all the way back to the tomb.

"Is there anything else you require, Lord Pheng?" the witch beside him asked.

"No. Leave us. Stand watch in the passageway. I will summon you if I need you."

He heard their footsteps as they shuffled out of the tomb's main chamber, the iron groan of the portal rising behind them. The drell was staring at him now, not only with fear, but a hint of recognition.

"You heard her name me? Yes, I was Shay-Ni Pheng, the commander whose mission you thwarted."

"And now you are changed by sorcery into a foul monster that eats human flesh."

He spread his hands, showing off his body. "*Phingarr* is the proper term." Her fear spiked deliciously. "Oh, don't worry, pretty insect girl. I'm not going to eat you—at least, not all at once." He drew a long pin from his robe and showed it to her. "A drell is a rare dish and should be savored."

His hand moved between the light bars. As he slid the pinpoint over her chest, her courage failed and she gave a sob.

But he drew the pin back without piercing her. "There is also another reason I want you alive. Since my transformation, I have acquired quite an interest in the deepshaping arts. In this regard, you interest me. When you escaped my bowmen in Fleevan, you did not just fly away. You disappeared in a globe of light. I have learned that this means you are gifted with the so-called *second flight*. Now that is a power I could certainly use—if I can learn how to draw it from you ...

He stroked his chin, glanced down at the pin between his fingers. Suddenly, viciously, he thrust the pin into her arm. The drell cried out in pain. Pheng drew the pin back, examined the bloody tip, then slid it over his tongue. He smacked his lips contemplatively.

"Different from human blood, but quite tasty. Yes, I shall enjoy keeping you alive for quite some time."

Twenty-Nine

E ben woke in the night, unable to budge. For an indefinite time he lay on his belly, willing his muscles to move without success. His face pressed down on wet grass. Shifting his eyes, he could just see a strip of the night sky.

By the time the sky brightened, his arms and legs were answering his straining will with spasms and twitches. In agony he fought the paralysis, finally rising onto knees and elbows. With a loud groan he forced himself to stand, wobbled, and fell over.

Dragging himself around on the grass, grunting and cursing, he succeeded in pulling on his clothing. On the third attempt to stand up, he stayed on his feet. He set off in a lurching, drunken walk.

The likeness of his condition to drunkenness settled in his brain with a stab of guilt. He had let enemies creep up and take him in his sleep—his *drunken* sleep. And poor Trippany had paid the price. As a warrior, it shamed him beyond words. He swore on his honor it would never happen again.

He spied enough disturbance in the grass to pick up the trail. He followed it along the lake front, then lost it at the edge of a paved walkway. Cursing, he staggered back toward the palace, legs still weak.

He found his mates on the terraced lawn where they practiced with sword and spear. Karrol and Lonn hooted and laughed when they saw him, but Glyssa noticed at once something was wrong. He stammered that he had been attacked down by the lake, that Trippany had been taken.

"... Three witches or mages, and a creature like a drog," he said. "Maybe it was that ogre that's been eating people out by the canal."

"Here on the palace grounds?" Lonn demanded.

The mates looked perplexed.

"You sure you didn't dream this?" Karrol asked. "Or maybe it's a joke?"

Infuriated, Eben took a swing at her, missed and fell sprawling on the ground. "Do I act like I'm joking?" he groaned.

Worried now, the mates bent and picked him up. Draven and Brinda brushed off his jacket.

"I lost the trail near the lake," Eben said. "The monster said he wanted to keep her alive, so there's a chance. But I don't know how to find her. What can we do?"

"Alert the Tuan," Glyssa said. "If this ogre was on the palace grounds, the Imperial Guard must be told."

The Iruks hurried through the gardens and courtyards to the gates of the Tuan's residence. There, a porter informed them that the imperial household had already departed for the Tournament of Witches. The Tuan was to participate in opening ceremonies at the House of the Deepmind and would then proceed to the plaza in the middle of the city where the contests would be held.

The mates spoke with the sentry on duty. They convinced the man to summon his superior. Presently, a sergeant of the guard appeared and listened to their story. He seemed puzzled as to what to do, but finally agreed to bring the matter to the attention of his lieutenant.

"This is getting us nowhere," Karrol grumbled.

"I have another thought," Eben said.

The residence of the Drell Ambassador was located in a separate building on the southern edge of the palace. Directed there by a steward, the mates arrived in late morning and relayed their story to a gatekeeper. Eben stressed the urgency, that the life of a drell maiden hung in the balance.

After a short time they were ushered into a tall, airy chamber that seemed to take up much of the building. Balconies, galleries, and beams sprouted at many levels from the walls below a ceiling sixty feet high. From one gallery, six drell warriors with lances and shields flew down and landed in front of the mates. They dipped the points in salute. Then another drell, a lone male fluttered down from an alcove high above. He was dressed in blue and gray silks and a jeweled headpiece. He spoke as soon as he landed.

"I believe we have met before, at state functions. I am Spegis Besu Keli, Prince of the Drell and Ambassador to the Tuan's Court. You nobles, I know, are friends of the Tuan and of the witch Amlina."

The Iruks offered stiff bows.

"Your highness, thank you for seeing us," Lonn said.

"I understand you bring disturbing news about my cousin, the Lady Trippany."

The mates turned to Eben.

"I did not know she was your cousin," Eben stammered. "But I—I was walking with her last night, during the ball, down by the lake. We were attacked. I was frozen by some sorcery and could not help her. She was carried off. They were men or women in robes and another, a creature like a drog. It might be the ogre that has murdered innocents in the outer city. I tried to track the attackers this morning but lost the trail. We have alerted the Tuan's household guard but ... I am not sure they took us seriously. That is why we have come to you, sir."

The drell prince touched his thin mustache. "I see. Most perplexing and troubling. Thank you for bringing this to my attention. Rest assured, if my cousin is in danger, I will do all in my power to rescue her."

"How can we help?" Glyssa asked.

The prince glanced at the warriors lined behind him. "Perhaps ... Perhaps if you go back and trace the ground again. I will send some of my guard with you. One of them, Lady Allenawey is, like Trippany, gifted with the *second flight*. She may be able to track her using that power. Meantime, I will make a personal appeal to the Tuan that the Imperial Guard conduct a search, and I will then inquire at the House of the Deepmind, to see if the acolytes of the Archimage might help us."

A short time later, Eben and his mates, armed with swords and throwing spears, marched west across the palace grounds toward Perfect Light Lake. Five drell warriors flew above them, the buzz of their wings disturbing the stillness of noon.

At the center of Minhang lay a giant plaza known as the Circle of Sublime Balance. Four wide avenues ran off from the plaza in alignment with the four directions. East Road led down to the main gates of the harbor on the river; North Road to the front door of the House of the Deepmind; and South Road to the House of Benevolent Justice, where chief magistrates codified and administered the laws of Larthang. West Road was a broad processional avenue leading to the Tuan's palace. It formed an exact line to the Castle of the Golden Land and finally to the Dark Bright Throne.

In the exact middle of the plaza lay the Pool of Perpetual Light, a circular fountain sixty paces wide, the waters aglow with witchlight. In front of the pool, on this First Day of First Winter, a curved stage had been erected for the Tournament of Witches.

Amlina stood at the edge of the stage with the other contestants— six witches of Larthang who had honed their talents and powers to a peak for this competition. In spite of her best efforts to empty her mind and concentrate on the moment, Amlina's thoughts flitted about in agitation. The excited mutterings of the crowd, the chilly brisk wind, trembling emotions within—all distracted her. Amlina shut her eyes and forced herself to breathe deeply. The crucial moment at last at hand, she could not allow distractions to erode her resolve.

In a row of chairs behind the seven contestants sat their sponsors, high witches all, Melevarry among them. Across the stage, five witches sat behind a curved table. Judges for the first event, they wore black robes with hoods, and veils concealing all but their eyes. One judge had an abacus for keeping score. Another held the end of a long apparatus set close to her ear. This device was a listening horn; it curled out several feet across the stage and ended in a wide-open funnel. The other three judges sat behind bound books, heavy volumes containing hundreds of pages.

A gong sounded and the plaza hushed. The Mistress of the Tournament stepped to the front of the stage. She announced ceremonial greetings: first to the Tuan, whose sedan chair loomed high at the center of the plaza; next, to the Archimage, who sat with her entourage in a curtained box adjacent to the stage; then to various other dignitaries.

Amlina waited, breathing deliberately, her palms sweating. Thoughts still jumbled through her mind: images of her friends, the Iruks. She had expected them to be among the spectators, but now could not sense their presence. Some trouble surrounded them, she could feel it.

When the speeches of welcome were concluded, the Mistress explained the day's contest to the crowd.

"*Wei-shen*, the deepseeing, the art of perceiving thoughts, images, and events through no physical sense but through the mind alone. On the table in front of our esteemed judges lie three books containing a total of nine hundred ideograms. Each contestant, by turn, will be hoodwinked and placed at the mouth of the listening horn. The judges will then randomly select and point to a character on a page, which the contestant must name. Correct answers will be totaled for each witch's score. The order of contestants has been chosen by lot. First is Liska Quenn of Hanjapore, sponsored by the Mage of Hanjapore."

From the front of the line, Liska Quenn walked to the mouth of the listening horn. She was a short woman with broad shoulders, dressed in robes of green and gray. She removed her hat, and two acolytes placed a black silk over her head. An official asked if she was ready to proceed, and she nodded.

A black curtain was drawn in front of the table—concealing the five judges from the competitors and spectators alike. The gong sounded, and all grew quiet. Presently, Liska spoke into the horn, her voice a soft murmur.

Eyes closed, Amlina focused on seeing each picture in her mind. Before long, she found attunement and believed she was watching the pages turn and fingertips touching the ideograms. Some believed it was an advantage to go later in the competition, as it allowed the witch to practice in just this way. Others asserted it was better to go early, lest the mind become overstrained. By lot, Amlina was sixth of the seven contestants this day.

When her turn finally came, she felt calm and focused. The silken blindfold slid easily over her head. Relaxed, she waited for the vibration of the gong to fade, then started announcing the pictures that came to her.

"River ... crown ... barking dog ... cherry blossom ..."

For a time, her deepsight remained clear, her heartbeat slow. But gradually, hardly perceptible at first, a mist rose in her vision. The characters darkened, edges blurred.

"Fallen wall ... motherhood ... tooth ..."

The darkness shimmered and thickened. The thought came that some force, some design, was deliberately obscuring her deepsight. That was supposed to be impossible. For an entire month preceding the Tournament, the House of the Deepmind brought vast energies to bear in fashioning barriers against such interference. A power able to pierce those barriers would have to be enormous ...

Amlina shook herself. That very line of distracted thought had caused her to miss four or five images. Grinding her teeth, she strained to pierce the thickening fog in her brain.

"Butterfly ... shield ... white cloud ..."

By the time her hundredth character had been presented, her deepsight was all but blind and she plucked wild guesses from the darkness. The hoodwink was removed. Crestfallen, she slumped over to stand with the other competitors, wondering how badly she had failed.

She was forced to wait another quarter-hour while the seventh contestant took her turn, and then the scores were tallied. At last, the Mistress of the Tournament walked to the edge of the stage.

"August Tuan, esteemed witches, nobles and citizens of Larthang: here are the results of the first competition. In first place, earning seven points, Ulleena Tuvari of Minhang ..."

Above the stage, a golden cloud condensed in the air. Written on the cloud in flaming red letters, the names, ranks, and points earned appeared:

	Deepseeing	Total
Ulleena Tuvari	1st - 7	7
Tolanga of Gon Fu	2nd - 6	6
Shen Tra Lo	3rd - 5	5
Elani Vo-T'ang	4th - 4	4
Amlina Len Tai	5th - 3	3
Liska Quenn	6th - 2	2
VonLui Tong	7th - 1	1

Amlina had finished fifth and earned three points. Given her relative skills in the four remaining arts, she had hoped for at least a third-place finish in deepseeing. Her trinket and formulation would have to score very high indeed. Even more troubling was the power that had interfered with her vision. Was it truly some hidden deepshaper intent on destroying her chances? Or was it yet another weakness in herself, arising at this crucial moment to cripple her hopes?

Returning to the House of the Deepmind, Amlina wondered disconsolately if she now had any chance at all of winning.

Strands of power like glittering ribbons flowed and shivered in her vision-space. At the center, radiating the strands sat a bulky figure in a mirror of polished bronze: the Phingarr. Yes, the anti-self was the source, but she, Clorodice, wove the strands. One old book likened the sorcerer performing this work to a spider at the center of her web. Clorodice appreciated the aptness of that analogy. She was spinning a web of fates, not only for herself and her allies and enemies, but for the Land itself. The power was intoxicating.

Outside, in the physical world, she felt a disturbance. She squeezed up her face in irritation, opened her eyes. A furtive knocking sounded on her study door. She had left orders not to be disturbed.

"What is it?"

The door slipped open. The steward's apprehensive face appeared in the crack. "Forgive me, my lady. Duke Pheng insists he must see you."

Before she could answer the door swung wide. The Duke, in cloak and plain garb, pushed past the anxious servant.

"Very well. You may go." Clorodice said.

The steward hurriedly closed the door. The Keeper of Keys made no effort to hide her irritation as Duke Pheng crossed toward her. Nor did she rise from her cushion.

Pheng loomed over her. "My lady, we must talk."

"What is so urgent, Lord Duke, that you disturb these critical workings?"

A sour frown crossed his face. "I'm afraid this ogre of yours, this *phingarr*, has gotten out of control. He apparently attacked last night on the palace grounds and carried off a woman, a cousin of the Drell Ambassador. Now the Imperial Guard is investigating."

Clorodice drew in her lips. "I am aware of it."

Pheng's forehead creased, his eyes bulging. "You are aware of it? And yet you sit so placidly unconcerned?"

"My Lord Duke, calm yourself. The phingarr, your *nephew*, remembers his former life and has an agenda of his own."

Irked and agitated, the Duke threw out his arms. "And what is his agenda?"

Clorodice showed a sly half-smile. "He seeks revenge on those he feels have wronged him—yourself and your sons among them."

"What?!"

"Take hold of yourself, my lord. Of course I won't allow harm to come to you or your sons. But if the phingarr is to serve our purposes, his cooperation must be maintained. Therefore, I have channeled his lust for revenge against others, ones he believes caused his disgrace—the drell witch is one, Amlina and her barbarian warriors are others."

"But he cannot be allowed to roam the palace at will!"

Reluctantly, Clorodice climbed to her feet. "I agree. I think he himself may have found a solution to that problem. He is seeking to adapt the drell's gift of second flight to his own use. If successful, he'll be able to transport his body outside the bounds of normal space—to appear and disappear at will, to some extent."

Pheng's jaw dropped. "So he will attack his next victim, at the palace or elsewhere, and then disappear?"

"Precisely."

"I am not sure how that is any less risky for us. And I fail to see why you allow him such dangerous freedom."

Calmly, Clorodice walked to a nearby table and picked up a crystal decanter. "I warned you at the start that the phingarr would have a will of his own."

"Yes. But you led me to believe you could control him."

"And so I am." With steady hand, she poured amber wine into crystal tumblers. "And let me remind you of the benefits we are reaping. The powers I am able to manipulate through this design are enormous—enough to overcome all the barriers put in place by the House of the Deepmind to prevent interference in the Tournament. Today, I was able to obscure Amlina's deepsight and lessen her score in the first event. In a few days more, Elani Vo'Tang will be champion and the Cloak will be ours."

She offered a tumbler to the Duke. He eyed it glumly, then accepted.

"I appreciate your abilities, my lady. As an ally, I value you most highly. Still, I advise you to keep the phingarr under better control. Delay any further attacks until after the Tournament. Then, if the ogre is discovered and killed, we are well rid of him."

Clorodice returned his hard stare. She had in fact obtained the ogre's promise to delay hunting any more victims until after the Tournament. But the Duke need not be appeased with this knowledge. Instead, she said: "I advise *you*, my lord, to leave the management of these matters to me. We are playing for high stakes, and some risks must be expected." Eyes not leaving his, she sipped her wine.

The corner of his mouth quirked, and she could sense his rage. Would he challenge her further? No, he would see no advantage in that. Instead he smiled thinly and sipped.

"As you say, Lady Clorodice, the phingarr is your creation and must be yours to control. I only ask that you minimize the risks as best you can—for the success of our most worthy causes."

He drained the tumbler and set it down.

The Duke departed a few moments later, leaving Clorodice to ponder his intent. Would he dare to denounce her and expose her sorcery? Unlikely. His hand was too deep in the affair. But the Duke was an expert conspirator. No doubt he had more than one scheme in mind to dispose of her and her circle should the need arise.

Clorodice touched a finger to her lips. The day might come when she would need to turn the tables on Duke Pheng, eliminate him and his sons.

No doubt, that would make the phingarr very happy.

Thirty

D on't you think we should at least *inform* Amlina?" Eben stared
belligerently at his mates around the table. "Trippany is her
friend too."

"No," Glyssa answered. "If there was something Amlina could do
that is not already being done, I might agree. But there is nothing."

The Iruks were sharing a spiritless supper with Kizier and Ting
Fo. The paneled doors of their common room were closed against the
evening chill.

"Besides," Draven added, "she is isolated in the House of the
Deepmind. The only time we might contact her is when she is on her
way to the next event. Should we rush up from the crowd shouting
our story to her, when she is trying to concentrate? It would only
distract her and hurt her chances."

"Your mates are correct, Eben," Kizier said. "The Archimage
assured Prince Spegis that she and her acolytes are applying all their
powers to discovering the ogre. I cannot imagine there is anything
more Amlina could do."

Eben gazed numbly down at the table, his food mostly untouched,
a wine cup he had refused to even fill. He had sworn off drinking
until Trippany was found. He knew his friends were right.
Everything that could be done was being done. Still, the helplessness
infuriated him.

All day the klarn, the Imperial Guard, and the Drell Ambassador's
guard had searched the palace grounds and along the lake shore. In
the afternoon, while the Tuan's forces examined the forests on the
southern shore, the Iruks and drells had crossed the bridge over the
north canal and inspected the vast City of Tombs. They had found no

trace of the ogre. Likewise, the drell Allenawey reported that she had discovered nothing using second flight, that potent concealments had obviously been invoked. Tomorrow, the Iruks and drells planned to search the city warrens beyond the canal, the district where the ogre's earlier attacks had been reported.

"There is one more thing we can do," Lonn announced.

Eben and the rest fixed him with expectant gazes.

"It seems we have been called to a new hunt," Lonn said. "I think it's time to raise the klarn."

The Iruks nodded. Without another word they rose from the table. Glyssa picked up a clean goblet and filled it with water. Lonn led the way to the terrace door and slid it open. Across the terrace and down the steps, they came to the corner of the garden where six spears stood, thrust into the ground. They formed a half-circle.

Eben watched, nerves humming, as Lonn took the cup from Glyssa's hand. Holding it, Lonn paused to look each of the mates in the eye.

"Now is the time for hunting," he said. "We awaken the klarn and call its strength into our hearts, our limbs, our blood." He took a sip, then poured a libation on the spot where his spear-point pierced the earth.

Lonn handed the cup to Glyssa. She repeated the ritual and passed it on to Brinda.

As each libation was poured, Eben attuned his mind to his mates, calling the klarn-soul into his body. The familiar presence rose in him, as it had so many times before, but not in these past few months. When his turn came, he spoke the words and sucked the air deep into his chest. Handing the cup on, he felt calmer and more filled with purpose than he had since coming to Minhang.

Under a gray sky, cold drizzle descended on the plaza. Discouraged by the chilly weather, a smaller crowd had gathered to watch the second event of the Tournament of Witches.

The Tuan occupied his usual place at the center of the plaza, a protective awning stretched over his high ceremonial chair. But the Archimage's curtained box beside the stage was vacant. From the rumor Amlina had heard, Drusdegarde and many of her Councilors were absent due to a critical security matter they were investigating. The members of the Inner Council who were sponsoring candidates in the Tournament occupied their usual seats on the stage, Melevarry among them.

After speaking hasty greetings and welcomes, the Mistress of the Tournament introduced the day's contest.

"The competition in *jai-dah*, known as formulation, the creation of mental constructs that are stored in the Deepmind and then released at a chosen moment. In the time prior to the Tournament, the competitors have woven their formulations. Now they will come forward, in the order chosen by lot, and cast them before our eyes. Our esteemed panel of judges will tally their scores based on the revered criteria of felt potency, presumed difficulty, and stylistic beauty. Although these evaluations may appear subjective, they are in fact based on ancient codified systems of measure. The judges' decisions are final."

Nervousness rising, Amlina scanned the crowd. Toward the back, she thought she spotted Kizier standing beside the Iruks' tutor, Ting Fo. But once again the Iruks themselves were not to be seen. Their absence caused Amlina not only curiosity, but a gnawing worry. She resolved to send a message to the palace after the competition to inquire after her friends.

The gong was struck, its solemn note reverberating across the stage.

The first contestant, Elani Vo T'ang, stepped forward. She cast upon the stage the illusion of a series of bronze and iron doors. Each door swung open amid smoke and flames and clashing sound. The final door opened to reveal the serene avatar of a goddess seated in perfect poise.

Next, Von LuiTong presented an orchestra of musical instruments which, though lacking players, produced a creditable rendition of a popular song.

Liska Quenn of Hanjapore misfired on her attempt, creating only vague outlines of a giant puppet play with blurred figures and muffled sounds.

Tolanga of Gon Fu's effort was more impressive. With the wave of two swords she cast forth a pair of automaton warriors who dueled and roared across the stage with convincing skill and ferocity.

Amlina observed the performances with a mild, detached air. Her pulse was slow, her mind focused on summoning her own formulation when the time came.

When her name was announced, she moved easily to the center of the stage. But as she shut her eyes and called the formulation to mind, a blankness descended—the same interference she had felt the day before. The act of releasing a formulation was simple; she had not expected the unknown force might trip her again.

After an instant of panic, she instinctively reached a hand to her wet hair and touched the moonstone fillet—the trinket of protection she had fashioned long ago. The touch reassured her. Flinging out her arms, she cast her power.

Her woven vision flashed above the stage. Auspiciously chosen for such a dreary day, it revealed a lucid blue sky illumined by a faint sun and streaming with flocks of spiraling birds. A vision from the far polar region of the world, it drew exclamations of awe and delight from the audience.

When the last witch had performed, the judges totaled their scores. Once again, the rankings for the day and the running total were displayed in a cloud above the plaza.

	Formulation	Total
Shen Tra Lo	1st - 7	12
Elani Vo-T'ang	2nd - 6	10
Amlina Len Tai	3rd -5	8
Tolanga of Gon Fu	4th -4	10
Von Lui Tong	5th - 3	4
Ulleena Tuvari	6th - 2	9
Liska Quenn	7th - 1	3

Amlina had finished third, not as high as she had hoped. The five points gave her eight overall, putting her in fifth place—but only two points behind the two witches who were tied for second. At least she was still in the running.

As she joined the procession back to the House of the Deepmind, she brooded over the obstruction she had felt again at the crucial moment of performance. She wondered if this mysterious force might be related to the security matter that had caused the absence of the Archimage and her Councilors.

Phingarr Pheng moved through a curling tunnel of cloud set with rings of orange flame. Of course, those visual manifestations were an illusion: in fact his body moved in a realm beyond space. Directed by will, steered by ravenous desire, he flew eagerly toward his prey.

Ahead, the tunnel ended in a jagged portal of light. Arriving there, Pheng stared down into normal space. He peered into a bedchamber of the Tuan's palace. Below on the bed two people slept—an Iruk man and woman. It was the woman he wanted.

Effortlessly, the phingarr's body seeped through the portal. Floating toward the bed, he reached down for the one named Glyssa. His claws had almost touched her when her eyes shot open. She gasped, then growled like a warrior in a sword fight. She flung up her arms to push him away. Sneering, Pheng floated toward her, talons extended.

But the man beside her moved with sudden speed. Roaring, the Iruk dropped an arm down beside the bed, then twisted his body and lunged, a sword in his fist. Pierced in the belly, Pheng gasped in shock and pain.

Instantly, he retreated back through the portal. It closed behind him in a burst of light and sizzling heat.

Cursing his failure, Pheng streamed up the tunnel of spaceless passage. Soon the rings of light dissolved around him. He stood once again in the underground tomb.

The belly wound caused a piercing ache; the Iruk's sword had struck deep. Hissing, Pheng wiped his belly with a huge hand, stared at the dripping purple blood.

"My lord, you are hurt?" The witch Arkasha stared at him, pale and worried.

"Yes, I failed. This time. Come, place your hands on the wound. Assist me in regenerating the tissues."

The witch hesitated, her face aghast.

"Come!"

Reluctantly, she sidled forward. Wincing, she placed both her hands over the wound and cast healing energies. As Clorodice's senior subaltern, Arkasha had lately been assigned to stay continually in the tomb, attending to the phingarr's needs. Plainly, she liked the duty less and less.

Pheng placed his hand over hers, adding his will to the staunching of blood and knitting of flesh. Opening his other hand, he examined the amulet still clutched there: a topaz stone set in a web of gold filaments.

He had taken this trinket from one of the lesser witches, then imbued it with the second flight talent stolen from the drell. At first, he had thought he would need to cut off the maid's wings, but that had proven unnecessary. Simply stroking the delicate wings had given him the ability to siphon off their power. From there, it was a simple matter to encase the power in the amulet. Whole new worlds of knowledge were opening to his mind. He could scarcely remember the time when he shunned the studies of magic and sorcery.

In this first foray, the amulet had worked flawlessly. He had known that the Iruks occupied a residence in the Tuan's palace. Once he mastered the skills of mental navigation, moving there through the corridors of light had been almost effortless. Had he not underestimated the barbarians' vigilance, he would have carried off his prize.

He remembered Glyssa all too well, the one who had wielded the Cloak that morning in Fleevan and routed his forces. He had chosen her to be the first of the Iruks to feel his vengeance. Next time, he would be better prepared.

Now he grabbed Arkasha's wrists and pushed her away.

"The bleeding has stopped. Enough for now. Bring food."

Cringing from his touch, the witch slumped off. Across the tomb's main chamber, she opened a cell and went inside. After a moment, she emerged, leading a small boy by the wrist. The child moved sleepily, his mind well-enthralled. The flesh would be tender. Pheng licked his lips.

His eyes roamed to the far wall, where the drell witch lay curled on a pile of straw in a corner of the light-cage. The phingarr needed the power drawn from her wings, and so he kept her alive. Still, he allowed himself a taste of her exotic blood every so often, scraping his talon over her skin. Soon, he thought, the Iruks would be caged beside her, and later, the witch Amlina. And when they all had been devoured, perhaps his cursed uncle the Duke and his equally treacherous sons ... Perhaps, in time, even the witch Clorodice herself. How he would enjoy torturing all those who had betrayed and humiliated him.

Pheng sat down on the floor and picked up the boy with both hands.

"Do we still think we should not inform Amlina about what's happening?"

Eben left the question hanging in the air for any of his mates to answer. The Iruks sat at the low table in their common room over a breakfast of rice cakes, fruit, and tea. They had just received a message from Amlina by courier, which Kizier had read aloud. The witch had noticed their absence at the Tournament events and simply inquired if all was well.

"All is *not* exactly well," Eben added. "We are facing an enemy who carried off one of our friends, and has now attacked two of the klarn in their bed."

"An enemy that Lonn's sword drove off," Draven pointed out.

Eben shrugged. "So you believe we should keep all this from Amlina?"

"I did not say that," Draven answered.

"I think we must tell Amlina the truth," Glyssa said. "She has a right to know. But we should not make the tale sound worse than it is, and not ask her to abandon the Tournament to come to our rescue. We are surely able protect ourselves, as Lonn proved last night."

Eben leaned a hand on his chin. "I hope you are right about that."

Their deliberations were interrupted by a butler approaching the table. "Your pardon, nobles. Guests are at the door: the Ambassador of the Drell and two of his attendants."

Shortly, Prince Spegis and two drell maidens flew into the common room. As they landed, Eben saw that one of them was Allenawey, she who possessed the second flight.

"My friends, please pardon the intrusion."

The Iruks rose from their bows.

"Of course." Glyssa gestured at the breakfast table. "Will you sit? May we offer you refreshment?"

"Thank you. No. We are here because Lady Allenawey sensed a disturbance during the night, which she believed resulted from a manifestation of second flight. She was able to trace the source to this wing of the palace. When I learned your residence is here, we came at once. Did anything unusual occur in the time after midnight?"

"You could certainly say that," Eben replied.

Lonn and Glyssa described the creature's appearance in their bedroom and how Lonn stabbed it and drove it away. Lady Allenawey asked to examine the room. After flying around and touching all corners of the chamber, she reported definite traces of spaceless travel, but that the trail was now too faint to follow.

"If I may make a suggestion," Prince Spegis said. "Having been thwarted in its purpose, the creature might attack again. If Lady Allenawey were on the scene, she might have a better chance of following."

The Iruks all indicated agreement with the plan. "Lady Allenawey is welcome to stay with us for as long as she wishes," Glyssa said.

Absorbed in her vision, Clorodice stared at the baleful countenance of the phingarr, reflected in the mental construct of a bronze mirror. Its form seethed with unbridled power.

The beast was becoming too hard to manage. Increasingly, the phingarr seemed to yield up the power grudgingly, to retain more and more for himself. In the formulation contest, Clorodice had succeeded in bolstering Elani's performance, such that she finished second and was now tied for second place overall. But Amlina had finished third. Clorodice's efforts to sabotage the renegade were not as successful as they should have been.

It might be necessary after all to destroy the phingarr once the Tournament was done. That course too had its dangers. Clorodice's life-force was now so enmeshed with the anti-self that killing the creature while preserving her own mortal life would, by all accounts, be a delicate operation.

But first she must tend to the Tournament and ensure that Elani won the Cloak. For a period of time she channeled psychic power to her apprentice, strengthening her for the upcoming contests.

Then Clorodice turned her thoughts on Amlina, whom Clorodice still perceived as the most dangerous threat. Tomorrow's event was trinketing, an art on which Amlina prided herself. The trinkets of all the contestants were already forged, of course. Clorodice's chance would come at the moment the magic of Amlina's trinket was unleashed. With pure shaping power drawn from the phingarr, she would tamp down the trinket's effect.

Then another idea came to mind—Amlina's sponsor, Melevarry. Was the Mage of Randoon casting hidden power to influence the Tournament, even as Clorodice herself? Highly improbable. Probing at the notion, Clorodice verified it was not so. And yet, Amlina plainly drew emotional support from her patron. Would removing that support undermine Amlina's confidence? Might that be enough to tip the scales for the Tournament's later events?

The idea appealed. Melevarry was herself a low-born witch from the provinces, her attitudes permissive, her positions in Council often hostile to those favored by Clorodice and the Thread of Virtue. It was only because of Melevarry's sponsorship that Amlina was even considered a candidate for Keeper of the Cloak.

Yes. Upon rightful reflection, Clorodice concluded she was justified in launching an attack on the Mage of Randoon. And this was something she could do without drawing on the phingarr.

Rising from her meditations, she walked to a secret cupboard and gathered the materials she would need—candles, a brass brazier, a witch's knife, tinctures, and oils. She filled the brazier with charcoal and placed it on a table. She set the candles in a half-circle in front of the brazier—all except one. That candle she carved into a rough approximation of a woman's form.

Whispering her intentions, Clorodice lit the charcoal and then the candles one-by-one. Chanting, she poured the oils and tinctures into the flames. As the fires burned she continued to chant, affirming again and again that the carved waxen image was identical to Melevarry, the Mage of Randoon.

Finally, the moment came. Clorodice unleashed her magic and dropped the carved candle into the flames. She gazed wide-eyed as it sizzled and burned.

Thirty-One

The seven witches competing in the Tournament had been assigned private rooms in a residential wing of Ting Ta Roo. On the morning of the third event, as Amlina dressed for the procession to the Circle of Sublime Balance, she was interrupted by a knock on her door. She opened it to find a chamberlain in the company of a courier from the palace. Amlina was handed a scroll bound by a wax seal.

Unrolling it, she found a letter written in Kizier's hand. In response to her message from the day before, he assured her first that he and the Iruks were neither sick nor injured. But Amlina read in growing alarm as the rest of the letter disclosed her friends' situation. Eben had been assaulted and Trippany carried off. Everyone believed the attacker was the same ogre reported to have committed murders in the outer city. Two nights later, the creature appeared from nowhere to attack Glyssa and Lonn in their bed. Kizier took pains to make it clear that the mates felt able to defend themselves and did not want Amlina to quit the Tournament. They had enlisted the aid not only of the Tuan's Imperial Guard, but the Drell Ambassador Prince Spegis and his warriors.

Amlina had not even finished the letter when another crisis snatched her attention. A neophyte witch appeared in the doorway to announce that Lady Melevarry begged Amlina to attend her. The Mage of Randoon had fallen ill and was unable to leave her apartment.

Hurrying to the Mage's chambers, Amlina found her sponsor lying in bed, attended by her apprentice Wenpheenae Chon and another witch who wore a healer's sash. Two maid servants stood nearby. The air held a close, sickly smell.

Melevarry appeared withered, as if her very life force had been drained. Amlina intuitively recognized the signs of a magical attack. Glancing warily at the others present, she kept that thought to herself.

In a parched and shaky voice, Melevarry asked to be left alone with Amlina and Wenpheenae. When the others had gone, the Mage took hold of Wenpheenae's hand. She fixed Amlina with a bleary eye.

"You see what has happened to me?"

"You were attacked, I think."

The Mage nodded. "A potent and malicious mind, scrupulously hidden."

Acting instinctively, Amlina laid her hands on the Mage's chest and used pure shaping to send healing energy. Melevarry looked surprised, then relaxed into a peaceful smile.

"Thank you, my dear. But you must save your strength for the Tournament."

Amlina stiffened. The Mage struck down, her friends at the palace attacked, an ogre out of ancient legend loose in the city. All of that added to the mysterious power interfering with her actions on the stage. All linked, she thought, by some hidden purpose.

"With all the potent evil at work," she murmured, "my ambition to win the Tournament hardly seems to matter."

"No, you are wrong," Melevarry whispered. "A conspiracy is afoot, to be sure. More, it comes from within the House of the Deepmind. Wenpheenae's deepsight and mine both agree on this. But as Mage of Randoon, I have little importance in Minhang. Why should the conspirators attack me—unless to undermine you? Whatever their ultimate goals may be, it appears ever more critical that the Cloak be won by a witch who can be trusted—trusted to act nobly and serve the Land righteously ..."

Her voice trailed off as she struggled to breathe. Amlina squeezed her hand. On the other side of the bed, Wenpheenae's face was etched with grief.

"My noble Amlina," Melevarry sighed. "I am sorry I cannot stand on the stage with you today. But you must go there and do your best."

"*Barang-xing*, commonly known as trinketing. In this art, the witch generates a magical design and binds it to a material object, allowing the power to be unleashed by herself or another person at a later time." Standing before the crowd, under a pale and cloudless sky, the Mistress of the Tournament described the third trial. "As chosen by lot, the seven contestants will display their trinkets to our esteemed judges and then unleash their designs here on-stage. As with yesterday's event, the effects will be evaluated on the bases of potency, presumed difficulty, and style."

Amlina scarcely listened, her thoughts lost and ominous. The friends she held dearest in the world were in danger. A compulsion to rush to their aid gripped her. Yet she had promised Melevarry that she would continue the competition. And that was what Kizier and the Iruks also urged. The Imperial Guard, the Archimage's Council were both battling the threat. For Amlina to believe she could do more was arrogant and foolish. No, she must keep her promise to Melevarry and do her best.

Her purpose was to serve the Land as Keeper of the Cloak. But was that still even possible?

Full of foreboding, Amlina watched as the witches walked forward one by one to show their trinkets.

Von LuiTong held up a lacquered tortoise shell. When she set it on the stage, a giant, living tortoise seemed to hover above it. Slowly, it rotated in the air, the shell flashing with ideograms foretelling good fortune for the Tuan and the Land.

Elani Vo T'ang displayed a snow globe, then dashed it on the floor. As it shattered, a blinding snowstorm blew out of the sky, winds shrieking. The blizzard lasted the space of several heartbeats, then just as suddenly vanished.

Tolanga of Gon Fu's trinket produced a warrior drog that strutted across the stage, waving twin swords. Shen Tra Lo opened a vial of green glass, producing a spume of purple smoke. From the smoke emerged a book with arms and legs, which walked about the stage and answered questions shouted by the crowd.

When Amlina's turn came, she produced from her robe her necklace fashioned of silver and garnets. Holding it high, she tapped each red stone in turn. The garnets emitted their cheerful music—tunes of harp, flute, and drum that echoed over the plaza.

Even as the charm spread, Amlina felt less power in it than she expected. Had the hidden interference struck again, diminishing the trinket's effect? Yes, perhaps. But she also had to admit that several of the competitor's entries were more impressive. In constructing her trinket, she had scrupulously avoided using techniques she had learned outside of Larthang, for fear they might be noticed and disqualify her work. Maybe she had been too cautious.

The final contestants displayed their trinkets, and then the judges tallied the scores. When the golden cloud appeared overhead, Amlina's heart sank.

	Trinketing	Total
Shen Tra Lo	1st - 7	19
Liska Quenn	2nd - 6	9
Elani Vo-T'ang	3rd -5	15
VonLui Tong	4th -4	8
Ulleena Tuvari	5th - 3	12
Amlina Len Tai	6th - 2	10
Tolonga of Gon Fu	7th - 1	11

All her hopes had been pinned on today's event. Finishing sixth, she now stood at ten points total, fifth in the list. Even if she won tomorrow's event, magical combat, she would most likely finish outside the top three.

She had done her best it seemed, and she had failed.

When the procession returned to the House of the Deepmind, Amlina stepped down from the chariot but did not go inside. Instead she wandered off, thinking a walk through the city, away from the House of Witches where she had been sequestered for so long, might clear her head.

Still wearing the ceremonial robes of the competition, she roamed back along the wide North Road, lined with civic buildings and mansions with their gated entryways and walled gardens. The crowds had thinned, festival goers heading off to their dinners or evening entertainments along the canals. The sky grew dim, a wet cold breeze blowing from the north.

Dusk had fallen by the time she returned to the Circle of Sublime Balance. The witchlight bubbling up from the huge fountain shimmered in the gloom. Amlina stared for a time at the center of the pool, where porcelain statues spouted their many jets of bright water. Eventually, she circled around and marched up the East Road. As she walked toward the Tuan's palace, a cold rain began to fall.

The sentries at the monumental gates were surprised by her appearance—a witch in fine robes arriving unescorted at dusk, soaked from the rain. Extra security was in force, and the guards held her until a captain could be summoned. This officer recognized Amlina from both the Tournament and her past residence in the palace. Still, because of his strict orders, he would not simply admit the witch to the palace grounds. Instead, he sent a guard to the Iruks' apartment. A while later the man returned, followed by Brinda. The Iruk woman wore linen clothing but carried sword and dagger in her belt. She confirmed Amlina's identity and that she was a welcome visitor.

"Your Larthangan is much improved," Amlina observed as they marched along the peristyle of a vast courtyard. Brinda, who seldom spoke at all, had conversed fluently with the captain.

The Iruk showed a faint smile. "Yes. We have all been working hard on the language. Even Karrol is improving. Why are you here?"

Amlina gazed straight ahead. "Because I needed to be with my friends."

"I thought you had to stay in the House of Witches."

"Not strictly speaking. The isolation is recommended, but not required or enforced. I received Kizier's letter. Is all well with you?"

"Yes. There have been no more attacks. We are keeping watch day and night, as we would on a boat. Draven and Lonn are sleeping now. There is also a drell warrior with us."

Traversing the courts and corridors, they arrived at length at the Iruks' quarters. Eben, Karrol, and Kizier gathered at the entrance to greet the witch. Glyssa ran up and hugged her.

"But you are soaking," Glyssa exclaimed. She asked the butler to fetch a towel, then led Amlina over to the marble hearth where pine logs burned. When Amlina was seated, feet propped before the fire, Kizier handed her a cup of hot tea. Lonn and Draven, wakened by the commotion, walked in from one of the bedrooms. The drell warrior flew in from another room to join them. Lonn introduced her as Lady Allenawey.

"What are you doing here?" Glyssa demanded.

Surrounded by her friends, Amlina felt warmed by more than the fire and tea. Draven stood behind her, hands resting on her shoulders. She pressed his hand.

"I needed to be here," she answered. "I missed you all."

"But what about the Tournament?" Eben asked.

"I ... did not do well today. My chances now of winning are very low. I will go back tomorrow but ... it's really not important. What *is* important to me is that all of you are safe and that I weave what protections I can to keep you safe."

Amlina listened while the mates recounted everything that had occurred, from the time Eben and Trippany were attacked on the lake shore. In turn, she described the attack on Melevarry, and the concealed power that seemed to be thwarting her at the Tournament.

"I feel these events are all connected," Amlina said, "tied up with some far-reaching purpose. The Archimage and her Councilors are supposed to be working on the problem, but so far it seems they have not been able to pierce the concealments."

When she had rested and warmed herself, she asked all of her companions, including the drell, to stand together in the center of the floor. Drawing the dagger from her belt, Amlina paced around the group, tracing a circle of witchlight. The blue radiance sizzled and touched the air with a faint, burning smell.

Standing within the circle, Amlina flung up her arms and murmured a chant. Through the power of pure shaping, she invoked a sphere of protection to cover them all. When she lowered her arms, the blue light was fading, but the atmosphere felt alive with magic.

"That is better," she said. "Now at least I have done what I can."

After thanking her, Lady Allenawey flew off to her room. Kizier returned to the fireside. The Iruks still hovered around Amlina.

"You look tired." Draven held her upper arm. "Would you like us to take you back to the House of the Deepmind? Or would you rather stay here tonight?"

Amlina hesitated. She had not thought beyond casting the protection. The thought of staying, of sleeping warm beside Draven, was hard to resist.

"There is one other thing we can do." Glyssa peered into the witch's eyes. "Two nights ago we raised the klarn-spirit. We can summon it again, and you can join us."

Amlina looked around at the Iruks, who watched her intently. "Would all of you agree to this?"

"Of course," Draven said. "Yes," said Lonn. Karrol, Eben, and Brinda nodded. "You were klarn with us before," Karrol added.

Amlina wondered: To merge her spirit with the Iruks' group soul again, to share their strength—the notion was as remote from authorized Larthangan witchery as one could imagine. But what did that matter, if it might strengthen her, help her protect Draven and Glyssa and the rest? She had scrupulously avoided all foreign influence in constructing her trinket—with the result an uninspired failure.

Her voice trembled. "If you will have me, then I will join you. Thank you all."

The Iruks laughed. Karrol and Eben patted her on the back.

A short time later, dressed in cloaks with hoods, Amlina and the mates walked across the terrace and down the steps to the garden. The Iruks had armed themselves and each held a spear. Draven had fetched an extra spear, which Amlina now carried.

The rain had slackened, but the wind was blowing colder. They stopped in a corner near the terrace and planted the spears in the ground. Glyssa handed the water cup to Lonn.

"The hunt continues. The klarn is with us." He drank and then poured a libation. "But now a mate returns to join us again. Amlina of Larthang, I remind you of your oath. Will you now take up your spear and join us with all your heart and courage?"

"I will."

"And do you swear on your soul, and on the souls of your ancestors, to hunt with us as one, to cherish our lives above even your own, to stand with your mates, protecting them with all your strength and skill, binding their wounds before your own, sharing with them even your last food or sip of water?"

"I swear it," the witch said.

"And do you take this oath freely and with a true and open heart?"

Her eyes met Draven's. "Freely and with all my heart."

"Then place your spear in the earth beside ours."

When she had done so, Lonn handed her the cup.

"Drink and give an equal drink to the klarn, and so become once more our mate."

The wind gusted as she lifted the cup to her lips. The wet cold reminded Amlina of the early days in Fleevan, when she had last felt this closeness with the Iruks. As she drank, the cold changed to a warmth that spilled down into her stomach and then swelled up into her heart. She watched as the cup was passed around, the mates drinking and pouring libations in turn. The warmth spread into an energy she remembered well, a tingling power born of the icy cold of the South Pole and the warrior blood of the Iruk folk. It brought Amlina peace and contentment, all her tensions slipping away.

So that, when the ritual had ended and they returned inside, a deep weariness possessed her. She leaned against Draven as they walked.

"You are exhausted," he said. "You had better stay here tonight."

Amlina gave a drowsy smile. "May I sleep next to you, dear Draven?"

For answer, he swept her up in his arms. "I would be glad of it."

Thirty-Two

For the fourth day of the Tournament, the stage had been reconfigured. A curved platform now extended on posts over part of the fountain, with gaps and narrow beams arranged over the bubbling water. Under a clear sky, the largest crowd yet filled the plaza, spectators pressing close to the stage and the fountain basin. Magical combat was always a popular event.

Once again, the Tuan occupied his tall golden chair at the center of the plaza. The Archimage and most of her Councilors had returned to the curtained box beside the stage. According to rumor, Drusdegarde's assistants and other high-ranking acolytes continued their investigations at the House of the Deepmind. Like yesterday, Melevarry was absent from the row of sponsors seated at the rear of the stage.

But Amlina did not feel alone. The spirit of her mates was with her. After a deep, untroubled sleep, she had risen strong and rested. The untamed energy of the Iruk klarn vibrated inside her like notes plucked on a lute. The music filled her with assurance and poise.

After eating breakfast together, the klarn had separated. The Iruks planned to continue their search for Trippany, this time tracking along the north shore of the lake as far as Noble Grandfather Mountain. Amlina, at their urging, had returned to the Tournament—though she recognized it was now highly unlikely that she could win. *Weng-lei*, which combined pure shaping with ritual fighting techniques, had never been her strongest art. With her slim body, Amlina lacked muscle and physical vigor compared to most of her opponents. Besides, even if she finished first today, the points earned might not be enough to place her in the top three and into the final. Having accepted the likelihood of failure, she had resolved to simply give her best.

On the far side of the stage, the panel of judges sat on a raised platform. Below them, twelve Warriors of the Chrysalis stood ready to challenge the contestants. The alatee were clad in their blue-scaled armor and armed with practice weapons—staffs, wooden swords, crossbows with blunt rubber-tipped bolts. Under the rules of the event, each witch would duel first one, then two, then three of the alatee together.

Inwardly still, Amlina stood at the side of the stage and watched as the first duels unfolded. Standing on a narrow beam over the water, staff in hand, Elani Vo T'ang easily kept her balance while holding off her opponent. After two parries, she jerked the staff back toward herself, a gesture that tangled the warrior's feet. The man had to drop his staff and place both hands on the beam to save himself from a dunking. Up on the platform, the judges slid the beads of abacuses. Elani had earned base points for the win plus additional points for the speed and style with which she dispatched her opponent.

The witches who followed also won their first duels, although these took longer. Surprisingly, the current overall leader Shen Tra Lo struggled defending herself with the staff. But finally she cast it, one-handed. This tactic caught the warrior off-guard. The staff struck his forehead before he could parry and the contest was over.

When her turn came, Amlina strode to the front of the stage, received her staff, and bowed to the judges. She climbed the wood steps to the balance beam, then edged to the middle. Her opponent was a woman, tall and thick-bodied, who grinned at her fiercely.

The moment the gong sounded, Amlina dove forward. Her weapon lanced out and struck the alatee's thigh. The woman jerked back, stance widening, rear foot retreating a step. Amlina was still crouched low. She pushed off with both feet and a burst of mental force, springing high above the warrior's shoulder. As the woman lurched, head rising to keep Amlina in sight, she again lost balance. Amlina landed behind her on the beam and thrust her staff between the warrior's legs. A quick wrench of the staff and the warrior toppled, falling into the pool with a loud splash.

The crowd burst into cheers. The Chrysalis warrior stood in the chest high water and saluted Amlina with a wave of her staff. Amlina rose slowly and paced back along the beam. The klarn-soul had inspired her bold and reckless attack. The very lightness of her body she had turned into a weapon.

Inwardly quiet, Amlina watched the last of the first-round duels and then the commencement of the second round.

Those combats took place at the front of the stage. without the hazard of the beam and water. Armed with two wooden swords, each witch now fought two alatee at once. A witch garbed in black stood nearby to referee.

Tolanga of Gon Fu showed the reason for her fame as a warrior. From the first moment she attacked ferociously, shouting, wheeling, cutting through the air with both curved swords, she kept her two opponents on the defense and easily won the match. Liska Quenn also put on a strong performance, while Elani Vo T'ang faltered a bit and Ulleena Tuvari actually lost her match.

Amlina went next. She hefted the two swords and marched toward the Chrysalis warriors, pointing a tip at each. When the gong crashed they charged simultaneously. Amlina was forced to retreat, leaping away from the swinging weapons. As she moved, a numbness seized her brain. With a pang of terror, she recognized the same sorcery that had thwarted her on previous days. But this time she met it with determination—the fierce determination of the klarn at the time of killing.

In her months with the Iruks, she had occasionally taken part in their arms practice and had learned some of their moves. She employed them now, lunging low, twirling with speed, parrying with one sword as she thrust with the other. The unfamiliar tactics made the alatee unsure. Amlina danced behind one of them and caught his back with a wide, hard cut. The referee ruled this one out of the contest. Amlina then turned both swords on the other warrior, jabbing and thrusting until he too was defeated.

Panting from exertion, Amlina lifted her swords in salute, first to the table of judges, then to acknowledge the spectators roaring their acclaim. So far, she had done better than she expected. Unless the judges marked her down for using the non-Larthangan battle tactics, she believed she must have scored high indeed.

The third and final contest moved again to the balance beam. Now the witches were required to stand at the center, alone and unarmed. From the platform opposite and the stage below, six warriors would shoot volleys at them with crossbows. The contestants must protect themselves with mind force alone, with extra points awarded if they could make the blunt-tipped arrows drop from the air or—a harder challenge—turn them back against the archers.

Amlina watched the first witches face the trial. Liska Quenn and Elani Vo T'ang emerged unscathed and managed to make a few of the bolts stop and fall into the water. Shen Tra Lo was less successful, her wide sleeves actually touched by a few of the bolts.

Then Amlina mounted the beam, feeling calm and ready. Once again, she felt a dim, hazy energy seeking to undermine her. As before, she was able to seize and reverse the force, turning it into power she could wield. When the gong tolled she slipped into a state of high awareness. The bolts seemed to drift toward her slowly. Amlina flung out her hands and steered them aside, plucking a few with her mind and turning them back whence they came.

Six times the volleys flew and six times Amlina commanded their motion through the air. At the last, she could hear roars of approval flowing across the plaza. Of the thirty-six bolts launched, none had touched her, and fully half had flown back to land among the archers. She turned and walked calmly back across the beam.

In nervous anticipation, Amlina waited for the judges to count the scores. This took longer than on the past days, and the panel of witches hovered together, conferring in low voices.

Finally, the Mistress of the Tournament received their consensus and strode to the front of the stage. As she announced the results, the gold cloud appeared above her.

	Combat	Total
Amlina Len Tai	1st - 7	17
Tolonga of Gon Fu	2nd - 6	17
Liska Quenn	3rd -5	14
Elani Vo'Tang	4th -4	19
VonLui Tong	5th - 3	11
Shen Tra Lo	6th - 2	21
Ulleena Tuvari	7th - 1	13

"The marks for the first four events have now been totaled. Be reminded, people of Larthang, that the top three contestants will go on to the final event tomorrow, which will determine the overall champion.

"In first place with 21 points, Shen Tra Lo, sponsored by Kanshi, Keeper of the Forge. In second place, with 19 points, Elani Vo'Tang, protégé of Clorodice, Keeper of the Keys. For third place, there is a tie between Amlina Len Tai, sponsored by Melevarry the Mage of Randoon, and Tolanga of Gon Fu, sponsored by Wicksa, Keeper of the Swords. By rule, these two, Amlina and Tolanga, will now compete against each other in a duel. The winner will claim third place overall and advance to the final event."

Elated, Amlina strained to keep her mien calm, her steps balanced as she and Tolanga walked forward. They were met at the center of the stage by the referee, who handed them not wooden weapons, but swords and daggers of steel.

"Honored sisters, you will meet at the center of the balance beam. The blades, as you see, are real. Though blood may be drawn, bear in mind it is neither necessary nor desirable to kill your opponent. But, unlike the previous combats, I will not judge fair blows or foul—All tactics are fair. The contest will end when one of you falls from the beam, or yields, or is incapable of continuing. Do you both understand?"

As they nodded, Tolanga stared smiling into Amlina's eyes.

"It is an honor to face in combat the slayer of the mighty Archimage of the East. I have watched you fight today, Amlina, and seen your canny tricks. Be assured, I will not be so easy to vanquish."

Amlina bowed. "I too am honored to face in combat the renowned warrior Tolanga of Gon Fu. Let the aegis of the Deepmind decide which of us is more fit to compete in the final event."

The gong sounded. The two combatants parted and marched to opposite ends of the stage. A hush lay over the Circle of Sublime Balance as Amlina and Tolanga mounted the steps and eased their way toward the middle of the beam.

Feet braced wide, sword and dagger pointed, Amlina faced her opponent. The moment the gong struck she lunged with the sword. Tolanga parried and thrust, keeping her dagger in reserve. Amlina was forced to retreat, waving her blade, watching for an opening to cast the dagger.

Tolanga was fast and strong. Once, twice, Amlina lost her balance and teetered on the edge of falling. She kept her feet by mind-force alone, but this cost her. Tolanga cast her dagger, steering it with her mind. Amlina yanked her head aside, not quite in time. The blade sliced her cheek as it hurtled by. Feeling the sting, Amlina dove low to avoid the dagger's flying return.

She could not win by the strength of her body, only by her mind. With that thought, she seized on a new strategy. Even as she dodged and parried Tolanga's fierce assault, she poured pure shaping into her adversary's muscles, numbing them, sapping their strength.

For a few moments, it worked. Tolanga's attack faltered. Amlina advanced, thrusting and then swinging her blade, touching Tolanga on the lower leg, though the cut drew no blood.

Tolanga realized what was happening. "You won't beat me this way," she snarled.

With a growl she shook her arms and resumed the attack. Once more, Amlina was forced to edge backward. Now her pure shaping met with strong resistance. Tolanga's blade swung faster.

Amlina's arms grew heavy, her defenses slowed. In moments, she would be finished. Only desperate, foolhardy measures remained. With all she had left, she grasped at a chance.

Drawing back her arm she cast the dagger. The instant after she released it, she also flung the sword—both aimed at Tolanga's face. Tolanga parried with both her blades, but the unanticipated action cost her a moment's imbalance. Amlina darted forward. Inches from her opponent, she shoved with both hands.

Tolanga's heavy body lurched. For a moment she teetered, then with a cry of despair she fell. As the splash erupted, Amlina stood precariously on the beam, flapping her arms to keep her own balance.

After steadying herself, she wiped her cheek and gazed at the blood wetting her palm. Loud cheering filled her ears.

Below in the water, Tolanga fixed her with a scowl. Then, shaking water from her thick arms, she burst into a laugh. She bowed to Amlina, her forehead touching the bright water.

Up on the beam, Amlina bowed in reply—carefully so as not to fall.

A short time later Amlina, with bandaged cheek, lined up with the rest of the contestants to receive their honors. Backed by an entourage, the Tuan presented gold medals to all seven witches, denoting their participation in the Tournament. The Archimage then named the three finalists, Amlina included, and placed over their heads medals of silver wrought with jade.

Thirty-Three

P hingarr Pheng flew down the tunnel of spaceless passage, one hand wrapped around the topaz amulet, the other clutching a staff imbued with the freezing power. This time he was ready for the Iruks' defenses.

Ahead and below floated the jagged doorway. As he approached, he gazed into the chamber beyond. Just as last time, the young Iruk woman Glyssa lay in bed, her lover asleep beside her—the one they called Lonn, the one who had pierced Pheng's belly.

Pausing a moment to gather his force, the phingarr sprang through the portal. Materializing, he landed heavily on the bed. Even as Glyssa let out a cry of shock and Lonn dove for his sword, Pheng froze them both with jabs of the staff. Shouts and footsteps sounded from outside the room. The phingarr snatched up Glyssa's inert body and flitted back into the wavering portal.

Another moment and he was streaming up the passageway of shining rings. The Iruk woman moaned and strained. Grinning, Pheng clutched her tightly against his massive chest.

Then a disturbance caught his attention. A glance over his shoulder showed a pursuer in the distance, a slim body with bee wings beating furiously. Another drell, it seemed, had the talent of spaceless passage. The phingarr hissed, wondering if he should stop and attack the drell. But he knew nothing of fighting in the spaceless realm, even touching her with the freezing staff might be futile. Instead, he cast all his strength into flight, surging toward the far end of the curving tunnel.

As he neared the portal into his lair, he could see that the drell was slowing. Suddenly her figure faded and disappeared. The concealments woven by Clorodice had succeeded once again.

Roused from sleep by the alarmed shouts of his mates, Eben sprang out of bed and grabbed sword and spear. Rushing to the common room, he met Karrol and Kizier. Draven and Brinda had been on watch, and he found them in the bedroom where Lonn and Glyssa slept. They had charged into the room on hearing a scream, only to spot a burst of light disappearing over the bed. Glyssa was gone. Lonn lay on his back, rigid, eyes staring at the ceiling. From time to time a faint growl of rage escaped his throat.

"He is frozen, as I was by the creature's staff," Eben declared. "Where is Lady Allenawey?"

"She flew in just after we got here," Draven said. "She shifted into second flight and gave chase."

"Go and put on your armor," Brinda told Eben and Karrol. "We'll try to rouse Lonn."

Eben returned to his room and quickly dressed in quilted shirt and trousers. He pulled on boots and strapped on his leather harness, adding sword and dagger to the scabbards. By the time he and Karrol returned to the other room, Lonn was sitting up, Draven and Brinda briskly rubbing his arms.

"Glyssa was taken," he grunted. "Did the drell follow?"

"She did," Draven assured him.

They were hoisting Lonn to his feet when a ball of light burst near the ceiling. Lady Allenawey swooped to the floor.

The Iruks shouted all at once: "Were you able to follow?" "Did you find Glyssa?"

"I could only follow part way," the drell answered. "Then a barrier appeared—unlike anything I have ever met in the spaceless realm. Strong sorcery, no question."

"Does that mean you lost the trail?" Eben cried.

"Not entirely. When I could not pierce the barrier, I dropped out of the spaceless place. I found myself near the lake, at the entrance to the City of Tombs. I believe the creature's hiding place must be near there."

"Go after her," Lonn croaked. "I will follow when I'm able. Go now!"

The Iruks agreed and left Lonn in the care of Kizier. While Allenawey flew off to alert Prince Spegis and bring more drell warriors, Eben, Karrol, Draven, and Brinda set off at a run across the gardens and lawns of the palace. Above them, full-faced Grizna hung near the summit of the sky. In the northwest, waning Rog shone like a red sword, beckoning them to the ancient tombs.

Phingarr Pheng stood smiling through the bars of the light-cage, gazing down at the helpless Iruk woman. Still wearing her nightclothes, she lay on the floor of the cell, straining to move her arms and legs.

"I remember you, *Glyssa*," he whispered. "I recall very well how you scattered my troops using the magic Cloak. But you are not so powerful now, are you, little barbarian?"

For answer, the girl grunted and rolled over, turning her face away.

"I will keep you here for a while, I think. I would like to capture a few more of your friends and imprison them. That way, they can watch from the cages as I eat you alive."

"My lord," the witch Arkasha spoke insistently at his shoulder. "Lady Clorodice urgently requires to speak with you."

"Bah!" The phingarr waved impatiently. "What does she want with me? It is still night."

"She has tried to reach you since you invoked the spaceless travel. She says it is most important."

With a grunt, Pheng turned from the cage. He held out his arm, and Arkasha dropped a ruby amulet into his giant paw. Clutching the ruby, he skulked across the stone chamber to a chair like a heavy throne, specially built to support his huge body.

Seating himself, he shut his eyes and called up the amulet's power. Immediately, his mind sank into a mild trance. He perceived a sky of gray mist and then, floating in the mist, the witch Clorodice seated cross-legged on a cushion. Her expression was vexed.

"I thought we agreed you would wait until after the Tournament."

"I agreed to nothing. You surmised." Actually, he did recall promising something of the kind. "I grew impatient. Anyway, it is done with no harm. I have the Iruk woman."

"By abducting her you have invited more scrutiny—and at this most critical juncture. The final event will be contested in just a few hours. Elani must emerge victorious. Yesterday, her performance in the combat was less than I hoped. Worse, I lacked the power to prevent Amlina from winning through to the finals. There can be no more failures."

"Very well," the phingarr grumbled. "What do you want of me?"

"We must draw more power from the Deepmind. We must begin weaving the ensorcellment at once."

Even as she spoke, Pheng felt the tendrils of her will reaching out, drawing him in to her design. He choose not to resist.

"I am at your service, Lady Clorodice. But remember: after the Tournament, Amlina and the rest of her band will be mine."

In the twilight before dawn, Eben and his mates stalked through the City of Tombs. Iruks disliked trespassing in the domains of ghosts, but any qualms they might have felt were banished by the urgency of the hunt for Glyssa.

They had searched half the night, by the pink light of Grizna and the faint, bluish glow of the nearby lake. They had traveled as far as the swampy woods on the western edge of the necropolis, then doubled back. Spread wide but within hailing distance of each other, they examined tracks on the grass and sandy trails, sniffed the air, and tried to sense Glyssa's presence through the klarn-soul. Lonn had found them an hour ago and joined the hunt, walking awkwardly, his body still stiff and sore. From time to time a hum of wings overhead disclosed one of the drell warriors searching from the air.

As the sun rose, the Iruks and drells gathered to rest in a circle of stone arches, the ruins of a mortuary temple. Prince Spegis and two of his servants had arrived, bringing water, dried fruit, and rice cakes. Sharing the meal revived the Iruks' flagging spirits.

"All of us here except Glyssa," Karrol muttered. "This reminds me of the other time we lost her. It took us months to find her then, but we did in the end, and she was all right."

"True," Eben muttered. "Amlina helped us find her in Kadavel."

"Amlina should be with us now," Lonn said. "She is klarn, after all."

The Iruks considered. "Today is the final event of the Tournament," Eben pointed out. "She is competing and can still win."

"No. Lonn is right," Draven answered. "She is klarn. She will want to know."

"How can we get word to her?" Brinda asked.

Eben looked up. "Perhaps one of the drells?"

As it happened, Prince Spegis was already planning to fly to the House of the Deepmind to inform the Archimage of the ogre's latest attack. He agreed to also convey the klarn's message to Amlina. As the others resumed the search, the prince and his servants flew off toward the city.

The sun climbed higher as the Iruks hunted through the northern districts of the tombs. Five of the drell warriors scouted from the air while the sixth, Lady Allenawey, tried again to pick up the trail through the spaceless realm.

By late morning, the mates were searching along the north wall— a far-reaching barrier built at various times of brick or stone blocks, crumbling in places, still solid in others. At one spot a stony road led through a gate and then over a bridge that spanned a dry gully. Eben knelt in the road, scrutinizing tracks left by cart or chariot wheels. Some of the tracks looked fresh.

Eben shouted to his mates. Lonn, and then others ran over to join him.

"I remember some cart tracks when we searched this place a few days back," Eben said. "Looks like more now."

Lonn nodded. "Seems a lot of traffic for a road so far from the city. I wonder we didn't notice it before."

"We were looking for ogre footprints," Eben noted. "Also ..."

"Also what?" Karrol asked.

"Well, if there is sorcery at work to hide the ones who made these tracks, they might have escaped our notice."

"Right," Lonn agreed. "Let's see where they lead."

Bent low, spears in hand, the mates crept down the trail, back among the tombs and low hills. The track crossed other paths as it wound past age-old monuments and walls shelved with urns. But most of the wheel- and paw-marks followed a definite path, which seemed to grow plainer as they went.

The trail ended at the base of a hill under a broken obelisk. In a gap of the hill, a flight of steps descended to a blackened iron door.

"It might just be wishing," Draven muttered, "but I have a sense Glyssa is under that hill."

"I feel it too," Karrol said.

She ran down the stairs, followed by Lonn and the others. The door was solid, framed by iron and stone. The mates examined the edges, but could find no lock or hinge or even a gap to pry.

Frustrated, Karrol banged on the door with the pommel of her sword. "Glyssa! Glyssa, can you hear me?"

Eben had another thought and ran back up the steps. Spotting one of the drells in the distance, he waved his arms and shouted. By the time the drell landed, the other Iruks had climbed out of the pit.

"Can you bring Lady Allenawey?" Eben asked the drell. "We may have found something."

Presently, Allenawey arrived, accompanied by the rest of the drell warriors.

"We think our mate might be down there," Eben told her. "Can you use second flight to get past the door?"

"I shall try," the lady answered. She lifted her arms and her wings came to motion, quivering with a high-pitched whir. An aura of light swelled and she vanished.

In a few moments, the drell reappeared, looking breathless and strained. "No. I could not pass within," she whispered.

Eben frowned. "There is nothing you can learn?"

Allenawey shook her head. "On the contrary. The thwarting of my second flight tells me this place is the center of the concealment."

"Well then," Karrol said. "We just have to find a way inside."

While the mates were debating whether to try digging around the door or to first search over the hill for another entrance, they spied more drells approaching. Prince Spegis and his attendants landed on the ground before them. Lady Allenawey quickly apprised him of the situation.

"That is excellent news," he said. "I will return to the city at once. The Keeper of the Keys, Lady Clorodice must be informed. She will likely have the means to open the tomb."

He was about to take off again when Lonn gestured to stop him. "Did you give our message to Amlina?"

"Ah. Regrettably, no. I did speak with the Archimage. But by the time I arrived the procession was about to begin. Lady Drusdegarde would not allow any communication with Amlina or the other contestants—an added precaution, she said, against interference in the Tournament."

Thirty-Four

All morning Amlina had been troubled. Suspicions hovered at the edges of her mind, but when she tried to examine them, the thoughts flitted away like phantoms.

She rode a chariot, rolling slowly along North Road. The way was lined with colorful crowds come to watch the final event of the Tournament. Dressed in a red and gold robe, wearing her moonstone fillet, Amlina stood beside the chariot driver and gripped the rail with one hand. With the other, she waved, acknowledging the cheers. Yesterday, she had considered herself out of the Tournament. Today, one of three finalists, she could hardly focus on being here.

Her mind kept turning to the Iruks and the suspicion that they were in danger. But no matter how hard she probed with witchsight, no matter how determinedly she tried to invoke the klarn-soul, she could perceive nothing definite—only a vague and hopeless despair. Was their plight concealed by sorcery? Or was her mind simply too scattered and confused by nervousness and exhaustion from all she had been through these past months?

After the recent rains, the air was crisp, the sky bright blue. Arriving at the Circle of Sublime Balance, the procession pushed slowly through a vast, milling throng. Once again, the staging for the event had been changed. Curtained boxes and galleries now formed a half-circle around the Pool of Perpetual Light. These seats were occupied by the Tuan and his royal court, exalted magistrates and officials, and the highest-ranking witches of the House of the Deepmind. The rest of the fountain basin was open to spectators who pressed and jostled close against the edge.

On an island at the center of the pool, porcelain statues of fish, dolphins, turtles, and sprites normally poured water in arcs and gushes. Today all were quiet. Instead, a giant column spewed from the mouth of a huge fish at the island's center. Three high seats were set up near the edge of the basin, widely spaced but equidistant from the water spout. A plank bridge and short ladder connected each seat to the fountain's rim. Before each seat, a wreath of golden flowers floated on the rippling blue surface.

Amlina and the other finalists were each led to their places, ready to cross the plank walkways and mount to the high seats. A flourish of trumpets sounded, followed by the tolling of gongs. The Mistress of the Tournament strode along the rim of the fountain and faced the crowed.

"Welcome, one and all, to the final event of the Tournament of Witches. *Quon-xing*, pure shaping, is the fifth revered art. It is the spontaneous use of mental power to create effects in the world. Today's contest is simple: from their chairs over the pool, the finalists will seek to bend the arc of the waterspout, to draw it toward them by mental force. Whichever witch succeeds in bringing the falling water to the center of her wreath of flowers will be crowned champion."

The Mistress introduced the finalists, beginning with Elani Vo T'ang. As Elani marched over the walkway toward her seat, Amlina stared around at the fountain and the crowd. Her vision wavered. Her ears burned and dizziness fluttered into her brain.

Amlina. Amlina.

Glyssa? Even as she recognized the voice, she sensed fear and terrible danger.

Amlina, we are one. Our minds are one.

Glyssa was seeking to forge a mental link, as they had done many times before. *Yes, Glyssa. I hear you. Are you in danger?*

I have been captured ... by the ogre. I am in a cage. I think our mates are outside.

In the Circle of Sublime Balance, Elani Vo T'ang had taken her seat. The Mistress was announcing the second finalist, Shen Tra Lo.

In moments, Amlina would be called to step onto the rim of the pool, to walk to her chair, and compete. She believed she had a chance to win.

But that would mean breaking the mind-link with Glyssa.

Winning the Cloak was supposed to be her purpose, her destiny. But if that meant abandoning her friends—That was no choice at all.

I hear you Glyssa. Reach out for me. We are one. Our minds are one.

Before her eyes, the fountain shimmered and disappeared. Amlina fell to her knees.

Her eyes blinked, strained to see—a wide stone chamber lit by candles and lamps. Hands rose into view. They were not her hands.

I am with you Glyssa. I see from inside your mind.

"Yes, Amlina. I feel you with me. I am so grateful."

Glyssa rose unsteadily to her feet. Amlina felt aches and stiffness. The chamber was dusty, a cavern or tomb, the air close and stuffy.

Nearby, radiant beams lanced between the floor and ceiling.

"The bars make a cage. They burn like fire." Glyssa showed a blistered hand.

Beyond the cage, at a writing table, a black-robed witch sat reading by lamplight. At the center of the chamber, a monster covered in coarse white hair sat slumped on a throne. Eyes closed, the creature appeared to be in trance. Perfectly still, it yet emanated immense, unfathomable power.

"The ogre," Glyssa whispered. "He is linked in mind with one called Clorodice. I heard him speak with her after he first brought me here. I could not move, but I heard him. The witch at the table serves them both. She is named Arkasha."

Clorodice. Arkasha. I know the names, Amlina answered. The puzzle pieces were falling together. Clorodice was tapping the power of this ogre, a creature engendered by sorcery, to bend the outcome of the Tournament—so that her apprentice, Elani Vo T'ang would win and claim the Cloak.

Glyssa turned her head and they peered into another cage nearby. A small, fragile form lay curled on a pile of straw. "Trippany is there. I think she is still alive."

We must get you out first, Amlina told her. *Then we'll come back.*

"Yes. I think our mates are outside. I heard Karrol shouting some time back."

Good. First we break open the cage. Then—Are you fit enough to overpower Arkasha?

"Oh, I should think so."

Good. We'll force her to let you out. And if our mates are waiting outside, they can come in and slay the ogre.

"What if he wakes before we get out?"

Amlina peered again at the creature. She didn't expect he would break out of trance, not while the Tournament hung in the balance. *I don't think he will. But we'll have to risk it.*

"How do we break the cage?"

Let's see.

Prompted by Amlina, Glyssa stepped closer to the beams. Their joined minds probed, searching. Amlina perceived jeweled disks embedded in the floor and ceiling, projecting each fiery bar.

Do you see the disks, Glyssa?

"Yes."

If we can dislodge just one, it will shut off that beam. I think cutting off one will be enough for you to slip out of the cage.

"Yes. I understand."

Together, they summoned power. Amlina had prepared herself to bend all her strength today to pure shaping. She could not have guessed it would be for this purpose. She and Glyssa focused on a single disk in the ceiling, prying and tugging. At first, the gemmed disk lay still, embedded in a sealant. Suddenly it shifted and specks of dust fell.

Over by the wall, the witch Arkasha sat up and stared.

Harder, Amlina urged.

Peering suspiciously, Arkasha got up from her chair, picked up a staff, strode toward the cage.

Amlina feared they would be too late. Arkasha would arrive and poke Glyssa's body, disrupting their concentration. But then Glyssa summoned a burst of will. The disk dropped from the ceiling, and the light beam flickered out.

Instantly, Glyssa charged through the opening. Arkasha gave a cry and raised her staff. But Glyssa was a trained warrior and eager for a fight. She leaped, grabbed the staff in both hands. As they grappled for the weapon, Glyssa regained her balance. Planting one foot, she lifted the other and thrust her knee into Arkasha's groin. The elder woman groaned and buckled. Tossing the staff away, Glyssa grabbed the witch's wrist and twisted it behind her back, yanking the arm up violently. Arkasha cried in pain.

Amlina exulted. *Tell her to show you the way out.*

A glance told her the ogre was still locked in trance, unmoving. Glyssa whispered threateningly to the witch and Arkasha, grimacing, nodded in surrender. Glyssa kept tight hold of the woman's wrist and shoulder. Staggering, Arkasha led her along the wall to a black iron door. From a shelf she took a bronze key and offered it over her shoulder.

Make her open the lock, Amlina said.

One arm still twisted behind her back, her other hand trembling, Arkasha placed the key in the air an inch from the middle of the square door. A lock of shiny mist appeared around the key, and Arkasha twisted. Chains creaked, and the massive door rumbled as it slid into the ground.

Beyond stretched a dim tunnel. Weakly, Arkasha pointed.

"Oh, no." Glyssa said. "You lead me out."

"Very well."

The witch pulled the key from the misty lock where it hovered. Glyssa shoved to move her forward.

The tunnel was ten or twelve feet high and at least ten paces across. The floor sloped up toward a distant metal door, just visible in the faint light from the chamber behind them. Faded murals adorned the walls, a procession of warriors and chariots. From the painting style, Amlina realized the tomb was ancient, from before the Age of the World's Madness. As Keeper of the Keys, Clorodice would know many such hidden places.

After about forty paces, they came to the second door. In the darkness, the key in Arkasha's had taken on a shine of witchlight. Once more, she raised the key before the center of the door, and once more a misty lock materialized. Arkasha turned the key.

With a hiss and growl, the door rolled downward. Bright daylight shone beyond, and Glyssa gave a cry of joy. From the steps outside, her klarnmates rushed to embrace her.

Thirty-Five

S natched from the mind-link, Amlina gazed up into a dazzling blue sky. She sat slumped with her back to the wall of the fountain. A sea of faces gaped down at her. Among those closest, Amlina recognized witches from the Inner Council—Drusdegarde, Clorodice ...

"Amlina Len Tai, are you back in this world?" The speaker was Drusdegarde, the voice impatient.

But Amlina was staring hard into the sharp face of Clorodice—the high witch, strict adherent of the austere Thread of Virtue, who had raised an ancient, murderous evil. Staring back at her, Clorodice's eyes narrowed.

"Amlina!" Drusdegarde called. "Are you well enough to continue?"

Amlina struggled to her feet, glancing around at the faces. *The Tournament of Witches, the final event ... But what about Glyssa and the Iruks? Did they still need her?*

"Your ... *fainting spell* has interrupted the contest for some time," Drusdegarde said, stern but not harsh now. "We must know if you are fit enough to continue."

"Perhaps she should be disqualified," Clorodice offered. "This bears the marks of suspicious practice."

Wicksa, Keeper of Swords, replied: "If tainted practice is at work, it would seem Amlina is the victim rather than the perpetrator."

"She cannot be disqualified without delaying the final event," said Crandora, Keeper of the Books. "There must always be three. So it is written."

"The one who finished fourth could take her place," Clorodice said.

Drusdegarde watched Amlina keenly. "No. We will allow Amlina to compete—if she is ready."

Amlina needed time to think, to try to reach Glyssa again. She could not do that with everyone watching. She brushed off her robe. "Yes. I apologize for my *fainting*. I am ready now."

Drusdegarde nodded. "So be it."

The high witches returned to their chairs. The Mistress of the Tournament walked back out before the crowd. She spoke apologies for the delay and then introduced Amlina as the third finalist.

Struggling to keep steady, Amlina stepped onto the platform. Cheers of acclamation rang in her ears as she paced cautiously over the plank bridge and climbed into her seat above the pool.

"Now that the finalists are all seated," the Mistress of the Tournament shouted. "Let the competition begin."

The crash of a gong reverberated over the water.

Amlina shut her eyes and called to Glyssa in her mind.

"Is Trippany here?" Eben shouted, as the Iruks and drell warriors clustered around the mouth of the tunnel.

"Yes. And the ogre too," Glyssa answered.

She turned her head and Eben saw the black-robed witch who had stood there a moment ago skulking away down the tunnel. Glyssa darted after the witch and jumped on her back, toppling the woman to the ground.

"Oh, no," Glyssa cried. "You'll not sneak away and shut the gate again." Squeezing the woman's wrist, she forced her to drop a gleaming key.

Snatching up the key, Glyssa wheeled triumphantly to face the Iruks. "Now, mates, let us go and kill an ogre."

Grinning, Lonn handed her a spear. The mates started down the tunnel at a run, the drell warriors flying overhead.

They had gone less than half-way when the air began to hum. The passageway shone with a weird gray light. Behind them, Eben heard a rhythmic chanting. He whirled to see the witch that Glyssa had overpowered, standing in the middle of the tunnel with arms thrust high. Her words echoed harsh and shrill, in a language Eben guessed to be an archaic form of Larthangan. The gray light flashed to silver and a shrieking wind tore through the tunnel. The Iruks stopped and huddled back to back, raising swords and spears.

The paintings on the walls had come to life.

Warriors seven- or eight-feet tall jumped to the floor, heavy boots thudding. Helmets with visors hid their faces. They advanced with pikes and long, curved blades. In the air above, the drell warriors hovered and darted, seeking openings to attack. Karrol roared as she charged, and then the rest of the mates sprang after her.

Deep in the foggy, glittering spaces of vision, Phingarr Pheng stared at the Pool of Perpetual Light. His mind bound with Clorodice's, he pulled the arc of water toward her apprentice, Elani Vo T'ang.

But something was wrong—an intrusion. Cocking an ear, he heard shouts of battle and the clash of weapons. His body, seated inside the tomb, stiffened and shifted as he perceived what was happening.

"The tomb has been breached," he growled at Clorodice. "We must break the trance."

"Not yet!" the witch cried. "We are close ... a few moments more."

"Stupid woman! We are under attack!"

With a brutish roar, the phingarr strained to tear his mind free. Clorodice gasped in pain and fought to restrain him. The gleaming ribbon of light that bound them in the vision snapped tight.

Seated above the pool, Amlina gazed at the arcing water spout. But she applied no effort now to the contest. Her thoughts focused on Glyssa, trying to reestablish the link. She sensed her friends were in danger again.

Closing her eyes, she sought the peaceful, contemplative state of trance.

Glyssa. Our minds are one. Our minds are one.

Amlina! We need you. We are losing the fight.

Reach for me Glyssa.

Heat burst behind Amlina's forehead. Blinking, she found herself again in Glyssa's body. Her eyes looked out on violent chaos.

The mates were surrounded, assaulted on all sides by giant warriors in armor from ages past. *The murals on the wall had come to life!* Standing back to back, the Iruks hacked and lunged. Glyssa held a sword she had taken from Karrol, who was down with a shoulder wound. From her knees, Karrol still jabbed left-handed with her spear. Lonn and the others fought on grimly, but Amlina could tell their limbs were growing heavy. As she watched, Brinda's blade sliced open a warrior's belly. The wound appeared with a sizzling sound and a blaze of light—and immediately closed.

They stepped out of the pictures, Glyssa explained. *Our weapons do not hurt them.*

Age-old sorcery, designed to protect the tomb, Amlina realized.

A glance down the tunnel showed one of the drells had fallen. Four others clustered around him, making their stand in a circle. Their strength too was flagging.

They must have a vulnerable place, a source of power, Amlina told Glyssa.

"Yes. But where?"

Amlina scanned the warriors with her deepsight. Drogs normally had a single point on their bodies where the animating force poured in from the Deepmind. But these ancient soldiers were no drogs.

Elemental beings, they hardly had physical form at all—like the very pictures from which they sprang. Amlina cast her gaze at a nearby mural. A thought occurred.

Glyssa, cast your spear at the wall, at a warrior's picture.

"What good will that do?"

Try it, please!

Glyssa dropped the sword, switched the hunting spear to her right hand. She crouched to get an opening and threw the spear. It flew the short distance to the wall and struck a painted warrior. The spear shuddered and hung there, as if it had pierced not paint and brick, but flesh. In the tunnel nearby, a warrior groaned and melted into the air.

"That's it!" Glyssa cried. "Mates! Strike their pictures."

The Iruks and drells both grasped her meaning. Soon they were darting and wheeling past the tall warriors to stab at the paintings. One by one the phantom soldiers shriveled in the air and faded like smoke.

When the last of their adversaries were gone, Glyssa and her mates stood panting, elated.

"Now for the ogre!" Glyssa cried.

Lifting her sword, she led the charge down the tunnel.

"We are attacked!"

Roaring in fear and rage, Phingarr Pheng tore his body out of the chair. On the far side of the vision space, he heard Clorodice gag with pain. Only a slim ribbon now connected them, at their hearts.

Wakening in the tomb, regaining control of his muscles, the phingarr snatched his staff from where it leaned nearby. Warriors rushed at him, Iruks with spears and swords, drells swooping from above with lances.

Growling, he leaped at them, swatting a drell from the air, poking the freezing staff at an Iruk's chest.

As his mates and the drells rushed down the passageway, Eben had stopped. A quick glance behind showed the black-robed witch skulking toward the outer door. Eben made a quick decision and darted after her. Catching the witch at the bottom of the steps, he grabbed her arm. She gave a cry of alarm as he spun her around. His sword-point prodded her throat.

"Come along," he growled. "We may need you yet."

With her wrist in his grip, sword edge at her throat, Eben marched her back past the now flat and motionless wall paintings.

At the end of the passage, they entered a wide, round chamber filled with wavering lamplight and the shouts of battle. Eben's mates and the drell warriors circled the ogre, who roared and waved his magic staff to keep them at bay.

Eben held on to the witch. His mates and the drells, he was sure, could handle the ogre. Scanning the edges of the tomb, he spotted alcoves and doorways and, along one wall, bars of yellow light forming a barrier. Just visible in the shadows lay a small winged figure.

"Come," he said to the witch. "You will free the drell lady. I hope she is still alive—for your sake."

His attackers were too many!

Seized by terror, Phingarr Pheng gazed past the darting and thrusting weapons, desperately seeking an escape.

An Iruk blade gashed his arm. As Pheng yanked it back in a spray of blood, a drell flew behind and drove a lance point deep into his back. Bawling in pain, Pheng tried to stab the drell with his staff. But now his front was exposed. With howls of their own, the Iruks thrust deep into his chest and belly.

The phingarr fell to his knees. His head lolled down, eyes staring at the plunging steel and spurting blood.

No! From far away, Clorodice shrieked in dismay.

Yes, witch. You have brought me to this!

The phingarr collapsed, sprawled on his belly. As his back was stabbed again and again, he retreated from the pain, back into the vision. Across the inner space, he saw the witch, their hearts still linked by a ribbon of power. With hate and spite, he poured the last of his strength into that link, binding the witch to himself.

As his life bled away, a glittering abyss opened beneath him. Falling, he gripped Clorodice and dragged her down.

Amlina's awareness poured back into her body.

The ogre was slain. Her friends were safe.

Dazed, she stared at the gleaming, rippling water. On the far side of the pool, the arc of the spout wavered. Splashing near the wreath of Elani Vo T'ang, it now crept toward Shen Tra Lo.

A commotion made Amlina turn her head. Behind her, in the Archimage's box, the witches gathered around one who had collapsed. *Clorodice,* Amlina thought, her life perhaps ended by the monster she had made.

Amlina looked back at the fountain. *She still had time. She could still win.*

Lifting her shoulders, she summoned power. All her heart, all the force of her soul, all the wild strength that rightfully belonged to her as a klarnmate, she poured into deepshaping. Casting her will across the pool, she focused, summoning the arc of water.

The spout quivered, wavering again. Then it shifted back toward the center, back toward Amlina. In her mind she felt her opponents tugging, fighting. Elani seemed baffled and frightened—perhaps sensing the loss of Clorodice's influence. Her strength was ebbing. But Shen Tra Lo was a strong and confident soul, a witch of deep power. Undisturbed by the changing circumstances, she continued her pure shaping from a place of inward calm.

The spout stalled near the central island, hovered, then drifted back toward the wreath of Shen Tra Lo. Amlina grimaced, sucking air between her teeth. She fought to steer the falling water.

The spout wobbled and shifted. Doubts nibbled at Amlina's confidence. If she weren't so exhausted, if she had not turned her attention away from the contest ... But she had no regrets. Glyssa and the others were safe—that was what mattered most.

Inexorably, the tumbling spray moved across the pool. The clamor and cheering around the plaza grew louder. Amlina watched, weary, serene, disappointed yet grateful, as the water fell into her opponent's wreath of flowers.

Shen Tra Lo had won the Tournament of Witches.

Thirty-Six

Two days later, Amlina was summoned to Ting Ta Roo to appear before the Inner Council. She was uncertain what to expect. She hoped she might receive honors for finishing as a finalist in the Tournament, perhaps be offered a post at the House of the Deepmind or in the provinces. She might be rewarded for her part in ending the threat of the phingarr. On the other hand, she might be censured for disrupting the final event, or for using foreign magic—if the presence of the klarn-soul had been detected in her. She might even be blamed for the death of Clorodice. Anything seemed possible.

After the final event, a banquet had been held at the Tuan's palace to celebrate the end of the Festival. Amlina had excused herself early, pleading exhaustion. Since that evening she had stayed in seclusion in the Iruks' apartment. Eating, resting in bed with Draven, feeling the joy and love of her mates—all had been wonderful. Eben in particular was heartened that Trippany had been found alive. The winged lady was now in the care of Prince Spegis' household and expected to recover.

Through the prince, the Tuan had been apprised of the events at the tomb, the slaying of the ogre, and the Iruks' part in the adventure. A flurry of investigations and conferences had ensued, but Amlina didn't know how far they had progressed—in particular, whether the inquiries had reached the House of the Deepmind or if the role of the deceased Clorodice and her circle been uncovered.

In late afternoon, under a clear sky, Amlina arrived at the gates of Ting Ta Roo. She wore her best witch's robe, the gold and red garment she had been given for the Tournament. She carried a dagger in her belt and wore her moonstone fillet. On a whim, she had plaited her long blond hair in the Iruk fashion. If she was to be reproached for foreign influences, she would own it boldly and without shame.

An attendant conducted her down the long pillared corridors to the chamber of the Inner Council. Presently, the doors swung open and she was called to enter. In a mood of curiosity but little fear, she crossed the alcove and strode over the invisible floor. Its image, like the sky outside, was pale blue with wisps of cloud. Amlina scanned the dais and the faces of the high witches, seated at their podiums with attendants clustered behind. Among the fifteen Councilors, she spotted Shen Tra Lo. Apparently, the Tournament champion had already been installed as Keeper of the Cloak and taken her seat on the Council. Amlina's twinge of regret over that fact vanished when she spotted Melevarry on the far left. Appearing much recovered, the Mage of Randoon offered Amlina a broad smile.

"Amlina Len Tai," the Archimage began. "Firstly, the Council wishes to congratulate you on your excellent performance at the Tournament."

Amlina nodded and said nothing.

"Secondly," Drusdegarde continued, "we require you to describe exactly what occurred prior to and during the final event. Publicly, we described your condition as due to a fainting spell. We charge you now to provide a full and truthful account."

Amlina drew in a breath and selected her words with care. "I sensed through the Deepmind that my friends, the Iruk warriors, were in danger. I managed to forge a mind-link with one of them, the woman Glyssa, whom I have trained in the magical arts. I discovered that she had been abducted by the so-called phingarr, and was being held prisoner in an underground tomb. I assisted her in breaking out of a light-cage and then opening the gates to the tomb. The rest of the Iruks were waiting outside, along with several drell warriors in the service of the Drell Ambassador. Later, I assisted them again in defeating elemental guardians that had emerged from murals in the tunnel. The Iruks and drells were then able to enter the tomb and kill the phingarr."

As she spoke, tensions flowed in the air. The floor streamed with fast-moving clouds. The shadowed faces of the Inner Council stared down from the dais.

"Most interesting," Drusdegarde said. "And it conforms with what Prince Spegis has reported to the Tuan."

"Most remarkable," said Kanshi, Keeper of the Forge. "If this is true, how do you account for the fact that you were able to pierce the concealments around the phingarr, when all the efforts applied by the House of the Deepmind failed?"

Again, Amlina trod with care. "I can only surmise it is because I have a strong affinity with my Iruk friends."

Crandora, Keeper of the Books, asked: "Can you explain the source of this most potent affinity?"

Amlina sighed—there was no avoiding the question. "The Iruks are barbarians, a wild people, close to nature. They form hunting bands called *klarns*. These klarns embody a group soul, a binding of their hearts and minds."

"And you were able to forge a mind-link with the Iruk woman through this group soul?" Crandora asked.

"Yes. Because I am part of it. I am a member of the klarn."

Soft gasps issued from several spots on the podium.

"I realize this is unorthodox, an alien magic," Amlina said. "But I have found no evil in it."

"Indeed," Melevarry noted, in a voice surprisingly firm. "In this case, the wild magic succeeded in overcoming a great evil—one which all of our orthodox practices failed to penetrate."

The other Councilors showed varied expressions: neutral, disturbed, curious, or intrigued.

"You might censure me for this," Amlina declared. "If so, I will accept your judgment. You may even revoke my right to practice as a witch of Larthang or send me back into exile. But I will not deny my friends or renounce our bond."

"Be not so hasty, Amlina," Drusdegarde said. "No one has spoken of punishment. Despite the unusual bent of your arts, I find only good in you. And, as Lady Melevarry has observed, in this case you have once again done great service to the Land. One further question though: Do I understand correctly that you *deliberately* chose to enter this mind-link a few moments before the pure shaping event? You must have known you were probably casting away any chance of victory."

"It is so. Much as I desired to win the Tournament, I would not risk the lives of my friends—my *klarnmates*."

The Archimage peered at her a moment longer. "Sisters. Let us withdraw to private council."

Around the dais, the witches grew still, their faces changing to blank masks. As they convened in psychic communication, the floor became a clear and empty void.

Amlina waited, glancing around the chamber, peering into the faces of the attendants and assistant witches, wondering what the Council would decide.

After a time, the high witches shifted in their seats. Melevarry smiled. Drusdegarde grunted to clear her throat.

"Amlina Len Tai, the Council has discussed your case and voted. First, as you likely have heard, the witch Clorodice died two days ago, at the very time the ogre was slain. It has been verified that Clorodice was psychically bound to the phingarr, that she created this evil being using forbidden sorcery. Now, as you know, it was intended that the champion of the Tournament would receive the honor of becoming Keeper of the Cloak of the Two Winds and take her seat on this Council. However, our sister Shen Tra Lo has declined that honor. Instead, she has elected to join us in the vacated post of Keeper of the Keys. Therefore, given your performance in the Tournament and history with the Cloak, and in honor of your great service to the Land, the Council has voted to offer you the post of Keeper of the Cloak. Will you accept?"

Stunned, Amlina glanced at Melevarry and then back at the Archimage. A wide grin spread across her face. "I will accept, most gratefully."

"Very good," Drusdegarde said. "Your investiture ceremony will take place this afternoon. A climate of danger and disruption still threatens the Land, and we should not leave so important a magical treasure unattended."

After three days filled with worry, Eben at last gained permission to visit Trippany. Carrying a bouquet of roses, he followed a steward down the corridor on the ground floor of Prince Spegis' mansion. Arriving in the high central hall, he stepped onto a platform of light bamboo. Two drell servants plied their wings to lift the platform to a gallery far above the floor. The drells' residence had no stairs.

In a bright and airy apartment, he found Trippany lying in a kind of hammock. Her wings extended below into a porcelain tub filled with some sort of healing liquid. Eben had been told that her torn and frayed wings were expected to regenerate, and the lady should be capable of flying again in two or three small-months.

Her eyes sparkled when she saw him. Noticing the roses, she smiled. "You brought me flowers?"

"Uh, yes. I understand they are an appropriate gift for one recovering from illness." Awkwardly, Eben looked for a place to set them down.

"They are lovely," Trippany said.

Eben handed the bouquet to a drell maid who flew forward to accept them. Another servant brought him a chair.

"Are you all right?" he asked.

"I am recovering." She lifted her arm, showed him the white remnants of claw marks. "I have scars now too, though not so bad as the one on your head. Do they make me less attractive?"

Eben laughed. "Not in the least."

"I am glad." Her voice thickened. "Oh, Eben. It was so horrible. Only five days, yet it seemed much longer. I thought he would devour me. Toward the end, I wished to die."

"I am ashamed," he said, "because I failed to protect you that night."

She frowned a moment, not understanding. "Oh, no! There is no shame. You are my brave warrior, my loving poet. I thought of you often. I knew you would keep searching for me. That thought gave me hope."

"I am glad. I was so happy when we found you alive."

They were quiet for a time, gazing into each other's eyes.

"What will you do, once you are healed?" he asked.

"Oh, I suppose I will return to the House of the Deepmind, continue my studies. What of you? Will you and your crew stay in Larthang?"

"I think so. Amlina is now a high witch. My mates and I will become her retainers ... I hope that means we can see each other sometimes?"

Trippany smiled. "I would be happy. When I am fully healed and can fly again, perhaps I might take you to visit my homeland. When the summers come again would be best. Our forests are so beautiful then."

"I would enjoy that very much." Eben grinned.

The drell nodded, pleased. "We shall see."

"Let the winds blow so they will?" Eben quoted.

She gave a faint laugh. "Oh, but I never told you the next line of that song."

"Is there a next line?"

"Let the winds blow so they will," she recited. "But fly against them when you must."

Four days after her investiture, in her first public duty as member of the Inner Council, Amlina attended a conclave in the Castle of the Golden Land. Wearing the Cloak of the Two Winds, she sat with the other high witches in a gallery adjacent to the Dark Bright Throne. The boy Tuan appeared like a small and shiny sun on the massive throne, clothed in gold raiment, flanked by close advisors. An assortment of ministers, magistrates, generals, and admirals filled the other galleries of the hall.

The session had been called to review the matter of the phingarr and the uncovered conspiracy. The witch Arkasha, found in the phingarr's lair, had been arrested by the Imperial Guard. Under the threat of torture, she had confessed details of the plot, implicating Clorodice and the other witches of her circle. Those women in turn had been arrested and interrogated. The ones who had participated directly in the abduction and murder of innocent civilians were to be tried by the Tuan's magistrates and likely beheaded. Others, judged of less culpability, would do penance in the House of the Deepmind.

Of course, the faction known as The Thread of Virtue included many who were not witches. Amlina listened as nobles, influential scholars, magistrates, and civil officials were brought before the conclave and interrogated. Naturally, all denied any knowledge of or involvement with the heinous sorcery of the phingarr. These men and women were given leave to depart with their freedom, though Amlina understood that their activities and writings would be monitored going forward. The Thread of Virtue, as a viable power in the Land, might not recover.

Also implicated in the initial confessions were certain military men. Late in the day, Duke Trem-Dou Pheng, Supreme Commander of the Larthangan Forces, marched into the audience hall. Two

Imperial Guardsman flanked him. The Duke was a stout, broadly built man of middle age. His hair and beard were perfectly groomed, his gait steady. Yet Amlina sensed the man was weary and unnerved. No doubt, he had already endured a long and pointed interrogation.

In a voice loud enough to be heard across the hall, the examining magistrate informed the Duke of the charges against him. Several witches of Clorodice's circle had implicated the Duke and his sons in their conspiracy. Arkasha, Elani Vo T'ang, and others had testified that the Duke personally delivered to Clorodice his nephew, Shay-Ni Pheng, as the victim whose body would be transformed into the phingarr.

Duke Pheng answered with unruffled aplomb. "Of course these charges are nonsense. I am Supreme Commander of the Tuan's Forces. What have I to do with the plots of witches?"

"Can you then account for the whereabouts of Admiral Shay-Ni Pheng?" the magistrate pressed.

The Duke evinced a shade of discomfort. "Sadly, no. My nephew disappeared from the Capital some time ago, without informing either his superior officers or our family. He had been distraught for some time, owing to reverses in his career ..."

"Then you did not hand your nephew over to the witch Clorodice?"

"Certainly not."

"For what reason should these witches, who face likely execution, dream up your involvement in their heinous conspiracy?"

"I cannot imagine the motivations of such deranged individuals," Duke Pheng replied. "But I say again, I am a military man. Those under my command have always served the Tuan and the Land. There are many high ranking lords in both the army and navy who will swear as to my honor and loyalty. Moreover, these lords command large numbers of troops, and are *loyal to me personally*."

The stress he placed on those last words suggested a threat: should Pheng be arrested, a mutiny might result. From the uneasy murmur that crept over the chamber, Amlina realized others had interpreted it that way as well.

"Duke Pheng." The Tuan spoke up in his clear, high voice. His tone was solemn yet serene. "*I am informed* of many occasions in our history when ambitious generals have led rebellions against their Tuans. Sometimes these men have succeeded. More often, they failed and paid with their heads." He let the words settle, then continued, once again using the ritual phrase that cited his mystical authority as avatar of all the Tuans. "I am also informed of the case of one Olam Vo Sing, a general under the 94th Tuan. This lord was implicated, perhaps falsely, in a plot against his monarch. Though he protested innocence, he wisely chose to avoid a trial and accept exile to the mountains of his native province. There he lived in seclusion to a ripe age, fished in the lakes, walked in his orchards, and wrote worthy books. Meanwhile, his sons were able to continue their service and his house to thrive."

Silence again settled over the hall. The Tuan had offered the Duke a way to save face while preserving both his head and the fortunes of his family. Removed from the affairs of the Capital, he could live out his life, no doubt under guard, at some country estate. His sons and their careers would be spared.

Head bowed, the Duke seemed to struggle over the idea. After a tense passage of time, he lifted his eyes to the throne. "August Ruler, I find General Vo Sing's story most engaging. Perhaps, with your permission, I will resign my post as Supreme Commander, and leave my noble sons to continue their service to your throne. Retirement to my manor in Tulong Province might prove most beneficial to my health."

The boy on the throne grinned. "We find your suggestion both wise and agreeable, noble Duke. You have our leave to depart to the country with all haste."

His face a neutral mask, Duke Pheng marched from the hall in step with the two guardsmen.

"August Ruler," the examining magistrate said, "I believe this concludes all matters for the conclave."

Many in the galleries shifted as if to rise. But suddenly the Tuan leaped from his throne. "One thing more," he cried, appearing less the divine ruler and more the nine-year-old boy.

When everyone was listening, he continued. "My noble councilors and officials of the Land, we would be amiss at this moment if we did not pause to convey our gratitude and respect to persons who have served us most nobly. I speak of Amlina, now Keeper of the Cloak, and her brave Iruk warriors, though they be not present. Months ago, these nobles brought one of our great magical treasures back to Larthang. In these past days, they have kept that treasure's power from falling into the hands of evil conspirators. I give you Amlina and her noble warriors."

Across the chamber, the ruling elite of Larthang stood as one, cheering and applauding. Cheeks burning, Amlina rose and bowed.

Epilogue

Before the Tournament of Warriors

C hill rain and sleet blew in from the north. Less than a small-month from the start of First Summer, yet the weather had turned cold. Standing before the wide crystal window, Eben watched the icy drizzle fall on the front yard and the avenue beyond.

The mansion deeded to Amlina as Keeper of the Cloak was located in a prosperous warren of widely spaced houses midway between the Tuan's palace and Ting Ta Roo. Three stories high, with carpeted halls, tall ceilings, and tapestry-covered walls, it had proven a most pleasant place to live—offering ample room for Amlina, her servants, and the Iruks who remained.

"Is she coming yet?" Karrol called from the staircase in the entry hall.

"You mean is *he* coming," Eben answered. "No. Not yet."

"*He, he!* Yes, I'll remember."

Karrol's boots thudded as she stamped back up the stairs. For all she tried to hide it, she plainly felt uneasy about today's gathering.

Just over a year ago the klarnmates had sailed from Fleevanport with Amlina. That year had wrought changes in all of them. Karrol had changed the least, Eben supposed, and so she was finding it hardest to adjust.

Eben wandered over to a chair by the fireplace and picked up his lute. He had started playing the instrument during Second Winter, as an accompaniment to his poetry performances. A beginner, he was far from proficient. Still, plucking out a tune soothed his nerves and made contemplation easy.

Of all the mates, he might have changed the most—well, except of course for Brinda now. Who could have predicted that a drunken

Iruk pirate would evolve into a successful Larthangan poet? Over the three winters, his performances had grown popular—some of his work was even printed and sold at bookseller stalls. Also, he was something of a scholar, spending pleasant afternoons in the palace library or in learned conversations with Kizier and other intellectuals. Sometimes he took tea with the Tuan and his coterie of savants—including Buroof the talking book.

Of course Eben remained a fit warrior, one of Amlina's household guard. He trained daily with Lonn, Draven, Glyssa, and Karrol—although that group would be changing now. Along with spear, sword, and dagger, the Iruks had taken up the crossbow. Lonn and Draven had even decided to compete in the upcoming Tournament of Warriors. That competition, unlike the Witches' Tournament, allowed large numbers to enter the opening rounds.

As for drinking, Eben had not taken a sip since that night six months back when Trippany was abducted. He had sworn it off and kept the vow. Trippany had, as she predicted, returned to her studies at the House of the Deepmind. She visited him on occasion, their love-making as sweet as ever. And she still spoke of taking him to tour the Drell Forests, though they never quite managed to fix a date. Eben stroked a sad note. She was a flighty thing—he had come to accept that as her nature.

A loud rapping on the front door interrupted his musings. He jumped up and headed for the foyer. Karrol was already rushing down the stairs, while Lonn and Draven marched into the hallway from another room.

Swinging open the carved ebony doors, they faced a young man of medium height dressed in the blue scaled armor of the Chrysalis. Though altered, the face looked familiar, sharper perhaps and now with short-cropped hair and a downy mustache.

For a moment, he stared at them, cautious, uncertain. Then Karrol burst across the threshold and hugged her former sister fiercely.

"There you are at last. Come out of the cold."

The letter had come six days ago. Brinda's time in the cocoon had ended, and she had emerged a male. Shortly after the Tournament of Witches, Brinda had announced her interest in joining the Order of the Chrysalis, to be transformed into whatever her ideal warrior might prove to be. She had mulled the decision all of First Winter, listened to her mates' thoughts and concerns, and the sometimes vociferous objections of her sister Karrol. By Mid-Winter, she had decided the move was truly what she wanted in her heart. and so had entered the Castle of the Chrysalis. She now went by the name Brinn of Ilga.

Joyfully, the Iruks welcomed their former mate. Embracing him, Eben noted a wider back with more muscle. By then, Amlina and Glyssa were descending the stairs. The witch ran to Brinn and took both his hands.

"You are most welcome, dear friend."

Glyssa came behind, moving more slowly due to her swollen belly. "I am so happy to see you," she cried.

Grinning, Brinn hugged her gently, then rested a hand on her belly. "The child is growing in you. That is so wonderful. And you are healthy?"

"Oh, indeed," Glyssa laughed.

Another of the klarn who had changed, Eben reflected. Still a warrior and a witch, Glyssa had chosen to add the role of motherhood to her life. She was due to deliver Lonn's child in another two months.

Candlelight danced over the long table, mingled with a golden glow from the hearth. Amlina, Kizier, and the six Iruks—the same eight companions who had sailed from Fleevan—feasted on rice and fowl, soup and vegetables, nuts and honey. The plum wine flowed freely, consumed by all except Eben, who drank hot tea.

Amlina was thriving in her role of Keeper of the Cloak and member of the Inner Council. Along with the klarn, her household included a half-dozen servants. There was also talk on her taking on an apprentice.

Kizier meantime had discarded, at least for the present, his desire to enter a monastery. He had taken employment as Amlina's secretary, a role that left him ample time for scholarly pursuits. He had finished his account of Amlina's voyages and adventures in Tann, Gwales, and Far Nyssan. Published at the start of Third Winter, the book had attracted a wide readership all over Larthang. Now, in his spare time, he was composing a philosophic work—based on his experience as a windbringer and the bostulls' unique mode of consciousness.

Between the wine and the cheerful acceptance of his friends, Brinn seemed at ease. The klarnmate who had left a woman had returned a man, but nothing else had changed.

"Have you thought about what path you will take after you complete training?" Amlina asked him. Fresh from the cocoon, Brinn still had six months before graduating as a full-fledged alatee.

He hesitated. "I have, yes. I would like—I would hope to be assigned to your household guard, Amlina. If you all will have me ...?"

The Iruks whooped and cheered, slapping hands on the table so the crockery rattled.

"You will be more than welcome," Amlina said. "I will make the request to the Castle at the first opportunity."

"The klarn will be complete again," Glyssa exclaimed, then quickly placed a hand over her lips.

All of the mates looked at Karrol.

"Do you think—" Glyssa asked her. "I mean, if Brinn returns to us, do you think you might reconsider ...?"

Karrol's mouth turned down. "No. I am sorry ... At least not right away."

Karrol had never been happy in Minhang. After Brinda left, she had talked about leaving Larthang altogether, sailing back to the South Polar Sea. None of the other Iruks showed any interest. Then, at the height of Second Winter, the mates had accompanied Amlina inland. They travelled to the northwest province of Shing Ton, where the witch used the Cloak to melt several lakes and streams, enabling winter fishing to augment the food supply. Karrol had enjoyed the wild, mountainous terrain. She had gotten to know some of the rangers who served as game wardens. They hunted and fished in the Tuan's imperial forests and kept the snow tigers and wolves under control. After returning to the capital, Karrol had talked about it often. Finally, she made the request to the Tuan that she might be appointed to join the Ranger Corps.

In fact, she was scheduled to leave tomorrow.

"Much as I love you all," she said, "this city is no place for me. I want to live in the open and hunt again. I know, I always seem unsatisfied, wishing to be somewhere else. But I must try this, at least for a time, to see if I like it any better. Perhaps I won't like it at all. I might come back after a few seasons ..."

The mates returned her gaze pensively.

"You will always have a home with us," Amlina said.

The party continued late into the night. The candles burned out and were replaced. The servants all went to bed. Fresh wood was tossed on the fire. The companions laughed and drank and talked of their adventures. Eben played the lute. They sang chants and songs, both Iruk and Larthangan. Eventually, the mates grew sleepy. First Glyssa and Lonn, then Draven and Amlina headed off to bed.

Eben stayed up with Brinn and Karrol—and also Kizier who diligently made notes about stories he had not heard before. Eventually, the scholar fell asleep in a soft chair by the fire. By then, a dull light was rising outside the crystal windows. The sleet had changed to snow.

"I'd best be leaving," Karrol announced.

Before the others could answer, she marched from the room and hurried up the stairs. A few minutes later she returned. She had changed from the quilted Larthangan clothing to Iruk garb—fur leggings and shirt, boots and leather harness, hooded fur cape over all. Sword and dagger hung from her belt, and she carried a quiver of hunting spears.

"But you haven't even slept," Brinn said.

"I will sleep on the canal boat. I mustn't miss it."

"Are you sure you won't change your mind?" Eben asked.

"I am sure."

Setting down the spears, Karrol hugged them each in turn.

"Good-bye, mates."

"We'll walk you to the gate," Eben said.

The snow fell in big flakes, and all the world was quiet. At the edge of the yard, Karrol embraced them both again. She strode off without another word.

The two Iruks watched their mate recede in the gray distance until she disappeared. Walking sadly back to the house, Eben noticed how the snow was already filling in Karrol's footprints.

In a day or two, the snow itself would be gone.

He would have to write that in a poem.

Glimnodd Calendar, Map, and Glossary

Glimnodd has two moons. Grizna, the larger, has a period of 32 days. The small moon, Rog, has a cycle of 11 days. A *month* always refers to the 32-day Grizna cycle. The cycle of Rog is called a *small-month* or simply a *rog*.

A year has six seasons, each two months or 64 days long:

First Winter
Second or Mid-Winter
Third or Late Winter
First Summer
Second or High Summer
Third or Late Summer

A map of Glimnodd is available online at
https://tinyurl.com/MapofGlimnodd

Glossary

Academy of the Deepmind - located in Minhang, the training school for Larthangan witches.

Age of the World's Madness - historical epoch preceding the current age, when the untrammeled use of magic produced chaotic effects and the rise of multiple sentient species.

aklor - a tall, six-legged animal used as a mount or pack animal in the Three Nations.

alatee - see Warriors of the Chrysalis.

Archimage - official title for the chief witch or mage of a nation.

blood magic - a kind of ancient sorcery using human blood.

bostull - see windbringer.

Bowing to the Sky - a ritual in which the deepshaper releases personal will and seeks the guidance of the Deepmind.

cantrip - a minor spell or 'mind trick.'

Cloak of the Two Winds - a magical garment created by the legendary witch Eglemarde, it gives the power to call the freezewind and meltwind.

dark immersion - a deep trance practice regularly by deepshapers to preserve their power.

Deepmind - the formative realm of which reality is a reflection.

deepseer - one skilled in the Larthangan art of deepseeing; that is, seeing outside the boundaries of time and space.

deepshaper - one skilled in the arts of shaping reality through magic.

design - any magical working.

desmet - a hanging trinket used to enhance mental power.

dojuk - Iruk hunting boat, agile on water or ice.

drells - a delicate winged people whose land lies to the south of Larthang.

drog - literally 'shell', a creature formed of magic, animated by the will of a deepshaper, guided by a single purpose.

ensorcellment - a great act of magic.

fire turtles - sea turtles that breathe fire. Normally considered non-sentient.

Five Revered Arts - The five authorized arts of Larthangan witches. They are 1. deepseeing (wei-shen); 2. formulation or "weaving" (jai-dah) 3. trinketing (barang-xing) 4. magical combat (weng-lei). 5. pure shaping (quon-xing).

Fleevan - Tathian colony in the South Polar region. The capital is Fleevanport.

flizzard - a small winged reptile.

formulation - the Larthangan art of creating and casting power through mental constructs.

freezewind - magical wind that changes the seas to ice.

House of the Deepmind (Ting Ta Roo) - located in Minhang, the center of power of the Witches of Larthang.

Iron Bloc - Larthangan faction advocating international conquest.

Iruks - hunting people of the South Polar region.

kiia - edible fern of the tundra; leaves are used to wrap dried fish.

klarn - Iruk sacred hunting group consisting of five to eight warriors. Members of a klarn share a group soul that gives them strength and courage.

lamnocc - large deer of the Polar region.

Larthang - westernmost of the Three Nations. Home to a race of powerful witches.

mage - any skilled practitioner of magic. When capitalized: the top-ranking Larthangan witch of a city or province.

magical combat - the Larthangan martial art consisting of both physical and mental tactics.

meltwind - magical wind that changes frozen water to liquid.

myro - sentient sea-creatures spawned from dolphins.

Nyssan - Easternmost of the Three Nations. Home to several races. Normally divided into Near Nyssan and Far Nyssan.

ogo - Larthangan name for the Deepmind. Literally, 'drift.'

phingarr or "anti-self "- a creature derived from a human but converted by sorcery in a source of vast power.

pure shaping - the Larthangan magical art of creating immediate effects through the power of thought.

second flight - a rare talent allowing certain drells to fly outside of normal space.

serds - a sentient race evolved from deep-sea fishes; powerful sorcerers who ruled Glimnodd during the Age of the World's Madness.

Tath - middle realm of the Three Nations. A group of islands, home to a race of seafarers and traders, ruled by independent city-states.

tali - a creature like a large tiger, domesticated and used as a dray animal in Larthang.

thrall - a sentient being whose mind and will have been subjugated by sorcery.

Thread of Virtue - Larthangan faction advocating strict laws to enforce morality and harsh punishment of offenders.

Ting Ta Roo - the House of the Deepmind.

torms - winged people of northern Nyssan, spawned from birds.

trinket - any object fashioned to contain or enhance magic power.

trinketing - the Larthangan art of constructing trinkets.

Tuan - the ruler of Larthang, a sacred king or queen.

Tysanni - Glimnodd's legendary third moon, which disappeared in the Age of the World's Madness.

volrooms - tusked, white-furred bears.

Warriors of the Chrysalis - an order of warriors dedicated to serving the Witches of Larthang, they undergo a magical transformation designed to produce their ideal self.

Way of the Wise Serpent - Larthangan philosophical tradition advocating mystical detachment and anarchy. Followers include alchemists, astrologers, and free magicians.

wei-shen - the Larthangan art of deepseeing.

wei-xing - general term for the Larthangan arts of deepshaping.

weng-lei - the Larthangan art of magical combat.

windbringer - a sentient fern-like plant; skilled at attracting winds and therefore prized by mariners of all nations.

witch - broadly any female mage; strictly, a woman trained in the Larthangan arts of the Deepmind.

yulugg - giant sea mammals, similar to whales.

Zindu - a land of forests and jungles south of Larthang.

Author's Note

Sincere thanks to my Beta Readers: Marilyn Massa, John W. Kelly, Richard Fisher, and Ben Kleven. Also to my cover artist, Shaun Stevens, who is truly a mage of design.

The Glimnodd Cycle includes these books:

>*Cloak of the Two Winds*
>
>*A Mirror Against All Mishap*
>
>*Tournament of Witches*

If you enjoyed this story, please consider leaving a rating and review on Amazon, as well as other sites. The algorithms of the publishing business make this extremely important to a book's success.

I love hearing from readers. You can connect with me at:

>Web: triskelionbooks.com or jackmassa.com
>Facebook: www.facebook.com/AuthorJackMassa/
>· X/Twitter: @JackMassa2

Also, check out my Substack at speclectic.substack.com.